Spellbound by the Single Dad

RACHEL BAILEY

LYNNE MARSHALL

NATASHA OAKLEY

MILLS & BOON

First Published in Great Britain 2019
By Mills & Boon, an imprint of HarperCollins*Publishers*
1 London Bridge Street, London, SE1 9GF

SPELLBOUND BY THE SINGLE DAD
© 2019 Harlequin Books S.A.

The Nanny Proposition © Rachel Robinson 2014
A Mother for His Adopted Son © Janet Maarschalk 2016
Wanted: White Wedding © Natasha Oakley 2008

ISBN: 978-0-263-27618-3

1119

MIX
Paper from
responsible sources
FSC C007454

FSC
www.fsc.org

This book is produced from independently certified FSC™ paper to ensure responsible forest management.

For more information visit: www.harpercollins.co.uk/green

Printed and bound in Spain
by CPI, Barcelona

THE NANNY PROPOSITION

RACHEL BAILEY

This book is for all the writing dogs who've kept me company. Not every dog I've had has been a writing dog, but a few have made it part of their role: Sascha, my first writing dog, who laid in her basket beside my desk and kept my writing time safe by growling at anyone – human or dog – who entered the room. Oliver, who sleeps nearby when I write and reminds me to keep my chocolate levels up (and to toss him a dog chocolate while I'm at it). Fergus, who likes to sleep under my desk, dreaming his dog dreams. Dougal, who ensures I don't spend too long at my desk in each stint by nudging me to take him for a game of dog tennis. Roxie, who sits on the lounge beside me during writing days at my mother's house. And especially Jazzie May, who passed away while I was writing *The Nanny Proposition*. In between perimeter patrols and naps by the office door, she'd sit by my desk and give me her big smile and ask if I needed anything – a dog to pat, perhaps? Hugs to you, my Jasmine Maybelline.

Acknowledgements

Thanks to my editor, Charles Griemsman who has a fabulous eye for story and the patience of a saint. Also to Amanda Ashby for the brainstorming and waffles, and Claire Baxter, who helped create a new country. And Cheryl Lemon for the information on California (though any mistakes are mine). But mostly, thanks to Barbara DeLeo and Sharon Archer, the best critique partners in the world.

One

Liam Hawke held the cell phone tightly against his ear, but it didn't help. The person on the other end of the phone wasn't making any sense.

"Mr. Hawke? Are you there?"

"Hang on a moment," he said and pulled his Jeep to the side of the road. At his brother's enquiring stare, Liam said in an undertone, "Listen," and hit the speaker button on his cell. "Can you repeat that, please?"

"I'm a midwife at the Sacred Heart Hospital and I just informed you that you've become a father. Congratulations." Liam frowned, Dylan's eyes widened and the woman continued. "Your daughter, Bonnie, is two days old and still here with her mother. Unfortunately, her mother has had some complications following the birth and has asked me to contact you. It would be best if you came right away."

A baby? Dylan mouthed as Liam loosened his tie

and undid the top button on his shirt, which had suddenly become too tight. There had to be a mistake. Babies didn't magically appear. Usually there was nine months' notice, for one thing.

The L.A. sun shone down on them through the sunroof as Liam swallowed and tried to get his voice to work. "Are you sure you have the right person?"

"You're Liam John Hawke?" she asked.

"I am."

"You were in a relationship with Rebecca Clancy?"

"Yes" —if you could call their arrangement a relationship— "but she wasn't pregnant when we broke up." Which had been a good while ago. He struggled to remember when he'd last seen her but couldn't bring a time or place to mind.

How long *had* it been? It could have been eight months ago.... An uncomfortable heat crawled across his skin. Then another piece of information registered. "You said Rebecca had some complications. Is she all right?"

The midwife drew in a measured breath. "I think it would be better if we spoke in person."

"I'll be there as soon as I can," he said and disconnected. He pulled the Jeep back out into the flow of traffic and made a U-turn.

Dylan pulled out his cell. "I'll cancel the meeting."

When Dylan ended the call, Liam threw him a tight smile. "Thanks."

"You had no idea?" Dylan asked.

"I still have no idea." He ran a hand through his hair, then brought it back to grip the wheel. "Sure, I was dating Rebecca back then, but that doesn't prove I'm the father of her baby." He'd heard she'd been dating again

soon after their breakup. First order of business would
be a paternity test.

After a frustrating delay in L.A. traffic, they arrived at the hospital. They made their way to the neo-
natal unit, where they were greeted by a woman in a
pale blue uniform. She led them through to the nursery.
"Ms. Clancy took a turn for the worse after I called you,
and she's been taken back to surgery. Her parents went
up with her, so they've left Bonnie with us here in the
nursery." She leaned over and picked up a bundle of soft
pink blanket with a tiny face peeping out.

"Hello, sweetheart," she cooed. "Your daddy's here
to meet you."

Before Liam could head the nurse off with an explanation about needing a paternity test, she'd placed
the baby in his arms. Large eyes fringed by long dark
lashes blinked open and looked up at him. Her tiny pale
pink face seemed so fragile, yet somehow more real
than anything else in the room.

"I'll leave you two to get to know each other for a
few minutes," the midwife said. "There's a comfy chair
over there in the corner."

Dylan cleared his throat. "I'll just…ah…pop out and
get us a couple of coffees."

But Liam was only vaguely paying attention to them.
Bonnie was all he could see. He couldn't remember the
last time he'd held a baby and he wasn't one-hundred-
percent sure he was doing it right, but he held her closer
and breathed in her clean, sweet smell. He could feel the
warmth of her body through the blanket, and a ghost of
a smile crept across his face.

All three Hawke brothers had their mother's unusual hair color of darkest brown shot through with
deep red—and Bonnie already had a thick crop of hair

exactly that shade. He'd still demand a paternity test, no question, and he'd need to have a full and frank discussion with Rebecca, but he was sure of one thing: Bonnie was his.

She was a Hawke.

As he sank into the chair and stared into the eyes of his daughter, the world stilled. *His baby*. His heart clenched tight, then expanded to fill his chest, his body. And for the first time in his life, Liam Hawke fell head over heels in love.

He lost track of time as he sat there, holding his daughter and telling her stories about her new family, of her two uncles and of his parents, who would adore and spoil their first grandchild rotten. An hour ago he was on his way to a business meeting with Dylan for their family company, Hawke's Blooms. How had his day gone from thinking about the business of growing and selling flowers to thinking about a having a little girl in his life?

A movement out of the corner of his eye made him look up to see a middle-aged couple enter the nursery. They stumbled to a halt just inside the door. "Who are you?" the heavily made-up woman demanded.

Instinctively, he held Bonnie a little tighter. This had to be Rebecca's parents. He'd never met them when he'd dated Rebecca—given the relationship had barely lasted three months before he'd ended it, the opportunity had never arisen. He guessed he'd be seeing more of them now.

"Liam Hawke," he said calmly, politely. "Bonnie's father."

Scowling, the man stepped forward on one Italian-shoed foot. "How do you even know about Bonnie?"

"Rebecca asked the nurse to call me." Not wanting

to disrupt the baby, he stayed in the chair and kept his voice level. "But the real question is, why *wouldn't* I know about her?"

"Rebecca would never have done that," the woman said, her eyes narrowing. "When Rebecca's discharged, she and the baby will be coming back to live with us— she moved in two months ago. We'll raise Bonnie together. In fact, you can hand her over now and leave before Rebecca gets out of surgery. If she'd wanted to see you, she'd have mentioned it before now."

Liam took a breath, prepared to give the couple some slack given their daughter was in surgery. But they were seriously mistaken if they thought he was going anywhere.

"So your plan was to never tell me I have a child?" he asked and met their gazes steadily.

"Rebecca's plan," the man corrected.

Their arrogance was astounding. To deliberately keep a baby's birth—the existence of a person—secret was beyond comprehension. "She didn't think I'd want to know? That Bonnie would need a father?"

The woman sniffed. "You can't provide anything that she won't already have. Your wealth is nothing to ours. And she'll have people around her *capable* of love."

He heard the unspoken critique of his family's wealth clear enough—the Hawke family didn't just have less money, they had *new* money. He felt his blood pressure rise another notch. He'd come across the prejudice often, always from people who'd never put in a hard day's work in their lives, whose riches had been passed down and all they'd had to do was spend and perhaps adjust the investments. He'd never been able to conjure up any respect for someone who'd inherited their money and position.

About to respond, Liam frowned and paused. Something in that last dig had been especially pointed. What exactly had Rebecca told them about him? They hadn't broken up on the best of terms, sure, but he hadn't thought it had been too bad. Though, now that he thought about it, hadn't Rebecca talked about her parents being cold and manipulative? Was this coming from Rebecca or from them…?

A man in a surgeon's gown appeared in the doorway. His face was drawn as he took off the paper cap that had covered his hair. "Mr. and Mrs. Clancy?"

"Yes?" Rebecca's mother grabbed her husband's hand. "Is she out of surgery? How is she?"

"I'm afraid I have some bad news. Rebecca fought hard, but her body had—"

"She's gone?" Mr. Clancy said, his voice hoarse.

The doctor nodded. "I'm sorry."

Mrs. Clancy let out a loud, broken sob and slumped against her husband, who pulled her against him. The noise made Bonnie's face crumple, then she began to wail. Stunned, Liam looked down at her. Her mother had just died. She was motherless. Her life would always be affected by this one tragic incident.

And he had no idea what to do.

The midwife rushed through the door, jostling to get past the doctor, who was still talking to Rebecca's parents, and took Bonnie from him. Liam watched her soothe Bonnie as if from a distance. As if it wasn't really happening.

"I'm so sorry about the news, Mr. Hawke," she said.

"What—" He cleared his throat. "What happens to Bonnie now?"

"Rebecca had already filled in the birth certificate and named you as the father. So as far as the hospital is concerned, you have custody of her. If you don't want her, I know Rebecca's parents were talking about raising her. How about I call the social worker to help you sort through your options?"

Bonnie had calmed down to a mild hiccup. Bonnie. His baby. She had worked her little arm free from the blanket and was waving it in the air. He reached out to touch her tiny fist, enclosing it in his.

"There's no need," he said and met the midwife's gaze. "Bonnie will live with me. I'll raise my own daughter."

The midwife smiled in approval. "We'll show you some basics, like how to feed her, then you'll be on your way. She's already had all her tests and passed everything with flying colors."

Liam blinked. Now? Just like that? He knew next to nothing about babies....

Suddenly Rebecca's mother was in front of them, making a grab for the baby. "I'll take her," she said, shooting Liam a defiant look. "We're going home."

Unperturbed, the midwife handed Bonnie to Liam. "I'm sorry, but Mr. Hawke is her father. Your daughter named him on the birth certificate. He has custody."

Mr. Clancy came to stand beside his wife and narrowed reddened eyes at Liam. "We'll see about that. He's not fit to raise a baby and I'll say that in court if I have to."

Liam didn't flinch. The Clancys could try whatever they liked. No one was taking his daughter from him.

As Jenna arranged the last of the weekly flower delivery—fragrant jasmine and sunshine-yellow lilies today—into a crystal vase, she heard her boss, Dylan Hawke, arrive home from an all-nighter. Judging by the voices coming from the penthouse foyer, his brother Liam was with him. Liam had a smooth, deep voice that always made her melt....

And that *is a completely inappropriate way to think about your employer's family.* Or any man. It had been falling for a man and forgetting her duty that had put her in this position.

She gathered up the flower stems she'd trimmed and ducked into the hall before the men made it into the living room. One of the things she'd learned growing up in a royal palace was that housekeepers were expected to keep a low profile—like magic cleaning and cooking fairies who were rarely seen.

From the adjoining kitchen, she heard a baby's cry and she stilled. It sounded like the cry of a newborn. Her arms ached for her own little Meg, but she was in day care, and at eight months old, her cry was different. Her boss, Dylan, and his two brothers, Liam and Adam, were all bachelors, and none of Dylan's friends had been expecting as far as she knew. She'd been pregnant herself for part of the time she'd worked here, so an expectant mother would have caught her attention.

Footsteps sounded down the hall, and then Dylan's face appeared around the corner. "Jenna, we could use your help with a slight baby problem."

"Sure," she said, wiping her hands and following him back out. The Santa Monica penthouse apartment's large living room was decorated in whites and neutrals so the only spots of color were the flowers she'd just arranged and the two men who stood in the center, one awkwardly holding the tiny bundle that was now crying loudly. Jenna breathed an "ohhh," her arms aching with the need to comfort the little thing.

As they approached, Liam glanced up at his brother,

then back to the baby he was gently jiggling. Even as her heart sighed at the sight of the six-foot-plus man with the tiny pink bundle, Jenna frowned. Who would leave their new baby with two clueless men? Despite being respected and feared businessmen, they were clearly out of their depth.

"Liam," Dylan said. "You remember Jenna. She'll know what to do."

Jenna glanced at her boss and asked in an undertone, "What to do about what, exactly?"

He stared blankly at her and then shrugged. "About the baby," he whispered.

Right. Well, maybe if she could calm the baby, she could find out what she needed to do.

"Yes," she said, her eyes on the little person nestled in Liam's strong arms. "Maybe I can help?"

Liam regarded her with an assessing gaze—he was less certain of her ability. He needed help—that was evident from the baby's cries becoming more desperate and the awkward way he was holding her—but his eyes held a fierce protectiveness. He wasn't handing this baby over to just anyone. She respected that—in fact, the sight of a man being so protective brought a lump of emotion to her throat. She'd have to lay his fears to rest if she was going to help.

"Hi, Mr. Hawke," she said, smiling brightly. "I'm not sure you remember me, but I'm Jenna Peters." She generally tried to stay out of the way when Dylan had guests, so she and Liam had never had a conversation, but she hoped he might at least recognize her.

He nodded in acknowledgment, but he then turned his attention back to the tiny, squirming girl he held.

"I have an eight-month-old daughter, Meg, and she cried like this when I first brought her home. Would you like me to try some of the tricks I learned with Meg on this little girl?"

Liam looked down at the baby, stroked a fingertip softly down her cheek, took a deep breath and oh-so-carefully placed the baby in Jenna's arms.

"Bonnie," he said, his voice rough. "Her name is Bonnie."

As he said the name, his dark green eyes softened and Jenna's stomach looped. He was still standing close, as if not wanting to be too far from the baby. Jenna shivered. She could feel the heat from his body, see the day's growth of dark beard, smell the masculine scent of his skin....

She stepped back, away from this man's aura. The priority here was Bonnie.

Jenna pulled the pale pink blanket a bit more firmly around the little girl, laid her across her heart so the baby could feel the beat and began to pace and rock, crooning as she went. The cries gradually quieted until a wet-faced Bonnie peered up at her.

"Hello, little one," Jenna murmured, unable to stop the smile spreading across her face.

Dylan crept across to look over Jenna's shoulder. "Good work, Jenna," he whispered.

But Jenna's gaze was drawn to Liam. He looked from the baby across to her, his features holding too many emotions to be easily deciphered, though gratitude was definitely one of them. He and this baby must have a strong link—perhaps they were related, or he was close to the parents.

He cleared his throat. "How did you do that?"

"I've laid her over my heart," she said, smoothing the fine, dark hair on Bonnie's head. "Babies like to feel the beat."

"Thank you," he said. His voice was low and full of sincerity.

She glanced up and opened her mouth to tell him he was welcome, but her throat suddenly refused to cooperate. She'd been around Dylan's brothers before, enough to know that good looks and hair like dark, polished mahogany ran in the family, but she'd never before been exposed to the full force of Liam Hawke's intensity. He looked like Dylan, yet nothing like him. Liam's hair gleamed in the sunlight streaming through the tall windows. His eyes didn't sparkle like her boss's; they simmered, a deep green maelstrom focused on her.

She swallowed and forced her mouth to work. "She's lovely. Are you looking after her?"

"You could say that," he said, his voice flat. "Her mother died."

Her heart breaking for the little girl, Jenna stared down at the baby who was drifting off to sleep. "Oh, I'm so sorry. Is she yours?"

"Yes," Liam said. A world of meaning was in that one word.

She lifted a hand to touch his forearm but thought better of it and laid it back around Bonnie. This man was still her boss's brother.

Dylan moved closer and looked over Jenna's shoulder. "Before we left the hospital, they showed Liam how to look after her. And while he was doing that, I ducked out and got a baby seat fitted to his Jeep. But once we hit the road, she started crying and nothing we did seemed to help. I suggested that when he dropped me off, he come up and see if you could get Bonnie settled before he drove home."

She sneaked a glance at Liam, curious about the circumstances that had led to this situation. Curious about why he didn't already have a car seat fitted when he went to pick up a baby. Curious about him. Instead she asked, "Could she be hungry?"

Liam shook his head. "She shouldn't be. We fed her last thing before we left the hospital."

"She's settled now," Jenna said. "Would you like to take her back?"

He nodded, but she saw the uncertainty in his eyes. Jenna positioned the baby across his chest, unable to avoid touching his shirt, then stepped back.

Bonnie squirmed, then settled as her father stroked her back.

"You live alone downstairs, don't you?" Liam asked, his gaze not leaving his daughter.

"On the bottom floor with my little girl." Dylan's apartment had three floors—Dylan slept on the top and she and Meg were on the lowest level. Luckily noise didn't travel in this apartment so Meg didn't disturb Dylan.

Jenna had been working as his housekeeper for more than a year now. She'd applied for the job at four-months' pregnant, and he'd been good to her, more than she'd expected from an employer. Having a job that gave her a place to live as well as an income was exactly what she'd needed in her situation.

An unmarried princess from the ancient royal family of Larsland falling pregnant had been intolerable, so Princess Jensine Larsen had left her homeland before anyone found out and started a new life in Los Angeles as Jenna Peters. But she had no support network, no family, no friends to fall back on. This job with Dylan had been a godsend and she didn't want to jeopardize it.

"I really need to get back—" she said as she turned away, but Liam cut her off.

"Where's your baby while you work?"

Jenna thought about the most precious thing in her life and held back a wince. "She's in day care."

"Wouldn't you prefer to have her with you?"

Jenna hesitated, looking from Liam to Dylan and back to Liam. The answer was obvious, but her boss was sitting in the room. "In an ideal world, of course I'd like to spend all day with my daughter." Even if she were at home giving Meg a royal upbringing, they wouldn't see much of each other—Meg would be raised by nannies and nursery staff, as Jenna herself had been. "But I need to earn a living to support us both, and I'm prepared to make sacrifices for that. Dylan's been good to me. I'm really grateful for this job. Speaking of which," she said, edging out of the room, "I have to go—"

"Wait," he said, and despite herself, she stopped.

Liam looked into the clear blue eyes of his brother's housekeeper. "I'm going to need help with Bonnie."

She nodded and smiled encouragingly. "That's probably a good idea," she said in her musical Scandinavian accent. "Being a single parent is a hard road. Will your parents help?"

That would have been best, and if he'd known he was about to become a father, he could probably have arranged it. He rubbed his fingertips across his forehead. "My parents are overseas for a couple of months."

Dylan let out an ironic chuckle. "They'd been looking forward to their big European holiday, but it turns out it was bad timing."

"You might want to think about hiring a nanny," Jenna said.

That had been his thought exactly. When the midwife had handed the tiny bundle to him, Liam had awkwardly accepted Bonnie and held her against his chest. He'd played a lot of sports in his life and coaches had often told him he had natural grace and agility. Yet he wasn't comfortable holding his own daughter. At least his heart knew no such awkwardness—in that moment, with his baby clasped to him, his heart had expanded as if it could reach out and encompass both of them with a love stronger than anything he'd ever experienced.

When they'd arrived at Dylan's penthouse, he'd held a fussy, sad-eyed Bonnie, and the sight had slayed him. He'd move heaven and Earth for this little girl, but she hadn't seemed to want anything from him. Now, if everything went to plan, he'd found somebody she would want—Jenna Peters.

And he was going to get her for Bonnie.

Liam looked at his younger brother. "You're going to do me a favor, Dylan."

"I am?" he said, folding his arms across his chest. "What is it?"

"You're going to let your housekeeper go without serving out her notice."

Dylan slowly uncrossed his arms and planted his hands low on his hips. "Why would I do that? I like Jenna."

Liam smiled, feeling the satisfaction of a good plan coming together. "She can't be your housekeeper because she's about to become my nanny."

"Your nanny?" Jenna said, her pale eyebrows drawing together. "I'm not leaving my job."

"Not just a nanny. You'll also teach me how to be a parent."

"You're already her father."

"I might be her father, but parenting is not part of my skill set." He shifted his weight to his other leg. Admitting a weakness so freely was tough, but he had to be completely honest if he wanted this to work. "I need to learn how to take care of a baby and bond with her. Circumstances mean I haven't had time to prepare for this and I'm not willing for Bonnie to suffer while I'm catching up. You'd be something of a parenthood coach."

Bonnie's grandparents had been furious that he'd been sent home with her, but he'd left them to their grief over losing Rebecca. He expected to hear from them soon about a bid for custody, and he'd deal with that when it happened. For now, he was focused on the immediate future. On being exactly what Bonnie needed.

"I'm no expert," Jenna said, shaking her head. "Many other people are more qualified for that. Agencies devoted to nannies and babysitters."

He glanced pointedly at his daughter, now sleeping soundly, then back to Jenna. "Bonnie seems to disagree."

"Getting a tired baby to sleep is one thing. I'm still working out so many other things as I go along through trial and error. Of course, I read books and articles." She tucked a strand of blond hair that had escaped her ponytail behind her ear, somehow making the simple gesture elegant. "But sometimes I'm just guessing."

He shrugged. None of that worried him—he'd already assumed as much. "You're many steps ahead of me. You'll share what you know and I'll pick it up as we go along. It won't take long before I'll know everything I need to know about babies."

Her eyebrows lifted to almost her hairline and she seemed uncertain about whether to laugh or not. She didn't believe him. That was fine—she didn't know him. He'd never shied from a challenge before, and this challenge was about his daughter. He wouldn't fail.

"So, you'll take the job?"

"Thing is, this is more than a job—it's my home too." She tapped her fingers against her lips, drawing his attention to their softly curved shape. "What will happen to me once you know all you need to know? I have a stable job and home for my daughter here, and I'm sure Dylan would replace me fairly quickly so I wouldn't be able to come back."

"Even when you've finished coaching me in the role of parent, I'll still need a nanny, at least until she goes to school. You won't be kicked out on the street."

She chewed on her lip, and he could see her mind going at a hundred miles an hour, thinking through all the possibilities. He liked that trait in his daughter's nanny. Hell, he liked that trait in anyone.

Jenna rubbed a delicate finger across her forehead. "Can I think about it?"

"I'd prefer you didn't. As you can see, I'm on my way home now. I only stopped in here to drop Dylan off and I wanted to try and settle her before the drive out of town. I'd like you to come with me and help with the feeding and bathing from the start."

"Now?" she asked, blue eyes widening.

"Pack a bag and we'll pick up Meg on the way. I'll send a moving company over to grab the rest of your things tomorrow."

"Hey, what about me?" Dylan asked, looking at them in bewilderment.

Liam waved the concern away with a flick of his wrist. "I'm sure you'll survive without a housekeeper until you can get an agency to send over a temp." He turned back to Jenna. "You'll take it?"

She lifted a hand to circle her throat, looking from him to Dylan and back again. "But—"

"Don't overanalyze it, Jenna. I have a job vacancy and you're qualified to fill it. I'll match the wage Dylan is paying you with a twenty percent raise, and the job comes with accommodation. Best of all, you can keep your baby with you during the day instead of having her in day care. Just say yes. Go on—" he smiled "—you know you want to. Say yes."

Her eyes flicked back to his brother. "Go on," Dylan said, clearly resigned to being housekeeper-less in the short term. "If you want the job, take it. I'll be fine. My brother and my niece need you more than I do right now."

"Yes," she said, then bit down on her lip, as if surprised at herself. Then more firmly, "Yes."

"Excellent." Liam stood, ready to leave now the solution could be put into place. "How long will you take to pack a bag?"

"If you give me your address, I can throw a few things together and catch a cab over in about an hour."

"I'll wait." He wanted her there when he and Bonnie arrived home. He was pretty sure Bonnie would need changing or feeding or both. "You and Meg can come with me and the movers can do everything else."

"Now," she said, a touch of wonder in her voice. "Okay, I'll go and pack a couple of bags as quickly as I can."

Liam let out a long breath as he watched his new nanny head down the hallway. There was something beautiful in the way she moved—he could watch her just walk all day. Having her under the same roof would be no hardship.

Before he could let that thought take hold, he gave himself a mental shake. He had bigger issues than attraction to a beautiful woman. In fact, attraction would be downright problematic. Now that he'd solved the problem of what to do with Bonnie, he wouldn't jeopardize that solution by acting like a teenager ruled by his hormones. He knew how to behave himself, knew what needed to be off-limits. Nothing would jeopardize this plan.

Everything was going to be all right.

He glanced down at Bonnie, sleeping in his arms. No, everything would be better than all right. He'd make sure of it.

Two

The trip in Liam's Jeep to his home in San Juan Capistrano was awkwardly silent after Meg's babble as she played with a crinkly toy in the back subsided and she eventually dozed off. By the time Jenna had finished packing a couple of bags of her and Meg's things, Bonnie had been hungry so they'd fed her before setting off. Now the baby was asleep too.

Behind the shield of her sunglasses, Jenna sneaked a look at her new employer. He sat tall in the driver's seat—she knew he had an inch or two on Dylan's six feet—and faint frown lines streaked across his forehead. Those lines were absent from his brother's face. But minor differences to his brothers didn't come close to explaining why it was *this* brother who'd always caught her eye. Why on those rare occasions his gaze had fallen on her at Dylan's apartment over the year, her heart had beaten that little bit faster.

What did she really know about him—well, besides that he was a man used to getting his own way? She'd been swept along by the speed with which he'd acted. She was used to autocratic people—not only was her mother a ruling monarch, but her father and siblings were all princes and princesses who were used to having people, including her, obey them.

She'd needed that job with Dylan, the settledness of it, the security of it for her and her daughter, yet here she was after only a matter of hours, minutes really, being relocated to Liam's house. Why had she let that happen?

As hard to resist as he was, she knew it was Bonnie's plight that called to her. And Liam's reaction to his new daughter—he was bumbling with his inexperience but so very protective and determined to do the best by the baby.

Most people had nine months to get used to the idea of parenthood. While she'd fed Bonnie at Dylan's apartment, Liam had admitted he'd had less than twenty-four hours since being thrust into the role of instant father.

And it was her job to help him acclimatize. Time to step into her role.

"I'm assuming you don't have any baby supplies at home?" she said, breaking the silence.

"Supplies?" He shoved one hand through his hair, then gripped the wheel again. "I have the car seat Dylan had fitted and the hospital gave me some things."

"Oh, well that will do for a start, but you'll need much more than that."

"I will?" he asked, his dark brows drawing together above aviator sunglasses.

"Yes." She fished around in her handbag, found a pen and scrap of paper and started making notes. They'd need everything from bedding to clothing to kitchen supplies…. "She'll need a few pieces of furniture besides a crib. A chest of drawers or a cupboard for her clothes, and maybe a chair we can put in her room for night feeds. But we can use whatever you have."

"I'll show you around and you can take what you need from other rooms." His voice was deep and business-like, as if he was organizing the logistics for a project. "Put everything else on your list and I'll get a baby shop to deliver."

"We don't need all of this right away," she said, looking down at the crumpled bit of paper in her hand. It was going to be a big delivery to get everything at once— she'd bought Meg's things slowly, in batches. "With some things, we can make do or she can use Meg's."

"Don't be shy about ordering new things for her. If Bonnie needs it, she gets it."

"Okay. We're going to need formula, diapers, bottles, a sterilizer, a crib, crib sheets, blankets, a diaper bag—"

Liam held up a hand. "What's a diaper bag? Don't they arrive in a bag?"

"It's to put all her baby supplies in when we take her out. Actually," she said, making a note, "we'd better get two." She scanned to find her place in the list. "Monitor, high chair, baby wash, booties, onesies—"

Liam stopped her again. "All of this for one seven-pound baby?" he asked incredulously. "Seriously?"

She held back a smile. "Amazing, isn't it? And this is just to start."

She kept reading, and though his eyes were hidden behind his dark sunglasses and he didn't interrupt her again, she sensed his air of bemusement.

When they pulled up in front of the house, Jenna was surprised. She'd expected something sleek and modern, like Dylan's penthouse, but this was older and ram-

bling. Two stories high, tall windows with sashed curtains, wide verandas of varnished wood and the air of
a family home.

Liam parked in front of the main door, under a por-
tico, and jumped out.

They unbuckled the babies and Jenna followed Liam
into the house, she carrying an instantly awake and
perky Meg, and Liam carrying a still-sleeping Bonnie
in one strong arm.

The house was spacious and open plan, with living
areas connected by archways. The whole was decorated
in neutrals with splashes of color, like the burnt orange
rugs on the tiled floor and olive green cushions on the
sofa. It was sophisticated but much more relaxed than
Dylan's apartment. More of a home. Jenna smiled. Bonnie would love growing up here.

A woman appeared through one of the archways,
tall, silent and grim-faced.

Liam glanced up and nodded at the woman. "There
you are, Katherine."

"Do you need something, Mr. Hawke?" she asked,
moving very few facial muscles in the action.

"Just to introduce you to our newcomers." He held
an encompassing arm out in their direction. "Jenna,
this is Katherine, my housekeeper. Katherine, this is
Jenna and her baby, Meg. As I mentioned on the phone,
Jenna is going to be Bonnie's nanny. I'm not really sure
how these things work. I understand babies create a lot
of washing and mess, so you'll need to work together.
Perhaps you also can take on a part-timer to help with
the extra workload."

Katherine didn't spare Jenna a glance. "I told you I
could take care of the little one, Mr. Hawke."

Liam didn't seem fazed. "You already have a full-time job, Katherine. You're essential to this household, and I won't have you overburdened."

Katherine sniffed, appearing to be partially mollified. "I assume there will be one extra for dinner?"

Liam nodded. "And for all meals now, thank you."

"I'll be in the kitchen if you need me." Still without acknowledging Jenna, Katherine turned and left.

Jenna watched the other woman leave. She hadn't been so thoroughly snubbed since she was twelve and her sister Eva had told her she was too babyish to come to her fourteenth birthday party.

"Did I do something wrong?" she asked.

"That's just Katherine," he said and shrugged casually. "She's run this place like a captain runs a ship for eight years and I'd be lost without her, but she can be a little…territorial."

Territorial was one word. Rude was another. "But you said she couldn't do both jobs anyway."

"Knowing Katherine," he said with the hint of a smile, "she would have liked to have made that decision for herself, then been the one who hired the new nanny."

Oh, good. That promised to play out well. Jenna took a breath and changed the subject. "Have you lived here long?"

"Since I was eleven. My parents bought it as a little farmhouse, not much more than a shack really, but it was the land they wanted. As the business grew, we added rooms." He looked around at the house as if it were an old friend. "I bought it from my parents five years ago when they wanted to retire and move off the farm. It is a good arrangement—they moved to a nice apartment in the city with no maintenance, and I can live here next to my work."

She followed his gaze, taking in all the tasteful elegance that oozed money. "It's hard to imagine this place as a shack."

"The original structure is now storerooms off the laundry. But for now, I'll show you the bedrooms I thought we could use as the nurseries."

"You're thinking of giving them their own nursery each?"

He put the keys to the Jeep and his sunglasses on a hall stand, then readjusted Bonnie to hold her closer before turning back to face Jenna. "If we don't, Bonnie will wake Meg when it's time for her night feeds and we'll end up having to get two babies back to sleep."

"It would be great if they could have their own rooms—I just wasn't sure how much space you had. I thought Meg might sleep in with me."

"Up here," he said as he walked up a staircase, "is the main bedroom wing. My bedroom is this one at the end." He opened a door and she peeked in to see a huge room decorated in strong browns and cream with a forest green wall behind the bed. Being at the end of the wing, it had windows on three sides that showcased amazing panoramic views of the San Juan Capistrano countryside.

He strode back down the hallway to the first room and ushered her in. "This is one of the guest bedrooms. There are three along this hall. I was thinking you could have this one. Then the next room for Meg, and the one beside mine for Bonnie."

The rooms were sumptuously decorated, each in a different color. The room that was to be hers had been done in lavender and wheat, with a satin comforter on the four-poster bed and a series of beautifully framed close-up shots of purple irises on the wall. It was gorgeous but didn't seem either Liam's or Katherine's style.

She stepped in and ran a hand over the silky bed cover. "Did you choose this color scheme?"

"No, my mother had the house redecorated before she and my father moved out a few years ago."

She walked into the next room along and turned around. Meg's new nursery had mint green walls and accents in rose pink. The bed had a multihued knitted blanket, and on the walls was a photo series of bright pink tulips. "We should easily fit Meg's crib and changing table in here along with the bed."

"No problem to move the bed out if you want."

Her eyes were drawn back to the bedcover. "Who knitted the blanket?"

"My mother," he said, a trace of a smile flitting across his face. "My brothers and I each have several of them."

"And the flower photos?" she asked, pointing to the tulips.

"They're mine. I take lots of photos in the greenhouse for records. My mother had some of them framed."

His tone was dismissive, but these were more than mere record keeping. The way the light had been captured hitting the leaves and the angle chosen to accentuate the shape of the petals were masterful. However, she didn't think he'd appreciate her pointing that out, so she let it drop.

The room next to his, Bonnie's nursery, had the same tasteful and elegant feel, but it was full of dark wood and tan walls. Masculine and heavy. Perfect for a male guest, but not so appropriate for a baby girl's room.

Liam winced and threw her an apologetic glance. "Perhaps you could organize this room to be painted."

"Absolutely. Any thoughts on color?"

"I'll leave that to you," he said, glancing out the window and seemingly distracted. "I'll organize a credit card—it will make redecorating this room and obtaining ongoing things for Bonnie easier. Though if it's something regular, like formula or diapers, let Katherine know and she can add it to the grocery order."

"Okay."

Bonnie fussed in his arms, and Liam's eyes suddenly had an edge of panic.

Jenna put Meg on the floor with a rattle from her handbag. "Do you want me to take her?"

"That might be best," he said and gently handed her over.

Jenna looked down at the sweet little baby and ran her hand over the soft, downy hair. "Her hair is so dark. Like yours, actually. Meg was bald when she was born."

A smile flittered across his mouth then left. "Bonnie's hair was how I knew for sure she was mine at the hospital." Frowning, he threw a glance to the door. "Listen, I know you've just arrived, but I need to duck out to the greenhouse. I hadn't expected to miss work this morning, so there are things I need to check on."

"No problem," she said, taking the cue. "You go back to work. We'll be fine here."

It seemed it had only been a couple of hours since she'd given Liam the list when a small truck with a stork emblazoned on the side pulled into the paved circular driveway. Liam had obviously found a place that was willing to deliver immediately. It probably helped that money talked.

Two young men jumped out and, with Meg on her hip, she met them at the front door. Bonnie was asleep in Liam's room in an old basinet Katherine had found. Since Liam's room was the farthest away from the rest of the house, she'd put the baby down there for the nap, hoping to not disturb her while they set up the nurseries. "We have a delivery for Liam Hawke," the older man said.

"You've got the right place. Thanks for being so quick."

"All part of the service," he said. They walked to the truck, rolled up the back and started to unload. Jenna showed them the way to Bonnie's nursery. The men assembled the new furniture in the living room and left piles of pastel pink crib sheets, blankets and other supplies stacked on the dining room table. Bonnie was lucky that her every need would be taken care of, that she wouldn't want for anything—yet, there was something a little sad about all her personal things being delivered like a work order. Nothing had been handpicked by someone who loved her.

Though…*had* things already been bought for her? Bonnie's mother must have been prepared for a newborn. Had she lovingly chosen little clothes, searched for and selected a charming crib and linen? Dreamed about playing lullabies as her baby went to sleep? Jenna's throat felt thick with emotion.

"That's it," the delivery man said from behind her. "Mr. Hawke paid over the phone, so I just need you to sign for the delivery." He handed her a clipboard with some papers attached.

"Thanks," she said, taking the clipboard then setting Meg down on the carpet.

As she put pen to paper to sign for the order, she hesitated for a moment before remembering her name. Jenna Peters. She'd had the name for more than a year now; surely soon it would become second nature to use it?

But even as she signed the fake name and handed the

form back, she knew the truth—she'd always be Princess Jensine Larsen, youngest of the five children of the reigning queen of Larsland. A princess who'd never put a foot wrong in her twenty-three years until she made one mistake big enough to obliterate that record.

She'd become pregnant out of wedlock.

At first the news hadn't been too bad—she and Alexander were in love and had been planning to marry one day. They'd just have to move the date forward. And tell their families. Their relationship had been a secret—after a life lived in the public eye, she'd just wanted one thing that was hers alone. She grimaced. People always said to be careful what you wish for. Now her entire life was lived in secret.

They'd planned on telling their families when Alexander came home from his latest military deployment. But Alexander hadn't come home. He'd been killed in the line of duty, leaving her grieving and pregnant, with no chance of salvaging her honor.

She hadn't been able to tell her parents and face their disappointment. Perhaps worst of all, once the local press found out, it would have tarnished the reputation of the royal family, something she'd been brought up to avoid at all costs. A royal family that had, unlike many of its European neighbors, avoided any hint of scandal in its modern history. The situation would have dealt Larsland royalty its final blow in an age when people were questioning the need for royalty at all.

She'd only been able to see one way out. She'd fled the country and set up a new identity in Los Angeles with the aid of a childhood friend, Kristen, who now worked in the royal security patrol. Jenna had originally planned to run to the United Kingdom because she'd been there before and it had a population large enough to lose herself in, but Kristen had a friend in the United States who'd worked with her on an exchange program a couple of years ago and was now in a position to help. Kristen and her U.S. counterpart were now the only two people who knew both who she really was and precisely where she was. She was sure her parents would have used her passport's trail to track her to the U.S., but it was a big country.

She'd been sending vague updates to her family through Kristen so they knew she was okay, and the press and citizens had been told she was overseas studying. In retrospect, the plan had several flaws, not least of which was that she couldn't be "overseas studying" for the rest of her life. But she'd been panicking and grieving when she'd made the plan and couldn't see a way out now it was in place.

She'd worried that she'd put Kristen's job in jeopardy, but her friend had assured her that her job was probably the safest of anyone's in the patrol. The queen needed Kristen right where she was in case Jenna needed specialized help, and to keep the updates coming.

As the truck turned a corner in the driveway and drove out of sight, she closed the door and picked Meg up.

"Shall we see what goodies were delivered for Bonnie?" she asked. Meg gurgled in reply and Jenna kissed the top of her head.

Liam came across the back patio, toed off his shoes at the door and waved to her through the open living areas that connected the front door to the back.

"Was that the baby supplies arriving?"

"Yes. They assembled the furniture so we just need to put it into position and bring the other pieces into the nurseries."

"We can do that now if you want," he said, resting his hands low on his hips.

"Bonnie's still asleep in your room, so it would be good timing."

They spent twenty minutes moving an extra chest of drawers into Meg's nursery and a single bed out of Bonnie's to make way for the new crib. Once they were done, they sat on the rug on the floor in Bonnie's nursery, Meg playing with a stuffed velvet frog that had been in the delivery, Liam taking sheets, blankets and baby clothes out of their plastic packets and Jenna unpacking the baby creams and lotions and setting them up on the new changing table.

Liam's deep voice broke the silence. "Is your accent Danish?"

She hesitated. Was telling him her true homeland risky? She'd been telling people she was Danish, just on the off chance they'd seen a photo of her before and the name of her country jogged their memory. But for some reason she didn't want to lie to Liam Hawke any more than it was necessary. Perhaps because he was trusting her with his daughter—the ultimate act for a parent—she felt that she'd be betraying him somehow with a lie she could avoid.

"I'm from Larsland. It's an archipelago of islands in the Baltic Sea. We're not far from Denmark and people often get our accents mixed up."

"I've heard of it. Lots of bears and otters."

"That's us," she said, smiling.

He fixed his deep green gaze on her. "Are you going home soon, or are you going to put down roots in the U.S.?"

"I'm seeing a bit of the world, so I'll probably move on at some point." That wasn't strictly true—she wasn't traveling, but she didn't yet know what the future held. Once she worked out how, she'd have to return to Larsland and face the music, and it was only fair Liam knew there was an element of uncertainty in her future. "But not until you and Bonnie are ready," she said to reassure him she wasn't flighty.

"This wasn't a lifelong commitment," he said. "As long as you give me notice, you'll be free to move on and see more of the world any time you want."

"Thanks," she said.

Liam stood, drawing her eyes up his tall frame. "I was serious when I said I'd increase your salary by twenty percent over what Dylan was paying you. And if you have any conditions, let me know."

"You don't even know if I'll be good at the job yet," she said, pushing to her feet before she got a crick in her neck.

Liam crossed his arms over his broad chest and rocked back on his heels, and once again he looked like the multi-millionaire businessman that he was. "Dylan wouldn't have kept you this long if you weren't a good worker, and Bonnie has been happy with you so far. Besides," he said with a lazy grin, "if it's not working out, I'll fire you and hire someone else."

She knew that grin was meant to soften his words. Instead, as it spread across his face, it stole her breath away. Boys and then men had tried a lot of tricks over the years to get her attention, hoping to marry into the royal family, but she'd always seen through them and been far from impressed. Yet Liam Hawke threw one careless grin her way, and she was practically putty in his hands. She held back a groan. This was not a good start to a new job....

"In the meantime," she said, bringing her focus back

to their conversation, "you want me to be happy in my work conditions on the chance I am actually good at the job."

He tilted his head in acknowledgment. "Exactly. A good businessman keeps his options open, utilizes the resources available and moves on when it's no longer effective or profitable."

Meg yawned again. "I'd better feed Meg and get her down for a nap because I think Bonnie will be awake soon."

She ran a fingertip across her daughter's button nose. Her eyes were getting heavy, so Jenna began softly humming an old Larsland lullaby that Meg liked.

Liam dug his hands into his pockets and turned to the door. "I'll leave you to it."

Without losing her place in the song or lifting her head, Jenna nodded. But once he was gone, she moved to the window so she could watch her new employer as he strode from the house toward the flower farm around back. And the question played over and over in her mind—why did she have to find this man, of all men, so appealing?

Three

Liam clawed his way through the nightmare. A child was crying, desperate, inconsolable, wanting—no *needing*—him to do something. He woke with a start, wrenching himself from the grip of the dream. Except the crying didn't stop. For a moment he didn't understand…and then it all came back.

Bonnie. His daughter was crying.

He stumbled out of bed, rubbing his face with one hand and checking he was wearing pajama bottoms with the other. Sharing night feeds with a woman meant making sure he was dressed twenty-four hours a day. He flicked on a light and saw the time—two a.m.—as he headed down the hall.

Just before he stepped into Bonnie's nursery, a light came on in the room and he saw Jenna, eyes soft with recent sleep, hair messed from her pillow and a white cotton robe pulled tightly around her body. She reached down and lifted his daughter into her arms as she whispered soothing words. Liam's heart caught in the middle of his throat, and for a long moment he couldn't breathe. The image in the soft light of the lamp was like a master's watercolor. The ethereal beauty of Jenna, her expression of love freely given to his daughter, and Bonnie's complete trust in return, was almost too much to bear. He couldn't tear his gaze away.

Jenna glanced over and gave him a sleepy smile as she soothed Bonnie, and he felt the air in the room change, felt his skin heat.

Bonnie's crying eased a little and Jenna said over her head, "She's hungry. Do you want to hold her while I make up a bottle?"

He cleared his throat and stepped closer. "Sure."

Jenna's fingers brushed the bare skin of his chest as she laid Bonnie in the crook of his elbow. The urge to hold Jenna's hand there, against his skin, was overpowering. He stood stock-still, not trusting himself to move. One thing was apparent—pajama bottoms weren't enough. For future feeds he'd have to minimize skin contact by making sure he also was wearing a shirt.

She gave Bonnie a little pat on the arm, then moved through the door and down the stairs. He followed, mesmerized by the gentle sway of her hips under her thin, white robe, but he purposefully drew his attention back to where it should be—the baby in his arms.

Stroking his crying daughter's arms in the same soothing motion Jenna had used, he followed Jenna into the kitchen and waited while she made up a bottle. She worked smoothly in his kitchen, as if she'd done this a hundred times before. Of course, she must have done exactly that for her own child. Had anyone else ever watched her and thought it was seductive? Her movements were simple, efficient, but with such natural grace it was almost as if she were dancing.

He was losing his focus again, damn it.

Was it the intimacy of the night that caused his reaction to his nanny? Normally the only women he saw at two o'clock in the morning—especially ones with sleep-tousled hair—were women he was involved with. Not that he often saw them here in his house. He preferred liaisons that didn't have too much of an impact on his personal life or intrude into his personal space. Dylan had once pointed out that Liam's philosophy was emotionally cold, but that had never bothered him—he wasn't naïve enough to think the women he dated were looking for emotional fulfillment or promises of forever.

Besides, women weren't interested in the real him, the man who was passionate about science and breeding new, unusual flowers, the man who had no time for the trappings of wealth beyond the security it could provide his family.

His oldest brother Adam had suggested that Liam had turned it into a self-fulfilling prophecy by choosing women he knew were attracted to him for his money or his looks, keeping things superficial and ending relationships before he allowed himself to be emotionally invested. Liam had ignored his brother—he was perfectly happy with things as they were. He'd never wake up to find he'd let his guard down and he'd fallen in love with someone who was using him for his wealth or had been merely entertaining herself with some twisted game the women he knew always seemed to be playing.

He leaned back against the counter and raised an impatient Bonnie to his shoulder. "Shh," he whispered. "It won't be long now."

He wasn't sure what game Bonnie's mother had been

playing. Her family was wealthy so she hadn't needed his money, but the very fact that she hadn't told him that she was pregnant showed she hadn't been a woman he could have trusted.

"Okay, sweetheart," Jenna said, turning her blue, blue gaze back to them. "Your bottle is ready. How about we go back to your lovely armchair to have it?"

She stroked her fingertips across Bonnie's head as she passed on her way to the hallway, and suddenly— and against all his advice to himself—Liam was in the ridiculous position of being jealous of a baby.

Warm bottle in her hand, Jenna rubbed her scratchy eyes and walked down the second-story hallway. Even though it hadn't been long since Meg had started sleeping through the night, she'd forgotten how demanding night feeds were.

As she reached Bonnie's nursery, she paused and asked over her shoulder, "Would you like to feed her or shall I?"

Liam cleared his throat. "You do this one. I'm still watching your technique with these things."

She nodded and settled into the armchair. She understood. Liam didn't strike her as the jump-in-with-two-feet sort of man—he was a scientist. He'd want to gather all the information first so he'd be best placed to succeed when he did attempt something new. She'd felt his gaze on her in the kitchen as if he were trying to memorize the method of preparing his daughter's bottle. Having the gorgeous Liam Hawke watch her every move was…unsettling, but obviously it would be part of the job as she taught him the skills to look after his baby and helped him bond with her. Surely she'd get used to it with time. A shiver ran up her spine, but she ignored it.

"You can pass her over now," she said, keeping her voice even.

As he leaned down, his bare chest came within inches of her face, and the scent of his skin washed over her. She took a deep breath to steady herself, but that only intensified the effect, leaving her lightheaded. Thankfully, he didn't linger as he deposited the squirming weight of Bonnie into her arms and stepped away.

As soon as Jenna gave the baby the bottle, she stopped flailing, all her energy focused on drinking. Jenna couldn't contain the smile as she took in the sheer perfection of this tiny girl.

Liam was silent for long moments, then he crossed his arms over that naked chest. "How are you finding motherhood?"

Such a loaded question. Thinking of Meg when she was Bonnie's age, Jenna lifted the baby a little higher and breathed in her newborn scent, then murmured, "It's more than I expected."

"More in what way?" His voice was low, curious.

"In every way," she said. "It's more challenging and more wondrous than I'd ever expected."

He leaned a hip against the chest of drawers. "Does Meg's father help?"

"No," she said carefully. "Her father's not on the scene."

He cocked his head to the side, his attention firmly focused on her now, not Bonnie. "Do you have family nearby to help?"

"It's really just me and Meg." Her pulse picked up speed at the half-truth, and she cast around for a new topic before she spilled all her secrets to this man in the quiet of the night. "So Bonnie's mother really didn't tell you she was pregnant?"

He scrubbed a hand down his face, and then looked out the window into the inky night. "I had no idea until I got the call from the hospital. Rebecca and I had broken up eight months ago and hadn't been in contact since. The next thing I knew, the hospital was calling to tell me that my ex-girlfriend had given birth to our daughter a couple of days ago and that Rebecca wasn't in a good way and was asking for me. But before we got to the hospital, she had passed away. They showed me Bonnie—" he cleared his throat "I took one look at her and...couldn't walk away. I'm sure you understand," he said gruffly.

Her mind overflowing with memories of her own, Jenna looked down at the baby who had caused such a reaction in Liam. "There's nothing quite as powerful as the trusting gaze of a newborn."

"Yes, that's it," he said, turning to face her, "along with knowing I'm the only parent she has left. I'm hers. And Bonnie is mine."

"That's a beautiful thing to say," she said, smiling up at him. It was true—as a single mother, she knew something of the challenges that lay ahead for him, but if he wanted his daughter, truly wanted her as it appeared that he did, then Bonnie was lucky.

"And now I have sole custody of a three-day-old baby." He speared his fingers through his already disheveled hair. "It still feels surreal. Yet the proof is currently in your arms."

"Oh, she's definitely real." Jenna smiled at him then transferred her gaze to Bonnie. "Aren't you, sweetheart?"

"It's a strange thing," he said, his voice far away,

"but the idea terrifies me, yet at the same time fills me with so much awe that I don't know what to do with it."

She knew that juxtaposition of fear and joy. Since she'd given birth to Meg, she knew it well.

Bonnie had finished the bottle, so she handed it to Liam, then lifted her against her shoulder and gently patted her back.

"What about Rebecca's family?" she asked. "Will they be involved in her life?"

He tapped his fingers against the empty bottle in a rapid rhythm. "When I was at the hospital, I met Rebecca's parents for the first time. They weren't happy to meet me." His expression showed that was an understatement.

"You hadn't met them when you were dating Rebecca?" She'd always been intrigued about how couples navigated the issue of each other's families when those families didn't include the reigning monarch of the country. She'd assumed—perhaps wrongly—it was much simpler for regular people.

He shrugged one shoulder. "We were only together a few months, and we hadn't been serious enough to meet each other's families. Apparently she'd been living with her parents while she was pregnant and had planned to take the baby back there after the birth," he said casually. Almost too casually. "They were going to help her raise my daughter."

"Without you?" Every day she wished Alexander had lived—for so many reasons, but most importantly so Meg could have met and known him. What mother would deliberately deny her child the love of its own father?

"My name was on the birth certificate, so I have to believe she was going to tell me at some point." But he said the words through a tight jaw. "And she did ask the staff to call me when she realized something was wrong, much to her parents' annoyance."

Watching the banked emotion in his eyes, Jenna put two and two together. "They're not happy that Bonnie is with you."

He let out a humorless laugh. "You could say that. In fact, I've already had a call from their lawyer about a custody suit they plan to file."

"The poor darling." Jenna brought Bonnie back down to lie in her arms and looked at her sweet little face. "To have already lost her mother, and now someone's trying to deny her a father."

"They won't win," he said, his spine straight and resolute. "My lawyer is dealing with it. Bonnie is mine. No one will take her away."

And seeing the determination etched in his every feature, she had no trouble believing him.

The next morning, Jenna tucked both babies into the new double stroller and set out to explore the gardens behind the house. The call of the outdoors was irresistible once the sun was shining. Besides, she was feeling restless.

After Bonnie's night feedings, she'd had difficulty falling asleep. Visions of the expanse of smooth skin on Liam's torso had tormented her. Memories of the crisp, dark hair scattered over his chest had dared her to reach out and test the feel under her fingertips the next time he was near. Which would be wrong on many levels, starting with Liam being her boss. She grimaced. She hadn't held many jobs—this was only her second paid position—but even she knew that making a pass at your employer wasn't the path to job security.

Beyond the patio, a small patch of green grass was hedged by a plant with glossy leaves, and beyond that, rows and rows of flowers stretched. Bright yellows, deep purples, vibrant pinks. So much color that it made her heart swell. Workers in wide-brimmed hats were dotted among the rows, and off to the side was a large greenhouse.

As they moved through a gap in the hedge onto a paved walkway, Meg squealed and reached her little hand out toward the nursery before them.

"That's where we're headed, honey," Jenna said to her daughter. "To see all the pretty flowers."

She'd known Hawke's Blooms had a large flower farm that produced much of the stock they sold in their state-wide chain of flower shops—and sent weekly deliveries to Dylan's apartment that she used to arrange—but seeing it in person was another thing entirely. It was as if she'd been watching the world in black and white when suddenly someone had flipped the switch to full Technicolor brilliance.

She pushed the stroller through the gate in the chain-mail fence that surrounded the whole farm and along the front of the rows, stopping at the top of each one to see what was growing there, bending an occasional flower over for Meg to smell. They hadn't made much progress when she caught sight of Liam making quick progress toward her from the greenhouse.

"Good morning," she said as he neared them. "We missed you at breakfast today."

"Morning." He nodded, his face inscrutable. "I wanted to get an early start to catch up on some work."

She took a deep breath of air fragranced with flowers and freshly turned earth. If she worked somewhere like this she'd probably be eager to start her days too.

"It's beautiful out here. Meg and Bonnie seem to love it already."

His eyes softened as he reached down to stroke each baby's cheek with a finger. "It's not a bad place to work."

She lifted Bonnie from the stroller and placed a delicate kiss on her downy head. "What do you think?" Jenna whispered. Bonnie's huge eyes fixed on Jenna's face, then as Liam came near, they settled on her father. "Do you want to hold her?" Jenna asked him, her heartbeat uneven from his closeness.

"Yeah, I do." He took his daughter and held her up for a long moment before murmuring, "Hello, Princess." Then he tucked her into the crook of his arm. "Thanks for bringing her out."

"No problem," she said, trying not to react to Liam using "princess" as a term of endearment for his daughter. To cover any reaction, she lifted Meg up onto her hip and asked, "Do you work out here in the gardens?"

"I come out to check on things occasionally, and sometimes I'm in the second greenhouse where we do the propagating, but mostly I work over there." He pointed to a long white building that looked more like an industrial complex than a gardening structure.

"What happens there?"

"The most interesting aspect of the entire business," he said with a grin. "Research."

Enthusiasm sparked in his eyes and she wanted to know more about what it was that made him happy, about what made this man tick. "Better ways to grow things?"

"We have people who work on that, but I prefer the plant and flower development side of things."

"Creating new flowers?" she said, hearing the touch of awe in her voice.

"Basically. Sometimes it's taking an old favorite and producing it in a new color. Or combining two flowers to create a brand-new one."

She tilted her head to the side and regarded him. "So really you're a farmer."

"No, I'm a scientist," he said in a tone that made it clear there was no doubt on this subject. "Though my parents were vegetable farmers before they moved here and started this business, and they always saw themselves as farmers."

She looked him over. His pants were neat and pressed, albeit with dirt smudges on the thighs. And his shirt was buttoned almost to the top, though there was no tie. There was definitely an aspect of "scientist in the field" about him. Which made her wonder about how he ended up here.

She switched Meg to her other hip to accommodate her daughter leaning toward Bonnie. "Did you always want to join the family business?"

"When we were young, we didn't have a choice. The business put food on the table, so we all helped. Dylan was a charmer even back then, and Adam always had an eye for a profit, so they usually manned the flower stall with Mom on weekends, and I helped Dad in the garden—digging, planting, grafting."

She chuckled. "Sounds like your brothers got the easier end of the deal."

"No, but I made sure they thought that." He shaded his eyes with his free hand as he looked out over the gardens, maybe seeing them as they once were, not as they were now. "I loved those days. Dad teaching me to graft, then leaving me alone with a shed full of plants to experiment. And once he realized I could create new flowers, things no one had seen before, he gave me room to experiment even more."

"Actually, that does sound pretty fun." She glanced down at a nearby row of red poppies and, suddenly wanted to sink her fingers into the rich earth and do a bit of gardening herself.

Following her gaze, he crouched down to the poppies, barely jostling Bonnie. He picked a single poppy with two fingers and handed it to Meg, who squealed with glee. "And," he said, still watching Meg, "there's nothing quite like the satisfaction of creating something with your own hands and knowing that it will contribute to keeping your family clothed and fed."

She could see him as a young teenager, focused on his experiments, carefully tending to the plants and recording the data in a spreadsheet. She smiled at the thought. "I'm guessing you were the serious one when you were kids."

"Adam was pretty serious too. It was usually Dylan leading us astray," he said, the corner of his mouth kicking up in a smile.

Having worked for Dylan for just over a year and watched him interacting with people, she could well believe that. Dylan Hawke had more than his fair share of persuasive charisma, and one day it would catch up with him.

Bonnie whimpered and flailed her arms, causing Liam to look from baby to nanny and back again. Without missing a beat, Jenna tucked Meg in the stroller and took Bonnie from her father as she asked, "So, have you worked here since you left school?"

Liam put his hands low on his hips, then dug them into his pockets, as if not sure what to do with them now. "I got a bachelor of science but kept my hand in here part-time. A double major in biology and genetics helped me with the development of new flowers."

"I think it's marvelous what your family has achieved here. What you've achieved here, Liam." He and his family had taken their destiny in their own hands. Until she'd left Larsland, she'd been on a course mapped out for her by others, and even now, she wouldn't trade having Meg for anything but she wasn't on a path she would have chosen if she hadn't gotten herself into a tangle. Liam was exactly where he wanted to be, doing exactly what he wanted to do. She admired that. "Thank you for sharing the story with me. It's amazing."

He shrugged. "Everyone's story is amazing if you take the time to listen. Take you, for example. You grew up on the other side of the world and now you're here. That's interesting."

Her heart skipped a beat. It was an invitation to share, and in that moment, she wanted nothing more than to tell him about her homeland, the beauty of a long summer sunset, how the winter's snow left a blanket across ages-old stone buildings or that the majesty of the Baltic Sea skirted the edges of her former world. But she couldn't. One slip and her whole story could come tumbling out. And then all the effort to create her new life would have been for nothing.

She leaned down and ran her hand over Meg's blond curls, not meeting Liam's eyes. "I really need to get Bonnie back inside for a bottle," she said as casually as she could manage. "It's been lovely being out here. Thank you."

Four

Five nights later, Liam arrived home just after eight o'clock, feeling an uneasy blend of anticipation and trepidation.

He'd always been something of a workaholic, staying up till all hours with his research, occasionally forgetting meals. And now he had an even bigger reason to ensure the productivity of Hawke's Blooms—Bonnie's future. He'd found her a good nanny, so now the best thing he could do for his daughter was make sure she'd always be financially secure.

Though, if he were honest, this evening's reluctance to come home early may have been more about gaining some distance from his newest employee. Four nights of sitting with Jenna while she attended to the night feedings in the intimacy of the silent, darkened house had led to four nights of lying awake, thinking of the woman a few doors down. Forbidden thoughts rising and swirling through his mind.

Of her mouth.

Her hands.

Her body.

Even though he knew she always dressed sensibly in her robe, the knowledge that she'd gotten up from her bed to attend to his daughter was proving to be alluring.

Yesterday it had become worse. The thoughts had leaked into his daytime activities, and visions of Jenna's skin, smooth and creamy, had distracted him from slicing the root of a plant he was grafting and he'd slipped and cut this thumb. An amateur mistake, and he'd been disgusted with himself.

He'd already been taking earlier breakfasts and ducking out of the house before Jenna woke each morning on the out of sight, out of mind theory. Today he'd taken it a step further; when he'd seen her strolling through the rows of blooms with the babies, he hadn't gone out to say hello, undermining their fledgling routine. But it wasn't just about him trying to regain control of his thoughts. This was also about Jenna.

He refused to jeopardize their arrangement by letting her know where his mind had strayed. If she guessed, she'd be uncomfortable living in his house, and he wouldn't risk her leaving for a less complicated job. Bonnie was his priority.

Not to mention that he was still a little uneasy about how quickly she'd left the other day as soon as he'd mentioned her background. If he wasn't mistaken, she'd used the excuse of Bonnie needing a feeding to avoid talking about her life. It sat uncomfortably in his gut that the woman taking care of his daughter might be hiding something, but he'd tried to dismiss it. There was probably a reasonable explanation. Though, to prove it to himself, he'd make sure he asked her about her childhood again.

Fifteen minutes ago, he'd called to tell Katherine he was on his way up to the house, and she'd said Bonnie was sleeping and dinner would be on the table when he got there. He dropped his briefcase in the living room and headed down the hall. With each step, he braced himself for the sight of Jenna.

So what if he was attracted to her? It was a simple case of mind over matter. His mind was infinitely stronger than anything his body felt.

Three steps from the dining room and he was a rock—wind and rain might pound at his surface, but nothing affected him. Two steps—solid stone, unwavering for anyone or anything. One step—he was impervious. He reached the door and walked through with a straight spine and head held high. Jenna stood gently rocking an old-fashioned white cradle that was set up near the dining table. The soft lighting made her eyes look enormous and her skin glow.

She's just a woman.

A woman of serene beauty, sure. But a woman just the same.

He paused to ensure his breathing was regular, his heartbeat even. He was a rock. Unyielding to outside influences.

He paused by the cradle. Bonnie's long lashes rested on her cheeks and he allowed himself a moment of tenderness as he watched her little chest rise and fall, her mouth move. Then he pulled himself back together and pasted on a polite smile for his employee.

"Good evening, Jenna." He pulled a chair out for her and waited.

"Hello, Liam." She took the seat and he pushed it in, careful not to touch her, as she sat down.

See? Easy. Now that he was over his initial reactions, he'd be fine. As the old saying went, familiarity breeds contempt, and though he didn't want or expect to hold Jenna in contempt, he did expect familiarity would breed indifference to her allure. It was practically scientific.

Several silver dishes with domed covers sat on the table. He lifted the cover off the first, revealing a fragrant curry. He passed the serving spoon to Jenna so she could put some on her plate.

"I'm sorry I'm late," he said, scooping rice from a second dish. "I hope it didn't put you out."

She didn't look up as she filled her plate with the food. "Not at all. It gave me a chance to talk to Katherine."

"How's that going?" Ideally, the two members of his household staff would have a good working relationship, but knowing his housekeeper and her preference for working alone, he was aware that was unlikely.

"I don't think Katherine approves of me eating with you." Her voice, normally lyrical with her Nordic accent, was somber, more careful. "I'm pretty sure she'd like to serve me in the kitchen."

"She's always been a stickler for propriety," he said in an attempt to soothe the waters.

"I'm more than happy to—"

"No. You're welcome at this table. I used to eat while reading journals or research papers, but now that I have Bonnie, it's time I started some new routines, like family dinner time. I want the tradition to be in place by the time Bonnie notices it. I told Katherine she's welcome, too, but she said she'd rather eat in her room."

Jenna ate another mouthful of curry before continuing. "Katherine will probably tell you herself, but she's hired a part-time maid to do the babies' washing and give her some support now she has a busier house."

"Good," he said and nodded. "I didn't want any of that falling to you when you're exhausted from keeping up with night feedings and looking after both girls."

Jenna settled her unflinching blue gaze on him. "You must be exhausted too. You've been getting up during the night and still going to work every day."

"Coffee has become my friend." She was right, but he wouldn't change a thing—Bonnie was worth it. He glanced over at the cradle, wishing his daughter was awake so he could hold her. Yet, even if she were awake, she'd prefer Jenna to him. His stomach hollowed and he turned back to his plate. "How was Bonnie this evening?"

"She cried a bit and didn't want to settle. I brought the cradle in here and had her with me while I made out the grocery order for Katherine, and she was happier with that until she drifted off." Jenna took the dish of spicy lentils that he passed and spooned some onto her plate. "Will you have any time free tomorrow? I'd like to start working on your bonding with Bonnie as soon as possible."

"Tomorrow will be difficult. What about tonight?" Creating a relationship with his daughter was a priority, but he also had to be careful about his work now that he was providing for a daughter. It was not the time to let things slip.

"That could work." She checked her watch. "She'll probably be awake for another feeding in less than an hour. We can do something then."

"Sounds good."

She spooned some more curry onto her plate. "Have you heard anything from Bonnie's mother's family? Are they still planning on filing for custody?"

"They've already taken the preliminary steps." In fact, they were becoming a royal pain in his butt. "My lawyer is on it and he doesn't think they stand a chance."

She nodded and looked back down at her plate. He took a mouthful of dhal and they ate for several minutes in silence. He and Jenna didn't know each other well, and conversation was hard to create. He wasn't good at small talk. Dylan was always telling him he needed to improve his ability to chat when they attended business functions or charity events. He drew in a breath. Now was as good a time as any. Plus, he could quiz Jenna about her background again.

"You asked me a few days ago what I wanted to be when I grew up, and I've been wondering the same about you." He picked up his water glass, took a sip and then watched her over the rim.

She bit down on her lip and looked at her plate for a long moment before replying. "Liam, if it's all the same to you, I'd rather not talk about childhood."

He sat back in his chair and swirled the water in his glass. Interesting. Perhaps she had a difficult time growing up and preferred not to think about it. Or perhaps she was keeping a secret. He couldn't force her to answer questions, but he would wait for the right moment to push further.

If she was hiding something, he'd find out what it was.

No one had ever asked her what she'd wanted to be—not as an adult or as a child. She was a princess. A princess with four older siblings would never be queen, but she was still expected to dedicate her life to her people. Her three brothers had served in the military, but that was about as far as the children of the monarch could move away from their royal duties.

Mewling from the cradle let them know Bonnie was waking. Jenna jumped up, eager for the distraction. "You keep her entertained, and I'll make her bottle."

She saw his quick doubtful glance at the cradle and suppressed a smile. He'd held Bonnie often but usually when she was fed and happy. And quiet.

When Jenna came back into the room with a warm bottle, Liam was sitting at the table, looking bemused as he held a screaming Bonnie. When he spotted her, the relief on his face was almost comical. "Thank goodness. She's been telling me that she's pretty desperate."

"At full volume." Jenna chuckled, took Bonnie from him and sat back in her own chair. "It's all right, little one. I have your bottle right here."

As she fed the baby, Liam finished his dinner, though she felt his steady gaze on her the whole time.

"Want me to take her so you can finish your meal?" he said when Bonnie was done.

"That would be great, thanks." She handed him the now happy baby. As Jenna resumed eating, she sneaked glances at man and daughter. The soft, loving expression on his face when he looked down at his baby turned her heart to putty.

In her world, men didn't have much to do with babies—there were nannies for that. Liam's murmured words, his stroking of her tiny cheeks, affected Jenna more than she would have guessed and made her grieve the loss of a father for Meg all over again. Her own little girl was missing out on this.

It also made her miss her own father and mother. It

had been more than a year since she'd seen them, since she'd heard their voices. This job with Liam would need to be her last in the States—soon, she'd have to work out a plan to return home. It still seemed impossible, but she had to believe that when the time came, she'd find the right way.

When she'd finished her meal, Liam returned Bonnie to the cradle so they could clear the plates, then stood with his hands resting on his hips. "So what's your plan for me with Bonnie tonight?"

She'd been mulling over that very question in her mind all day. Where to start was important. "I was thinking we could try you and Bonnie with her baby carrier."

"Baby carrier?" He rubbed a hand across his raspy chin. "I thought you'd have us doing something more…"

"Hands-on?" She reached for the gray and white carrier she'd slipped behind the cradle to have it accessible.

He shrugged a shoulder. "Yes, actually."

"If we fit the carrier straps to your size and you're comfortable in it, it will give you a certain amount of independence with her. You'll be able to duck in and pick her up during the day if you want, and you'll have your hands free. The easier that becomes, the more time you'll be able to spend with her."

"And the more time I spend with her, the stronger our bond. Got it. Hear that, Bonnie?" The baby was lying back in her cradle, her little arms flailing as she watched them. "This is the first step to our new bond."

Jenna gave the cotton and mesh a shake. "If you're ready, the first thing we need to adjust the carrier straps to fit you."

He looked dubiously at the contraption in her hand. "Is it the right size?"

"They come in one size and we adjust it." She lengthened the strap, then reached up to loop it over his head but hesitated. She'd done this countless times on herself, but pulling it over Liam's thick mahogany hair seemed an act of intimacy that was beyond the boundaries of their relationship.

"Er, you might be a bit tall for me to reach...." It was an obvious lie. He was taller, yes, but if he ducked his head there was no reason she couldn't manage the task. She held the carrier out to him, and Liam seemed to take her assessment at face value.

He took the carrier and slipped it over his head and threaded his arms through, then held the pouch section out in front of him. "This will hold her?"

"She'll be well supported." The carrier needed to be a little tighter so that Liam could hold Bonnie more firmly against his chest, but the threaded buckle was at the back, so it would be awkward for him to do it himself. Perhaps Jenna should have asked Katherine to help with this part. "If you turn around, I'll adjust it."

Suddenly she was presented with the expanse of pale blue shirt fabric pulled firmly across his broad shoulders. A prickle of heat raced across her skin. She wanted to allow her hands to roam, to trace the shape of him under the material, to luxuriate in the warm solidness of him.

He didn't move—patiently waiting for her to help him with something for his daughter. Which was enough to snap Jenna out of the mood that had descended. Quickly, she tightened the straps to fit firmly around him, ignoring the exquisite torture of her fingers brushing against him.

"Okay, I think that's about right," she said brightly. "I'll pop Bonnie in, and check the fitting again then."

As he turned back around, Jenna picked Bonnie up, gave her a quick kiss on the cheek and slid her into the pouch strapped to her father's chest. Bonnie's neck arched against the head support and she locked her gaze on her father's face.

"I think she likes it already," Jenna said.

Liam put a hand up behind Bonnie's head, as he examined as much of the carrier as he could see, as if making an assessment about its construction and the safety of his daughter. "I thought I'd seen babies facing the other way."

"As she gets a bit older, we can adjust it and have her facing forward. Older babies like to see the world, but right now she'd rather be snug against you."

Liam whispered something to Bonnie, and Jenna saw his Adam's apple move slowly up and down. Tears of tender emotion pressed at the back of her eyes, but she blinked them away and busied herself reading the instruction leaflet that came with the carrier, despite having read it several times already, and allowed father and daughter to have their moment.

"Did you wear one of these much with Meg?" he finally asked, glancing up.

Jenna smiled as she circled him, testing the straps and the fit. "She practically lived in one. After work, I was busy trying to get our washing and cooking done. But I hadn't seen her all day, so I didn't want to be apart from her either."

He nodded in understanding. "And with the carrier, you could do both things at once."

"In theory," she said wryly. "Often I'd get distracted by Meg and end up with no washing or cooking done and I'd eat a banana for dinner."

She felt the low rumble of his laugh as it vibrated

through his chest and quickly dropped her hands. "I think she's safe and snug in there," she said, stepping back. "How does it feel?"

He leaned a fraction to one side, then the other and swiveled at the waist, as if testing the carrier's scope. "It's surprisingly comfortable. I mean, I know she's there and my center of gravity is different, but I'd expected it to feel more cumbersome."

"That's great. Why don't you take a walk through the house? See if it feels secure while you move around."

He wandered off, ambling from room to room, leaving her watching him. But she felt more like a voyeur than someone supervising the process. His body moved with such masculine grace, and the carrier straps emphasized the set of his shoulders.

Her heart clenched tight. Why was she having such inappropriate thoughts about her boss? And, maybe more important, why was she so ineffective at controlling them?

She sank into the dining chair and covered her face with her hands, forced to acknowledge that she was quite possibly in over her head.

Two days later, Liam met Jenna and the babies at the door to his research facility. On a whim—one he was still struggling to understand—he'd sent a note to the house inviting them down to see where he worked.

"Hi, Liam," Jenna said brightly. "Thanks for the invitation." She'd worn a summer dress and an orange wide-brimmed hat, and for a moment he felt a pang at not being able to see her silky blond hair.

"Hi," he said, looking at the double stroller. "It might be better if we carry them. And you won't need your hat in here either." He slipped off his white lab coat, threw it over one arm and scooped Meg up in the other. Meg was the heavier of the babies, so he'd instinctively reached for her to save Jenna's arms, but he'd surprised himself lately by liking Meg in his arms almost as much as Bonnie. She had such a sweet personality even at this young age.

Jenna picked Bonnie up and followed him through the doors.

"I'm glad you could make it," he said as they walked down a corridor.

"We wouldn't have missed a personal tour for anything, would we, girls?" Meg gurgled in his arms at her mother's voice.

Beyond family and his research staff, he'd never allowed anyone into his rooms. Corporate espionage was always a concern—if there was a flower he'd developed and was about to patent, a competitor would love the opportunity to see it and try to trump him.

But there was a personal element too.

Since the day his father had given him a plot of land and free rein to breed his own flowers when he was fifteen, he'd always grown his plants with a fair amount of privacy. He had staff to help now, to carry out tasks such as replicating his experiments to ensure the plants would throw the same flower every time and that the cultivars were healthy. But, in his own lab on a day-to-day basis, he still worked alone. It was a more personal space to him than his home.

So why he'd invited Jenna Peters into his inner sanctum was anyone's guess. He inwardly winced. He could rationalize it and say he was letting his daughter visit him at work—something he hoped she would continue to do as she got older—and she needed her nanny to bring her, but he knew that wasn't the truth.

There was something about Jenna that he trusted. Sure she'd been reluctant to talk about her childhood when asked, but he'd decided it must be painful for her. She simply wasn't the type of person to hide anything from him.

As they walked down the sterile white corridor past rooms filled with activity, a few of his staff rushed over to coo over the two babies, but even those who didn't watched his progress. Having non-research or admin staff in the building was enough of a surprise to raise eyebrows, but his personal assistant had told him that his instant fatherhood had been a hot topic of gossip among the staff, so he was sure the rumor mill had filled everyone in on whose baby was in the nanny's arms. He found he didn't mind the extra attention as much as he usually did.

They passed through a set of double doors into the area where he worked. Usually he was the only one in these rooms unless he called on an assistant to lend a hand. His heart rate felt uneven and he realized he was uneasy, waiting for Jenna's reaction.

Jenna stood in the middle of the first room, Bonnie in her arms, and turned around in a full circle. "This is where you work, isn't it?"

His attention snapped to her. "How did you know?"

"It…" Her voice trailed off as she looked from the surroundings back to him. "This is going to sound crazy, but it feels like you in here."

"Feels like me," he repeated dubiously. He narrowed his gaze as he took in the rows and rows of seedlings that he hoped would grow up to be something special, the whiteboards covered in diagrams of the generations of the cultivars, the computers and microscopes. "I'm not sure how it 'feels' any different in this room from the other rooms we passed along the way."

"That's the crazy part." She grinned at him. "Maybe—" She leaned in and sniffed his shoulder, and Meg made a grab for her hair. "No. I was thinking maybe it smelled like your cologne in here and my subconscious picked it up, but you're not wearing any."

He tried to get his lungs working again after she'd leaned so close. "None of the staff wear cologne to work," he said, hoping his voice was normal. "We often need to smell fragrances from a flower, so we don't want outside influences floating around."

She shrugged. "I don't know what it is then. I'll keep thinking about it." She wandered over and peeked through the glass panels in the door to the next room. "What's through here?"

A small swell of pride filled his chest—this project had been his greatest success so far. "Something I've been working on."

Watching her face so he didn't miss her reaction, he opened the door and waved her through.

Five

As Jenna stepped through the doorway of Liam's laboratory, her breath caught in her throat. The windowless room had artificial lighting beaming down on rows of benches covered in small black pots that were bursting with glossy green leaves, each with the same flower on long stalks rising elegantly. It was a single, curved petal of a lily, but this bloom was darkest blue. It was stunning.

"Liam, you created this?" she asked once she'd found her voice.

He nodded. "Well, it was a joint project with Mother Nature."

"It's amazing." She walked along the benches, looking at flower after flower, each as perfect as the last. "Has anyone else seen them?"

"Just the staff here. And Adam and Dylan, so they're ready for when we release it to the public."

She couldn't stop looking at the lilies. She'd never seen anything like them. "This will create a sensation."

"Thank you," he said. "I'm hoping so."

Unable to resist, she reached out and ran a fingertip over a thick, waxy petal. "What sort of launch are you planning for it?"

"I leave that to my brothers, but Dylan's office usually has window signs made up for all the Hawke's Blooms stores when we release a new flower, and Adam's office will probably put out a press release. Gardening magazines and TV shows usually pick up on it, and occasionally we get lucky and the mainstream media mentions it."

This flower deserved more than a poster and a press release. This flower deserved fanfare and fame. "Have you ever done anything more to promote your creations?"

"What more is there?" he asked, frowning.

Her mind kicked into gear, suddenly full of possibilities. "Maybe an event. Something to really make a splash. Something that would get you a lot of publicity and make the blue lily the most sought-after flower in the state."

Liam handed Meg a rubber stress ball from his desk as he asked, "What are you thinking?"

If there was one thing Jenna knew about, it was events. She'd been attending large-scale occasions since she was a child. "It could be almost anything, like a media stunt, or maybe a snazzy release, like the way a bottle of champagne is smashed against the bow of a boat." She'd christened her first ship when she was sixteen. It was more fun than cutting a ribbon, but there was always the danger of splashing her dress. "Perhaps something elegant. How about a ball?"

"For a flower?" he asked dubiously. "People would go to that?"

"Sure they would if you promise them a good time. Make it the party of the year."

Meg reached up and grabbed a fistful of his dark, wavy hair, but Liam barely flinched. "What exactly constitutes a 'party of the year'?"

She thought back over the successful events she'd attended. "Location, guest list, entertainment, food. Just the basics, but done really well."

He arched an eyebrow. "You seem to know a lot about this sort of thing."

"I've attended a few in the past. I had a boyfriend who was often invited to big parties and events." Which was true. In her previous life, whichever guy she'd been seeing had been invited to the events she attended as her plus one.

Apparently accepting her explanation at face value, he sank into a chair in front of a messy desk and leaned back, Meg on his lap. "What else would you do?"

Good question. To start with, they'd need a theme. "Have you named the flower?"

"I was planning on calling it Midnight."

"That's perfect," she said, feeling a little buzz of adrenalin. "You could make midnight the theme of the ball. The decorations would all be in midnight blue, and maybe the official launch would be at the stroke of midnight, perhaps someone cutting a ribbon, and every guest could be given a gift and a cut Midnight Lily. Naturally, you'd make sure there was press coverage, perhaps some influential bloggers, anyone who would talk it up beforehand and afterward."

He made some notes on a jotter on his desk, then turned to her as Meg tried to grab his pen. "I'll run it past Adam and Dylan, but I think it's a great idea. Thanks."

"My pleasure." She smiled. It had been a while since she'd used her brain in that way and it was fun. "I'm sure you'll make it a success."

He ran a hand over his chin, then tapped a finger against his jaw. "Would you consider overseeing the event? You have your hands full with Bonnie and Meg, but my admin staff can put all your plans into action. It would be more about being the ideas person and giving advice about the whole thing."

Jenna chewed the inside of her cheek. The very last place she could be was a party covered by the media. If a single photo of her leaked back to her homeland, her whole plan would come crashing down around her and she'd have to return before she was ready.

"The thing is," she began, thinking on her feet, "I hate being in front of people, talking to the media, that sort of thing. And crowds. So I'm not the best person to organize it."

He shook his head, obviously not seeing her objection as an obstacle. "Adam or Dylan would do all the public speaking, and Dylan's office, which oversees the Hawke's Blooms stores, has a PR person. She can be the liaison with the media. And if you're worried about the crowds, you wouldn't even have to attend. You can be as behind the scenes as you want to be. It's your ideas I want."

A bubble of excitement filled her chest just thinking about it, and she held her breath for a beat as if that could contain it. She had heaps of accumulated knowledge about events, which was currently of no benefit to anyone. She could make use of her knowledge and help Liam and Dylan, who'd both given her a home and a job when she'd needed them.

Then again, her conscience protested, she'd never actually organized an event of this size on her own. She'd feel like a fraud. Her excitement deflated.

Reluctantly, she admitted the truth. "The best thing would be to hire an event organizer, someone with experience and training."

"True, but I've never been known for traditional hiring practices. Just look at the process of hiring my brother's housekeeper to be my nanny, and that's working out just fine. Besides," he said with a pointed look, "you're the one who convinced me that we should do it differently this time, so it's pretty much your responsibility to see that through."

She laughed at his attempt at levity. "Okay, all right. I'll give it a go, but I can't promise that I'll do it as well as a professional would."

A spark of triumph flared in his eyes, and he grinned. "You just do it your way—that's all I'll be expecting. I'll run it past Adam and Dylan and get a team together to meet with you."

A few minutes later, Jenna pushed the stroller out of the building into the brilliant sunshine and the scents of the flower farm and wondered what she'd just gotten herself into.

"Girls," she said, looking down at the two babies, "sometime soon I might need to learn to say no to Liam Hawke."

When Liam arrived home that night it was almost eleven o'clock. The house was quiet, calm. He felt an ironic smile creep across his face. A few months ago, quiet and calm had been his house's natural state. Then his daughter had arrived, bringing sunshine and happy chaos with her. Meg had only added to that.

Jenna, however, had interrupted his calm in a different way. In a wholly unexpected and unwelcome way. Even now, thinking about her, his pulse accelerated against his will.

He headed up the stairs and down the hall and noticed the light in Bonnie's nursery was on. Bonnie must be having her bottle, which was good timing—he could stop in and help with that before falling into bed. But when he reached the room, it was empty of furniture and Jenna stood with her back to him as she painted the walls daffodil yellow. In a simple white T-shirt and cut-off denim shorts stretching nicely over her rounded bottom, she was the most alluring woman he could remember seeing. His mouth was suddenly dry. He swallowed once, twice.

"Well, this is unexpected," he said, leaning on the door frame.

She whirled to face him, eyes startled and face covered in splatters of bright yellow. A large spot sat lopsided on her nose, and drips decorated her white T-shirt.

"I thought you said it was okay for me to paint this room," she said in a rush. "The dark browns—"

He held up a hand. "It's fine. You're right, I wanted the nursery redecorated—I just thought you'd get a contractor in to do it. Painting walls isn't in your job description."

She shoved some hair that had fallen from her ponytail away from her face, but it flopped back straight away. "I wanted to do it. I've never painted a room before."

He couldn't hold back the laugh—she was so earnest. "It's hardly up there with life goals like climbing Mt. Everest or touring a medieval castle."

"I suppose," she said with a secret smile dancing around her mouth, "it depends on what a person has and hasn't experienced before."

"I suppose so." He pushed off the doorframe and wandered around the room, scrutinizing her handiwork.

"It's not too bad, is it?" Her hand fluttered as she tucked the stray strand of hair behind her ears. She seemed more uncertain than she had about anything since he'd met her.

The edges were crooked in places, but given it was her first time, it looked remarkably neat. "You've done a good job."

She beamed at the simple praise as she pointed to the windowsill. "I know the edges need some work. I'll go over them when I've finished here."

"How about I change my clothes and give you a hand? I know some tricks that will make it easier." He was sure he'd regret this later, but in that moment, seeing her glowing from within, he couldn't walk away.

"Oh, no," she said emphatically. "I couldn't ask you to do that after a long day at work. I'll be fine."

"I assume you've also put in a long day already. Speaking of your job," he said mildly, "where exactly is my daughter?"

Jenna rubbed her forehead with the back of her hand, leaving another adorable smear of yellow. "Sleeping in Meg's room. I moved Meg's crib into my room until I've finished in here and Bonnie can move back in."

"Okay. I'll do a quick check on her, then change into some old clothes and be back."

He slipped out and into the room next door and saw

the perfect little face of his child. She still made his breath catch in wonder every time he saw her.

She was a miracle, and she was his. Would he ever feel worthy of her?

Jenna sighed heavily after Liam left the room. Spending time with him on a joint project sounded like sweet torture. It was hard enough being with him late at night when she fed Bonnie, but at least they had the baby to focus on and clearly defined roles. She was the nanny, awake for a night feeding.

Though, truth be told, she was often at sea in Liam's house. When she'd lived in the palace, she also had a clearly defined role—she was the daughter of the queen and she had access to certain areas, knew who worked where and how things should be. When she'd lived in Dylan's apartment as his housekeeper, she'd had her own space downstairs and clearly defined boundaries—she cleaned Dylan's living areas but she didn't spend time in them, and her own rooms were hers and private.

Yet here in this house, she was sharing Liam's personal space, despite barely knowing him, despite being his employee. Liam had encouraged her to make herself at home, but that wasn't realistic.

Could that be why she reacted to her boss as a man? The boundaries of home and work were so confused that the boundaries between the man who signed her paychecks and the man who filled out a button-down shirt like no one's business were destined to be equally as confused.

Liam strode back into the room wearing an old T-shirt that fit him perfectly and a pair of blue jeans that had become soft with washing and hung low on his hips, molding over his thighs. A low, insistent pulse beat through her body. It seemed that it wasn't just when he was wearing button-down shirts that he affected her....

"Where would you like me to start?" he asked, his voice deep and rich.

She swallowed, trying to get her voice to work. "Maybe on the edges. As you pointed out, I'm not particularly good at them."

"No one's perfect at something the first time they try it, Jenna. It takes practice." He rested his hands on his hips as he assessed the spots he'd be working on. "You've done a good job for your first time."

"That's kind of you to say," she said, feeling a blush creeping up her cheeks.

He picked up a paintbrush and dipped it in the sunshine yellow paint. "Just truth. I'm a simple black-and-white, facts-and-figures kinda guy."

She wondered if he truly believed that or if it was a throwaway line. He'd said it in all seriousness, but surely the man who'd created the Midnight Lily and taken the photographs that adorned the bedroom walls couldn't see himself as only a "facts-and-figures kinda guy"? She had so many questions about Liam Hawke.

They painted in silence for a few minutes before she found the courage to pose one of them. One she owed it to Bonnie to ask. "Can I ask you something personal?"

"You can ask," he said, his voice teasing as he crouched to reach a corner. "However, I'll reserve the right not to answer."

She paused with her roller midair, trying to get the words right. "You work such long hours. Wouldn't you prefer to spend more time with Bonnie?"

He shrugged and kept painting. "Of course I would, but I have other responsibilities too."

"You told Katherine to take on a helper because the

situation had changed," she said as politely as she could. She knew she was treading on dangerous ground, questioning her employer, but she had to say something for Bonnie's sake. "Shouldn't the same principle apply to you, so you can balance your obligations to the business with those to Bonnie?"

He reached into his pocket, brought out a roll of masking tape and began to tape around the edges of the window. "Part of the role of a father is to ensure his children have everything they need in life. I know what it's like to start out poor, and I won't let that happen to my daughter. So sometimes, yes, I need to work harder and longer so I can make sure she has every opportunity in life that I can create for her."

Taking her cue from him, Jenna kept working as she spoke, despite wanting to watch his expression. "You know, my parents prioritized their work over spending time with their children." Their work had been royal duties, but the principle was the same. "Bonnie doesn't care if her sheets are 1,500-thread count cotton or 300-thread count. She doesn't care whether she gets to use a designer diaper. She just wants the thing taken off after she's made a mess. Bonnie cares about you being there, about being held, loved, fed."

She could feel his gaze land on her. "Correct me if I'm wrong, but isn't that what I employed you for?"

"Yes and no." She moved to the next wall and kept painting. The fact they weren't looking at each other was probably making this personal topic easier to discuss. "Nannies aren't for life, and after I'm gone, Bonnie will only have you. *You* will be the constant in her life, the one whose love and attention she'll crave."

The silence on the other side of the room made her risk a quick glance at him. She caught him letting out a long breath and rubbing the back of his neck with his spare hand.

She winced, but she'd come this far, so she may as well finish what she'd started. The roller tray was nearly empty, so she tipped more paint from the can as she spoke. "You want to know what I think?"

"Shoot," he said wearily.

"I think it would be easy to hide in science," she said, choosing her words with care. "Babies and love are unpredictable and messy. Science is logical. In some ways, science would be simpler than real life."

"Science has rules. It has order." His voice was grave with the weight of conviction. "Science is measurable. Science doesn't lie."

The silence in the room was heavy, as if they both realized the depth of this accidental revelation. Part of her wanted to leave him alone, not to push on something so personal. The other part couldn't let this little window into a man who fascinated her go.

"People lie?" she asked softly.

She sneaked a glance and saw him shrug. "They've been known to."

"Like Rebecca not telling you she was pregnant?"

"That's one example," he acknowledged, his voice even. Then he shifted position to paint around the windowsill as if this wasn't a big deal.

Jenna hesitated, again torn between wanting to let him talk and not pushing. Finally, she decided to leave the decision to him. "Liam, you don't have to tell me anything. I'm just your daughter's nanny. But if you want to tell me, I'd be interested in listening."

He didn't say anything for long moments, then cleared his throat. "When I was eleven, we moved from the Midwest out here to California. I'd been in elementary school and started here in my first year of middle school. My parents thought I'd be fine—all the kids my age were in a new school, so we were all in the same boat."

"But you were in a different boat altogether," she guessed.

"I was," he acknowledged ruefully. "The kids I used to be friends with had helped out on their parents' farms after school, like we did. The kids in the new school had no responsibilities and were obsessed with labels and other status symbols."

Her heart broke a little for that boy who was a complete fish out of water, but she tried to keep the sympathy from her voice, knowing he wouldn't want it. "It sounds like you would have had culture shock."

"Perhaps I did." He added more masking tape further along the edge and went back to painting. "Then the flower farm started doing well, and our parents moved the three of us to prestigious private schools."

She grimaced, imaging what was to come. "Which was worse."

"Absolutely," he said on a humorless laugh. "Full of rich kids who were spoiled brats. Bragging and exaggerating were normal parts of conversations, and they were always playing power games. Everything came with a price. Nothing was as it seemed."

She'd met kids like that when she was young—they'd say they wanted to be her friend, but it was all about her title, not the person she was. "Self-centered and not afraid who knew it."

"That's about it." His voice wasn't bitter or accusing, simply matter-of-fact. "For a country boy, it was all so foreign. My brothers and I were unfashionably family-oriented."

"Yet, now you're probably richer than many of them," she said, knowing she was pointing out the obvious.

"There's a difference between self-made wealth and inherited wealth. People who are born to wealth and privilege are a different species."

Her heart clenched and sank. "And those born to wealth and privilege are a species you have no time for," she clarified, but his tone had been clear enough.

"It's a culture of one-upmanship. It's dishonest."

If he knew the truth about her, she'd only reinforce his theory—she had been born to wealth and privilege and her life now—even her own name—was a lie. And it mattered. For some reason Liam Hawke's opinion of her mattered way more than it should. A tight band seemed to clamp around her chest, making it difficult to draw in breath.

"You know," she said, putting down her roller, "it's quite late. I'll finish this tomorrow. Thanks for your help."

She heard a muffled groan and turned. He stretched up into standing and rubbed a hand over his eyes. If he knew she was another one of the people who lied to him, there would be disgust in his gaze. Disgust at her. How would she be able to stand that? She looked back to the roller tray.

"Jenna," he said softly.

Even knowing what he'd think of her if he knew the truth, she couldn't help turning back to him when he said her name.

"I shouldn't have laid all that on you. I'm sorry." He reached a hand out to rest on her shoulder. "It's my crap, not yours and now I've made you uncomfortable."

His nearness made her pulse race, and her shoulder tingled where his hand rested. The contrast between that excitement and the heaviness in her chest about her deception was almost too much to bear.

"No, you didn't say anything wrong. I'm just tired. Probably too many paint fumes."

"Here, I'll help you clean up," he said, turning and picking up the brushes.

Five more minutes this close to him was out of the question. She had to get some space or risk losing control, pushing him against that wall and kissing him with all the crazy, confused desire inside her. Or she might even break down and confess the secret she'd been keeping. Then he'd see her as the same as all the other people who'd lied to him. Either option was unthinkable.

She pasted on a fake smile that she knew didn't reach her eyes.

"It will only take me a minute. Really," she said, with as much conviction as she could muster. "I'll see you tomorrow."

For a long moment, he didn't move, just watched her with a frown line crossing his forehead. Then he nodded slowly. "Tomorrow." And he walked out the door.

Six

The afternoon sun streamed through the window of Bonnie's nursery, silhouetting Jenna as she painted the final touches on the newly white window frame.

She hadn't heard him, so for a moment Liam took the opportunity to watch her work, to appreciate the sheer beauty of this woman who'd so suddenly become a part of his life. A woman who made the world a little brighter wherever she was.

He must have made a sound because she started and turned. "Oh, it's you," she said in her musical accent.

"Just me." He stepped into the room. "No babies?"

She rested her brush on the side of the paint tin and rose to stretch. "Bonnie's asleep and Katherine has taken Meg for a walk."

"Katherine?" he asked, incredulous.

Jenna shrugged one shoulder, causing the pale blue cotton of her T-shirt to stretch across her breasts. "She offered. She said she could see I wanted to finish the painting, but I think she and Meg have developed a certain devotion to each other."

In the eight years Katherine had worked for either him or his parents in this house, he'd never seen her display devotion to anything other than her job. "Wonders will never cease," he said and considered whether he'd been underestimating his housekeeper.

"Don't be too surprised," Jenna said with a lopsided grin. "She still doesn't particularly like me."

He laughed as much for Jenna's self-deprecation as for the humor in the situation. "Then the universe still makes sense."

She picked up a rag and wiped her hands. "If you're just dropping in to see Bonnie, I can—"

"No," he said, interrupting her. "I'm home for the day."

Her eyes were wide when they met his. "At four o'clock?"

He dug his hands into his pockets and nodded. He'd given this a lot of thought during the day and had made a decision. "You were right last night. I've been seeing this from the wrong angle. Bonnie needs her father around. It's time I made that happen."

Jenna's blue eyes glistened, then she blinked and smiled. "She's a lucky little girl."

The pureness of the emotion in her eyes resonated through him, seemed to take hold of his heart and squeeze, and he had to clear his throat before he could reply. "I appreciate that, but we both know that as a parent, I have a long way to go."

"It takes practice," she said, repeating his words from last night.

He smiled wryly. "True. That's why I've rearranged

things at work and handed some tasks and projects over to my staff." His two senior research assistants had been surprised but keen for the extra responsibility, and he'd also talked to his PA about handing some tasks to her. "My plan is to be home by four o'clock every day."

"That's amazing, Liam. Bonnie will love having the extra time with you." She looked at him with admiration shining in her eyes, and he had to wonder if he'd partly made the decision because it was Jenna who'd suggested it. He'd like to think he'd have realized the right thing to do on his own, but he couldn't deny the effect she had on him.

He let out a long breath, wanting to respond only as a father, not a man who was having trouble focusing anywhere but on his nanny's lips.

He shrugged as casually as he could manage. "I can't promise how successful it will be, that I'll be home by four every day, but I'll definitely aim for that."

"We'll be able to work much faster on your bonding with Bonnie."

He'd been thinking about that and knew just what he wanted to do next. "I'd like to learn to feed her on my own. There's no reason we both have to get up every night."

"I've been thinking the same thing." She put the lid on the paint tin and gathered up her brushes as she spoke. "I'm sure you'll find that those late-night feedings, when it's just the two of you, can be a special time."

They probably would be. Plus, this plan had the advantage of not feeling tempted by seeing Jenna in that thin robe when he was only half awake and his defenses were low. "How soon can we start?"

"Tonight, if you're ready," she said, looking at him

with those clear blue eyes, beguiling him with those cupid's bow lips.

"That will be great." He headed for the door before he did something stupid, like kissing her here in the freshly painted nursery. "Let me know when she's ready for her next bottle."

He walked down the hall to his room, loosening his tie as he went. Now he just had to survive one more night of the temptation that was his nanny and he was home free. Well—he hesitated with his hand on the doorknob to his room—that covered the nights, but he couldn't be sure of coping with the temptation that was Jenna during the day. He threw the door open and once he was in, he leaned back and hit his head against the door behind him.

Liam spent the late afternoon hours sprawled in the living room playing with Meg and asking Jenna her opinion on topics he'd come across in the baby books he'd been reading, such as routines and when to introduce solids into Bonnie's diet. Her opinions were well considered and interesting, and he found himself simultaneously agreeing with her and thinking he should take notes. He thanked the fates he'd stumbled across someone like Jenna to care for his daughter. Their situation was ideal. Well, it would be as long as he could keep his rogue attraction to her at bay.

Dusk was settling over the landscape when Bonnie's little cries came over the baby monitor.

"That's my cue," Jenna said, unfolding herself from the sofa and heading for the stairs.

He scooped Meg up and followed. "Come on, Meg. Group trip to the nursery." The baby gurgled and babbled her agreement.

Liam walked down the hall after Jenna, trying not to watch the sway of her hips but failing. There was something very particular about the way she walked—it was almost gliding. Had she had deportment lessons as a child, perhaps?

In Meg's room—which was still temporarily Bonnie's—Jenna reached into the crib, but Liam put out a hand to stop her. "I'll do it all this time. You just talk me through it. It's the only way I'll become self-sufficient."

Jenna took Meg from him and nodded. "Okay."

Slipping his hands under the baby to support her in all the right places, he lifted her to his chest. Her little face was red and her arms flailed. "Shh," he said. "You might need a bit of patience for this, but I promise you'll get fed in the end."

Jenna sank down into the armchair with Meg, who was playing with her own toes. "First, she'll want a clean diaper," Jenna said.

He'd had some practice at changing diapers, so he was fairly confident and managed to complete the task without incident.

"Done," he said and held his diapered daughter in the air.

"She'll be perky for a little while since it's still early, so she'd probably like a bit of time on her play mat."

Play mat. Right. He looked around and nothing jumped out at him. "Where do we keep the play mat?"

"It's folded in the bottom drawer. It has a mobile that arches over the top and she loves it when you play on that with her."

He found the mat, laid it out on the carpet, put Bonnie on top and then clicked the arms of the mobile together. Bonnie seemed happy, but how, exactly, was he supposed to play with her? He wasn't a complete idiot—he'd worked out how to play with Meg, but she had more control over her limbs and a rudimentary understanding of games. Bonnie was a different matter.

He rubbed a hand over his chin. "What—?"

"The soft animals hanging from the mobile arms all make different sounds if you handle them and Bonnie loves it when you touch them for her. Try the ladybug—she's crinkly."

Liam crinkled the ladybug, then surprised himself by losing track of time as he lay on the floor playing with his daughter.

"I think she's getting tired," Jenna finally said. "She'll appreciate a bottle and a sleep."

Reluctantly Liam packed up. When he'd spent time thinking about being a father to Bonnie, he'd mainly thought of himself as a caregiver in this phase of her life and not really being able to interact with her until she was a bit older. He'd never suspected that he'd be sorry to put a play mat away.

"Right," he said, "we're ready."

Jenna stood back so he could pass her and head for the kitchen. She talked him through making up his first bottle. On the other night feedings, he'd held Bonnie while Jenna had made the milk, so the juggling act of holding a baby while carrying out the task was more of a challenge than the bottle itself.

Back in the nursery, he settled down into the armchair, bottle in one hand, his now fussy daughter in the other. "You know, they showed me how to do this at the hospital the day I met Bonnie, but I'm afraid I was so overwhelmed, I didn't pay enough attention."

"No matter. It's all worked out perfectly fine," Jenna said with a smile. "Lay her back along your forearm. And tilt the bottle to her."

Getting the bottle past those angry fists was easier said than done, but once Bonnie had the teat in her mouth, she stilled, as if all her focus was on the food. Triumph surged through him at being able to successfully feed his daughter; it satisfied something primal inside.

"Have you heard anything more from Rebecca's parents?" Jenna asked softly.

He sighed. "Our lawyers had a phone meeting today to see if they could negotiate an agreement."

"No luck?"

"The Clancys aren't interested in anything but full custody."

"But anyone could see Bonnie belongs with you," she said, gesturing to his hand holding the bottle.

"My lawyers think this is about anger. They're angry their daughter is gone. And they want the last link to her."

She nodded. "Bonnie."

"Yes," he said, gazing at his baby girl. "And they're angry at me because I have her."

"I'm sorry, Liam." Her voice was full of compassion, and just for a moment he let himself accept what she was offering. But only for a moment.

"Thank you, but don't be sorry for me—cheer me up instead." He grinned as he glanced up, wanting to just sit and listen to her speak in her beautiful accent. "Tell me about Larsland."

Her eyelids drifted closed as she rocked Meg. "It's beautiful," she said, her voice dreamy. "The sky is a blue I haven't seen since I left. The birds are different, so the birdsong early in the morning is distinctive. And the old cities on the main islands are a mixture of modern buildings and stone structures, some dating back hundreds of years."

As she continued to describe the sights, he glanced down at his daughter. Bonnie blinked at him as she drank, as if mesmerized. Her gave her a smile, then looked back to Jenna as she talked about her homeland, and suddenly he knew how Bonnie felt. Enthralled. He was enchanted by Jenna in the soft lamplight, by the glow of her skin and the emotion in her eyes. His body heated with heady warmth.

He'd never wanted to kiss a woman more.

Of course, the irony was that he'd never met a woman more off-limits. She was an employee, and he'd never cross that line and become a boss who made advances to women who worked for him. That type of behavior was deplorable.

Worse, Jenna Peters was the employee he particularly couldn't afford to scare off. Bonnie was the most important thing in the world to him, and Bonnie needed Jenna. If he made a pass at Jenna and she left, he'd never forgive himself. Being able to handle a night feeding on his own was a far cry from being able to look after his daughter's every need. Sure, he could get another nanny, but could he guarantee he'd be able to find one Bonnie liked as much? Whom he could trust as much?

No, kissing Jenna would be bad on so many levels. He held back a groan. Perhaps he should change the subject to something more practical, something she'd be less passionate about.

"I heard you met with Danielle again today." He'd asked his PA to meet with Jenna as soon as she could schedule it to get moving on the launch of the Midnight Lily and they'd now had two meetings in two days.

"She's great," Jenna said brightly. "We had our meeting while I changed diapers and carted babies around. She didn't flinch or lose her train of thought once."

Liam was pleased but not surprised. Hawke's Blooms was known for paying its staff well, but in return, they had high expectations of every employee. "Did you get far with the plans?"

"We made a list of what needs to be done in the next week, and she's going to liaise with people in Adam's and Dylan's offices. She's already booked The Gold Palm as the venue and they're talking about the guest list. I think everything's on track."

"Thank you again for agreeing to help with this. I appreciate it."

"You're welcome," she said, smiling. "It's actually been fun."

From the expression on her face, he didn't doubt that, but she was still doing him a favor. "I've been thinking, since you're handling this on top of your nanny duties, you should be compensated accordingly."

She held up a hand, her eyes suddenly serious. "I couldn't take more money. I'm barely doing anything—Danielle is doing most of the work."

"I'm not comfortable with you getting nothing. If you won't take extra money, then what?" He settled his gaze on her, wishing he could see inside her mind. "Tell me what you want, Jenna."

Jenna couldn't catch her breath. With his dark green eyes on her like that, her body quivered. What did she want? Him. No question. Just him.

But that wasn't what he meant. She bit down on her lip and looked away. "I can't think of anything."

He raised an eyebrow. "Then you're a rare person. Everyone wants something. What about a trip home to Larsland? We could wait until Bonnie's a bit older and get someone to fill in here for you for a couple of weeks."

Jenna stroked Meg's head as the baby's eyes grew heavy. "I'm not ready to go home just yet."

"Well, a trip somewhere else. Or if you don't want to travel, then perhaps a night out. Dylan's always getting tickets to Hollywood premieres and offering them to me. Fancy a night on the red carpet?"

An event swarming with media? She suppressed a shiver. The very last thing she needed was to be snapped in the background of a celebrity shot by a paparazzo and have the photo beamed around the world.

"I'll just take Meg next door," she said, glad her daughter had fallen asleep. She needed a moment to think of something to distract Liam.

After laying her daughter in her crib and kissing the top of her head, she went back to Liam and Bonnie. "The only thing I can think of is a puppy. Bonnie could have her own dog to grow up with her, and the puppy would be another constant in her life."

The royal court had several dogs, and one of the happiest memories of her childhood was when her parents had let her have a puppy of her own. The only stipulation had been on the dog's size. Because it would be living in a palace, it needed to be small and easily controlled. Her little Sigrid had been white, fluffy and her best friend. One day she hoped to be settled enough to get a dog for Meg, but there was no reason Bonnie couldn't have a little puppy soon—they'd just need to carefully supervise their interactions while Bonnie was so small.

Liam's gaze told her he hadn't been fooled for a second. "I have no problem with Bonnie having a puppy, but that's not something for you."

"I'd love a dog," she said earnestly, "so having one for Bonnie would be like having one for me too."

The corners of his mouth twitched. "Still not good enough. It has to be something else."

She released a breath and put up her hands. "Liam, honestly, this job is like a godsend to me. I have a home for my daughter and can spend all day with her." She looked down at the precious baby cradled in his arm. "Bonnie is the icing on the cake. I truly love her, and so does Meg."

Liam lifted the empty bottle from Bonnie's lips. "You'll have to teach me to burp her now, but—" he looked up at her, eyebrows raised "—we haven't finished on this topic yet."

"Noted," she said, hoping she'd have worked out what to say by the time they got back to it. She took the bottle from him and set it on the table, then grabbed a little towel. "Here, put this over your shoulder, then lift her so it's in front of her mouth."

He lifted Bonnie very carefully and positioned her. "Okay, now what?"

"Tap her back lightly, so she can bring up any air bubbles that went down with the milk."

The towel wasn't sitting quite in the middle of his shoulder and her fingers itched to smooth it out, but she knew he wanted to do this completely on his own, so she left it.

After a few taps, Bonnie brought up a small amount of white liquid, which, unfortunately, landed squarely on Liam's shirt. Jenna smothered a laugh as she said, "Don't worry, it's happened to me more times than I can count."

He turned his head to try and see the damage. "We might have to work on your aim, Bonnie Hawke. Or more likely, on my towel placement skills."

Jenna chuckled. "Here, let me take Bonnie so you can get that shirt off."

"Thanks," he said, passing his daughter. "She's one wink away from sleep anyway."

Jenna took the baby, whose eyes were already closed, rocked her a few times to make sure, then laid her in the crib. "Good night, beautiful," she whispered.

When she turned around, she was confronted by Liam's bare chest. He was standing several feet away, but he was all she could see, and a tiny spark of electricity shot straight through her. He was balling the shirt in his hands and looking around the room, probably for the dirty clothes basket, which gave her precious moments to observe him unnoticed. She took advantage of them without thinking.

His chest was solid with faint lines of definition and a sprinkling of dark hair. Her fingers itched to test the strength of the muscles there, to feel the crispness of the hair. Then she realized he'd stilled. She raised her gaze to his face only to find he was watching her. Her stomach fluttered. He took an infinitesimal step forward, as he reached out to stroke the side of her face then cup her cheek. His gaze fell to her mouth, and the nerve endings in her lips sprang to life, tingling. Yearning.

This was wrong, she knew it was wrong, yet in this moment she couldn't bring herself to care. All that mattered was Liam, and he was close, so close that her heart battered against her ribs.

He lowered his head, ever so slowly, until his lips brushed hers. Delicious warmth spread through her body and she couldn't contain the moan that escaped her throat. When his mouth settled more firmly and his tongue touched hers, she knew she'd reached heaven.

She fell into the kiss—into Liam. His heat and scent. Sensation danced across every nerve in her body. She reached up, touching his bare chest with her fingertips, and she felt a shudder rip through him. The shirt he'd been holding fell to the floor as one of his hands snaked out to press her fingers more firmly against his skin, the other to wrap around behind her, hauling her against him.

This kiss was more than anything she'd ever experienced—more intense, more uncontrollable, more glorious. Just more. And she'd never get enough. Of the kiss. Of Liam. He sucked her bottom lip into his mouth and she would have melted into the floor if he hadn't been holding her up.

And then he wrenched away, breathing heavily but with his gaze still locked on her. The air was cold on her chest where he'd been pressed only seconds before. The sudden absence of a kiss that had felt like her whole world caused her head to spin, and to stop herself reaching for him again, she rubbed her fingertips over her still tingling lips.

His eyes tracked the action, then he speared his hands through his hair. "Jenna," he said, groaning and stepping further away. "We can't do that again."

"I know," she whispered, trying to remember the reasons why. The job. She couldn't jeopardize the job and Meg's home.

Furrows appeared across his forehead, as if he was trying to force his brain to work. "Kissing an employee," he paused, swallowed, "is a breach of Hawke's Blooms' sexual harassment policy." His voice was a monotone, as if he was merely reciting the policy, while his eyes were still on fire.

"I don't work for Hawke's Blooms," she pointed out, then winced. What was she doing arguing a point she agreed with? They *couldn't* do it again. Shouldn't have done it in the first place. It was madness.

"No, but the principle is the same." He rubbed a hand down his face. "You have a right to a workplace free of inappropriate advances."

The guilt on his face tore at her heart. "Liam, don't get me wrong, I don't think it should happen again either, but just to put your mind at ease…you didn't pressure me. It was mutual." She'd been dreaming of his kiss for too long to deny it.

"Mutual?" he asked, eyes pained. "I'm not sure if that makes it better or worse."

She sighed, knowing what he meant. Resisting him would be so much harder now she knew he was thinking the same forbidden thoughts. She circled her throat with both hands as she willed her brain to kick into action. "Thing is, I can't start something right now anyway. Not with my life in such disarray."

He frowned. "What's in disarray? You have a job and a home. You and Meg seem relatively settled."

The blood in her veins froze. Had she given herself away? She silently cursed. This was the problem with letting your guard down—once it was down, there was no self-protection. No filter to protect your secrets. Thankfully, Liam seemed curious but not suspicious.

"You're right," she said as breezily as she could manage. "We are. I meant that I'll be returning to Larsland at some point, so starting something with you or anyone—it couldn't go anywhere."

"Well, at least we're in agreement," he said, ruefully.

She bent to pick up his shirt, needing to escape before she changed her mind. "I need a shower. I'll take this down to Katherine—"

"No, I've got it," he said, his voice low. He reached for the shirt and for a long moment, they both held the fabric, connected through it. She could feel the air pulse with the heat between them.

Then she quickly dropped her end. And fled.

Seven

"Princess Jensine?" said the voice on the other end of the line.

Jenna settled back into the sofa and held her cell phone closer to her ear. "Hi, Kristen. Yes, it's me," she said in her native language. "Can you talk?"

"Hang on." There was a pause and a muffled noise. The time difference and Kristen's shift work always made these calls to her friend in the royal security patrol difficult to plan, but they were the only way her family knew she was all right.

"Okay, I'm back," Kristen said.

Jenna tucked her feet underneath her, looking forward to a conversation in her mother tongue. "How are you?"

"I'm fine, but never mind that. How are *you*?"

"I'm good. We're good. This new job has been great—it has everything I need." Although it also had something she didn't need—an inconvenient attraction to her boss. An image of Liam rose in her mind: the way he'd looked two nights ago after he'd kissed her, his breathing heavy, chest bare, eyes brimming with desire. Jenna's skin suddenly felt warm.

"I'm glad to hear it," her friend said. "Any news on when you'll be coming back?"

Jenna's stomach dipped. She'd have to go back, but her parents wouldn't necessarily be pleased by her return. They'd definitely be angrier than they were with her now when they found out she'd had a baby out of wedlock. She'd been brought up to remember one golden rule: duty before all else. Duty before fun, duty before friends, duty before personal dreams, duty before everything.

And after they'd recovered from their personal disappointment, the focus would shift to how to protect the monarchy. In days gone by, they would have put Meg up for adoption or quickly married Jenna off to a husband willing to overlook her indiscretion and fudged the dates on official documents. With the advent of the internet, it was much harder to hide indiscretions unless she went completely underground, as she'd done. And she'd never consent to giving up Meg.

She just needed to find a solution that suited everyone.

"Not yet," she said, wincing at how inadequate that sounded.

"Your mother is becoming more insistent in her questioning when I give her your updates."

Jenna's heart hurt. When she'd first left, she hadn't considered how many people would be affected by her plan. "I'm so sorry to have put you in this position, Kristen."

The other woman blew out a breath. "I don't regret helping you, but I can't hold your parents off forever. So far they've respected your request for privacy, but I think that won't last too much longer. I wouldn't be surprised if your father is already planning to have someone in the Patrol track you down."

"Oh." Seeing them again and telling them everything would be hard enough, but being confronted by surprise, when she didn't have her thoughts in order, would be so much worse.

"You'll have to reveal the secret sometime," Kristen said.

"I know." And, despite knowing how disappointed her parents would be in her, she still longed to hear her mother's voice, to see her father's face.

"What can I tell them this week?" Kristen asked, breaking into Jenna's thoughts.

"Tell them…" What exactly? She chewed on her lip. That she was scared she was falling for the wrong man? That she wished she was a normal woman who could simply fall in love and not have to consider her duty in every situation, even when she was AWOL? "Tell them I'm fine," she said wearily.

"You know they won't be satisfied with that."

"I'm sorry, but it's the best I can do." Without a doubt she was going to have to find a way to fix the situation she'd caused, and soon. "Kristen, I'm sorry again—"

"Don't worry about it. I can handle this. It's no worse than that day when we were eight and you pushed me into the mud. My mother was furious I'd ruined my dress before the party."

Jenna laughed at the memory. "I was such a brat, even if you had just called my ringlets stupid. But you never told anyone it was me."

"That's not my way," Kristen said in her trademark matter-of-fact tone.

A ball of emotion welled up in Jenna's throat. "I miss you."

"Then come home." Jenna sensed an exasperated smile in Kristen's voice.

"I will," she promised, hoping to heaven that was true. "I just don't know when."

Liam walked through the back door and paused. Jenna was on her cell phone talking in her native language. The accent was light and musical, and without realizing it at first, he was smiling. The language suited her. Made him want to hear her whisper those musical words near his ear, to kiss the mouth that sang its sentences, to run his fingers through her blond hair as she spoke. He adjusted his collar, which was suddenly too tight.

Jenna looked up and saw him, and her face fell in unmistakable guilt. He stilled. Why? She was using her own phone, and he didn't doubt Bonnie was sleeping or taken care of or she wouldn't be relaxed and chatting. What else could she feel guilty about?

Was it a boyfriend? He shook his head as he dismissed the idea. One thing he knew—Jenna Peters wasn't a woman who would kiss him if she was already involved with a man.

Jenna ended the call and smiled at him, but it was a thin mask. Perhaps it had been what she was discussing that made her feel guilty. Had she forgotten the conversation wasn't in English so he had no idea what she'd said?

"Liam," she said overly brightly. "I didn't expect you home in the middle of the day."

He watched her face for any telltale signs as he spoke. "I thought I'd take Bonnie for a walk in the baby carrier. Maybe keep her with me for a while."

"That's a great idea," she said and slipped her cell phone into her pocket.

"Were you talking to someone from home? Your family?" He knew he had no right to pry, but still, he couldn't resist prodding just a bit.

"Er, no." Her eyes slid to the left. "Well, yes—a friend from home."

He prowled a few steps closer. "Is your friend in America now? I don't mind if you have visitors here at the house."

"Um, no. She's still in Larsland." Her voice was even, but the pulse at the base of her throat was rapid, her pupils too large.

"Do your family ever come over?" he persisted. "You're more than welcome to offer them the spare room next to Katherine's."

"Thank you, I'll keep that in mind." But her expression said she wouldn't. "I'll just get the baby carrier and Bonnie," she said, edging out of the room.

Liam watched her go, his gut in knots. Obviously more was going on with Jenna's family and homeland than she was prepared to admit. It shouldn't feel like a slap in the face that she hadn't shared that with him— she was under no obligation to tell him her life story.

But it felt uneven somehow.

He'd trusted her by letting his guard down and being open with her on more than one occasion—about Rebecca, about his fears of being a father, even about work and the Midnight Lily, which was still a secret from most people. Yet Jenna hadn't let him in on pretty much any level in return. Meg was the only person in her life that she talked about. Why was that?

And why did it sting like hell?

He raked his hands through his hair, swore under his breath and followed her up to Bonnie's room. Maybe they'd both be better off if he stopped obsessing about his nanny and let her have her damn secrets.

From this moment on, Jenna Peters was an employee, no more.

Two days later, Liam pushed away from his desk and pocketed his cell. His parents were about to board a flight that would take them to Oslo—the first leg of their journey home. He'd managed to track them down a day ago in the Faroe Islands to tell them about their new grandchild and they'd immediately cancelled the rest of their trip and bought new plane tickets. They were thrilled with the news and his mother was already planning presents and a belated baby shower.

He walked out of his office building into the sun and through the garden beds, on his way up to the house. Jenna would want to know that his parents were planning to visit as soon as they'd landed and been home to drop their bags and freshen up. He could have rung up to the house, but he was happy for the excuse to see his daughter.

As he walked across the back patio and neared the door, he could hear Jenna's clear, sweet voice; she was singing in her own language. When he reached the doorway, he could see her in the living room, sitting on the floor in front of both babies, who were propped up on the sofa, so their faces were all at the same height. And she was singing something enchanting.

Jenna glanced up, paused in her song and smiled.

"Hello, Liam. There's a little girl over here who will be delighted to see you."

Unable to resist either his daughter or her nanny—despite his promise to himself only two days earlier—he ambled over to the little group, picked Bonnie up and sat on the sofa with her on his lap. He'd done so well for those two days, keeping things professional with Jenna—though part of him had suspected he was only fooling himself, and any semblance of control would snap with one little crook of her finger. Still, another part of him clung to the belief that he was one hundred percent in control.

Jenna followed his lead, sitting beside him on the couch with Meg in her lap.

"Well, we're lucky, aren't we, girls?" she said, her voice playful. "A visit from Bonnie's dad during the day."

"Don't let me interrupt what you were doing with them," he said, putting his fingers out for Bonnie to grab with her little fists. "I only dropped by to tell you that my parents will be coming by tomorrow to visit."

Her eyebrows lifted in surprise. "I thought they were in Europe."

"They have been. It's taken me a while to track them down because they've been moving around so much, but they're coming home early to meet their first grandchild." He'd told them he didn't mind if they wanted to finish their trip, but they wouldn't hear of it. They could visit Europe again, they said, but only see Bonnie at this age once.

"Oh, that's lovely." Jenna smiled broadly. "And you weren't interrupting—I was just singing them a lullaby from Larsland."

Something deep inside him wanted to hear her sing

again...whether he was happy about that or not. He'd been charmed by her Scandinavian accent from the start, but hearing her sing had now taken his fascination with her voice to another level.

"Don't mind me," he said as mildly as he could. "Feel free to do whatever you'd be doing with them if I weren't here."

"All right then." She looked from Bonnie to Meg. "Where were we?"

As Jenna crooned the lullaby again, the babies stilled, transfixed. And Liam was just as affected. She smiled softly as she sang, looking at each girl in turn. And when she finished, she kissed each baby on the cheek.

"That was beautiful," he said once he could get his voice to work again.

She turned her bright smile—as dazzling as spring's first blossom—to him. "They like to hear singing, especially if it's our voices. You should try it."

He shifted in his seat. Her expression was so earnest that he hated to disappoint. "I don't know any lullabies. Well, I know fragments, but I can't say I remember any the whole way through."

She tickled Meg's sides, eliciting a giggle. "I'd sing one with you," she said, "but I only know them in my own language and that might be a bit hard for you to sing along with."

He tried not to seem thrilled that he couldn't be expected to sing. "You just go ahead on your own, then, and I'll listen."

"Bonnie would adore hearing you sing her something." Jenna tucked some of her silky blond hair behind her ear. "What about a song instead? How about 'California Girls'? No, something simple to start with. Do you know 'Edelweiss'?"

He nodded, resigned. "My childhood was filled with my mother watching musicals, so I could probably manage that one."

"What do you say, girls?" Jenna asked, tickling a baby with each hand. "Shall we give it a go?"

Jenna's hand brushed his thigh and his heart skipped a beat, but no one else seemed to notice. Meg squealed her delight and Bonnie's little legs started pumping.

"I think that's a yes," Jenna said.

She began the song, and after a few words, Liam joined in, uncomfortable at first, but once they reached the chorus he became more confident with the melody. Jenna moved into a harmony and his eyes strayed from Bonnie to her nanny. He'd never sung in front of anyone before, let alone in a duet, but it felt natural and... strangely, good with Jenna.

Her face shone and her angelic voice wrapped around him, lulling him into a magical place where anything was possible. She smiled when their last note faded away, so obviously enjoying having sung together that he closed the few inches separating them and kissed her.

At first, she didn't kiss him back, but she didn't pull away either, just let herself be kissed, and he was more than happy to oblige. Her lips were sweet, sensual, but not enough. He'd never get enough

Meg squealed in glee and they both froze, then quickly broke apart.

As he tried to regain his mind, Jenna blinked, then a fleeting frown marred her forehead and she turned to Meg and Bonnie.

"Did you know he could sing like that?" she asked them in a breathless voice. "We'll have to encourage him to sing more often, won't we, girls?"

It took him a bewildered moment to realize she was

going to ignore the fact that they'd kissed. He should have been pleased that she wasn't making a big deal out of it, but, for some reason, he *wanted* her to make a big deal, to be more affected. As affected as he was.

He drew in a breath, trying to get some oxygen to his brain. "I'm not so sure—"

"Bonnie loved it," she said, smoothly cutting him off. "While I'm thinking of it, you should take some photos of Bonnie soon too. You take such gorgeous, professional shots and you should capture this age. She'll grow up quickly."

"What do you mean by professional shots?" he asked, trying to catch up on the conversation. "I can take some snapshots of her."

"If you use the camera you use in your work, you could get some lovely portraits. We could hang one or two on the wall in here." She swept an arm, taking in the pale walls of his living room.

He shook his head. As a diversionary topic that she'd pulled out of thin air, it wasn't bad, but he needed to set her straight. "I don't have any experience in photographing people, but feel free to call a professional out, and make sure you get some of Meg for yourself, too."

"Liam, those photos on the bedroom walls aren't just snapshots. The lighting, the angles you've chosen, the whole package—they're good. Really good. You might see yourself as a scientist, but you're more than that. You have a creative soul. And deep down, I bet you know that."

For long seconds, Liam couldn't talk. Could barely think. Jenna had seen him in a way no one else ever had. Perhaps she'd seen through his façades more than anyone. Being with Jenna while he was with his daughter and learning about fatherhood meant he'd let his guard down. Kissing her was dangerous. He should never have done it once, let alone twice.

If he let his guard down and fell in love with someone who saw the real Liam and she rejected him—*rejected the real him*, the man he hadn't shown another woman—that would be a thousand percent worse than anything he'd suffered in the past.

Which was the reason he'd always kept things superficial with women. And one more reason he needed to back away from his nanny. Quickly.

"About that kiss," he said, his voice heavy with the emotions pulling at him. "I'm sorry. I won't do it again."

The corners of her mouth twitched. "You said that last time."

"And I meant it last time. I'm sorry for both times."

She sighed. "So am I. We have good reasons not to do it again."

"Your life is in disarray." Though he still didn't know what that meant exactly. "How about we don't bother with the reasons, and we simply agree that it's not a path forward that either of us is interested in exploring."

"That might be best," she said softly.

The aching sadness in her voice tore at his heart. "Jenna, just because I don't think we should repeat the experience doesn't mean that wasn't an amazing kiss." He looked her directly in the eyes. "It was. Amazing."

"It was," she agreed, then wrenched her gaze away.

He stood, gave Bonnie a hug and laid her back in the position she'd been in on the sofa when he'd arrived. "I'd better get back to work." He slid his hands into his pockets. "I'll see you tonight."

Then he turned on his heel and strode from the house.

* * *

The next day Jenna was sitting cross-legged on the floor in her bedroom playing blocks with Meg when Liam appeared in the doorway.

"My parents are here early," he said with an apologetic glance. "I should have expected they wouldn't be able to wait and would come straight from the airport."

Jenna jumped up, her mind clicking into gear. "Bonnie's asleep, but she shouldn't be for too much longer. I can bring her down when she wakes up."

Liam nodded. "I thought she might be. They said not to wake her if she was sleeping, but they'd like to meet you."

"Oh, right." It was reasonable they'd want a chance to assess the person looking after their granddaughter. She'd met them in passing when she was Dylan's housekeeper, but she'd never had a conversation with either of them. And now a proper introduction to Mr. and Mrs. Hawke took on more meaning—after all, she'd never kissed Dylan....

Liam scooped Meg up and tickled her under the chin. "What do you say, Meg? Want to meet my mom and dad?"

Thrilled to be in Liam's arms, Meg squealed and babbled, probably telling him about her day. It made Jenna's heart ache that Meg would never know Alexander and would lose Liam from her life when they left his house.

"Are you ready?" he asked, turning to Jenna.

She looked down at what she was wearing—a long floral skirt and a red tank top. She wanted Mr. and Mrs. Hawke to think their granddaughter was in safe hands. Would these clothes make a good impression? She had splatters on her skirt from the finger painting she'd done with Meg earlier, and her top was covered with creases from where Bonnie had gripped it in her little fists, but she figured because she was trying to make an impression as a good nanny, the look was probably appropriate.

She smoothed the skirt and tucked her hair behind her ears. "Yes, I'm ready."

Picking up the baby monitor, she followed him down the stairs, blowing Meg a kiss as her daughter watched her over Liam's shoulder.

When they entered the living room, Liam's mother came over and grasped Jenna's hands. "It's so lovely to see you again, Jenna."

Pleasantly surprised at the familiar greeting, Jenna squeezed the older woman's hands. "You too, Mrs. Hawke."

"Please, call me Andrea." She swept her arm towards her husband. "And this is Gary."

"All right. Andrea. Gary." She nodded at each one as she said their names, relieved that they already seemed to approve of her as their granddaughter's nanny. "I'm sorry that Bonnie's still asleep, but I don't think it will be long before she wakes."

"That's okay," Andrea said. "We can wait. In the meantime, we can keep ourselves busy with this beautiful girl. You must be Meg." She put her hands out to the baby in Liam's arms, then hesitated. "Do you mind, Jenna?"

"No, please feel free to hold her. Meg loves new people."

Andrea took the baby from Liam, and Meg looked around with quick movements until she spied Jenna, then smiled. Jenna gave her a little wave. Satisfied, Meg turned back to the new person she'd found.

Liam dug his hands into his pockets. "Do you want to freshen up while you wait?"

"No, we won't be here long." Andrea sank down onto the sofa with Meg, playing a game on the baby's fingers. "We just wanted to meet Bonnie, then we'll get out of your hair."

Gary turned to Jenna, his hands in his pockets, mirroring his son. "You're from Scandinavia somewhere?"

"Larsland," she said, nodding.

Gary broke out in a smile. "Ah, Larsland. That was on our itinerary, but we missed out when we heard about Bonnie and cut our trip short."

Jenna thanked the stars that Larsland had been one of the countries they'd missed. If they'd made it and seen her photo somewhere, they might have recognized her today. "It's a shame you missed it," she said, "but Bonnie will be more than worth it. She's an adorable baby."

Gary's eyes softened. "I'm really looking forward to meeting her. Perhaps we'll make it to Larsland next time. We'd even booked a tour at the royal palace. Have you been there before?"

Jenna froze. "Um," she said and swallowed. "Yes. Most people in Larsland have been at least once." She hated lying, but both statements were technically true.

Soft crying sounds came through the baby monitor. "I'll go," Liam said.

Jenna would have welcomed the opportunity to escape from a conversation that was veering into dangerous territory, but Liam was already gone. Besides, it was probably important to Liam to be the one who introduced his daughter to his parents, and she wouldn't want to deprive him of that.

Once Liam left, his father wandered over to the huge sliding glass doors at the back that looked over the flower farm and let out a deep, contented sigh. "The stock is looking good," he said.

His wife rose, Meg on her hip, and joined him. "There's nothing quite like that view."

Jenna followed them and gazed out at row after row of bright flowers that she'd come to think of as her own personal garden. "I don't know how you ever left it. I love waking up and seeing the flowers from my window."

Meg reached for her and Jenna put her arms out so Meg could monkey-crawl from Liam's mom across to her. Andrea smiled softly as she watched the baby. "After years of having the responsibility of a farm, we'd been dreaming of an apartment with no garden maintenance. No lawn, even."

Gary chuckled. "That sounded like freedom to us."

"I can see that," Jenna said, thinking of the times she and her brothers and sisters had talked about the freedom of a different life. "Sometimes responsibilities can feel overwhelming."

"The grass is always greener," Gary said, heavy on the irony.

Jenna cocked her head to the side. "It's not working out that way?"

Andrea shrugged delicately. "Oh, we're more than happy. And the change has probably been good for us. But I have to admit that, at heart, we're farmers. We're happiest with the feel of the soil between our fingers."

Gary draped an arm around his wife's shoulders. "There's nothing like tending to a seedling that grows and flowers into something bursting with color."

Liam's parents glanced at each other, and a look of sweet nostalgia passed between them. Jenna swallowed the lump of emotion in her throat. They so clearly had a deep love for each other, and their love for their career was inspiring. Had she ever felt that way about stepping into royal duties? Had her parents? When she'd been growing up, she'd taken it all for granted, which seemed such a waste now. If she had her time over, she'd look for the aspects of her role to love, find the joy.

She glanced up as Liam came through the door with Bonnie cradled in his arms. The sight made her breath catch, as it always did. He was so tall and broad that the tiny baby appeared even smaller, even more delicate, and the care he took as he held his daughter made Jenna's heart swell. In a few long strides, Liam crossed the room and passed Bonnie to his mother, the pride in his features unmistakable.

"So precious," Andrea whispered in a voice clogged with tears as she took her granddaughter. His father swiped at his own eyes, then hugged Liam tightly.

Touched by the private moment, Jenna held Meg closer and slipped toward the archway that led to the kitchen. Liam tracked her movement with his eyes. "Where are you going?"

"I thought I'd give you some family time together," she admitted.

"Oh, don't leave," Andrea said. "You and Meg are a big part of our granddaughter's world."

"Yes, don't leave on our account," Gary said. "Unless you have something else to do, of course."

Jenna readjusted Meg on her hip, torn. As Dylan's housekeeper, she would have melted into the background long before now. The thing was, she was still an employee, not a friend or family member. Yet part of her—the part that missed her own family with such aching sadness—longed to stay with the Hawkes a little longer, even if only as an observer.

Giving in to that feeling for once, Jenna sat down on the end of the sofa.

Seemingly satisfied, Andrea went back to inspecting her granddaughter, kissing her cheeks, rubbing her little arms. "Such a tragedy about her mother," she said. "For herself and her family, but also for Bonnie."

"It was," Liam said, his voice tight. Jenna knew that he'd do anything to be able to give Bonnie her mother back.

Andrea smoothed the dark hair on Bonnie's head as she looked up at her son. "What about her other grandparents? Have they been to visit?"

Liam's gaze flicked to Jenna for a split second, then back to his parents. "It's complicated. They're getting ready to file for custody. My lawyers tell me it should be any day now."

"They're *what*?" his parents said in unison.

"Apparently, they've been collecting evidence to prove I'm an unfit parent." He held up a hand to forestall their outrage. "Don't worry—my lawyers are on it."

"I should hope so," his father said indignantly.

Meg squirmed in Jenna's lap, so she put her on the floor and the baby crawled straight to Liam. As if without thought, Liam hoisted her into the air while still talking to his parents, explaining his meeting at the hospital with Rebecca's parents. His mother watched the move, then her appraising gaze swung to Jenna before a ghost of a smile flittered across her face.

Her stomach clenching at what Liam's mother thought she'd seen, Jenna abruptly stood. "I'll just get a bottle ready for Bonnie."

Liam nodded. "I'll help you."

Andrea Hawke broke out in a proper smile and asked her husband to take Meg from her son. "Don't hurry back. We'll enjoy our time with Bonnie and watch Meg for you."

Jenna felt the heat rise up her neck to her cheeks. Now she wasn't just hiding who she was from the world, but also how she felt about her boss. As she made her way down the hall, she cursed the tangled web she'd woven.

Eight

When they reached the kitchen, Liam noticed Jenna's cheeks were pink. "Are you okay? You look flustered."

She touched the tip of her tongue to her top lip, obviously debating whether she'd share what was on her mind. Then she winced and said, "Your mother thinks there's something going on between us."

"Does she?" He frowned and glanced toward the doorway that led to the hall. "What makes you think that?"

Jenna shrugged one shoulder. "There's a look in her eyes."

Perhaps he should have been paying more attention to his mother rather than watching Jenna. He scrubbed a hand through his hair. "Well, I suppose she's right. There is something between us. It's just something we've agreed we won't explore."

Her gaze flicked to his as she moistened her lips with her tongue, and all the blood in his body headed south.

"Jenna," he said, aware it sounded more like a growl than a word. "Since we both agreed it's not what we want, it would help if you didn't look at me that way."

Her eyes widened and she spun away to open random cupboard doors. "Your parents seem to have hit it off with Bonnie," she said in a rush.

"Yeah." He smiled, thinking of his daughter out there with her grandparents. "They've been hinting about grandchildren for a while. Probably since they retired and sold me this house."

"You know," she said slowly, turning back to him, "I think they regret that."

"Retirement?" He rubbed a hand over his chin. That didn't seem right—they'd been looking forward to retirement and the things they'd be able to do.

"I'm not sure about retiring, but I think they regret moving away from the farm."

He thought back over all the family conversations about his parents stepping down from the business and moving to an apartment. "That doesn't make sense. They'd been looking forward to a life of no daily responsibilities. A nice apartment in L.A. where they could walk to places and let the farm go."

"Maybe it hasn't lived up to expectations?" She took one of Bonnie's bottles from the cupboard and went to the pantry for the formula. "I don't know. It might be worth talking to them about it."

He narrowed his gaze as he tried to ascertain what she was getting at. "You think I should sell them the house back? Leave here?"

"No, sorry, I didn't mean that," she said, frowning. "It's your home now. Besides, maybe I'm wrong. Or maybe there's some other solution."

He leaned back on the counter and crossed his arms.

Could his parents be having second thoughts? And if they were, why had it taken an outsider to pick up on it? Jenna had only just met them.

"I'll keep it in mind," he said, surveying his nanny. This woman was constantly surprising him. And he wasn't at all sure how he felt about that.

It was just after seven that evening when Liam arrived home. Jenna had bathed both babies and gotten them ready for bed, and Katherine had helped her carry them down to the living room so she could get Bonnie's bottle and let the girls say goodnight to Liam. To Jenna's surprise, Katherine had taken to helping out if Jenna was struggling, which often happened if one of the babies wanted some attention while the other was having her bath. Jenna generally tried to bathe Meg when Bonnie was napping, but it didn't always work out.

"I'm sorry I'm late," Liam said as he came through the back door.

Jenna threw him a smile. "You don't answer to us, Liam. Besides, most nights you've been pretty close to the four o'clock finish time you said you'd aim for."

Katherine stood and hoisted Meg onto her hip. "Since we're doing apologies, I have one of my own."

The pronouncement seemed so out of character, Jenna was momentarily stunned.

"Katherine?" Liam said.

The housekeeper stood in front of them, expression as grim as ever, chin raised. "I haven't made anything for dinner tonight."

Jenna frowned. She'd ducked into the kitchen earlier to get a snack for Meg and seen a pot of pasta sauce bubbling away on the stove.

"But I saw—"

"As I said," Katherine said, cutting Jenna off, "I'm sorry. To make amends, I'll look after the babies, Mr. Hawke, while you take Ms. Peters out somewhere to eat. I'll keep Bonnie down in my room with me tonight and put the baby monitor in Meg's room, so don't you two be worried about how late you stay out."

Liam rubbed a hand over his chin. "I'm sure we'll make do. You don't have to—"

Katherine's spine stiffened and she fixed Liam with a glare. "Ms. Peters has been working herself ragged, between night feedings, painting the nursery and running around after these two. It's about time she had a night off and did something nice. We'll be fine here, won't we, girls?"

Jenna wouldn't have been more surprised if a bird had landed on the windowsill and given that same speech. Katherine had just come out on her side. Katherine, who seemingly still begrudged her presence in this house. Katherine, who'd not said a nice thing to her since she and Meg had arrived.

"Why are you looking at me like that? I have eyes. I've watched you work. Now, go," she said, making shooing gestures. "Go out for dinner somewhere nice."

Jenna still didn't move. Was Katherine trying to set this up as a date?

Liam grinned indulgently, then turned to Jenna. "Katherine makes a good point. How about it? I'll have a quick shower and throw on some clothes."

Katherine nodded, satisfied. "While you do that, I'll make you a reservation at George's place."

Jenna knew her mouth was gaping but was helpless to do much about it. One minute she was getting babies ready for bed, and the next, people were making plans around her.

Liam turned to Jenna, his eyes dancing with amusement. "Wear something nice. Katherine's brother is the chef at the hottest restaurant in L.A."

"That's assuming he can find you a table," Katherine said, clearly not willing to appear too kind all at once.

Liam gave Bonnie a kiss and then left, taking the stairs two at a time, and Katherine picked up the phone, leaving Jenna standing as if in the middle of a whirlwind, unsure of how her night had so drastically changed.

She was going out to dinner with Liam.

To the hottest restaurant in L.A.

Most worryingly, even though Katherine had planned it, why did that sound like a date?

Liam sipped his wine and looked around the restaurant, with its trademark high ceilings and pink marble and chrome interior, bustling with waiters and patrons. Katherine must have twisted her brother's arm to get this table—Liam knew they were normally booked out months in advance. And with good reason. His meal had been delicious, and if he wasn't used to Katherine's excellent cooking skills, he'd have been even more impressed.

A waiter cleared their plates and left the dessert menus.

"Would you like dessert?" he asked Jenna. Their conversation during dinner had been interesting. She was well informed on world affairs and they had discussed several scientific discoveries made in other countries.

Yet even while discussing topics as impersonal as science and world affairs, the insistent pull of attraction for her had lurked, and he'd had to be careful not to let his guard down and say something stupid. Something like, *Come back to my room tonight. I want to peel that pink silk blouse off you with my teeth.* His blood heated at the thought, and he tried to distract himself by studying the menu.

"I can never go past a cheese platter," Jenna said. "Would you like to share?"

"Sure." He indicated to the waiter that they were ready and placed their coffee and dessert order.

"You know," she said, looking around the restaurant with an expression of happy bewilderment, "I think this is the first night I've been out without Meg since she was born."

He cocked his head to the side, trying to imagine that. "Not once?"

She shrugged as if it were no big deal. Perhaps it wasn't to the many single mothers across the country. And probably half the married ones too.

"When I worked for Dylan, I took trips for groceries and errands while Meg was in day care, but nothing social. I never went out in the evening."

He didn't know how she did it. She seemed so calm and confident about being solely responsible for her daughter whereas he was filled with horror at all the perils that lay waiting for his baby girl out in the world.

He swirled the last of the wine in his glass as he asked a question that had been preying on his mind. "Do you think much about the future with Meg? About how you'll handle it on your own?"

She was silent for a moment before replying, and he became more aware of the background noise of glasses clinking and the dull murmur of a room full of people. Then she said, "Sometimes. Do you?"

He nodded. "And it scares the hell out of me."

The waiter returned with their cheese platter and

drinks. Jenna spooned sugar into her black coffee and stirred slowly as she regarded him. "I'm sure you'll find someone to share the parenting with, a stepmother for Bonnie."

She popped a piece of pear in her mouth and chewed. Liam put a finger in the restrictive collar of his shirt and tried to look anywhere but at her mouth.

"I'm not so sure," he said, wincing at both his reaction to her and his admission of the truth.

She threw him an ironic glance. "You're attractive and wealthy. Don't try to tell me you have trouble getting dates."

"Getting dates is one thing." He helped himself to a piece of blue cheese. "Finding a woman I'd be happy to have as Bonnie's mother is another thing entirely."

She trapped her bottom lip between her teeth and frowned. "She might not be the next person you date, but surely at some stage you'll find someone who would be a good fit."

"I tend to meet rich women, many of them professional socialites." He cut a piece of triple brie and put it on a cracker. "Or women who want to be," he said dryly.

"I hate to break it to you," she said, unable to hide her amusement, "but you're kinda rich too."

She was right. But he hadn't started that way. Maybe to Jenna, the difference wasn't obvious, but to him it was everything.

He took a sip of his coffee. "I grew up without much—some of the time my parents really struggled—and my brothers and I still have our working-class values. Any woman I'd consider as Bonnie's mother would have to have those same values, no question."

She arched an eyebrow. "There are a number of assumptions in your argument."

He knew that. He didn't doubt that it was possible for someone to grow up with wealth and privilege and still remain grounded, but he just hadn't met a woman like that yet. And if he hadn't met one so far, what were the chances of it happening in the near future, let alone that they'd hit it off and get married?

"Perhaps," he admitted, "but I'm sure you've seen the women Dylan dates. Glamorous and high profile. He attends red carpet events and knows who's who in the world of the rich and famous."

Jenna flinched. It was so quick that he would have missed it if he hadn't been watching her so intently. Then she composed her face into the dignified mask she usually wore for everyone except the babies.

"It's not a world you want to be a part of." It was a statement, not a question. She understood.

"I can think of nothing worse than attending events and having to smile and make small talk. Yet, like Dylan, that's how I meet women socially." He speared a piece of pear. "I think Bonnie and I will just have to make do on our own. And in the meantime, we have you, so all isn't lost."

"Yes," she said, her voice free of inflection. "All isn't lost."

But his gut felt hollow. Jenna was an employee; she wouldn't stay with them forever. He looked at her again and had an idea. Katherine had been with his family for years, and she seemed settled. Happy. What if he could make Jenna's working conditions so good, she stayed just as long? Starting with a raise. She'd certainly earned it.

The heaviness that had been sitting on his shoulders eased a fraction. Of course the flaw in the plan was that employees were off-limits, especially ones he was trying to retain in the long term. His plan presumed he could live with her down the hall for years and not kiss her again. Not touch her.

And he wasn't even sure he was going to make it through this dinner without doing that.

As they pulled up in Liam's Jeep in front of the house, Jenna tried to stave off her disappointment that the night was ending. It wasn't a real date. She couldn't let herself think that, and the sooner she was tucked up in her bed—alone—the better. Safe from fantasies that Liam had actually invited her out and that she was free to follow her attraction in whatever direction it led…

Then Liam leaned across and stroked her cheek with a feather-light caress, and all her attempts at being reasonable went up in smoke. She felt herself tremble under the touch but she didn't dare move, hope and doubts and anticipation warring inside her.

"Thank you for a lovely evening," he said and let his hand fall. That didn't seem to break the connection, though—it was as if the very air in the Jeep crackled.

There was no use denying she wanted him to kiss her, had never wanted anything more. And it didn't seem as if he was bothering with denial anymore either. His eyes darkened as he focused on her mouth. Her lips parted and she drew in a shaky breath, but he didn't come closer. The moment felt suspended in time, neither of them moving. Then his eyes changed, became pained, and his head swung away.

"We'd better go inside and check on the babies," he said and opened his door.

Suddenly cold, she blinked. The babies. Of course. She was the nanny, after all, not someone he was dating. But her traitorous body wasn't as easily convinced.

She pulled herself together and went with him into the house. Katherine had left a note on the hallstand saying that everything was fine, and Bonnie was sleeping soundly with her. They crept up to check on Meg, who was also fast asleep.

Jenna gave her daughter a soft kiss on her round head, then hesitated in the hall, unsure of how to end the night. There was so much unfinished between them that she had no idea of what to do, and Liam didn't seem to be in a rush.

Perhaps simplest was best. "Well, good night, then," she said.

"I always walk a date to her door." He waved an arm toward her room.

"Okay," she said, not really sure how to take that.

They took the few steps to reach her room, then she turned to look up at him. He propped a shoulder against the doorframe, his gaze smoldering. A wave of heat rushed over her skin, and suddenly she didn't want to do the safe thing anymore. Taking a risk was by far the more interesting option. She moistened her lips and hoped her voice sounded steady. "Isn't a kiss at the door part of that tradition?"

Liam stilled, studying her face. "You want me to kiss you, Jenna?" His voice was low and rough.

"Oh, yes," she said on a soft breath.

He groaned and his eyes closed for a heartbeat, and she thought she might never breathe again. Finally, his head came closer until his lips met hers in a kiss that was sweeter than any they'd shared before. Their other kisses had been stolen and had been all about attraction. This was more of an exploration, and more intense for it.

His hands found hers and their fingers entwined. When her knees wobbled, she leaned back against the door, and Liam pressed against her, not letting her fall. His body was scorching hot through her clothes and she wanted more, wanted everything.

Liam wrenched his head away, gulping for air, but his gaze didn't leave her. She'd never wanted anyone more in her life; her entire body vibrated with need. It was time for another risk.

"Can I invite you in for a coffee?" she asked as casually as she could manage, resting her hand on the doorknob.

His green eyes darkened, but the corners of his mouth twitched. "Thing is, because this is my house, I happen to know you don't have coffee-making facilities in that room."

"That's true, though I could probably rustle up a chocolate bar and a bottle of room-temperature water." She turned the knob and pushed the door open behind them.

"As it so happens, scrounged chocolate bars and room-temperature water are my favorite things in the world," he said, wrapping a piece of her blond hair around his finger. "But in all seriousness, Jenna, do you honestly want me to come in? Say the word and I'll see myself to my own room. It's your call."

She let out a long breath. "Liam, I can give you about five good reasons why we should say goodnight out here in the hall. And I suspect you have a list about the same length."

He raised a hopeful eyebrow. "But…?"

"I don't want to," she said simply. She'd been denying and fighting this attraction long enough.

His Adam's apple descended slowly, then came up again. "So what do we do?"

Good question. They couldn't go forward and they

couldn't not go forward. There had to be another way. "What if we give ourselves a free pass for tonight?"

Heat flared in his eyes. "The reasons we shouldn't do this aren't going anywhere," he said, tracing a fingertip down her throat. "We could park them in this hall and they'll be waiting here patiently to be picked up again in the morning."

"We wouldn't be doing anything wrong, because—"

He cut her words off with a kiss full of the passion they'd been holding back. She raised her hands to grip his shoulders, and his body shuddered.

"Because we're not brushing those reasons aside," he said against her mouth. "We're just—"

"Parking them for a few hours," she finished, her fingers tightening on his shoulders.

"Well, if we're parking them, it will be just as easy to park them in the hall in front of my room as yours. And my room has a bigger bed." He tugged on her hand and she followed him down the hall, anticipation bubbling in her belly.

When they reached his room, he drew her inside, then closed the door, pushed her back against it and kissed her again. "Maybe your room would have been better," he eventually said, leaning his forehead against hers. "That was a long wait between kisses."

With nimble fingers, he undid the buttons of her blouse. As he moved the fabric aside, his fingers skimmed and swirled from her stomach up over her bra, to reach the column of her throat. Her heart rate went soaring, her senses on overload.

"Jenna," he said, his voice uneven. "I've wanted you since the day you moved in."

"Only that long?" She gave him a crooked smile. "I feel as if I've wanted you forever."

He groaned and slipped his hands behind her to un-hook her bra, then tossed it to the side. The air was cool on her breasts, but he soon cupped them, bringing all his warmth and the delicious friction from his work-roughened palms.

She slipped her hands under his shirt, feeling the play of muscles across his chest as he tensed in re-action to her touch. It wasn't enough. Trembling, she pushed the shirt from his shoulders and it dropped to the floor, then she leaned in and placed a kiss on his chest, thrilled when he sucked in a breath and held it. As her hands became bolder, roaming, exploring, he groaned and buried his fingers in her hair.

Part of her still couldn't believe she was here with Liam, the man she'd been watching, wanting for so long. But he whispered her name and she knew she wasn't dreaming. This was him, and it was even more perfect than she'd imagined.

He skimmed his hands up her thighs, bringing the skirt as he went, then hooked his fingers in the top of her panties and pulled down until she could step out of them, then out of her shoes. She was naked before him and he stared down at her with such longing that she felt as if she were floating.

He toed off his shoes, pushed his trousers and box-ers off in one smooth motion, and then came back to her, kissing her until her head was spinning. She let her hands roam, wanting to touch him everywhere she could reach, from his biceps, up to his shoulders, and down the smooth skin of his back. While her hands explored, she kissed a trail down his body, loving that the muscles in his chest and abdomen tensed when her mouth made contact. And when she flicked her tongue out to taste the skin, he moaned her name.

He pulled her back up by the shoulders and held her in place with a kiss as his hands began their own journey, slowly moving down her sides, skimming the slope of her breasts, across her rounded stomach, and down farther. He broke off the kiss and dipped his head to take the peak of a breast into his mouth, just as his fingers found the apex of her thighs. She gasped, and he retreated, teasing, promising.

Just when she thought she could stand no more, he gently pressed her back on the bed and prowled over her, kissing and licking and nipping wherever he could reach. Then his mouth reached the core of her. At the first touch of his tongue, she moaned deep in her throat. His fingers joined the assault, and she could barely contain herself, as if she'd grown too big for her skin.

She clutched the sheets, helplessly giving herself over to sensation. Her hips flexed of their own accord, but his hands and mouth continued, slowly driving her out of her mind with the sweet torture, until all feeling coalesced and peaked at a point higher than she'd known existed and then shattered into a thousand shiny fragments.

She heard him opening a drawer in the nightstand. He retrieved a condom and quickly sheathed himself. But instead of coming straight back to her, he hovered, his weight resting on his hands on either side of her shoulders, his gaze locked on hers. The clarity of the look—no masks, nothing to hide behind—made something move inside her chest. It was if she was seeing into his soul. She reached up and ran her fingertips down his cheek, along his jaw, and when they reached his mouth, he tenderly kissed them.

Then he leaned down and captured her mouth in a kiss that was pure heat and desire and urgency. Without breaking the kiss, he positioned himself between her thighs, and she moaned deep in her throat. He entered her slowly, giving her time to adjust, but she wrapped her legs around his waist, urging him on, reveling in the warm rush of sensation as he began to move.

He rocked in a rhythm that she wanted to last forever and her body strained for his, wanting more, meeting every thrust of his hips.

She struggled for air, shifting restlessly on the sheets as the world pulsated around her. She gasped his name, over and over, could think of nothing else. Her body tightened around him. She was on the edge of something so intense, she wasn't sure she could handle it when it came, but if they stopped now she'd lose her mind.

And then he changed the angle and she fell over the edge of the world, falling, falling, soaring up, soaring as the world exploded around her, and she heard his words of release as he joined her.

Nine

Jenna woke slowly, surrounded by heat and male limbs. Still drowsy, and with the memories of their lovemaking lingering, she was perfectly content. More than that—in this glorious moment, blissful happiness filled every cell in her body.

She slid to the side, away from the weight of arms and legs, and propped her head on her hand so she could see Liam better. He mumbled something in his sleep and adjusted his body, and then his breathing became even again.

With his gorgeous face smoothed in sleep, he seemed relaxed as he never did when awake. But awake or asleep, there was no doubting his strong heart, his fascinating mind, his noble sense of honor. This was a man she could fall in love with…if she let herself.

A shiver ran across her skin. Of course, she would never let herself do that. It was time to sort out her life. She had to go home.

She had no idea how her family would react to her arrival, to Meg, but she had to at least tell them. Seeing Liam's parents with Bonnie had rammed that point home like nothing else could. Both her parents and Alexander's deserved to meet Meg. And Meg deserved to meet them.

Softly, she touched a fingertip to Liam's dark, wavy hair. She would give him notice so he could find another nanny, but she wouldn't deceive herself that he was merely her employer. Not while she lay naked in his bed.

She didn't know what they were to each other now, but one thing she knew without question—Liam deserved to know the truth. If she was prepared to share her body, then she should share the rest, too.

And she needed to tell him today. Before she gave notice, before anything else happened, she had to tell him who she really was.

She slipped out of the bed and found her clothes. After getting dressed and checking on Meg—and ducking into the nursery before remembering Bonnie was still with Katherine—Jenna grabbed her robe from her room and crept down to the conservatory to try to think of the right words. The words that would help Liam understand everything she had to tell him.

Unfortunately, she had to wonder if words that magical even existed.

Liam woke alone in the dark.

In general, that wasn't an unusual occurrence, but it wasn't one he expected to face tonight. Not after sharing his bed with Jenna.

Still drowsy, he'd reached out, hoping to find her ready to make love again, but instead he'd found the sheets cold. He'd grabbed his trousers and, zipping them up, headed for the hall.

His first thought had been that Bonnie had woken, but he'd checked the nursery, belatedly remembering she'd been with Katherine overnight. Then he'd checked Meg's room and Jenna's and, coming up empty, had started to worry.

He'd finally found her in the conservatory, sitting on the overstuffed green striped sofa, her arms wrapped around her knees in front of her. Her gaze settled on him, but she didn't move.

"Is anything wrong?" he asked warily, sending up a little prayer that she hadn't had second thoughts about sleeping with him.

"No." She chewed the inside of her cheek. "It depends. Maybe."

"Regrets?" he asked and held his breath.

Her eyebrows lifted. "About making love? No. I wanted you so badly I couldn't see straight."

He'd suspected as much but was glad to hear it confirmed. The feeling had been entirely mutual. "I like the sentiment, but I don't like how it was in the past tense."

"There's something…" she said with a slight tremor in her voice. "Something you don't know."

"Whatever it is, it can wait till morning. Come back to bed." He held out a hand and gave her a lazy smile. "I had plans for the rest of the night, involving you, me, my bed and none of these clothes we've accidentally acquired."

A smile flittered over her face, then was gone, leaving her features sober once more. "No, it really can't wait. In fact, I should have told you before I invited you into my room."

He wrapped his hands behind his neck and stretched.

"All right, shoot. But be warned, as soon as we're done here, we're going back to my bed." The heat began to spread through his body at the thought. "Those plans I have? They'll take the rest of the night."

She looked down at her interlaced fingers resting on her knees. "I need to tell you the truth. About me."

The truth about her? He stilled, suddenly focused. "Go on."

"Jenna is short for Jensine." She moistened her lips, swallowed. "My real name is Jensine Larson."

"You changed your name? Why?" That didn't seem so bad, if that's all there was, but seeing how serious she was, he stood a little straighter.

She looked up and met his gaze squarely. "I have a title that goes before my name. Princess. I'm from the royal family of Larsland."

Liam lost his breath for a full second. A princess? Here in his house. Less than an hour ago in his arms, welcoming him with her body. Of all the scenarios he might have expected, this had never rated a thought. A princess. Seriously?

He folded his arms over his chest. "I'm sorry, I haven't brushed up on my royal protocol lately. How close to the crown does one need to be, exactly, to be called a princess?"

She ran her fingers through her hair, pulling it back in a ponytail, then letting it go to fall over her shoulders again. "My mother is the queen, the current monarch. My father is the prince consort. My eldest brother is the crown prince."

Right. The daughter of the queen. It was so ludicrous he could have laughed. But he didn't. "And Meg?" he asked, though he had a feeling he already knew.

"If she had been born at home, and I had been married, she would be Princess Margarethe. Maybe she still is—I don't know how this will play out when I go home."

"Royalty," he said, still trying to get the concept to compute in his head.

She picked up her cell from the coffee table beside her and held it out to him. "Check online. I know you want to."

When he didn't reach to take the phone, she clicked a few buttons, then held it up for him. "That's me second from the left," she said as she passed him the device. This time he took it and gazed at the screen. "The photo is a couple of years old and my hair was longer, but it's still me with the rest of my family."

She had pulled up the official website of the Larsland royal family. "Princess Jensine Larson," he said slowly.

"Yes." Her eyes held a world of pain, and he didn't understand any of it.

He rubbed his eyes and sank down onto a sofa across from her. It really was true. His brain wasn't awake enough for this. "So what happened? How did you end up as Jenna Peters, nanny to Bonnie Hawke?"

"I was in love with a captain in the national army," she said, her voice so faint he had to strain to hear. "He was from an old family, and though we hadn't talked about it specifically, I think we both thought we'd get married one day."

His mind jumped ahead and suddenly he had a vision of Rebecca, pregnant with Bonnie, choosing not to tell him. His stomach hollowed. "Does he know about Meg?"

"He was killed in action before I could tell him I was pregnant." She seemed so small, so alone. He crossed to her sofa and wrapped an arm around her shoulders, but she didn't seem to notice.

"I'm sorry, Jenna." Such ineffectual words, but he could offer her nothing else. She'd said she was in love with Meg's father, which was so much worse than what had happened between Rebecca and him. He cast around for something to say. "I didn't know Larsland was at war."

She drew in an unsteady breath. "He was part of our contingent in a United Nations peacekeeping mission."

He nodded. Of course. This would have been a much smoother conversation if he had caffeine in his system. "So you were pregnant and single," he said, picking up the pertinent thread.

She shuddered. "Which is worse than it sounds. Larsland's royal family has prided itself for many years on the lack of scandal. You've probably seen that some of the other European royal houses have made head-lines, so our parents instilled in us that it was our role to stay above that. Be better than that. We were never to give the people of Larsland a reason to question the need for a monarch."

Understandable but unnervingly hardhearted. "So they packed you off?"

She flinched, then tucked her hair behind her ears as if to cover for the reaction. "No, I left. I didn't want to put them in the position of having to make a decision about what to do with me."

"Hang on," he said, pulling away so he could see her face more clearly. "They don't know where you are?"

She winced. "Not exactly, no."

He thought of Bonnie disappearing when she reached her twenties and his blood turned to ice. He shifted away a little and rubbed a hand down his face, now really wishing they had waited till morning for this.

Then another thought struck. Without the use of diplomatic channels between the two countries, it would be beyond difficult for her to be here. "How have you pulled this off? Living here under another name is not an easy thing to achieve."

"I entered the country using my own passport, and since then, well, it's probably better that you don't know the details, so let's just say I have friends in high places."

He narrowed his eyes. "Friends who let a princess work as a housekeeper and a nanny?"

"It's what I wanted." She shrugged one shoulder. "I needed to be incognito for a time while I worked out what to do with my life."

Incognito. His chest clenched tight. She'd been using him. Toying with him and his family, starting with Dylan, then Bonnie and him. She'd lied, like every other woman he'd been involved with. The difference was, he'd trusted Jenna—she even knew how he felt about lying—but it turned out she was no different. His stomach turned.

"You've been using me, my family, as cover." Nothing since they'd met was what he'd thought. Their every interaction had been dishonest. She'd been playing him for a fool. "No one would suspect a nanny or a housekeeper," he said, disgusted.

She raised an eyebrow. "If you remember, you offered me this job. Pushed quite hard to get me to take it."

He shook his head, refusing to take that as an excuse. "You lied to me. I suspected you were hiding something, but I never imagined it would be on this scale."

"I know. I'm so sorry, but surely you can see why

I had to." She reached out a hand to him but he didn't take it, so she put it back in her lap.

"I can see why you had to lie to strangers, but to me? All this time, we've been living in a house together, and you've said nothing." He strode to the glass wall of the conservatory, acutely aware of how vulnerable they were in here—it seemed no better than being out in the open. "Do you even realize the risk you put Bonnie in?"

"No one knew I was here," she said, frowning.

"What if someone had found out? All it would take is one person who alerts the world's media that a princess was hiding out in L.A. as a nanny. If the media had descended on my house, we would have had no warning to prepare, to have enough security in place." The scene was almost too horrifying to contemplate. "You could have put Bonnie in the middle of a media frenzy."

Her face paled. "I honestly didn't think—don't think—that's a feasible risk."

"But it's possible," he persisted.

Her shoulders slumped slightly. "I guess so."

Liam felt so tense his muscles were vibrating. Tomorrow he'd meet with the head of security for the farm and work out an excuse to put in some extra safety measures. Even if Jenna left tonight, if the paparazzi ever figured out she'd once been here, this place would be crawling with the press. He'd never let Bonnie be a target.

"So what happens now?" he asked. "Do you want me to pretend to everyone that you're a regular citizen while you keep working for me?"

She unfolded herself from the sofa, wandered over to a stand of ferns and rubbed a frond between her fingers. "I need to go home and sort this out."

Something slid into place in his mind. "That's why you said your life was in disarray when we first kissed."

"Yes." She squeezed her eyes shut, and when she opened them again she seemed about ten years older. "I was always going to have to return home, and once I do that, I have no idea what the future will hold for me and Meg. It's not a time in my life when I can start a relationship."

"Right." He nodded once. The last thing he wanted was a relationship, either. Especially not with an incognito princess who'd been lying to him. "So you're leaving," he said, his voice flat.

"Not right away, unless you want me to." She raised her hand to circle her throat. "I thought I'd wait till after the Midnight Lily's launch, and I'll help you interview new nannies. Once everything's in place, I'll go."

He scrubbed his hands through his hair. "You know, this is not how I saw the rest of the night panning out."

"Liam," she said softly and waited till he looked at her. "I'm sorry."

"Tell that to Bonnie when she's crying for you after you leave." He knew that was an unfair thing to say, but he wasn't in the mood to be fair.

He pushed to his feet and headed back to his room.

Jenna didn't see Liam again until the next night at dinner. He arrived late, and she didn't blame him—if their positions were reversed, she'd have wanted time to process the bombshell she'd dropped last night, too.

"Good evening, Jenna," he said, his tone and expression excruciatingly polite. Which meant they were back to the mask he wore with other people but he'd stopped putting on for her. The realization stung but didn't surprise.

"Hello, Liam." She tried to be bright to compensate. "Bonnie's asleep, but she had a good day."

Katherine came in with bowls of steaming minestrone and freshly baked bread on a tray. Liam thanked her, Jenna said the smell coming from the bowls was divine and Katherine left with a satisfied smile.

Liam broke off a piece of bread. "I checked on her before coming in here and she's sleeping soundly. I had hoped to come in and get her and the carrier, but I was in meetings most of the day. Perhaps tomorrow you could ring Danielle when it's a good time for Bonnie, and I'll swing by and pick her up."

"That would be great. I know Bonnie would enjoy it." The mention of his PA reminded her of the meeting she'd had a few hours earlier. "Danielle came by this afternoon and we went over the plans for the Midnight Lily's launch. It seems to be coming together nicely."

"I've been thinking about that." He put his spoon down and met her eyes squarely. "The reason you don't want to attend is you're worried about being caught in a photo, isn't it?"

"Yes," she admitted, only just resisting the urge to fidget.

"What if we made it a masked event?" His voice was low, his gaze serious. "The Midnight Masque."

She gaped. "You can't make a change that big five days out from the event."

"It's not changing anything substantial," he said, shrugging one shoulder. "More like adding something. And sending the update to people who've already been invited will serve as a reminder about the event itself. I talked to Danielle about the feasibility earlier and she thinks it could work. In fact, she said there's a certain mystique to the flower already, so this will play up that element."

A masked event? She could see it in her mind's eye—guests wearing half-masks, the mystery, the glamour, the fun. They could bring their own or wear one that Hawke's Blooms provided in midnight blue. It could work, and she'd be able to see the fruits of her labor firsthand. It was perfect.

Without thinking, she reached out and laid a hand over his forearm. "You'd do that? After everything that I—"

He glanced down at her hand, his eyes pained, and she quickly withdrew it. Then he let out a sigh. "Regardless of what's occurred between us, this event wouldn't be happening without you. You deserve to be there," he said, his voice softening for the first time since he'd walked in the door.

A ball of emotion lodged in her throat, and she dabbed at her mouth with her napkin to give herself a moment. "I appreciate that. There's something I'd like to talk to you about too." If she were to leave, she wanted to ensure she left things the best that she could for Bonnie. "What do you know about Rebecca's parents?"

"From my own experience, they're rude and have a sense of entitlement. Although," he admitted, "they probably weren't at their best given their daughter had just died. From the private investigator's report, they seem like average people who have friends who think highly of them and others who are happy to speak badly. They've crossed people in business but also made allies. And the investigators couldn't find anything dirty going on in their company."

She wasn't surprised he'd had a private investigator look into them, or that they'd come out relatively clean.

She'd started to wonder if they were as bad as Rebecca had painted them. "What did Rebecca say about them?"

He buttered another chunk of bread. "She often made snarky comments about them, but the only specific thing I remember is that they're cold and manipulative. She said that when she was growing up, they were emotionally distant." He frowned. "Is there a reason you're suddenly so interested in the Clancys?"

"I've been wondering," Jenna said carefully, "if they were awful, why was she living with them?"

"That's a good question." He scraped a hand across the day's growth on his chin. "I guess I hadn't stopped to consider things from her point of view. In fact, she was apparently going to continue living with them when she left the hospital with Bonnie."

"And," she said, "more to the point, if they were such dreadful parents, why would she let them help raise her own daughter?"

Liam was struck by the comment. "You're right—that doesn't make sense."

"Did she have money of her own?" Jenna asked, gently probing.

"She did." He nodded, thinking back over Rebecca's situation. "And a part-time job in fashion. I assume she was on maternity leave, but she was hardly destitute. With her contacts, she should have been able to get another job easily when she was ready." Which meant there was no reason to believe she was with her parents for financial support.

"And she always had you as an option. Even if you parted on bad terms, surely coming to you for help with your own daughter was better than letting her cold, manipulative parents near her child, right?"

He wasn't comfortable speaking ill of the dead, but Rebecca had always had a touch of the drama queen about her. Exaggeration wouldn't be surprising. He'd assumed that part of her need for drama was because her parents had been the way they were, not the other way around.

He frowned. "Now that I think about it, it's possible, perhaps even likely, that she exaggerated their faults."

"And if she's exaggerated about them to you, can you imagine what she's said about you to them?"

He dropped his spoon to the table with a clatter as things finally made sense. "No wonder they're determined not to let me have Bonnie. Rebecca could have said anything."

He thought back over his first meeting with them in the hospital on the day of Rebecca's death. They'd been angry and scared for their daughter and had probably been told he was something of a monster, so when they saw him with their newborn granddaughter, of course they'd reacted strongly. In their shoes, he'd be suing for custody too.

Jenna tapped a finger to her lips, bringing his attention back from the past to the woman sitting in front of him. The woman he burned to touch again despite everything that had happened. He picked up his spoon and took a mouthful of Katherine's minestrone.

"You know," Jenna said, her voice puzzled, "I get that she might have talked badly about you to her parents, but not telling you she was pregnant is more serious. That's a passive-aggressive way of lashing out. Did your relationship end badly?"

Liam sighed. He'd been over and over this in his mind since he'd found out about Bonnie. "I didn't think so. I'd made it clear from the start that I don't do forever, that we'd never be serious. And she was okay with that. Said she preferred it that way."

"So why did you break up?" she asked gently.

"Nothing dramatic." He shrugged. "It just ran its natural course."

Jenna took a last mouthful of soup, then pushed her bowl to the center of the table. "Whose decision was it?"

"Mine." His chest hollowed out as he put two and two together. "I became uncomfortable when she wanted to spend her nights here. She started to push for more than I was willing to give."

Jenna laced her fingers on the table in front of her, brow furrowed in concentration. "Would she have known she was pregnant then?"

He shook his head. "I doubt it. I've counted back and it must have happened just on the cusp of us breaking up. She was getting clingy, but it wasn't because she was pregnant."

"Liam," she paused till he looked at her, "she fell in love with you."

"It's possible," he said, his gut churning.

"And you broke things off. Broke her heart." They were harsh words but not said unkindly. He knew Jenna was only trying to help, but it was still a brutal wake-up call. God, what had he done?

She'd loved him and he'd discarded her. He'd been a jerk. No, worse.

He groaned and sat back in his chair. "I never meant to hurt her."

She gave him a sympathetic glance. "I know. But when she found out she was pregnant, she couldn't bring herself to tell you. She punished you."

"I still deserved to know," he said fiercely.

She held up her hands, palms out. "No argument

from me. But we're discussing it now in a calm, rational manner. People make all sorts of bad decisions when they're emotional. Especially a woman who's pregnant with her first baby and panicking."

Something in her tone made him suddenly alert. "Are we talking about Rebecca or you?"

"Rebecca. Me." She rubbed her eyelids with her fingers. "I don't know."

Suddenly all the anger at her deception that had been bubbling away under the surface dissipated. This was harder for her than it was for him. "What are you going to do?"

She took in a shaky breath. "I shouldn't have waited this long to go home. Seeing your parents with Bonnie has made me think about my parents missing out on Meg. And Alexander's parents—they have a link to him that they don't even know about."

"The same link to Rebecca that her parents could have through Bonnie," he said, finally understanding where she was coming from.

Jenna gave him a crooked smile. "Why don't you hold out an olive branch to them? See if you can work out some arrangement?"

"They're suing for custody," he pointed out.

"If they thought they could be part of her life, and if they believed you were the best person to raise their granddaughter, perhaps they wouldn't feel the need to carry on with that case."

His father had often told him that if something sounded too good to be true, it usually was. It was a nice idea in theory, but reality was something else altogether. Too much water was under the bridge now. "I can't see it working."

"Isn't it at least worth a try?" Her voice was optimistic and damn difficult to resist.

He blew out a long breath. Anything was worth it for Bonnie. "You're probably right."

"You'll call them?" she asked, practically bouncing in her seat.

"I'll call them," he confirmed and just prayed this plan didn't make things any worse than they already were.

Ten

It had been six days since she'd told Liam her secret. Six days since they'd made love. Six days since her world had changed.

Each night after he arrived home from work, she'd coached Liam through another aspect of Bonnie's care, and last night he'd bathed his daughter. There wasn't much left for her to teach him, which was bittersweet. On one hand, everything was just as it should be; on the other, her presence was becoming less necessary by the day.

She'd made a deal with herself that if Liam's meeting this morning with Rebecca's parents went well, she'd be free to go home to Larsland.

There would be no more excuses left if Bonnie's entire family was intact and her father had all the skills to care for her. The last piece to fall into place would be to find another nanny, and if everything went smoothly with the Clancys, she'd talk to Liam about that today. She wanted this sorted out before the Midnight Lily launch event tomorrow night.

The doorbell rang and she heard Liam answer it— he'd asked Katherine to leave it for him. Jenna sat on the sofa in a long white summer dress holding Bonnie, who wore a bright pink dress and purple headband. Beside her was Meg in her best dress of tangerine and lime green checks, happily playing with her favorite plush dog toy.

Jenna's stomach was in knots. So much was riding on this visit—Bonnie's future relationship with her grandparents, the custody suit, the healing of a family. And the vow she'd made to herself about leaving...

She heard Liam's smooth, deep voice. "She's in through here, in the living room with her nanny, Jenna Peters."

Then Liam appeared through the archway, a tight smile on his face, followed by a middle-aged couple. The woman was carrying a teddy bear the size of a five-year-old child, and the man's face was obscured by a bunch of about twenty helium balloons in an assortment of pastel colors.

"Bonnie," the woman squealed as she rushed to the sofa. "Oh, my darling girl."

Jenna looked to Liam for guidance on how he wanted to handle Rebecca's mother, and in two strides he was beside her, lifting Bonnie from her lap.

"Would you like to hold her, Mrs. Clancy?" he asked.

"Desperately." She thrust the bear at Jenna with barely a glance and took Bonnie into her arms. Meg gurgled her pleasure over the teddy, and Jenna positioned it on the sofa so Meg could climb on it.

"Oh, my sweet, sweet girl," Mrs. Clancy said with

tears in her voice. "If the world was fair, your mother would be with you."

"I completely agree," Liam said, his tone and expression somber.

The woman jerked her head up, narrowed eyes fixed on Liam. "If only you'd shown that sort of consideration to my daughter when she was alive."

Liam bowed his head in a conciliatory gesture. "Mr. Clancy, Mrs. Clancy, I have to tell you I couldn't be more sorry with the way things have worked out."

Rebecca's father harrumphed. "You're only saying that because you want to convince us to drop the suit."

"I would like you to do that, yes, but it doesn't make what I'm saying any less true. I've recently realized," his gaze flicked to Jenna, "that Rebecca and I probably had different perceptions of what our relationship was."

Jenna's heart swelled to bursting. He'd taken their conversation seriously and was doing his best to make amends. He was a good man. An honorable man.

"You toyed with her," her mother spat at Liam. "It's what you do with women."

"Perhaps that's a fair comment, but Rebecca and I were always open about the limits of our relationship." He slid his hands into his pockets. "If I could go back and change things, I promise you, I would."

Mrs. Clancy looked pointedly down at the baby she held. "And Bonnie?"

"I love Bonnie with everything inside me. More than I thought it was possible to love." His eyes shone with genuine emotion. "She might have only been part of my life for a short time, but now she's my everything. My reason for getting up in the morning and my reason for coming home early in the afternoon. The center of my world and all my plans for the future."

Mr. Clancy scoffed. "I suppose this is what you're planning to tell the judge. Someone else probably even wrote those words for you to say." But Jenna could see they were softening, that Liam's heartfelt words had hit their target.

Bonnie grew restless and Mrs. Clancy tried to soothe her, but Bonnie had obviously reached her limit of time spent with an unfamiliar person and started to cry. Mrs. Clancy turned to hand her to Jenna, but Liam stepped forward.

"I'll take her."

The room stilled. Even Meg, always sensitive to the moods of the adults around her, stopped playing and looked around. The only sound was Bonnie's plaintive cries. The Clancys obviously hadn't been expecting Liam to back up his words with action.

Liam reached over and took Bonnie, putting her up on his shoulder so she was close to his face. Then he began to croon "Edelweiss" very softly. The love in his voice and in his every move was unmistakable and Jenna couldn't hold back the tear that had slipped down her cheek. Bonnie stopped crying and turned to see her father's face.

Jenna drew in a long breath. She couldn't deny it any longer. She loved him. Loved Liam Hawke with everything inside her.

She'd told herself not long ago that she wouldn't let herself fall in love with him, but that had been a staggering case of denial. How could she avoid it? The love was so big, so strong, she couldn't have outrun it. It simply was.

Not that he'd welcome her revelation. He'd been so exquisitely polite since the night they'd made love, she didn't know whether she'd killed any feelings he'd had for her, or if he'd smothered them in his anger. Either way, he'd made it quite clear that they had no future.

She gave herself a mental shake. The focus right now needed to be on helping Bonnie's family to come together.

Jenna looked at Rebecca's parents to see how they were reacting to Liam soothing Bonnie. Mrs. Clancy's jaw gaped, and her husband's aggressive stance eased before he dropped into a chair, the balloon strings still protruding from his fist. Meg clambered backward down from the sofa and over to Liam, trying to crawl up his leg. With his free hand, Liam reached down and scooped Meg up, and the babies' delight in seeing each other after an absence of minutes was clear in the noises they made.

Mr. Clancy cleared his throat. "Is there somewhere I can put these damn balloons?"

Katherine appeared in the archway, threw Jenna a wink and said, "I'm Mr. Hawke's housekeeper. I'll take them for you."

He handed them over without making eye contact. Seemed the Clancys weren't big on talking to underlings.

"Now, listen here, Hawke," Mr. Clancy said. "I'm not promising anything, but if, and I say if, we dropped the suit, we'd have conditions."

Liam didn't look up from the two babies in his arms. "Such as?"

"Regular visiting rights," Mrs. Clancy said.

"Input into decisions on her school," Mr. Clancy added.

Mrs. Clancy folded her arms across her chest. "You wouldn't move out of the area."

"A say in all important decisions in her life," Mr. Clancy said, pointing a finger to emphasize his demand.

Liam finally looked up, his gaze fixing on Mrs. Clancy before coming to rest on Mr. Clancy. "I will make all decisions about my daughter's future on my own. That's not negotiable. However, I'll take your opinions seriously, and I'll ensure you have access to her as often as is practical. A strong relationship with both sets of grandparents is a good thing for Bonnie."

Jenna watched the interaction with her heart breaking. Liam looked so strong, refusing to be bullied or swayed, yet fair and kind in his conditions. Oh, yes, there was no doubt she loved this man. He was going to make everything perfect for his daughter, and all Bonnie's family would be able to work together. This was exactly what Jenna had wanted for her little charge—a father with the skills to care for a baby and now a healthy, strong extended family.

But Jenna wouldn't be around to be part of it. She wasn't family.

She needed to go home, to see if she could salvage her own family bonds and give her parents a chance to know their granddaughter. She had no idea if that was even possible, but she had to try.

"Well," Mrs. Clancy sniffed, "I'll concede that it appears Bonnie is happy here. We'll consider the situation and let you know our decision."

"I appreciate that." Liam nodded once, confident, considerate. "Would you like some time with her now?"

Mrs. Clancy nodded but didn't rush to take her granddaughter, probably remembering that Bonnie had grown restless with her only minutes before. Catching Liam's eye, Jenna retrieved a play mat from the corner of the room and spread it on the floor, then relieved Liam of Meg.

He laid Bonnie in the middle of the mat, then turned to Mrs. Clancy. "Bonnie likes it when you play with the hanging toys. Especially the ladybug."

For half an hour the Clancys played on the floor with their granddaughter—occasionally whispering to each other—until Bonnie was ready for a nap. Jenna had already made her bottle and settled in on the sofa to feed her.

As they left, Mr. Clancy shook Liam's hand. "We're prepared to drop the custody suit, Hawke. But we expect you to follow through on your promise of regular access."

"You have my word," Liam said. "We'll stay in touch."

Once they were gone, Jenna turned to Liam and smiled, hoping to hide any hint of the realization that she loved him. "That went better than I expected."

As he let out a long breath, Liam sank down on the sofa beside her and lifted Meg onto his lap. "Thanks to you."

She shook her head. "You did all of that. I think you blew their socks off with your relationship with Bonnie."

"I meant in making all of this possible. This visit would never have happened without you. You'll always have my gratitude for that." For the first time since she'd told him her true background, he looked at her with something other than the polite mask he wore for most of the world.

In that precious moment, she glimpsed the real Liam again, saw his heart in his eyes, and knew he was as affected by her as he'd always been. So she had her answer—she hadn't killed whatever feelings he'd had for her. But then he severed the connection by glancing down at Meg. Clearly, he was unhappy about those feelings. Which was probably for the best. She needed to leave the States, and soon.

She pasted on a smile. "No need to thank me—I'm just glad that Bonnie will have as much of her family around her as possible. And now that that's resolved, we need to talk about hiring a new nanny."

His head jerked up. "You're really going?"

"I have to, Liam." Bonnie finished her bottle, so Jenna put her up to her shoulder, using the action to avoid eye contact with him as she said the hardest thing. "And to be honest, I don't think you're comfortable with me here anymore. Not after…" She trailed off, unable to say the actual words.

"No one could do a better job with Bonnie," he said, his voice rough.

She blinked back the emotion that threatened. "A good nanny will do fine, and you'll be more at ease without me here. I'll call an agency on Monday and set up some interviews."

Not replying, he took Meg over to the play mat and gently set her down. "Listen, I'll need to head into the hotel early tomorrow to help set up for the launch, and I'll take my clothes and get ready there. Will you be all right if Dylan takes you?"

Jenna said a little prayer of thanks that he'd changed the subject. She might have lost the fight against tears had they talked about her leaving for much longer. "Tell him not to worry. I can catch a cab."

"He's already offered." Liam shrugged and dug his hands deep into his pockets. "He'll pick you up at seven."

"Then thank you," she said. "That would be nice. The babysitter will arrive at six, so that will be good timing."

He started to leave, then turned back. "One other thing—I've arranged for a personal shopper to come out today with an assortment of dresses so you can choose one for the launch."

She frowned, unsure where that was coming from— the idea of him providing her with clothes made her think of mistresses. Did he feel guilty about sleeping with her? Or was it some misguided thought about her needing fancy clothes because she'd been brought up in a palace? "You don't need to buy me a dress, Liam." She had a perfectly serviceable black dress she'd been intending to wear.

"Jenna," he said, his gaze not wavering, "you're part of the organizing team, so your outfit is Hawke's Blooms' responsibility."

She narrowed her eyes. "You're buying a dress for Danielle and the others?"

"They'll all be wearing branded formal clothes, so people can seek them out and ask questions. So, yes, the company is clothing them for the night. And you as well."

Her lungs deflated. That made sense. And...part of her wanted to wear something other than the black dress. Wanted Liam to notice her again, no matter how unwise that was.

"Thank you," she said. "I appreciate it."

He gave her a tight smile. "I'll see you there."

Clinging to Dylan's arm, Jenna walked through the foyer of The Golden Palm, one of the most stylish hotels in L.A., and tried not to fidget with her masquerade mask. She hadn't seen Liam since he'd left after breakfast this morning, and all her deportment lessons couldn't save her, thanks to frustrating restlessness.

She'd chosen a silver dress with a fitted bodice and flowing skirt, but now she was wondering if it was the wrong choice. Perhaps she should have worn the satin yellow sheath with a split up the thigh that the personal shopper had recommended. The yellow dress had certainly been sexier—

"How are you doing, Princess?" Dylan whispered with a grin, interrupting her thoughts. Jenna had told him her secret on the ride over. Because he'd been kind to her as an employer, she wanted him to hear it from her. She trusted him, and she was going home soon.

She slapped his arm lightly. "It might be better if you don't use that word." She gestured to the throng of paparazzi clustered near the door up ahead, waiting for glimpses of celebrity guests.

He nodded his understanding and whispered, "I still can't believe my floors were cleaned by a royal princess. And that time I asked you to—"

"Dylan," she said firmly, "you gave me exactly what I needed at the time—a job and a home. You accepted me when I was pregnant, and you were a great boss. I honestly can't thank you enough."

Even though the photographers weren't interested in her, and she was wearing a mask that covered the top half of her face, she still looked down as they passed them and casually covered her mouth and chin with her hand.

"Tell me something," Dylan said as they entered the hotel foyer. "Is your new boss giving you what you need?" The mischief in his tone made the skin on the back of her neck prickle.

Unsure of where he was going with this, she chose

her words with care. "Liam's been good to me. And good to Meg. I can't complain."

"My mother thinks we might be welcoming you and Meg into the family soon. And just so you know," he said conspiratorially, "I couldn't be happier."

A wave of sadness, of powerful longing, washed over her. She knew Liam had no intention of proposing to her, and even if he had, she didn't have the freedom to simply accept. No matter how much she loved him, she had to do what she should have done from the beginning. Face the music.

She was going home as soon as she could find a new nanny for Bonnie, and as long as her parents didn't try to separate her from Meg, she'd consent to whatever plan they thought best for the good of the country, the monarchy and her family. This time she'd do what she'd been raised to do—put duty first.

But Dylan didn't know any of that. She hadn't told him her family was unaware of her location, just that she'd been incognito and that he needed to keep the secret.

She waved her wrist in a gesture she hoped seemed casual. "There's no chance of that happening, Dylan. I'll be returning to Larsland soon. But, for what it's worth," she said, smiling up at him, "you'll make a great brother-in-law to someone."

As they approached the doors to the ballroom, a woman in a midnight blue dress handed Dylan a Phantom of the Opera style half-mask.

"Thank you," Dylan said, slipping the elastic over his head. "How does it look?" he asked Jenna.

She grinned. "Stylish."

As they pushed through the double doors, Jenna couldn't hold back the gasp. The enormous room had been transformed into a night-time fairytale scene. A huge glowing moon hung in one corner, and shadowed clouds hovered in the air, suspended from the vast ceiling. Stars and constellations shone from above and from the walls, and occasionally a shooting star arced across the sky.

Tables set with crisp white tablecloths and covered in glassware, bordered the room. Huge stands of cascading flower arrangements, using a variety of white flowers, were artfully placed. Dylan and Jenna were a little early, so not many people had arrived yet, but a waiter glided over and offered them glasses of champagne. Dylan took one but Jenna shook her head. Her mother had never let them drink at official functions and the habit had stuck.

Dylan let out a low whistle. "Jenna, I think you may have just changed the way Hawke's Blooms announces a new flower forever."

"This wasn't all me," she protested. "Honestly, Danielle and the staff from your and Adam's offices have done all of this. This is so much more than I imagined."

"No," he said, holding up a hand. "You were the spark. It was one hell of an idea."

She gave him a gracious smile. "Thank you. I'm glad to have helped."

From the corner of her eye she spotted a familiar figure and, without thought, she turned. Liam was on the other side of the room, not yet wearing his mask; he was deep in conversation with Danielle, but his gaze was locked on Jenna. The sparkling room faded and it was as if he was standing within touching distance. Her skin warmed, and her pulse was erratic. Liam said something to Danielle, who nodded and left, and he began to cross the room to them.

"Oh, yeah, nothing going on between you two at all," said a voice beside her.

A dark frown crossed Liam's face and his gaze shifted to his brother, the warning clear.

"So," Dylan said when Liam reached them, "I was just leaving to investigate those ice sculptures. Lilies made of ice. Genius." Then he darted off before either of them could say anything. Not that Jenna would have been able to—she'd lost her voice around the time she'd spotted Liam in a tuxedo. Possibly lost her mind at the same time.

He cleared his throat. "You look sensational." He leaned in to kiss her cheek, lingering a little too long.

A ripple of heat ran across her skin, but she tried to ignore it. "Thank you for the dress. I love it."

"It looks great on you," he said, his eyes lingering as long as his kiss had. "Can I get you a glass of champagne? Or something else to drink?"

Her restless fingers needed something to do, so holding a drink was appealing, but she really shouldn't have one. Instead, she smoothed a hand over her French twist. "No, thank you. I'm fine."

His gaze followed her hands to her hair, then back to her eyes. "How were Bonnie and Meg when you left?"

"The babysitter had arrived and Katherine was in her element, explaining what she was required to do and showing her in no uncertain terms who was boss."

Liam chuckled. "We really should put on more household staff so Katherine can exercise her management skills." Then his face sobered. "I'm glad you came."

She felt a tremulous smile form on her lips. "I can't tell you how much I appreciate you making it a masquerade so I could be here.

Frowning in concentration, he picked up her hand

and held it between two of his. "Jenna, I know you're going home soon." He paused, cleared his throat. "I have the key to the hotel's penthouse room in my jacket pocket, and both the babysitter and Katherine are at the house all night with the babies."

Her breath was trapped in her lungs and she couldn't get her voice to work, but he didn't wait for her to reply.

"Stay with me tonight." His hands tightened around her fingers. "Being with you again…it's all I think about."

"Yes," she whispered before she'd thought it through.

His eyes flared, then he checked over his shoulder and winced. "I'm sorry, I have to help Danielle with some arrangements, but I'll be back."

Frozen to the spot, she watched him walk away. How would she ever make it through the night now she knew how it would end?

Eleven

Liam took a glass of white wine from a passing waiter as his eyes scanned the crowd for Jenna. The event had been in full swing for a couple of hours and he was only just getting a chance to catch his breath. Future events would likely be the responsibility of Dylan's or Adam's offices, but because the idea had come from his office this time and Danielle had been coordinating everything, he'd been the point man for the night. He wouldn't be sorry to lose the role—it had been hectic, especially when he'd only wanted to spend the time with Jenna.

Then he saw her, not too far away, chatting with his parents. Her silver dress shimmered; the fitted bodice drew his eye to her exposed collarbone, down over the slope of her breasts, to where the fabric tucked in at the waist then floated down to her ankles. His heart thumped erratically.

From the moment he'd seen her enter the room on

Dylan's arm, he'd been mesmerized. He'd never wanted a woman more. He was well aware that part of this need was a factor of the forbidden—not only was she his daughter's nanny, but also she was leaving. Tonight would be simple and pure, away from the complications of reality, as if away from time itself. Like Cinderella at the ball—except, of course, she was the princess and he was no prince.

A man walked into his field of vision, so Liam moved to the left and found Jenna again...and his movement made it obvious she was watching him from under her lashes. His entire body heated. Drawn as if by magnetic force, he found himself moving through the crowd until he reached her side. Their shoulders brushed and his heart all but stopped its beat.

"Liam," his mother said. "There you are. I was just telling *Jenna*," the subtle emphasis showed that she knew Jenna's real identity, "that if she needs to leave before you have a new nanny in place, I'd be happy to fill in."

Liam stiffened. She was thinking of leaving before they'd even employed a new nanny?

"There's no need," Jenna said quickly, her blue eyes shifting to him from behind the mask. "I have enough time to help Liam interview for the next nanny."

His mother nodded, smugly satisfied. "Have you noticed there's a dance floor over there? No one's using it yet. Perhaps you two should get it going."

He couldn't tear his gaze from Jenna and had only been half listening to his mother, but there was a pregnant pause in the conversation, he realized he must have missed something. "Sorry?"

His mother patted him arm. "Take Jenna over to the dance floor, Liam. Someone needs to start the dancing."

He grinned. That was a great idea. Danielle had been particular about having a dance floor, but no one was using it yet, so she'd appreciate him doing something about that. In fact, it was practically his responsibility as the point man to stand on that dance floor with this woman in his arms.

"Jenna," he said, holding out a hand, "would you like to dance?"

A slight blush tinged her cheeks as she laid her hand in his. "I'd love to."

Anticipation simmered in his veins as they threaded their way through the crowd to the two stairs leading to the raised parquetry platform set aside for dancing. He prayed the deejay didn't play a fast dance number first up. He wanted to be able to hold Jenna close.

The deejay saw them step onto the dance floor and changed the track to a Righteous Brothers ballad. Liam nodded his thanks.

As he put his arms around her, he sighed and pulled her close, and she wrapped her arms around his waist. She felt so good against him, as if she were made for exactly that spot.

He dropped his head to whisper in her ear. "I've barely been able to think of anything besides meeting you after this is all over. Tell me you haven't changed your mind."

"I have," she said and drew in an uneven breath. "About thirty times."

Another couple joined them on the dance floor, and, heart in his mouth, Liam navigated Jenna away from the interlopers so they couldn't be overheard. "And where do you stand right now?"

The tip of her tongue darted out to moisten her lips

and it almost undid him. "I…" she said, then swallowed. "I want to be with you one more time."

He closed his eyes and groaned. "I've been thinking the same thing." She would be gone soon, which was how it had to be—she didn't belong in his world and he didn't belong in hers—but in the meantime, they could make magic.

Two more couples began to dance, so she leaned up to whisper in his ear. "In fact, if you tried to lead me out of this room right now, I'd probably let you."

A shudder ripped through his body. "Don't tempt me. The official part of the evening is in half an hour and Danielle will murder me if I leave before then. She's putting me up on the stage."

"Half an hour isn't long," she said, tracing a finger down his lapel.

Not long? Incredulous, he looked down at her. "It's an eternity."

She smiled softly at him, her blue eyes dark. "You're right. It is."

More than forty minutes later, Jenna stood in the crowd as the well-known actor Danielle had arranged to appear cut the ribbon and a dark blue satin curtain fell, revealing the Midnight Lily. The audience cheered and clapped, but Jenna couldn't take her eyes off Liam, who was standing to the left of the group on the stage.

As the emcee explained how the flower was the work of Liam Hawke and his research team, Jenna finally turned to take in the audience's wonder and approval. She also admired the seamless presentation that Danielle had organized for the formal proceedings. But mostly, she was aware of Liam's gaze resting on her.

A message. A promise.

Her skin quivered deliciously.

After a witty final comment from the actor that sent the crowd into fits of laughter, the music began again, and Jenna's heart picked up speed. Liam would come for her now. She didn't take her eyes off him, willing him to walk faster.

As he threaded his way through the throng of people to her, he was waylaid every few steps by well-wishers. He spoke a little to each person, smiled, nodded and moved on, all while keeping her within sight.

Her hands trembled as she watched his approach and she put her water glass on a waiter's tray before she dropped it.

When he finally reached her side, he whispered in her ear, "Are you ready to go?"

The brush of his lips against her earlobe turned her insides to melted honey. "I was ready two hours ago," she said.

He took her hand and led her out into the foyer, then into the elevator. As soon as the doors swooshed closed, he put a hand at the nape of her neck and kissed her. She gave herself to the kiss, wanting nothing more than to be in his arms, to feel his lips against hers.

His breathing was heavy as he leaned his forehead against hers. "Jenna, I have no idea what I just said to those people. All I could think about was getting to you."

"I would have died if one more person stopped you."

The elevator doors glided open and he dropped his hand to her waist and inserted the keycard to the door of the penthouse suite in front of them.

When they entered the room, Liam didn't turn the lights on. There was no need. Every surface, from the coffee table to the side tables, was covered in flickering candles. Her heart tripped. The bed was a four-poster, with white diaphanous material draping the sides and tied back, and the white comforter was strewn with rose petals. A wave of goose bumps shimmered over her skin. It was even more magical than the ballroom.

Liam stood behind her with his arms wrapped around her waist and nuzzled the side of her neck. "What do you think?"

She slipped her mask off and let it drop from her fingers as she leaned her head back onto his shoulder. "When did you have time to arrange this?"

"I made the time." His hands strayed from her waist up to trace the slope of her breasts and the valley between. "Don't tell anyone, but this portion of the evening was my main priority."

She pressed back along his body and felt the thick ridge of his arousal against her lower back. He groaned in her ear, sending warmth blooming in the pit of her stomach.

"I've wanted you so badly all night," she said, turning in his arms so she could see his face. "No, before then. Since we last made love."

His breath rasped. "I haven't been thinking straight since that night. Tonight, seeing you in this dress, knowing you were coming up here with me after…it's been hard to focus on anything else."

She'd wondered if he'd been as affected as she, and it was a thrill to know he had. That this raging desire was mutual.

She pressed her lips to the skin on his throat. "I wanted you to kiss me when we were on the dance floor."

"I wanted to do this on the dance floor," he said, cupping her bottom and pulling her close. Being pressed against him so intimately sent a flutter low in her belly.

He kissed her gently, tenderly, and his chest rose and fell beneath her palms. His fingers burrowed through her hair, freeing it from the pins holding it in the French roll, and even her scalp tingled at his touch. Then he kissed her again, unleashing a hunger inside her that was fierce and demanding. She kissed all the way down his neck to nip at his collarbone, her eyes fluttering shut so she could focus on the feel of him below her lips, the taste of his skin.

Then she moved lower, opening the buttons of his shirt as she went, kissing the skin she exposed. His hands fell restlessly to his sides and then curled into fists, a shudder ripping through his body, as she reached his abdomen. When she undid the last button, she straightened and pushed the sides of his shirt over his shoulders. The candlelight threw a golden glow across his chest, accentuating the muscle definition, enticing her.

He reached for her but she stayed his hands. "Let me have a moment," she said.

Last time, he'd undressed quickly and she hadn't had a chance to enjoy the gradual reveal of his body. This time would be different.

She slid the button of his trousers through its hole and slowly lowered the zipper. His entire body tensed as she slipped her hand into his boxers and wrapped her fingers around him. This was one of the things she'd missed last time and had thought about since in the darkness of her own room. She glided her fingers along his length, luxuriating in the feel of him, glancing up as a breath hissed from between his teeth. The trousers lost traction and fell down his legs to pool at his feet, and she pushed the boxers down so he could step out of them.

Standing there, strong and glorious in his nakedness, giving her control of the situation, the power, simply because she'd asked, he was everything she could ever want. A ball of emotion lodged in her throat, but she swallowed it away—now was not the time. She lifted his hand and placed it on her shoulder and he took the cue, moving forward and kissing her softly. This was what she wanted—him. Just him.

He sank down to the edge of the oversized bed and pulled her to him until his cheek rested against her belly, and his thighs bracketed hers. She combed her fingers through his thick hair, losing herself in the sensation of his hands tracing her shape beneath the dress, over the curve of her hip, gathering the fabric, then dropping it again. The sweet torture was slowly driving her insane.

The warmth of his breath through the thin material sent shivers across the skin of her stomach. He turned her and unzipped her silver dress at the back, leaving it gaping. He turned her again until she faced him before he drew the straps from her arms and the gown slithered down her legs to land in a puddle. He kissed a trail across her stomach, the slide of his tongue sending electric heat rippling through her body, his evening beard rasping deliciously against the sensitive skin of her belly.

He hooked his fingers in the sides of her panties, dragging them down her legs, then turned her again to unhook her bra. When she faced him, he didn't touch, he merely looked, and the expression in his eyes—the hunger, the reverence—almost undid her. The peaks of her breasts tightened under his gaze, and shivers of anticipation rippled across her body. He cupped her breasts, brushing the tips with the pads of his thumbs, and her knees buckled. She was on sensory overload; it was too much.

"Liam," she said, knowing it was closer to a whimper than a word.

He tugged her off balance into his lap and she wrapped her arms around his neck, reveling in the hot, hard press of his erection against her thigh.

He brushed a strand of hair from her cheeks and whispered, "You feel so good in my arms."

"Well, your arms feel good around me."

He nudged her back onto the bed and stretched out beside her. Heat and anticipation rolled across her skin. She wanted him so badly—how would she live without him when she left? The thought was too awful, so she banished it as she scraped her nails across his skin, focusing only on Liam and the present moment.

He opened a bedside drawer and found a condom.

"That's convenient," she said, arching an eyebrow.

"When I ducked out to check on the room earlier, I dropped it off. I didn't want any obstacles for tonight."

She glanced around at the flickering candlelight. "You really did think of everything."

"As I mentioned, it was a priority," he said and rolled the condom on.

He aligned their bodies. His muscled thigh parted hers, and she trembled with the force of her need. She wrapped her legs around his waist, inviting him, and as he entered her, she moaned, dying at the pleasure but wanting more, always more. She wriggled, adjusting her position to take him fully, and then he slid further and the breath rushed from her lungs.

He began to move in a dance of advance and retreat, making her body sing. He moved faster, binding the coil of need inside her tighter, and she begged him to put her out of this sweet misery. His hand snaked down to where their bodies joined and suddenly she was tumbling, free-falling but completely safe because he would be there to catch her. He would always catch her. In that moment she knew that in her bones. And she would catch him.

Liam called her name as he found his own release, then slumped beside her and pulled her close against him.

Later, after she'd returned to Earth and Liam had fallen asleep, she realized she'd been wrong—they wouldn't always be there to catch each other.

She was going home.

And the longer she let it drag out, the more entangled they'd all become and the more she'd hurt everyone— Liam, Meg, Bonnie…herself.

A dark cloud seemed to engulf her as she thought about her future, but she had to be strong and make the right choice, not the easy choice.

Tomorrow she'd leave Liam's house for good.

When they reached home the next morning, Liam got changed and headed into work. It might have been a Sunday, but the launch had taken up a fair bit of time and his nursery team was behind on some orders, so he needed to spend a few hours in the greenhouse. And, hopefully, work out what he was going to do about Princess Jensine Larsen. Digging his fingers into soil always helped him think.

The first time they'd made love, he could excuse it as being impulsive. Giving in to temptation.

The second time? Not so much. They'd both had several hours to change their minds, hours to find an excuse, yet neither of them had. And he had to admit, he was glad. Their night together had been amazing, even better than their first time. And during the early hours of the morning, they'd made love again.

But...what happened now?

He lifted a tray of seedlings onto the wooden bench among the lush greenhouse plants and got to work.

He and Jenna couldn't go back to what they'd been before yesterday. Not after the intensity of their night together. But where were they headed? Where *could* they head? He might want her like crazy, but that wasn't enough.

A movement at the door had him looking up. Wearing a bright orange sundress, Jenna was walking past the African violets and orchids. She was more beautiful than the flowers she passed, but he noted a haunting sadness to her features. His belly dipped.

"Jenna," he said, "did you need me for something?"

She laced her hands together in front of her stomach and moistened her lips. "If you have a moment, there's something I need to tell you."

"Sure." He brushed his hands off on the towel beside him. "What is it?"

"I'm leaving," she said softly. "Today."

"What?" His head jerked up as ice hit his veins. "What about Bonnie?"

Pain and regret flashed across her features. "I'm sorry I won't be here to help you interview for a new nanny, but I've arranged with your mother that she'll look after Bonnie until you get someone. She's on her way over." A tremulous smile tried to form on her mouth. "She says she's looking forward to it."

Everything was moving too fast. "You promised you'd give notice."

She took a breath, her blue eyes meeting his squarely. "I'm asking you to waive that promise in these circumstances. I'm not leaving you without someone to look after Bonnie, and we both know this isn't a normal boss–employee situation."

Panic clawed inside his gut. She really was going today. "What if I asked you to stay? You've been happy here."

"I can't go on like this, Liam," she said, her voice breaking on his name. "It's tearing me apart."

"What if you stay but not as the nanny?" He cleared his throat, braced himself. "What if you stayed as my wife?"

A proposal hadn't been in his plans, but now that he'd been backed into a corner and made the offer, it felt right. She'd make a good mother for Bonnie and he'd have her in his bed every night. He should have thought of it sooner.

She raised her eyebrows, creating frown lines across her forehead. "And live the rest of my life incognito as Jenna Peters?"

"No." He straightened his spine. "Jenna Hawke."

"I can't live my entire life as a lie." Her hand fluttered up to circle her throat. "I'd be in hiding every day, wondering if anyone recognized me. And what about my family? They'd never know where I was. Besides," she said ruefully, "I think my father would have me tracked down eventually."

"I can't be part of your life if you go back," he warned. It was a deal-breaker for him.

"I know." She sighed, resigned. "You told me once that people born to wealth and privilege are a different species, one you have no time for."

"You can't believe that I think of you that way." Surely, after all they'd shared…

"No, but it's how you think of my family, of my real life. And I'm sorry you feel that way. You had bad luck and went to a rotten school when you were a kid, but I have friends and family who aren't like those people you experienced."

"I was raised with working-class values, and that's the way I want to bring up Bonnie." He'd put a lot of thought into this since he'd become a father, and his value system was the best thing he could pass to his daughter. He wouldn't compromise that, not for anyone.

"Not the way I was raised, you mean," she said pointedly.

He rested his hands low on his hips. "I won't commit Bonnie to a life in a royal family. It's the life you ran away from not so long ago. How could you expect me to allow that for my daughter?"

"So, we're at an impasse." She nodded, as if she'd expected this. "I can't stay, and when I get home, I'll be subject to my parents' decision about what to do with my life. And you won't be part of that."

A band clamped around his skull and tightened. He rubbed at the sides of his head—there had to be another way. His career was based on thinking outside the box and finding creative solutions. "What if they want you to stay out of the spotlight? To go on living incognito? You could come back."

"So, you'll have me under those circumstances?" Her blue eyes flashed. "You want to know something, Liam? I might have lied to you, but at least I saw you. What we had was more honest than anything I've had with anyone else, despite the lie."

He stilled as the truth of that statement flowed

through him. She was right. She'd been the first person outside his family to see the real him. And she might have even seen more of him than they had.

"I know," he said, his voice low. "I saw you too."

Her bottom lip trembled and she bit down on it before she replied. "You did, yes. But if I came back to a man who would only have me under certain conditions, what would that say about our relationship?" She swiped at a tear that made its way down her cheek. "It wouldn't be about the real me or you, the whole person. It would be about only accepting the parts that suited you. What sort of foundation for the future is that?"

He thrust both hands through his hair and held them there. What more did she want from him? He'd offered her marriage, then said she could come back if her parents didn't want her in Larsland, and still it wasn't enough. That was all he *could* do. Bonnie's welfare had to be paramount. What sort of father would he be if he sold out his daughter's future for his own happiness?

He set his jaw. "I can only offer you what I've already laid out."

"And I won't settle for less than what I need." She rubbed her eyes and turned to look up toward the house that was only just visible through the net walls of the greenhouse. "I've rung the friend who helped me move here, Kristen, and arranged to go home."

The weight of everything that had just happened suddenly fell down on him and he struggled not to let it press him into the ground. *She was going.* Jenna was leaving him and he couldn't stop her.

He covered the few feet between them and ran a hand down her arm to tangle her fingers with his own. "I'll miss you and Meg."

"We'll miss you and Bonnie," she said, her voice

wobbling. "If you need me, I've left Kristen's cell number on your bedside table. She'll be able to get me a message, no matter where I end up."

He leaned down to kiss her cheek, but, unable to stop himself, he drifted across and kissed her sweet lips instead. She moaned his name as she gripped his shoulders and he pulled her closer. She tasted of tears and everything he wanted, and he wondered if he'd have the strength to let her go or whether he'd hold her here in the greenhouse forever.

He wrenched his mouth away while he still could, stepped back and dug his hands into his pockets to keep himself in check. "Do you need any help packing?"

"No," she said, folding her arms tightly under her breasts. "I've packed a suitcase to take, and Katherine said she'd send the rest on for me."

"God, Katherine," he said, wincing. "She'll probably kill me. She's turned into your biggest fan."

She smiled, but it didn't reach her eyes. "I have to go. Your mother should be up at the house with the babies by now."

"I'll walk you up." He turned to his workbench and pushed the seedlings into the middle so they were safe while he was gone, then looked back to Jenna.

"Please don't," she said, gulping air as the tears flowed more freely down her face. "I don't think I could stand saying goodbye to you in front of other people."

He could barely speak past the lump lodged in his throat, but seeing her cry really tore him up. "Goodbye, Jenna."

"Goodbye, Liam," she said and rushed through the rows of flowers, away from him, gone.

Twelve

"Well, you're a sorry example of fatherhood."

On hearing his brother's voice, Liam scowled.

In the couple of weeks since Jenna had left, he felt like he'd merely been going through the motions of living, and Bonnie had been the only light in his dark. He hadn't felt like seeing anyone else and had barely spoken to the other researchers at work. So on a Sunday morning when he should have been surrounded only by his daughter's baby sounds, the last thing he wanted was visitors. Guests would expect him to talk and interact like a normal person, a person whose heart hadn't been torn in two, with one half on the living room floor here with him, and the other on the other side of the globe.

Resigned, he leaned over and picked up Bonnie from her play mat and faced them. "I'll be telling Katherine to check with me before letting you two in again. What's that comment supposed to mean, anyway?"

Adam shot Dylan a glance. "I see what you were talking about."

"What?" Liam demanded. He didn't have the patience for cryptic games.

Dylan winced. "Well, there's that bark for a start."

Adam reached over and took his niece. "A father should at least pretend to be enjoying time with his daughter."

Liam folded his arms over his chest. Who were they to question his parenting? "I was enjoying my time with her. Until you two showed up."

"Could have fooled us," Dylan said. "You look like you just lost the love of your life." His eyes widened in mock innocence. "Oh, wait…"

Liam felt his temper rising and cut his brother off before he could say something else and make it worse. "Why, exactly, are you here?"

"We wanted to see how you're doing," Adam said, concern in his voice this time. "Since Jenna left."

Dylan folded his arms, mirroring Liam's stance. "And if you're going after her."

Going after her? As if he hadn't thought about that option at least a million times. "I'm doing fine, thank you very much, and I'm not going anywhere."

Adam narrowed his eyes. "Then you're a fool."

"Hey!" Liam said, surprised. This was going beyond their normal fraternal teasing.

"You know," Dylan said conversationally, as if the other two weren't squaring off, "I was reading a Larsland newspaper this morning and I saw a story about our Princess Jensine."

Liam found his scowl again. Perhaps they'd been bored and were here to torture him for their own entertainment.

"They said," Dylan continued, "that she'd spent some time in seclusion after losing her boyfriend, Alexander."

"I'm not interested," Liam said, lying through his teeth. He'd wanted to check the newspapers too, but he hadn't allowed himself—it would be the start of a slippery slope that could easily end with him abandoning all his values and following Jenna to her homeland.

Dylan took Bonnie from Adam and spoke while he played with her fingers, as if this wasn't big news. "And it turns out that she has a baby, Princess Margarethe. The Larsland people have embraced them." He frowned. "I had to put it through a translation program, but I'm pretty sure that's what it said. Of course it could be they've got two new otters at the zoo called Jenna and Margarethe and the Larsland people have fed them. In some places it was hard to decipher."

Liam's chest expanded. Jenna had been worried about how it would all go down when she returned, but it seemed she'd been able to make peace with her family—at least enough that they'd presented her to the people again. She would be able to live the life she'd been brought up to live.

The life that was far away from his.

"That's good to hear," he said, ensuring his voice was even.

"Come off it, Liam," Adam said, throwing his hands up. "Don't try to deny you love her. We all saw it at the launch of the Midnight Lily."

Every muscle in his body clenched tight at being confronted with the truth in such a cavalier way. "Of course I love her. What's that got to do with it?"

"Are you intimidated because she's a princess?" Adam asked, rocking back on his heels.

Dylan nodded. "I can see why he would be. She was

too good for him before we found out she was a princess. Now she's totally out of his league."

"The door's that way," Liam said, planting his hands low on his hips and nodding to the front door. "Don't let me keep you from whatever it is you usually do on a Sunday morning."

"Yep," Dylan said, turning to Adam, "definitely grouchy. Seems we arrived just in time."

"She lied to me," Liam said before he could stop himself. "You can't build a future where there's no foundation of trust."

Adam sent him a mocking glance. "She had to. When she started here, she didn't know you from a bar of soap. Did you expect her to divulge a secret like that to a virtual stranger?"

"I saw you two together," Dylan added. "I don't care that she was lying about her name or her family. You two had something real going on."

"You know, I might have lied to you, but at least I saw you. What we had was more honest than anything I've had with anyone else, despite the lie."

Everything inside him seemed to tangle into knots. He used to think the relationships he'd had in the past were shallow yet honest. Both parties knew going in the game they were playing and the rules. But he'd been wrong. Very wrong.

He'd exposed his soul to Jenna, and he'd seen the essence of hers. Their time together had been nothing like the meaningless trysts he'd had in the past. Names didn't matter when the connection had been that deep.

But, he reminded himself, their connection wasn't the issue here. He straightened his spine and met his brothers' gazes squarely, one after the other. "Bonnie is my number-one priority."

Dylan looked down to the baby in his arms, then back to Liam. "Are you kidding? Bonnie adores Jenna and Meg. Letting her have them in her life *would* be prioritizing her."

"This situation is bigger than individual people. Anyone involved with Jenna would live their life in the public eye." He held back a shudder; he could think of nothing worse. "Remember the life Jenna has resumed is the one she ran from in the first place and ended up being your housekeeper. I categorically refuse to put Bonnie in that situation."

Dylan looked at Adam. "And you were right too. He *is* an idiot."

"Hey!" Liam said again.

"No family is perfect," Adam said on a sigh. "The best you can hope for is a family full of love. You love Jenna, and you love Meg. Bonnie loves Jenna, and Bonnie loves Meg. And Jenna and Meg love you both right back."

Had his figures-and-spreadsheets brother just used the phrase *family full of love*? At any other time, Liam would have laughed out loud.

Dylan nodded his agreement. "And you and Jenna are ridiculously well suited to each other. Any fool can see that."

"What more could you possibly be holding out for?" Adam said, exasperated.

Liam looked from one brother to the other, partly infuriated and partly touched that they cared enough to stage something of an intervention, and suddenly a thought hit him. The bonds with his brothers had been one of the most important things in his life, no question.

Bonnie had that with Meg. It was clear they had a bond—they already acted like sisters. And Bonnie responded to Jenna as a mother. She'd already lost one mother, so why was he letting her lose another one? Family was family.

Having Meg and Jenna in her life was more important than whether they might have to make a public appearance or deal with Jenna's family. Besides, Bonnie would have him on her side, which was one advantage that Jenna didn't have growing up. He'd protect her with a fierceness that anyone standing against her best interests would come to fear.

And if Bonnie would be happy because she'd have Jenna and Meg in her daily life, loving her, then the decision about their future rested solely on what *he* wanted.

He finally freed himself to admit it.

He loved Jenna.

Loved her and wanted her in his life, no matter that her royal lifestyle was the last thing he would have chosen. She was a package deal, and he was fine with that. More than fine. He'd put up with worse to have her in his life.

It was as if the world moved back onto its proper axis and clicked into place. This felt right. Felt good. Now that he knew what he wanted, he just needed to make it happen.

He lifted his daughter from Dylan's arms. "You two need to leave," he said.

Dylan was outraged. "I wasn't finished cuddling my niece yet."

"You want to stay," Liam said, throwing them both pointed looks, "then you can help. *Without* making comments. One of you can book me a ticket to Larsland. The other can find Katherine. I have arrangements to make."

His brothers slid each other a smug sideways glance, then jumped into action.

Liam watched them, trying to ignore that his heart was in his throat. Would Jenna still want him? Would her family approve of the match? Would he even get in to see her?

He took a steadying breath. He had more questions than answers, but he owed it to both Bonnie and himself to at least give it a try.

Holding his daughter against his chest and trying to keep his heart from beating through his ribs, Liam entered the palace's Throne Room. He refused to glance around, keeping his attention focused on the woman and man seated on the oversized chairs twenty feet away in front of a giant red velvet curtain with gold trim.

It wasn't hard to see the room had been built to impress and intimidate, with its two-story ceilings held up by huge columns, ornate moldings and decorations, and intricate murals.

The number Jenna had left in case he needed her had led to her friend Kristen, who, in turn, had started the ball rolling to get him here, meeting with the Queen of Larsland and the Prince Consort. After all the background checks and meetings he'd had with palace staff to get to this stage, Jenna's parents would be thoroughly briefed about him. If he wanted a future with Jenna and Meg, he needed to handle this royal thing head on.

And he did want a future with her, if she'd have him.

"Mr. Hawke," Jenna's mother said coolly. "So very lovely to meet you."

"Lovely to meet you as well, Your Highness," Liam said.

Jenna's father huffed out a breath. "We don't have

long. We've had to delay a meeting to give you these few minutes, so you might want to get to the point."

Liam held back a smile. No small talk. That suited him just fine. He adjusted Bonnie and faced them. "I spent some time with Princess Jensine and her daughter while they were in L.A."

The queen raised a regal eyebrow. "We know who you are, Mr. Hawke."

Right. Of course she did. But how much did they know? Just the facts from the background checks or had Jenna told them about him?

Had they told Jenna he was here…? His stomach looped. No, he had to focus on the present moment to be able to make it past this first hurdle.

He swallowed, then laid his cards on the table. "I'm here to request permission to ask Jenna for her hand in marriage."

Her majesty's face didn't move so much as an eyelash. "My husband and I are grateful for the assistance you and your brother gave to our daughter during her time in the United States. However we cannot give our consent."

The world fell away beneath his feet. He wouldn't let their refusal stop him from asking Jenna to be his wife, but he knew they'd just drastically reduced the chances that she'd accept him.

He straightened his spine. This wasn't over until Jenna told him it was.

Jenna stood with Meg on her hip, hidden by the thick velvet curtain behind her parents' chairs, trembling with the power of the emotions coursing through her.

Her mother had asked if she wanted to be present during this meeting, but Jenna had declined. Liam had contacted Kristen and asked to meet with the queen and prince, not with her. At first she'd been surprised, but she was also intrigued to find out what he wanted— she'd thought they'd said everything they had to say to each other before she left L.A.—so she'd accepted her father's suggestion to listen in instead.

When Liam requested permission to ask her to marry him, she gasped, then covered her mouth with her hand. Luckily, no one seemed to have heard, so she eventually let herself breathe again.

Those words had been the last thing she'd expected him to say. Was he serious? What could have possibly changed since she left?

Liam cleared his throat. "May I ask why I'm refused permission?"

"When Jenna returned," her father said, "she told us everything."

That was true. She'd resolved that going forward there would be no more secrets. She'd had enough to last her a lifetime.

On her first day in the country, Kristen had smuggled her in to meet her parents in private. She hadn't wanted anyone else to see her until her mother and father had decided what they wanted to do. She'd embarrassed them with a child out of wedlock, so it was their right to decide the next step.

The most likely outcome had been that they'd ask her to stay out of the spotlight—perhaps move to another country permanently—and come up with a cover story to explain her absence. Or perhaps they would let her raise Meg in the palace but tell the press she was someone else's child and that Jenna had adopted her. Or perhaps they'd come up with a plan she hadn't even considered.

But the parents she returned to were not the same parents she'd left. They'd been so frightened while she was gone, and blamed themselves for her disappearance, that many things had changed. They'd welcomed her with open arms and had been thrilled to find out about their first grandchild.

Then they'd called a family meeting with her siblings, the first one they'd ever had, and had an open discussion about what they all really wanted for their own lives. Not every wish could be accommodated, but the fact they'd been listened to meant her brothers and sister felt better about going ahead with devoting their lives to their country—something none of them questioned.

"And when she told us about you," her father continued, "we asked her if she'd like to marry this man from America, and she said no."

"She did?" Liam asked, his voice rough.

"She did," her mother confirmed. "And now that we have our daughter back, we'll be prioritizing her needs. So, no, you do not have our blessing."

Liam was quiet for a moment, as if absorbing that information. "You have to understand," he finally said, his voice like steel, "I won't give up. Not unless Jenna herself tells me she won't marry me."

Jenna's heart stopped beating. She couldn't wait another moment. She stepped out from behind the curtain. Meg squealed and reached for Liam, but she soothed her.

"Jenna," he said on a long breath. He didn't move toward her, which was just as well—she wouldn't have been able to think if he had.

She moistened her lips and found the courage to ask the question she needed to before they went any further. "Why do you suddenly want to marry me, Liam?"

"Jenna, you and Meg are half of my family," he said simply but with a world of emotion in his eyes. "I love you both, more than I thought was possible."

The air was suddenly too thick to draw into her lungs, but she persevered. Things were far from settled.

"My parents have offered me a full-time public role in Larsland." With them getting older and wanting to step back from some of the duties, and three of her brothers away in military training, they'd said at the family meeting they'd welcome the help. "How does that information affect your offer? A life lived in the public eye. Day after day, night after night, by my side, engaging in small talk."

She lifted her chin, challenging him, daring him. She needed to know if this was a misguided attempt to reclaim something that had been good while it lasted, or if he really could handle her life.

He swallowed, but he didn't waver. "Wherever you are, I'll be there. If you want to take on a job in Antarctica, Bonnie and I will join you. I realized after you left that family is family, regardless of whether the blood is red or blue. You and Meg are our family."

She took a step forward. "You would?"

"Without hesitation." He moved within touching distance and smoothly took Meg when the baby reached out and murmured a personal hello to her. With a baby in each arm, telling her she was his family, he'd never been more desirable. She'd never loved him more. "But I have a suggestion," he said and cast a glance at her parents.

Jenna waved away his concern. "You can speak freely in front of them. No more secrets. If we're to find a way forward, I want everything out in the open in my family from now on."

Liam shrugged a shoulder, then nodded. "In some ways, Bonnie and I will be grafted onto your family. In other ways, you and Meg will be grafted onto the Hawke family. You've already made changes to mine. My parents are meeting with an architect while I'm away to draw up plans for their new house on the farm's land. That's thanks to you."

"I'm so glad!" she said, thrilled that they'd be back where their hearts truly were.

"Sometimes," he continued, "families can be complicated, with their rules and expectations, as well as what we imagine the rules and expectations are. Especially when there are, ah…family businesses involved."

She couldn't contain a laugh. "I think both our families fall into that definition."

He tilted his head in acknowledgment. "So I have a proposition for you."

"I'm listening," she said and took Meg back when she kept thwacking Liam in the jaw. She needed to hear what he had to say before Meg did any damage.

"You and I can create a hybrid family." A hint of a smile turned the corners of his mouth up for the first time. "We negotiate with both our families. See how much my family needs me for Hawke's Blooms and how much they can do without me. I've already been handing over some of my role, also thanks to you. And we do the same with your family. We also do it with the Clancys, because Bonnie will still need access to her other grandparents. Then we look at what we want. You and me. And we create our family. One that suits us both."

For a moment she was speechless at the beauty of the plan. It was so obvious now that he laid it out, yet at the same time it was so quintessentially Liam with its hybrids and grafting. She tapped a finger against her lips and watched him watch the move.

Then she grinned. "You know, that could work."

She looked to her parents, who were listening to the conversation with indulgent smiles. They nodded their assent to his proposition.

Liam took her free hand with his and squeezed. "However we work it out," he said, low enough that she was the only one who could hear, "if you marry me, I'll spend the rest of my life making sure you don't regret it."

She felt the love she had for him rise up and fill her body, so much it overflowed and a tear, then two, slipped down her cheek. "You don't have to do anything to make sure of that," she whispered. "Just love me. Love us."

He cleared his throat twice before he could reply. "I can promise that, Jenna. I'll love you, Meg and Bonnie till my dying breath."

She'd forgotten the world around them existed, but suddenly her parents were beside them, and her mother kissed her cheek. "I'm happy for you," she murmured in their native language. "This is the right man for you and the right man to be Meg's father."

"Welcome to the family, son," her father said, patting Liam on the back, then taking Meg from Jenna. "This is a family that might take some getting used to, but Jenna will help you through it. And we'll be here if you need us."

Her mother put her arms out to Bonnie and Liam handed her over. "It seems we've acquired another granddaughter," she said to her husband.

The prince kissed his wife's hand. "It's been our lucky month."

Then her parents, holding one baby each, faded into the background, giving them some privacy.

Jenna reached up and cupped his cheek in her palm. "I can't believe you're here. I've dreamed of this so many times since I've been back that it still doesn't seem real."

His smile was slow and sexy, and it melted her insides. "Not only am I here, but I'm not going away. Not unless you come too."

Liam threaded his hands into her hair, then lowered his head and kissed her. The feel of his lips touching hers once more was sublime. She flexed her fingers into the front of his shirt and gave herself over to the kiss. Over to him. And when she felt the shudder that ran through him, she knew he was giving himself over to her too.

"From now on," he said against her mouth, "we're a team. You, me, Bonnie and Meg. A family."

Her heart swelled. "That sounds like a recipe for heaven."

Then she tipped her chin up and found his lips again.

* * * * *

A MOTHER FOR HIS
ADOPTED SON

LYNNE MARSHALL

To foster and adoptive parents worldwide who open their homes and hearts and make a difference in young lives.

CHAPTER ONE

SAM MARCUS STOOD in the observation room above the OR suite in St. Francis of the Valley Hospital, waiting for his child to lose an eye. He'd seen his share of surgeries before, being a pediatrician, but never for someone he loved. This time he needed an anchor, so he leaned against the window to see his son better and to offer support against the threat of his buckling knees.

He watched as the anesthesiologist put his tiny boy under and while the surgeon measured the eye globe and cornea dimensions, the length of the optic nerve. His heart thumped in his chest, and a fine line of sweat gathered above his lip as the surgeon made the first incision. He swiped it away with a trembling hand, trying his best to get his mind wrapped around what was happening.

Enucleation.

His barely three-year-old newly adopted son had retinoblastoma and needed to have his left eye surgically removed. He swallowed hard and shook his head, still unable to believe it.

He'd fallen in love with Danilo, an orphan, on his last Doctors' Medical Missions trip to the Philippines. The mission had been in response to their latest typhoon, to tend to the countless new orphans. He hadn't been in the market for a son or daughter. No, it had been the last thing on his mind then. Yet there had been one particular one-year-old boy who'd lost his entire family in the typhoon and who'd miraculously managed to survive for forty-eight hours on his own. A little hero.

Over the days of the two-week mission, Sam and the other doctors had performed physicals and minor proce-dures, as well as arranged for other children who had re-quired more extensive medical care to be transported to where they needed to be. Dani had used his new walk-ing skills to follow Sam everywhere. It'd made Sam re-member one of his favorite childhood books, *Are You My Mommy?* A story his own mother had read to him, where a little bird who'd fallen out of the nest went looking for his mother, asking everyone, even machines, if they were his mother, and it had broken his heart.

All the children on this mission were orphans dealing with their losses in their own ways, yet this child, Dani, seemed to have chosen Sam. He gave in and took the boy with him everywhere at the orphanage clinic, cautiously opened his heart, then fell in love in an amazingly short period of time. Then it was time to leave. Dani cried in-consolably, and one of the sisters at the orphanage told Sam that it was the first time the child had cried since ar-riving there six weeks before.

What was a man supposed to do? He knew how it felt to be homeless. He'd been taken away from his mother when he was ten. She hadn't abused him, but she'd had to leave him alone most nights so she could work a second job. Her plan had backfired and the authorities had taken Sam and put him into foster care. Yeah, he knew how it felt to be left all alone.

Fortunately for him he'd been placed into a big happy family and currently suffered from missing them, with everyone fanned out all across the United States. There'd been five natural siblings in all, and he'd become kid number six, yet his already overworked foster mother had insisted on bringing in more foster children—a long, long list of foster kids had come and gone over the years. *Why?* he used to ask whenever he'd been instructed to share his bunk bed with yet another new kid. *We don't have room for more, Mom.* She'd always insisted he call her Mom.

Even after all these years her response never left his subconscious. "We don't always know how we'll make ends meet or where they'll sleep, Sammy, but we just know we've got to bring them in because the child needs a home."

The child needs a home.

He'd been one of those children. And he'd been trying to prove himself worth keeping ever since.

When he'd returned home from the Philippines, he'd been unable to get Dani out of his mind. Missing his infectious smile and unconditional love, he'd decided to try for the adoption in honor of his deceased foster mother, because that child needed a home.

Though it had taken a year and a half to jump through all the hoops to arrange for Dani's adoption, six months ago he and Dani had teamed up and never looked back. And what an adjustment being a single father had been. It'd always been hectic, growing up with so many foster siblings, yet under the chaos there had been stability. Something he'd never had when he'd been a young boy. That was his goal for Dani, to give the boy stability, but he'd never been a parent before and they were both on a stiff learning curve, working things out, juggling the logistics of his busy career, child care and father-son time.

Then this cancer nightmare had happened, and any stability they'd established had been replaced with utter mental and emotional turmoil.

They'd discovered the tumor on Dani's very first eye examination in the United States. The simple yet disturbing fact that his pupil had turned white instead of red when the ophthalmologist had shone a light into it had heralded the beginning of more and more bad news. The child had intraocular retinoblastoma.

The team of doctors, headed by the pediatric oncologist, had recommended the surgery after all other avenues of treatment—each with drawbacks and no guarantees—had been considered and rejected. Dr. Van Diesel, the pediatric eye surgeon, had come highly recommended, and since there wasn't a chance that Dani's vision could be saved, they'd opted for enucleation.

Sam watched from behind the viewing window as the surgeon, through a dissecting microscope, removed the outer covering of the eye. Next the four rectus muscles were detached from the eyeball, then the surgeon placed a hemostat on the stump of the last severed eye muscle. With special long, minimally curved scissors, he cut the optic nerve. Sam's battered heart sank, realizing the monumental change that single surgical incision had made to his son's vision. He stood motionless, unable to take in a breath, emotion flooding through his veins as next the surgeon removed the eyeball.

Unable to swallow the thickening lump in his throat, Sam watched as a nurse stood nearby with a small specimen container to collect a tiny piece of the optic nerve for histopathologic study. For their next huge hold-your-breath diagnosis—had all of the cancer been removed or had it spread? His stomach pinched at the potential outcome. The doctor worked painstakingly to also open the eye globe to harvest tissue from the retinoblastoma. Before closing, he placed a plastic temporary conformer into Dani's eye socket to avoid a shrunken look and maintain a natural shape. They'd discussed in advance how this would be done in preparation to ensure the proper size and motility for the future eye prosthesis.

When he finally could, Sam took a deep breath. The worst was over, no, check that, the worst had been getting the damn diagnosis of cancer in the first place. Since he wanted to keep a positive outlook, he'd deemed today the first step in Dani's healing. He watched like a hawk as the anesthesiologist prepared his son for transfer to the recovery room and the surgical nurse bandaged Dani's left eye with a special patch to help decrease swelling.

He rushed out of the observation deck and hustled down the stairs to be the first to talk with Dr. Van Diesel when he exited the OR.

"All went well," the white-haired man said, as he tossed his gloves in the trash and removed the surgical cap then the mask from his face. "No surprises." He forced a smile that looked more like a squint. "Should be a couple of days before we get the pathology reports."

"Thank you." And Sam probably wouldn't sleep until he knew whether the tumor had spread or not. But he was determined to keep that positive attitude. As of right now the tumor was gone, his son was free of cancer. That was how it had to be.

The doctor continued on to the locker room. Sam stood outside the OR doors and waited for the team to transport Dani. Several minutes later the doors swung open and his son, looking so tiny on the huge gurney, got rolled toward the recovery room.

He followed the medical parade out of the surgical suite, down the hall and into Recovery. As he was a staff member as well as a parent, he was also allowed to accompany the boy rather than be instructed to wait outside until he was ready for discharge. The receiving RR nurses bustled around the gurney, transferring him to their bed, disconnecting Dani from the OR equipment and attaching him to theirs. Heart monitor, blood-pressure cuff, pulse oximeter, oxygen.

Sam remained by his son's side, taking his tiny yet pudgy fingers into his own, feeling their chill and asking for a second blanket to cover him. Every once in a while his son moved or took a deeper breath. His heartbeat was steady and strong, blipping across the monitor screen; his blood pressure read low for a three-year-old, but he was still sedated. One particular Filipino nurse looked after Dani as if he were her own. That gave Sam reassurance.

"Is your wife coming, Doctor?" Her Filipino accent made the sentence staccato.

"No." Sam shook his head. "No wife."

He'd lost the woman with whom he'd thought he'd spend the rest of his life. She'd walked away. But he'd committed to adopting little Dani and he couldn't bear the thought of disappointing the boy who would finally have a home and a family of his own. Even if it was just the two of them.

"I will watch him," the nurse said. "Don't worry. You should take a break."

He stretched and glanced at her name tag. "Thank you, Imelda. I could use a cup of coffee about now."

She nodded toward the nurses' lunchroom. "We just made some."

He thought about taking her up on the offer but realized how much he needed to stretch his legs, to get his blood moving again. To help him think. To plan. Maybe with more circulation to his brain he'd be able to process everything that'd happened today. "Thanks, but I'm going to take a walk."

He stood and started to leave, then blurted the first thought in his mind. "By any chance, do you know where the prosthetic eye department is?"

Imelda pulled in her double chin. "Do we have one, Doctor?"

He tipped his head. Good question. Hadn't Dr. Van Diesel mentioned it at one point? "I hope so."

As he left the recovery room, he made eye contact with the charge nurse. "I'll be back in twenty minutes but beep me the instant Dani wakes up, okay?"

She nodded, so he pushed the metal plate on the wall and the recovery room department doors automatically swung inward. With one more glance over his shoulder to his sleeping son, and another pang in his heart, he stepped outside.

The one-hour operation under general anesthesia was fairly routine, and because the eye was surrounded by bone, it made it much easier for Dani to tolerate. If all went well, his son could even be discharged later that afternoon.

He walked down the hall, entered the elevator. His mind drifted to Katie, wondering if this pain would have been easier to take sharing it with someone else, but that was never to be. Katie had stuck with him all through medical school and his pediatric residency at UCLA while she'd tried to launch her acting career. Sure, they'd talked about marriage and children, but mostly he'd avoided it. He'd been left by the most important woman in his life, his mother, at a tender age, and it had marked him for life. Toward the end of their relationship, she'd kept insisting on wedding plans and he'd kept sidestepping them. When he'd finally brought up marriage because of the adoption, after screaming at him for making such a huge decision by himself Katie had suddenly decided her acting career needed her full attention.

He'd screwed up by not consulting her, but he'd thought he'd known her, and she'd very nearly wrenched his heart right out of his chest when she'd walked away.

Not a great track record with the women he'd loved. At least his foster mother, Mom Murphy, had never sent him back.

The elevator stopped at the first-floor lobby and he headed to the information desk. "Don't we have a department that makes facial prosthetics here? You know, things like eyes?"

The silver-haired gentleman's gaze lit with knowledge. "Yes, as a matter of fact, I believe we do." He scrolled through his computer directory, then used his index finger to point. "It's called Ocularistry and Anaplastology." The man had trouble pronouncing it and made a second attempt. "And it's in the basement, with Pathology." He placed his hand beside his mouth as if to whisper. "I think it's next door to the morgue."

"What's the name of the head of the department?" Sam asked.

"Judith Rimmer. Or, as we volunteers like to call her, Helen Mirren without the star power. Hubba-hubba, if you know what I mean."

Sam's brows rose at the thought—so even old guys had crushes—but off to the dungeon he went. Once he exited the elevator, he wondered why the fluorescent lights even looked dimmer down in the hospital basement, but pressed on. He passed the Matériel Management department, then Central Service—the cleaning and sterilization area. He knew where Pathology was—he'd visited there regularly to get early reports on his patients and to discuss prognoses with the pathologists. He'd also unfortunately been to the morgue far more often than he cared to in the line of duty. Nothing cut deeper than losing a child patient, and for the sake of science he'd sat in on his share of autopsies to help make sense of the tragedies.

Sam sidestepped the morgue double doors, refusing to even glance through the ocean-liner-style windows for activity, then squinted and saw the small department sign for Ocularistry and Anaplastology in bold black letters. How many people would even know what it meant?

The office was shoved into the farthest corner in the hallway, as if it had been an afterthought. The panel of fluorescent lights just outside the door blinked and buzzed, in need of a new tube, making things seem eerier than they already were. He wasn't sure whether to knock or just go inside. He glanced at his watch, he'd wasted enough time finding the department, so without a moment's further hesitation he pushed through the door of the "prosthetic eye people's" department.

A dainty, young platinum-blonde woman with short hair more in style with a 1920s flapper than current fashion arranged flesh-colored silicone ears under a glass display case, as if they were necklaces and earrings in an upscale jewelry store. She looked nothing like Helen Mirren but might pass as her granddaughter. What had that volunteer been talking about? On the next table sat a huge model of an eyeball. He narrowed his gaze at the odd juxtaposition.

The woman glanced up with warm brown eyes surrounded with dark liner and smoky underlid smudges. Not the usual look he noticed in the hospital, and the immediate draw caught him off guard. His son was in Recovery, having just lost an eye, for God's sake. He had no right to notice an attractive woman! The fact he did ticked him off.

"I'm looking for Judith Rimmer." Okay, so he sounded gruffer than necessary, maybe impatient, but it wasn't even noon and he'd already been through one hell of a no-good, very bad day, to paraphrase one of his son's favorite books.

"She's currently in Europe," Andrea Rimmer said. The intruder had barged in and brought a whole lot of stress with him, and her immediate response was to bristle.

The brown-haired man with intense blue eyes, of which neither was prosthetic, stared her down, not liking her answer one bit. He may be a head taller than she was, but she wasn't about to let him intimidate her. She'd had plenty of practice of standing up to men like that with her father.

"When will she be back?" He seemed to look right through her, which further ticked her off. Wasn't she a person, too? Was her grandmother the only one who mattered in this department?

"Next week." She could play vague with the best of them.

"I'll come back then."

It hadn't been her idea to take the apprenticeship for ocularist four years ago. Nope, that had been good old Dad's plan. She'd barely graduated from the Los Angeles Art Academy when he'd pressured her into getting a "real job" while she found her bearings in the art world. Now that she was in her last year of the apprenticeship, and since Grandma was threatening to retire and was expecting Andrea to take her place, she'd felt her back against the wall and resented the narrow choice being shoved down her throat. Work full-time. Run the department. The place didn't even have windows!

What about her painting? Her dreams?

Had the demanding doctor brushed her off by assuming she was an inexperienced technician because she was young? She didn't think twenty-eight was that young, but being short probably made her seem younger. If he thought he could be rude because she was young or a nobody, this guy with the tense attitude had just pushed her intolerant button.

"She may not *be* coming back." She sounded snotty, which wasn't her usual style, as she rearranged the ears again. But she didn't really care because this guy, who may be good-looking but seriously lacked the charm gene so who cared how good-looking he was, had just ruined her morning for no good reason.

She glanced up. He raised a brow and stared her down

in response to her borderline impudent reply, and she saw the judgment there, the same look she'd seen in her father's eyes time and time again. *I'm a doctor. You dare to talk to me like that?*

The imaginary conversation quickly played out in her head. *What? Am I not good enough for you?* A feeling, unfortunately, she'd had some experience with on the home front most of her life. After all, wasn't she the daughter of a woman with only a high-school education? A stay-at-home mother keeping a spotless house for a husband who rarely visited? A woman so depressed she'd turned into a shadow of her former self? Half of her DNA might be genius, but the other half, often insinuated by her father, was suspect. Well, good ol' Dad should have thought about that before knocking up her mother if it meant so damn much to him.

The invading doctor continued to stare down his nose at her. Andrea wasn't about to back down now. The nerve. Did he think she was a shopgirl, a department receptionist minding the store while Granny frolicked in France? She'd just spent a week making this latest batch of silicone ears, measuring the patients to perfection, matching the skin color, creating the simplest and most secure way to adhere them to what was left of their own ears. And unless anyone looked really closely, no one would notice. Just ask the struggling musician Brendan, who'd had his earlobe chopped off by a mobster, what he thought about her skills!

"What do you mean, she may not be coming back?" His tone shifted to accusing as if he should have been privy to the memo and voted on the decision. Wasn't that how demanding doctors, just like her father, behaved? *I need this* now. *Don't annoy me with facts.* He stood, hands on hips, his suit jacket pushed aside, revealing his trim and flat stomach—wait, she didn't care about his physique because he was rude—refusing to look away from the visual contact they'd made. Something really had this guy bothered, and she was the unfortunate party getting the brunt of it.

"It's called retirement."

His wild blue stare didn't waver, and, as illogical as it seemed under the circumstances, something was going on with the electrical charge circulating around her skin because of him.

A beeper went off on his belt, breaking the standoff and the static tickling across her arms. He glanced at it. She was glad because she really didn't know how much longer she could take him standing in the small outer office, and most especially gazing into those intense eyes.

It was her job to notice things like that. Eyes. Yeah, she'd become quite an expert during her apprenticeship. If she kept telling herself that, maybe she wouldn't scold herself later for falling under the spell of a completely pompous stranger based solely on his baby blues.

"I've gotta go." Obviously in no mood to deal with her touchy technician act, he turned and huffed off, right out the door.

Wilting over her bad behavior, she tossed her pen onto the countertop and plopped into the nearest chair. Why had she behaved that way with him? She'd knee-jerked over the intruding and demanding doctor, but wasn't he acting exactly like her father? Arrogant and overbearing. Lording his station in life over her. *Where's the head of the department, because you're not good enough. Step out of my way.* He didn't need to say the words; she'd *felt* them.

Andrea caught herself making a lemon-sucking expression and let it go. Maybe she was the one with the attitude, and she hadn't even tried to control it. That man had just got the brunt of it, too. Truth was, she needed to be more accommodating to clients and doctors, especially if she actually ever agreed to take over as the department head.

Which she sure as heck wasn't certain she wanted to do. Especially if catering to demanding doctors like that guy would be part of the routine.

She hadn't expected a young doctor with such interestingly pigmented irises—because that was what she'd learned to notice since beginning her apprenticeship—and penetrating eyes as that guy's to set her off on a rant. And she'd acted nothing short of an ass with him.

Shame on her.

Guilt and longing intertwined inside her. She'd fallen short of the mark just now, and it was a symptom of the battle she fought every day when she came to work. This was her job, creating prosthetic eyes for people who needed them, silicone ears, noses and cheeks for cancer victims and veterans, too, and it was a noble profession. She actually loved it. Loved the patients and making their lives better. But she liked things the way they were—working four days a week at the hospital and painting the other three. Her heart yearned to paint, not run a windowless department in the bowels of a hospital.

Andrea put her elbows on the counter and rested her forehead in the palms of her hands. If Grandma ever retired, some lousy department head *she* would make.

A week later...

It had taken Sam a good day and a half to calm down after his ridiculous encounter with the young woman in the O&A department. Where did they find the employees these days anyway? But to be fair, she didn't have a clue that he'd just come from watching his son have his eye removed in surgery. He may have been more demanding than usual, but he'd been in no shape to judge how he'd come off to her, or, at that moment, to care. All he'd wanted had been to ensure his boy could have the best person possible make a realistic-looking eye to replace the one Dani had lost.

That woman couldn't have been more than in her early twenties. How could she possibly have the skill…? Yet, he reminded himself, he'd eventually realized that Judith Rimmer had a reputation known all over the country for excellence in her specialty. He'd read up on her online while little Dani had napped one afternoon. She wouldn't leave her beloved department in the hands of a novice. Would she?

Now, having completely calmed down, and being back on the job with a miraculous break in his schedule that morning, thanks to a no-show patient, Sam prepared to return to the basement to discuss Dani's need for an eye.

He reached the ocularistry and anaplastology department door, took a deep breath and entered with a plan to apologize for inadvertently insulting the still-wet-behind-the-ears ocularist—if that was even what she was. How could he know for sure? They hadn't gotten that far. Because his foster mother hadn't raised an ungracious son—she'd knock him upside the head from the grave if she found out, too. Nor had she raised a son to judge a book by the young cover—not with the revolving door of foster kids with whom he'd grown up. He smiled inwardly, then swung open the door, and much to his surprise found Helen Mirren's double, not retired but standing right in front of him beside a row of unblinking eyeballs in all colors in a display case. She wore something that looked like a sun visor but with magnifying glasses attached and a headlight, examining one specific eye as if it were a huge diamond.

Sitting with an expectant gaze on her face was the girl, who, on second encounter, and with all that eye makeup, looked more like the iconic 1960s model from Great Britain. Twiggy, was it? But not nearly as skinny. This girl had curves. She obviously waited for Judith's approval on something, a project she'd made? Maybe, but, no matter what the scene was about, Sam was ticked off. Again.

The young woman finally noticed someone had entered and glanced at him, a quick look of surprise in her double take. Yeah, he'd caught her in a childish lie, so he glared back. He could act as juvenile as the next person, thanks to his four older foster brothers and two younger foster sisters, countless other foster siblings constantly coming through the family revolving door and foster parents who hadn't been afraid to make threats in order to tame the often out-of-control tribe.

"Reconsidering retirement, Ms. Rimmer?" His vision drifted to a perplexed Judith.

Judith's gaze flitted back and forth between the woman and Sam, obviously trying to figure out what their history had been.

"Technically I wasn't lying, because my grandmother plans to retire as soon as I'm ready and *willing* to take over." She stood, which hardly made a difference. What was she, five feet, tops? And jumped right in with an explanation. "And, for all I knew, she could've been swept away by the beauty of Europe and decided not to come home. To retire on the spot. It could've happened."

Her outlandish cover nearly made him smile. Nearly. But he held firm because he found himself enjoying her flushed cheeks and her mildly flaring nostrils as she explained, her raccoon-painted eyes taking on more of a fawn-ready-to-bolt appearance.

"Which makes it okay that you lied to me?" He wasn't ready to let her off the hook, though.

She stepped around the counter, taking two steps toward him, never breaking the visual connection, which was surprisingly stimulating. "You came in with a nasty attitude that day and proceeded to make me feel like a novice who couldn't possibly be of help to you. So I decided not to be any help at all."

So that's how she'd read him. For a second he felt like a chump, but she deserved the full story. An explanation for why he'd been that jerk. "I'd just come from watching my son's enucleation. I needed reassurance he could look normal again."

Her challenging expression instantly melted into an apologetic peacemaking plea. "Oh." Those huge eyes immediately watered. "I'm so sorry to hear that."

"Dr.—" Judith read his name badge "—Marcus, I'm sorry the two of you got off to a rocky start, I'm also very sorry about your son, but I assure you Andrea is as skilled as they come. And because I'm completely booked up with projects, having just returned from vacation, she'd be happy to help you with your son's eye prosthesis. I assure you, with her artistic background, she'll make a perfect match and fit."

Andrea sent a quick questioning glance toward her grandmother but immediately recovered, as if she'd gotten the clear message to play along. *Was* she a novice? Sam still wasn't convinced. She looked so young.

"So, what I'll need to do—" Andrea used an index finger to lightly scratch the corner of her mouth "—is make an appointment for you to bring in your son. Is he completely healed yet? We shouldn't take measurements until he is."

"It's only been a week, but he's doing really well."

"Let's make it next week, then, to be safe. I'll need to take photos of his other eye and make a silicone cast of his healed eye socket. After that I'll make a wax version, which I'll be able to mold as needed to fit. What's your son's name?"

"Danilo, but he goes by Dani."

She nodded, sincerity oozing out of those huge brown

eyes. "What day is good for you?" She brought up a calendar on the computer—back to business—and he fished out his pocket phone, tapping through to his work calendar.

Back and forth they went, politely trying to work out an appointment day and time. His schedule was overbooked, since he'd taken off a week to be with his son after the surgery, which was why he was aggravated that one of his patients was a no-show today and would need to be rescheduled, further keeping him backed up. Yet that was the only reason he'd been able to sneak down here at this moment, which had turned out to be a good thing. Which would all be beside the point if he couldn't make an appointment.

At least for now, since his return to work, his former foster sister Cat could be Dani's caregiver during the day. She lived within five miles of him and was a stay-at-home mom who needed the extra cash. Their arrangement worked out for everyone, since she also had two children under the age of five, and Dani loved to play with the other kids. He scratched his head, at a loss.

Why hadn't he considered his work issue when he'd known Dani would need the prosthetic eye right off? The bigger question was why hadn't he considered how difficult it would be to become a single father in the first place?

Of course, that hadn't been his original plan...

Yeah, he was in over his head, but it made no difference, because he was proud and happy to be Dani's father, no matter how hard and complicated life had become because of it. Add another point to foster Mom's tally, *the kid needed a home.* "Do you do house calls, by any chance?"

Andrea dipped her head, thinking for a second. "No. But since I gave you a hard time last week, I'll make an exception for you, Dr. Marcus."

All was forgiven. Sweet brown-eyed angel from

heaven. "Call me Sam, please," he said, on a rush of relief. "I really appreciate that."

Their earlier glowering contest faded to a distant memory when she smiled at him. It was more of a Mona Lisa smile, but it drew his attention to her mouth and he noticed a pair of classic lips with the delicate twin peaks of a Cupid's bow.

"So how about this day next week, at your house, say, sevenish?"

"Sounds like a plan, Ms....?"

"Rimmer, but please call me Andrea."

"Are you related to Dr. Rimmer?" The tyrant of Cardiac Surgery?

"Yes. Andrea's my granddaughter," Judith spoke up, reminding Sam that Dr. Rimmer was her son. Why he hadn't made the connection earlier was beyond him.

"I hope you won't hold that against me," Andrea said drily, as though reading his thoughts and bearing the weight of her father's perilous reputation. She glanced sheepishly at her grandmother, a good sign that Andrea cared about her and didn't want to insult her son, though it seemed clear she knew what Sam's surprised reaction had been about.

Since they'd skimmed over last week's argument and had moved on to peace talks, he wouldn't bring up his multiple grievances about the curmudgeon cardiac surgery department head who wanted to throw his weight around the entire hospital. Instead he dug deep into his bag of tricks and pulled out a smile. Admittedly, since his breakup with Katie, and Dani's diagnosis, he'd nearly forgotten how, but seeing Andrea's immediate relieved reaction, her expression brightening and those lovely lips parting into a grin, he was glad he had. Plus he'd meant that smile and it felt pretty damn good.

Because she was the first lady to get him riled up in ages, and he liked how that jacked up his ticker. She'd made him feel nearly human again.

"Next Tuesday, then. Seven. It's a date, Andrea."

CHAPTER TWO

ANDREA TAPPED ON the white front door of the boxy mid-century modern home in the hills above Glendale. She was about to ring the bell when the door swung open. Admittedly nervous about facing the handsome Dr. Sam Marcus on his turf, she grinned tensely until she saw him with an adorable little boy balanced on his hip and wearing an eye patch, then she relaxed.

"Come in," he said, seeming more hospitable than she would have imagined considering their first two encounters.

"Hi," she said, stepping inside onto expensive-looking white tile in the narrow entryway. "This must be Dani." She moved closer to the little boy, raised her brows and gave a closed-mouth smile. He buried his face in his father's shoulder. *Ack, too much.*

"Bashful," Sam mouthed.

She nodded and pretended to ignore the adorable little person after that, as Sam bypassed the living room and walked her into the more inviting family room. It was large, square, open and with excellent sources of natural light from tall windows nearly covering one entire wall of the boxy '50s architecture. As it was late April, the sun stuck around longer and longer, and though his house abutted mixed-tree-covered hills and stood on metal stilts at the front, the angle at this time of day was perfect for maximum light. A thick brown carpet made her want to kick off her shoes and walk barefoot. Not sure what to do next, she set her backpack and art box aka fishing-tackle box on the classic stone fireplace hearth, then glanced up at Sam. The previously upturned corners of his mouth had stretched into a genuine smile.

She'd given herself a stern talking-to the afternoon they'd made the appointment for letting herself send and pick up on some kind of natural attraction vibes arcing between them. The man was a father! Probably married. How many do-overs would she need with this guy?

Shifting her gaze from Sam, she secretly studied Dani so as not to send him into ostrich mode again. She was admittedly surprised that Dani wasn't a mini-me of Sam. He looked Asian, Filipino maybe? Was he adopted? And Sam didn't wear a wedding ring, which made her wonder if he might not be married, but she figured she'd find out soon enough once his wife or significant other made an appearance.

"That's as good a place as any to set up," he said, easing Dani down onto his own two feet. "I hope the lighting is good enough."

"This should be perfect."

Dani immediately ran toward his stack of toys.

"Um, should I wait for your wife?"

"I'm not married. I adopted Dani on my own." Sam sat on the large wraparound couch and put his feet up on the circular ottoman at the center.

"That's fantastic." *Don't sound so enthusiastic!* "The adoption part, I mean." The only men she knew in Los Angeles who adopted kids on their own were gay. Dr. Marcus clearly didn't fall into that category if she read that subtle humming interest between them right.

"I knew what you meant." A kind gaze came winging

her way, and she felt her anxiety over making a dumb remark take a step down.

"Does he speak English?"

"They spoke both English and Tagalog at the orphanage. He's superbright and picks up more and more words
every day." Spoken like a proud papa.

She found the boy busy with a colorful toy TV control-
ler, punching buttons and listening to sounds and jingles,
and dropped to her knees. "So, Dani, may I look under
your patch?"

The black-haired toddler, who was small for his age,
kept his head down, staring at the gadget in his hand, as
he let her gingerly remove the child-sized patch. She'd
seen empty eye socket after empty eye socket in the four
years since she'd started the apprenticeship, but this was
her first toddler. Grandma had given her a pep talk that
afternoon about how much she believed in Andrea's talent
and technical skills, and truth was she knew she'd caught
on quickly to the long and tedious process of re-creating
matching eyes for the eyeless. But this was a beautiful
little kid, and her heart squeezed every time she looked at
him, thinking this was way too early for anyone to need
a prosthetic. But was there ever a good age?

She'd worn stretch slacks, so she sat cross-legged beside him in order to be at his level. "I need to make a little cast to fit your face, Dani. Will you let me do that?"

The boy looked at his father, who reassured him it was
okay with a slow, deep nod.

"It won't hurt, I promise, but it might feel strange and
cold for a little while." With adult patients it was so much
easier to explain the process. She'd just have to wing it
with Dani. "May I take some pictures of your eye, too?"

"Eye gone," he said, slapping his palm over the left
socket, as if she didn't know.

"This eye." She pointed to the right one.

"Okay." She could hardly hear him.

"Thank you." She blinked when he glanced up. "Do you ever play with clay?"

He nodded shyly.

"This stuff is kind of like clay. Want to watch?"

"Okay."

"Here, you can touch it."

He did but immediately pulled back his hand at the feel of the foreign, gooey substance.

Andrea worked quickly to make enough casting gel to press into the empty socket area, and when it was time, Sam held Dani's head still while she gently pressed it into the completely healed cavity. "Cold?"

"Uh-huh."

"But it doesn't hurt, right?"

He shook his head and they smiled at each other. He understood she hadn't lied. A sudden urge to cuddle the boy had her skimming her clean palm across his short-cropped hair instead. "How'd you get to be so sweet?"

"Don't know."

A surge of emotion made her eyes prickle. This precious guy had already lost an eye to cancer. How was that for a huge dose of reality to a toddler? She swallowed against the moisture gathering in her throat. "I bet you were born sweet." Was this how it felt to flirt with a little kid?

The statement wasn't the least bit funny, but Dani thought it was and he giggled, his remaining almond-shaped eye almost closing when he did. She hadn't been around many children since way back when she used to babysit for movie money, but something about Dani made her want to kiss his chubby cheeks and touch the tip of his rounded nose with her pointer finger.

She wiped her hands clean and dug out her camera from the backpack. "May I take your picture?"

"Uh-huh." He watched her as if mesmerized, but also maybe a little afraid to move with the cast in place and taking form.

"I have to get really close to your eye. Is that okay?"

"Yes."

She leaned in toward his cute out-sticking ear and whispered, "I promise not to touch your eye, just take pictures."

He sat perfectly still and stared at her camera as she focused and zoomed in and shot photo after photograph of his dark brown orb. Later she'd study that eye until she had it memorized, then, and only then, would she attempt the intricate painting of his iris. Making eyes was a long and tedious process that took anywhere between sixteen and occasionally up to eighty hours, even though there was a big push to go digital these days. Mistakes weren't acceptable in Grandma's world. Neither was digital technology. Andrea had learned early on to take the extra time and effort at the beginning to save hours of do-overs. And she loved that part of her job.

By the age of three she knew the human eye was just a hair smaller by one or two millimeters than it would eventually become, and that by the age of thirteen it would reach the full adult size. Danilo would probably need a new prosthesis at that time, if not before, but she planned to make this one to last a full decade. The boy deserved no less.

After four minutes the timer went off, alerting her that the silicone was set. Tomorrow, back in the O&A department, she'd duplicate it in wax and later reform it until it fit Dani perfectly, which would give her another excuse to see the adorable little guy. There'd be multiple reasons to see Dani, since he'd have a trial period of wearing a clear acrylic beneath his patch for fitting purposes for the next month while she re-created his iris.

"I'm all done. What do you think about that?" She

gently eased out the silicone cast from his eye socket, brow line and upper cheek.

"Okay."

"And it didn't hurt, did it?"

He shook his head. She showed him what the cast looked like and he made a funny face, which made her laugh, then she carefully put the partial facial and eye-socket cast into a protective carrying case. Dani watched every move she made, as if she might be taking part of his face with her. She handed him a mirror to see she'd left all of him behind. He stoically studied himself, missing eye and all, which made her want to brighten him up.

Andrea raised her brows and pressed her lips together before talking. "Did you know I brought you a present?"

His other eye widened. "No." So serious.

"I brought you my favorite stuffed frog." She reached into her backpack and pulled out the bean-stuffed toy that used to sit on her computer monitor at work. She'd grabbed it on a whim just before she'd left tonight. "His name is Ribbit."

Dani giggled again. "I like him."

"Here. He's yours. You earned him for being so good." She offered him the toy, and he reached for it without hesitation.

"What do you say?" For the first time in the entire process Sam spoke up.

"Thank you."

She couldn't help herself and kissed his forehead. "You are welcome."

Sam cleared his throat. "Can I make you some tea or coffee?"

"Tea sounds good. Thanks." There was a strange expression in Sam's eyes when theirs met, as if maybe he'd been touched by the interchange with her and Dani as much as she had.

Dani played happily with his frog as Andrea helped put the eye patch back on. "There. Now you look like a pirate."

"I don't like pirate."

"When I make your new eye, you won't need to wear the patch anymore."

He touched the patch and tugged on it. "Okay."

"Hey, is this your truck?" She crawled over to a pile of toys in the corner of the room. "May I play with it?" The boy quickly followed her and laughed when she made a vroom-vroom sound, pushing the red truck around the carpet, while waiting for Sam to make the tea.

Next they played building blocks, and Dani took great pleasure in letting her build her colorful tower, only to knock it down the instant she'd finished. She pretended to be upset, folding her arms and pouting, but the boy saw right through her. Mostly what they did was laugh, giggle, tease each other and horse around until Sam showed up with the tea.

"I hate to break up the play, Dani, but it's time to get you ready for bed."

Dani acted upset. He pushed out his lower lip and crossed his chubby arms just like Andrea had done a few moments before, but she knew it was all a show. He'd been rubbing his right eye when they'd played, like any little kid who was getting sleepy. When he thought she wasn't looking, he'd even yawned.

"Oh, jammies," Andrea said, to distract him from his pout. "I bet you've got really cool jammies."

"My jammies have trucks," he said, his sweet single-eyed gaze waiting for her reaction.

"Trucks! I think you already know how much I love trucks."

She was positive she saw him puff out his chest. Sam offered his hand and Dani took it, looking happily up at his father. The moment went still in her mind like a photograph, as she admired the sweet boy with the loving new parent he'd had the good fortune to find. But before he left the room she called after him. "Dani, don't forget your frog."

He trotted back to take it and gave her one last smile before running off to his father's waiting hand, then walking with him down the hall. Andrea sat on the plush carpet and sipped her fragrant chamomile tea, her heart aching for a precious little boy with one eye. The warm tea helped smooth out the lump in her throat, but there was no way she'd soon forget Dani.

A large framed black-and-white photograph on the opposite wall caught her attention. She carried her tea over to it and counted eight kids with a mother and father, all grinning, on someone's front lawn. She studied the enlarged grainy family photo and determined that the boy third from the end might possibly be Sam Marcus. Or maybe he was second in? Come to think of it, there wasn't a very strong family resemblance.

A tallish woman with a broad smile and clear-looking eyes stood next to a droopy-shouldered man with a soft, kind face. They both had dark hair. Two of the kids looked even less like the rest, a blonde girl and a gangly boy with a buzz cut, but somehow those two had earned the favored position of each standing under a draping arm of the mother. Maybe that was Sam under her right arm? Who knew? The date at the bottom of the blown-up picture read "1990." That would make Dr. Marcus somewhere around thirty.

Andrea's gaze wandered to another wall and a shiny silver frame with beautiful cursive penmanship on a weathered scroll inside. The title read "Legend of the Starfish" and the short allegory taught that though a person might not be able to save everyone, in this case starfish, they could at least help one at a time. She stood pondering the words, sipping her tea, wondering what this told her about Dr. Samuel Marcus, the single guy who'd adopted a little boy from the Philippines.

Ten minutes had passed. She'd put all of Dani's toys back where they belonged and had almost finished her herbal tea when Sam returned. He wore comfortable jeans that still managed to hug his hips and thighs, and a white with black stripes polo shirt he hadn't bothered to tuck in. It gave her a glimpse of his broader-than-she'd-expected chest and surprising biceps. He walked around in his socks, proving he was totally at home in his castle. His cell phone rang. He checked the caller and said, "Sorry, but I've got to take this. It's my sister." She nodded her approval.

"You're up late," he said, then walked around the room in brief yet very familiar conversation. She tried not to listen, though envying him having a sister to share things with.

His hair was less tidy tonight, and Andrea liked the effect, especially when a clump fell forward onto his forehead when he bent over to pick up an overlooked toy block. And the eyes that had practically drilled a hole into her the last time they'd met seemed smoky blue tonight without a trace of tension around them. She'd often heard the term "boyish good looks," but never understood what that meant until now. How could that uptight man who'd barged into her department be the same guy standing in front of her? A man who'd adopted a little boy on his own and appeared to genuinely enjoy a conversation with his sister. A man like that had to have a good heart.

She took in a tiny breath as he ended the call and approached, her enjoying every step. So this was what an everyday hero looked like. Feeling nothing short of smitten, she let out a beyond-friendly smile.

Sam didn't know why he'd choked up just before he'd

put Dani to bed, but seeing Andrea with his son, and how effortlessly they'd gotten along, made him remember how much Katie had let him down. Evidently having her own kids would have been one thing, but it'd been too much for her to consider adopting someone else's child. "You never know what you'll get," she'd said. "You could be adopting a million problems." He'd argued that the same could be said for any child. Besides, he'd seen with his own eyes what wonders selfless understanding and generosity of love could work on most kids. His foster mother had been the queen of that, not only with her own children but with all the kids she'd brought into their home.

He wasn't about to go down Katie's road of disappointment and pain again, especially right now, not when the dramatic-looking, height-challenged blonde with big overly made-up brown eyes sat waiting for him. He smiled and she gave a flirtatious beam right back. He definitely liked that, even though he knew a smile like that could be dangerous.

"You've made quite an impression. Dani said to tell you good-night."

"Great. He's an awfully sweet kid."

"Yeah, he has a gentle nature." Now wasn't the time to go all soft over the misfortune of his beautiful adopted son, and how sometimes it reminded him of his own situation as a child, so he focused on his tea. "My tea's gone cold. Can I refill yours?" He scooped up his cup and took hers when she offered it to him, then headed for the kitchen. Surprisingly, she followed along in her bare feet. He liked it that she'd made herself at home.

He put their cups on the kitchen counter, and as he turned on the front burner to heat the teapot, he felt her expectant gaze. He glanced over his shoulder and found her still smiling at him, so he smiled back, letting her warmth pass through him. If they kept up this goofy grinning, things could get awkward.

"It's really obvious you're a good and loving father."

"I don't know how true that is, but he deserves no less." He kept busy, opening and closing drawers and cabinets, but talked freely.

Something about her easygoing and encouraging style helped him open up. "You know my greatest fear is that Dani might lose his other eye. They say the odds are low with a single retinoblastoma, but having gone through this with him I guess I'm still afraid it could happen again. And the kid so doesn't deserve any of this." He bit back his frustration.

Andrea kept quiet, cuing him to keep talking, so he did. "No matter what happens, my goal is to make as normal a life as possible for Dani."

"I can tell how much you care about him." She folded her hands on the quartz surface, and he thought the counter was high for her stature. She'd need a little stool to wash dishes at this sink. The thought tickled him and made the corner of his mouth quirk, imagining her standing on a stool in his kitchen, washing plates. So domestic, so different than the artistic impression she gave. Where had that thought come from?

She couldn't be more than five feet, but what a powerhouse. She'd probably never be caught dead washing dishes for a guy. He sensed she'd never let anyone take advantage of her. She sure as hell hadn't let him that day. Thinking back to her stern father, he was sure she'd probably had to grow a steel spine to survive. Yeah, no way she'd be a happy dishwasher.

He poured them both more tea and they sat at the kitchen table, and because she was so easy to be around, and seemed so sympathetic toward Dani, he decided to really open up. "I'm afraid people will look at Dani and pity him, which, by the way, you absolutely didn't do. Thanks for that."

She dipped her head and blinked slowly, then took a sip of her tea, so serious. "I've had a lot of practice with our clientele."

"I'm sure you have." He sipped, but the tea was too hot, so he put the cup on the table. "I also worry that other kids will be curious about his fake eye and make him self-conscious."

"I think all kids are self-conscious about something."

A quick flash of him being around seven or eight and having to wear faded thrift-store shirts that didn't fit to school, because that was all his mother could afford, reminded him firsthand about self-consciousness.

"The thing is, I don't want him to slip into the mindset of feeling inferior. That could set the tone for the rest of his life. I'd hate for that to happen." He'd been fighting those feelings his entire life, and he'd obviously said something to move Andrea, because she leaned forward and her hand cupped his forearm and tightened.

"I'm going to make the most perfect eye ever for him. The other kids won't even notice."

"Then it'll be my job to teach him to be totally independent, not afraid to try things." His crazy, lovable foster family came to mind. "Hell, if he takes after any of his new uncles, he'll give me gray hair before my time."

"I think your plan is perfect. Dani's a lucky boy to have you as his father. By the way, is that your family in that big picture?"

He considered the Murphys his family, especially after he'd been taken away from his mother at ten and she'd officially given him up when he'd been twelve—which had hurt like nothing he'd ever experienced before and could never be matched until Katie had walked away—

and they'd kept him until he'd been eighteen, then sent him off to college.

"Yep. The big clan, circa 1990. I was around ten in that one."

"Ah, you were the middle brother. I thought I recognized you." She laughed lightly, and he was glad she'd taken the time to look at his family picture, but didn't feel like going into the complicated explanation of who they really were. He hardly knew her. He'd let her think what he let the rest of the world think—he'd come from a big, happy family.

"Yeah, try being in the middle of four daredevil brothers. Those guys were tough acts to follow. Probably why I went into medicine." His professional choice had also been part of his determination to prove the positive impact fostering could have. It had been his way of giving something back. But she didn't need to know that, either.

She smiled and he grinned back. He found his smiles coming more often and easier, spending time with her. It felt good.

"I can only imagine." She went quiet.

They sat in silence for a while, him in deep thought about the responsibilities of being a single father, about how his parents had taught by example the importance of routine and stability in every kid's life, and having no clue what Andrea was ruminating about. Soon the tea was gone and she stood.

"Time to go?" How could he blame her? He'd gone quiet after the topic of his family had come up, then had gotten all maudlin about his lack of parental skills. Great company. Who'd want to stick around for more of that?

"Yes. I want to get an early start on my project tomorrow."

He stood now, too. "I'm really glad you're doing it."

"Really?"

"Yeah, you're not nearly as bad as I originally thought."
They laughed together, and it lightened the shifting mood.
He wanted that earlier ease back between them.

"Oh, yes, the impertinent ocularist strikes again," she
teased. "But I could have sworn you started it."

"I was uptight. Give me a break."

He could tell from the benign look on her face that
she *was* indeed giving him a break, that she totally understood, especially now having met Dani, and he truly
appreciated that.

They headed for the family room, where her tackle box
and backpack had been left, Dani's silicone cast safely
tucked inside. "And I had no idea what you'd just been
through." With the backpack over one shoulder she faced
him, an earnest expression softening her serious face.
"Please forgive me for being rude to you that day."

"I've already forgotten. Besides, after the way you and
Dani became fast friends tonight, I kind of have to."

That got another smile and a breath of a laugh out of
her.

He walked her to the door and allowed one quick
thought about how great she looked in those black slacks
and the pale blue sweater hugging her curves. It was so
much better than those faded scrubs and that frumpy white
lab coat.

They said good-night, and he asked when he'd need to
bring Dani in for reshaping of the wax mold she planned
to make.

"I'll be in touch," she said, "as soon as possible, I promise."

"Then I'll take you at your word."

They said their goodbyes. He closed the door and
scratched his chin and let his mind wonder about the possibility of something more working out between him and
the perky ocularist. That was a first since Katie, too, and

a good thing. Wasn't it about time to start dating again? For an instant he realized how single mothers must feel, wondering if a man wanted to get involved with a lady with kids. Was that how it worked the other way around? Would it matter to Andrea, as it had mattered to Katie, that he was an adoptive father?

CHAPTER THREE

SAM STROLLED INTO the hospital employee cafeteria to grab a quick lunch before his afternoon clinic. He'd barely finished playing catch-up with his electronic charting and had about twenty minutes to spare. Going through the line, he grabbed the fish of the day, and his guess was as good as any as to what type of white fish it was. He went for the least overcooked vegetables, green beans, grabbed a whole wheat roll and a tossed green salad and was good to go.

After paying, he juggled his cafeteria tray and searched around the noisy and crowded room—which smelled entirely too much of garlic—for a place to sit. A pleasant surprise awaited him when he spotted the light blond hair of his new favorite ocularist, especially after the slam-dunk impression she'd made on Dani last night, and he made a straight line to where she sat. Fortunately, she was eating alone. And reading a book, so she didn't notice him coming.

"Is this seat taken?"

Andrea glanced up, totally distracted by whatever novel she'd been reading. "Oh, hi." An instant flash of recognition and a welcoming smile made him think he'd made the right decision. "No, join me."

"Thanks." The invitation, which he'd clearly forced, still managed to make him happy. He sat, but not before removing the dishes from his tray and balancing that against the leg of the table. From this angle he could see the book was a biography on the artist Jackson Pollock. "Reading picture books, I see. No wonder you and Dani got along so well." He could always manage superficial conversations easily enough, had learned early on it was a survival technique in the foster care system, which had been pointed out to him by his "mom" when he'd tried the old you-can't-reach-me routine at first. The quiet and withdrawn kids got moved around more than the ones who knew how to socialize. All he wanted to do was prove he was worth keeping. That was the truth.

She rolled her eyes at his awful attempt at humor. "America's cowboy artist. Our very own van Gogh, torment and all." She closed the book and gave all of her attention to him. He liked that. Her naturally beautiful eyes were less distracted by makeup today, which he definitely also liked.

"How's our project going?" He pushed around the green beans rather than taking a bite, then decided to pile them on top of the piece of fish, thinking it might help the bland cafeteria food have a little more flavor that way.

"I'm off to a good start. I'll need to see Dani again, though, to exactly fit the wax mold."

"I can have my sister bring him by this afternoon, if you'd like." Yeah, piling the food together hadn't helped enhance the flavor at all, but watching Andrea, hearing her voice, made the taste far more palatable. Next he dug into his salad.

"I should be able to work that in. Can she bring him around two-thirty?"

"I'll see." He got out his mobile phone and texted Cat, his foster sister, the one he felt closest to. Being a mother of two toddlers herself, plus the fact she lived five miles from him, it'd made sense to ask her to be his child-care provider when his parental leave came to an end and he had to go back to work. Not to mention the fact that her husband, Buddy, a welder, had agreed to her staying at home with their kids. They lived on a tight budget, and she could use the extra income that watching Dani brought. The way he saw it, it was a win-win situation.

Andrea took a dainty bite of her salad, and he smiled at her, then tore into his roll, slathering it with butter, then taking a bite. "So, do you eat here every day?"

"Not usually, but I came in early today to start Dani's mold and forgot to pack a lunch."

"Thanks for that." He got a return on his text. "She'll be here. Now I'll have to explain that you're located in the dungeon next to the ghoulish morgue." He finished his text and looked up to see her studying him. Had he been insensitive about her department and its location? Had he insinuated that hers was an inferior department? Hell, it didn't even have windows, even when right at this moment in time it was the most important department in the whole hospital for him and his son. "I'm sorry if that sounded mean. I have jerk tendencies. I blame it totally on the influence of four brothers."

"You do have a big family, I can't argue with that."

"Crazy big, but it made me who I am. Major flaws and all." He grinned at her and really liked what she returned. "Sorry." If he'd offended her about her department being in no man's land, she'd easily forgiven him, judging by the sweet smile that highlighted those gorgeous lips. He allowed himself a moment or two to check them out. And when was the last time he'd gotten carried away with wild ideas by a woman's mouth?

He took another bite of his food to distract him from thinking of what it would feel like to kiss her. "This has got to be the worst lunch I've had in a long time," he said, to cover his real thoughts. *But thanks for that luscious mouth of yours.*

"The salad's not bad."

He pushed his plate aside and pulled the salad bowl closer, deciding to take her up on her tip and stick with that and the roll. "Right about now I'm dreaming about Thai food."

"I love Thai food." She matched him bite for bite with the salad.

"Yeah? You like pineapple fried rice? Pad Thai?"

"Love it, and satay, peanut sauce, all of it."

"But have you ever had coconut curry with braised chicken and egg noodles?"

"No, and now my mouth is watering, thank you very much." She played with her salad, no longer taking bites.

"Sorry. Didn't mean to ruin your lunch, but sometime I'm going to have to take you to Hollywood Boulevard for my new favorite dish."

She tossed him a questioning glance over the vague remark. And, yes, he was testing the water. Playing it safe was a knack he'd developed, and always preferable to getting rejected.

"Uh, yes, I guess theoretically that was an invitation. You interested?"

"Well, you can't very well dangle coconut curry in front of me like that without inviting me. Theoretically speaking, that is. It wouldn't be polite."

"Agreed. And we both know I'm nothing if not polite." Considering their rocky beginnings, with his being pushy, demanding and rude and her giving him a taste of his own medicine right back, his absurd comment hit the mark and she laughed. He joined her. Good. She had a sense of humor. He'd try to keep her smiling, because she really was gorgeous to watch that way. "Truth is, since adopting Dani I don't get out much anymore. So are you really up for this?"

"Absolutely. But who'll watch Dani?"

Thoughtful of her to wonder. "I'll ask Cat again, since I haven't introduced him to Thai food yet." *And I'd like time alone with you.*

"Okay. Theoretically, that sounds good."

"Yeah, some Dutch beer, coconut curry—heaven."

"I know it's a gazillion calories, but I prefer Thai iced tea."

"Chicks." He tossed his paper napkin across the remaining half of his salad. "Only a lady would pass up good Dutch beer for sweet tea." He wasn't sure why he liked to tease her so much, but the instant she grinned he remembered. They were having something he'd almost forgotten. Fun.

"My prerogative." She feigned being insulted. "And guys. Always competitive. Please, don't tell me you'll force me into a hot curry tasting contest. I'm not one of your brothers."

He leaned forward and gazed into her truly enticing eyes. "How do you know us so well? You have a bunch of brothers, too?"

She shook her head. "Nope. I'm an only child."

"Really? I don't know many of those. What's it like to have a house all to yourself. To know what the sound of a pin dropping is? To never have to cross your legs and dance around in the hallway, waiting for the bathroom?"

After a brief and polite smile on the last comment she went serious, met his gaze and held it. "Lonely?"

That answer made him sad. He knew that kind of loneliness, plus fear, having been left alone at night for a couple of years before he'd been taken away from his mother—he hated the memory and tried to suppress it as much as possible—plus, he wanted to put a positive spin on the conversation to keep things upbeat. "And quiet. I bet it was really quiet at your house, you lucky dog." Though the quiet used to scare him to death as that left-behind kid.

She'd finished her lunch and moved her salad bowl away to prove it. "So you grew up in a noisy house, big deal. Isn't that why they invented earbuds and playlists?"

Being around her kept him from going to that old and awful place in his mind.

"Headphones back then at my house with portable CD players. And anytime I used them one of my brothers would sneak up and pull them off my head. Made me all flinchy, waiting. Couldn't even enjoy the music."

He'd made her laugh lightly again and he really appreciated her putting up with his silliness, because he needed to get far away from bad memories. The fact that he'd fudged about his "family" really being a foster family didn't seem relevant now. "You know, if I didn't have to get back to work, I'd invite you to have lunch there right now."

"But I've already had lunch. Just finished."

She tipped her head, a suspicious gaze, clueing him in that he needed to do something. After all this big buildup about the great Thai food, the almost-but-not-quite invitation, he'd better make his move beyond the theoretical. And as his foster father used to say, there was no time like the present.

"Will you have dinner with me tomorrow night, then? I'm thinking Thai food. Hollywood. Beer or iced tea, but definitely fried bananas for dessert." He'd just asked out the first woman after his breakup with Katie and becoming a father, and it felt damn good. He was ready for this. Except maybe he should hold off on the triumph part until he got her answer.

A why-not expression brightened her rich mocha eyes, but only after a long moment's hesitation. This one wasn't looking for a date or a boyfriend—a good thing in general, but right this moment a little unnerving. "Sure," she said finally. "I'd like that."

Both surprised and happy, he grinned and rapped his knuckles twice on the cafeteria tabletop. "Great. It's a date, then."

"I'm sorry, Mom," Andrea said over the phone after lunch. "I've just made plans for tomorrow night." Why she'd agreed to have dinner with Sam Marcus was beyond her, but he'd lured her with a great-sounding meal, and to be honest the thought of spending a few hours with him hadn't seemed like such a bad idea at the time. Not even fifteen minutes later she doubted her decision.

Chalk another one up to dear old Dad, the first and worst man in her life.

"With a man?" Mom didn't even try to hide her surprise.

Andrea snickered. Yes, it was a rare occurrence for her to accept dates, so she couldn't blame her mother's honest outburst. Jerome Rimmer had done a number on both of them. "Yes, Mother, a man." A doctor, no less. Was she crazy?

"Well, that's wonderful."

"I don't know about wonderful, but there is Thai food involved, so it won't be all bad." No, she wasn't looking for a relationship, that was for sure, especially not with a doctor. Her overbearing, demanding, perfectionist father had pretty much messed her up forever in the male/female department. But a simple evening out, gazing at a way more than decent-looking guy, who also happened to smell really good—she couldn't help noticing during lunch—wouldn't be a total loss of an evening, would it?

"Oh, now, Andrea, maybe he'll be nice."

And maybe Dad was actually the greatest guy on earth,

but somehow Andrea had never noticed it before? "He seems nice. But let's not read more into this than necessary. I'm making an eye for his adopted son, so I think he may just want to pay me back somehow."

"Oh, I see." Mom went quiet.

Her mother rarely invited Andrea to dinner, but now that she was on the new medicine regimen for her debilitating depression, she seemed to have more energy and to be more interested in interacting with people. Andrea hated to put her off. "Can we get together Friday night?"

"Oh, Friday is a bad night for your father. He's got a weekend conference to attend in Sacramento and he's leaving that afternoon."

"We could make it a girls' night out, just the two of us." Andrea had learned as a child how fragile her mother was emotionally, especially after marrying a guy like Andrea's dad, and her insecurity about being loved was still a weakness. The last thing Andrea wanted to do was blow her off without making replacement plans. Besides, she'd much rather have dinner with just her mother than both of her parents.

"That might be fun, but let me fix dinner," her mother said. "We can stay in and eat here."

Aware that her mother was still dealing with her reclusiveness and anxiety issues, Andrea wouldn't push it. "That's fine. I just want to spend time with you. Plus you know I love your cooking." Growing up, watching her mother always trying to impress her father with her cooking skills but always coming up short for her perfectionistic father, had taught Andrea not to even try to learn to cook.

"I'll keep it simple, but it will be great to see you. Seems like forever." Her mother's "simple" was fifty times better than anything Andrea could come up with.

"Barbara! Where's my gray tie? Did you iron those

shirts for me?" Andrea's father's voice boomed in the background, demanding as always.

"Oh! Um, let me do that right now," Barbara said, her voice shifting toward trying-to-please mode from the relaxed state a second before. "I've got to go, honey. See you Friday. I'll tell Dad you said hi."

"I'll bring dessert!" She'd buy it from the local bakery.

And that was that. Dad bellowed, Mom jumped. Too bad antidepressants couldn't change that well-worn routine, too. And for the record, she hadn't said hi to her dad.

Sam picked up Andrea after work on Thursday, having removed his tie from a gray denim shirt and wearing a sporty black lightweight zip-up jacket and dark jeans. She'd dressed nicer than usual for work, had even worn wedge-heeled sandals, knowing tonight was their date, and had rushed to change when the department closed. She'd hoped her straight-legged beige pants and gentle yellow boat-necked sweater would be nice enough for dinner out, and, seeing his casual appearance, she decided she'd made the right decision.

"Hey." His genuine expression gave her the impression he was happy, and maybe a little excited about seeing her.

She was flat-out nervous, since he was the first guy she'd wanted to go out with in months, and worked hard to cover her nervousness and focus on the meal part, not the date. "Hi. I'm starving—how about you?"

"Definitely. Hmm, you smell great."

"Thanks. Sometimes I worry I smell like acrylics and wax after working here all day. I didn't overdo it, did I?" She'd used a sample she'd gotten at a cosmetic counter the last time she'd bought eyeliner. It had an almost stringent citrusy scent in the container, but softened on her skin. Or at least she hoped so.

He stepped closer and sniffed the air, but she got the

distinct impression he'd wanted to test her neck, which kind of excited her. "Smells great to me."

Their eyes connected and something fizzed through her body. "Thanks." She pretended to hunt for her purse while she regained her composure. What was it about Dr. Sam Marcus that shook her up so much, especially since she'd seen him in another light at his house? This guy wasn't all boom and bluster, like her father. He was obviously a caring father who'd taken in a special-needs kid. One of the good guys, and good guys were even scarier than the bastards.

When they arrived at the Thai restaurant, it was only six, but the place was already crowded. Wall-to-wall tables lined up with little care for intimacy, just straight row after row from one end to the other of the modern Asian eatery. Though there were more secluded tables outside, enclosed by an intricate white wrought-iron fence to separate them from the boulevard, Sam thought the street noise would be too distracting and said so. So they took a table inside by a window with tall bamboo on the other side.

"It's not much for ambiance, but I endorse the food one hundred percent."

"I can't wait."

They grinned at each other all through dinner. Sam obviously enjoyed his Dutch beer, and Andrea savored her sweet Thai iced tea. She liked the end-of-day stubble on his cheeks and chin, and how his hair wasn't neatly combed. She thought the creases around his mouth made him look distinguished, but the one-sided dimple kept him cute, all-American-boy cute. She'd never call him classically handsome because he had so much more appeal as a good-looking, everyday kind of guy. The part of his face she hesitated to study was his eyes. Those baby blues seemed to reach right inside her whenever they talked, and she got occasional prickles down the back of her neck. It was a feeling she'd nearly forgotten, that "thing" that only certain men set off. Between eating all the great food, their conversation still managed to be nonstop.

Who'd have thought a stuffy, overbearing doctor could be so easy to talk to?

"No, no. I can't," she said, when he offered her one last bite of the fried bananas. "I'll burst." She was definitely thankful she'd worn her semi-loose envelope-hem sweater.

So he popped the last bite into his mouth and chomped down, shaking his head over how good it tasted. He sat back in his chair. "Do I look like a satisfied man? I'm just asking."

His frequent, silly outbursts always made her grin. "You definitely look like a man who's enjoyed his food so much he has a bright yellow curry stain above his pocket."

He pulled in his chin and glanced down, then frowned. "I swear, I think Dani's eating habits are wearing off on me." He dipped his cloth napkin into the remaining glass of water and attempted to do a quick cleanup, which only drew more attention to the stain, which struck her as downright sweet.

"Dr. Sammy! Dr. Sammy!" A high-pitched child's voice cut into the moment. Sam lifted his brows and followed the sound.

So his patients call him Dr. Sammy, how adorable. Could this man be any more appealing?

"Hi!" He waved at a little redheaded boy who looked no more than eight, as he walked by with his parents on their way to being seated. The mother stopped.

"That new medicine you prescribed has done wonders."

Like a true gentleman, "Dr. Sammy" stood and spoke quietly to the boy's mom, though briefly. Andrea looked on with a strange feeling growing inside. Admiration. This was a good guy who took his job seriously, and who didn't just talk the talk but walked the walk. He cared about people. He was single and he'd adopted a son. With his profession, he could have indulged himself with everything from travel to grown-up toys like cars and boats to women, but he'd chosen to go on medical mission trips, settle down and raise a son…who'd lost his eye and needed special care. She'd never met a man like Dr. Sammy before.

The negative side of her allowed one little thought to slip past. What was the catch? Was he too good to be true? Maybe she'd seen the real Dr. Marcus the first day she'd met him, and for her taste that'd been way too much like dear old Dad. Maybe he was on his best behavior tonight and it was all a facade.

Andrea hated how her father still negatively influenced her life and her thinking toward men.

She took one last drink from her tea and stood when Sam offered her his hand. "We ready?"

"I'm going to have to waddle out of here," she said, "but, yes, thanks."

The odd thing was he didn't let go of her hand as they walked back to the car. The warmth of his solid palm flat against hers turned out to be far more distracting than the loud car noises, brakes and horns along Hollywood Boulevard, or the ugly earlier memories of being raised by a man like Dad. Sam's grip felt warm, and if hands could actually do this, it also felt sexy. She pursed her lips, wondering what to make of everything.

Sam walked Andrea to the apartment door. The sturdy Spanish-styled beige triplex dwelling had two units downstairs and a larger single unit upstairs. Andrea's was on the lower right, with rustic red Saltillo tile on the entry porch and an azalea shrub in a huge terra-cotta container right next to the door. He'd been surprised to learn she often took public transportation to work, and he wondered happily if maybe today she'd chosen to do it because they'd had plans for dinner and she wanted a ride home from him. He wouldn't let that fact go to his head, but it sure made his outlook optimistic about what might come next.

"Would you like to come in?"

Of course! "Sure. Thanks."

She unlocked the solid dark wooden door and flipped on lights. The funky yet hip apartment showed a different side of the Andrea he'd come to know at the hospital. The walls were covered in paintings that he knew for a fact he couldn't afford, and he wondered how she could. Rather than sit down in one of the boxy chairs or on the trendy urban home-styled sofa, he walked around the room and admired each one of the amazing conceptual modern paintings that featured mostly bright colors and abstract designs and patterns. "These are something else."

"Thanks."

Then his eyes caught sight of another one, very different from the others, in a corner by itself. It was a long rectangular canvas featuring a single eye peeking through a keyhole in an old door. From his own reading on the topic, he recognized this style as something called photorealism. "I'd buy something like this. It's really special." It spoke to him, seemed to nail how he'd felt as a foster kid at first, watching life through a keyhole, not really a part of it. Sometimes he still felt that way.

"Thank you."

"Who painted all of these?" He squinted to read the tiny signature but couldn't quite make it out.

"Oh, let's see. Um, me." She pointed to one of the bigger paintings, then another. "Me. Oh, and me and me." She ended by pointing to the door and keyhole, his favorite. "Me."

He did a double take and his brows had to have risen a good inch. "Wow. You're really talented." *She's an artist?* Hadn't he sworn off the artistic types after Katie, the actress, had chosen a recurring bit part on a TV sitcom to being his wife and an adoptive mother? "Now I get why you were reading that book on Jackson Pollock yesterday." Andrea possessed significant talent, he couldn't deny that.

"I don't paint anything like him, but I love his renegade approach to art." She threw her jacket over a chair. "He inspires me to take chances."

"So, let me get this straight. You're an artist who works at the hospital, making prosthetic eyes for people."

"Correct."

"But—" he glanced around at the spectacular paintings "—painting is your first love."

She stopped and sighed. "I have to be honest and say yes."

Uh-oh. Been there with Katie. "So if a millionaire bought all of your paintings, you'd walk out the door of St. Francis of the Valley and never look back?"

She stood perfectly still, clearly weighing the truth of her answer. Her eyes drifted over the walls of her apartment, studying her own work for just a moment. "In a perfect world, yes. But I have a grandmother I respect and a father who would hound me to death if I dared. And, honestly, I love my patients and the fact that I can improve their lives."

He didn't like the sound of the first part of her answer one bit. It meant she worked in the O&A department against her will. In fact, he hated the answer so much that a yellow flag waved in the recesses of his mind. Artists were flighty. People you couldn't depend on. Sign him on to the grandmother and dad's side. The thought didn't seem fair to Andrea, though. It felt kind of selfish, if he was honest, but after his experience with Katie his perspective was blurred. Then there was the second part of her answer—she loved helping people and obviously got a lot out of the job in that respect. Life was never black-and-white, and in her case he preferred the gray areas.

There was something about Andrea that called out to him. He genuinely liked her, she was attractive, talented, fun to be around, and she gave a damn about people. She also happened to turn him on. Very much. His instinct said to go for it, kiss her. Damn. Why couldn't he think straight? He'd blame it on the carb high from the Thai food, but the concern about her being an artist was still enough to trip him up.

"Would you like some coffee or wine?"

"The wine sounds great, but can I take a rain check? I need to pick up Dani." His son was a logical excuse, and an honest one. He really did need to go get him.

Sam glanced around the living room. He liked the feel of her home, especially liked her, and would've liked to stick around, yellow flag or not, because she was so damn hot. But he was a father and knew for a fact that Dani slept best in his own bed. Which was a great argument for finding a babysitter besides his foster sister—who couldn't do nights—one who would come to his house. Being a parent, especially a single father, had been a steep learning curve, and this moment had just taught him something else, besides caution about the new lady in his world—the value of a teenage, pay-by-the-hour babysitter. Did they still exist? He'd make a mental note to follow up on the idea ASAP so he wouldn't have to miss out on another invitation like this from Andrea, if she ever gave him one.

He noticed Andrea's disappointment over his rain check on the wine. It was in her nearly Keane-like eyes, which surprised and pleased him at the same time. Was she as interested in him as he was in her?

But she recovered quickly. "Sure. After that huge dinner I should put some time in on the treadmill anyway. A glass of wine would definitely interfere with that."

He'd enjoyed every second of watching her tonight over dinner. She'd eaten like a champ, and she'd parted her hair on the side and swept her bangs, the only long part of her hair, to one side, accenting her round face, big eyes and sharp chin. The short-haired style was definitely growing on him. She'd held up her end of the conversation throughout the evening, too, and he'd never felt the need to fill in lag time. She hadn't said a thing about her talent, either. Humble. Another good trait.

It made sense that a trained artist would be right for the job of re-creating eyes, and he assumed every eye was unique in some way, and an artist would be best to detect the difference. Now he was glad grandmother Judith had assigned her to his son's case. Glancing around her walls at the bright colors and splotches of paint that, though seeming random, still managed to grab an immediate reaction from him, he realized that Andrea was special, someone he wanted to know more. Even though he'd been kicked hard in the relationship solar plexus by Katie. Andrea was different. He had to keep that in mind.

Hell, Cat would be the first to chew him out for comparing the two women. And he didn't know Andrea well enough to pigeonhole her anyway, but she'd admitted art was her first love. She'd be willing to walk away from ocularistry if the artistic opportunity arose. Theoretically. But why should that matter? He wanted to get to know her better, and that part, the glutton-for-punishment part, the part that still insisted women didn't stick around for him, made him nervous. All because she was so damn appealing.

He was a father now, with a son who needed much of his attention and a job that needed the rest. Was there even room for a woman?

The silent pause had grown long and awkward. He'd been overthinking things, like always. That was another thing that being a foster kid had taught him—consider all possibilities, because life could change at a moment's notice. "I guess I better be going."

"Okay," she muttered, resigned. Disappointed? He hoped so because he sure was.

"Nice apartment, by the way," he said, thinking how lame he sounded, and turned to leave.

Andrea strode toward him with those crazy-sexy platform sandals tapping on the Spanish tile and something on her mind, and he stopped dead in his tracks. If he wasn't mistaken, she was giving a clear sign, so when she got close enough he held her upper arms and moved in for a kiss that evidently she had already been planning on. Great, the feeling *was* mutual. But was he sure it was a good idea?

Right now, who cared?

Her hands wrapped around his neck and that sexy fragrance he'd picked up on back at the hospital lingered in the air. He liked it. A lot. Her mouth felt fresh, tasted sweet, like her tea, and full of life. Every worry about her being an artist flew from his head. She kissed like a curious explorer, and he dived in with enthusiasm and soon did some serious investigating of his own. He liked the warmth of the inside rim of her lips, the feel of them on his, the fact that she opened her mouth and invited him in, then put him under her spell. She was a creative kisser, as she was a creative painter, and he soon got swept away.

With her body pressed against his, her heat and softness melding to his chest, a forgotten hunger came out of hiding. He wanted more of her. Confusion about pursuing his lust and whether it would be wise or not, and the more practical need to pick up his son at a reasonable hour, soon crept back into his thoughts and ruined the moment. He couldn't get carried away now. Was she trying to seduce him? Or had he made way too much out of her inviting kisses? She was a naturally passionate person, probably couldn't control it, so it made sense that she'd kiss like this. He was the one who'd blown everything way out of proportion because he was so out of practice, and still smarting, thanks to Katie. He cupped Andrea's soft cheeks and regretfully ended the kiss.

Neither said a word. He stared at her warm brown eyes and she stared back. The unspoken, mutual message being *Wow*. Yeah, there was definitely something there. Something between them. Sparks and fireworks and all. He couldn't very well jump into the sack with her, as he might have done back in medical school, not now that he was thirty-five, and a father, but he definitely knew, good idea or bad, he wanted to, and that was definitely a step forward.

"Will you have dinner with me tomorrow night?" he asked, his voice throaty with desire.

Her eyes went bigger, as if they could, and she smiled. Something told him to sell the deal, just in case there was any hesitation on her part about seeing a new guy two nights in a row. Three if they counted the night she'd measured Dani for his prosthetic eye. Oh, and lunch yesterday... But who was counting?

"I'm a great cook, and I plan to dazzle you with my culinary skills. And after Dani goes to bed, we can do more of this." He kissed her lightly but, practicing restraint, only once.

Her eyes went dreamy. Good, she liked his pitch.

"I'd love to but I've made plans with my mother for tomorrow night. I'm sorry."

What? At least she hadn't blown him off outright, but plans with her mother?

"Would Saturday work?" she said, before he had the chance to think any further.

"It does. As a matter of fact, it does." The blush on her

cheeks may have been fading, but he was glad he'd put it there in the first place, and he was especially happy about her taking him up on his invitation, even if it was a day later.

Yeah, he was in trouble.

"Then I'll see you at seven on Saturday. How's that?"

"I'll be there."

He wasn't sure what he was getting himself into, seeing a woman—a yellow-flag-raising woman—several nights in a row, and maybe taking Friday night off would be a good thing, to cool down, but right at this exact moment he liked the possibilities.

"That was the greatest meal I've ever had," Andrea said on Saturday night, wiping her mouth with a paper napkin and pushing back from the table. "Even counting the Thai food Thursday night."

"You're awfully easy to please," Sam said, smiling. They were sitting at the small round table in the kitchen alcove, and he loved it that she liked his cooking. "Since it's the weekend I probably should have made something fancier."

"Are you kidding? I loved the shepherd's pie. The chicken was a nice switch, the spring vegetables were fresh, and I could tell your crust was homemade."

"You're okay with a guy who makes his own crust?" It was one of the first ways he'd bonded with his foster mom, by helping out in the kitchen. He'd wanted to be that good, likable boy whom they wouldn't send back, and helping in the kitchen had paid off. Not that they'd ever threatened or anything, but he'd been sent to a couple other foster homes before he'd wound up at the Murphys'.

Andrea gave a quick throaty laugh, one he'd already come to like. "I don't cook, so any homemade meal is a treat."

She didn't cook? Being artistic, he'd half expected her to be a gourmet chef, even worried she'd find his basic home cooking boring. Turned out that line of thinking had been a waste of time, since he was the one with the kitchen skills. "Then I'm especially glad you enjoyed it." He pushed another tiny yellow waving flag to the back of his brain. One: artist. Two: doesn't cook. And changed the subject.

"See, Dani? She cleaned her plate."

The little boy had eaten less than half of his dinner when he'd pushed away his bowl. Sam, being a pediatrician and often reassuring stressed-out mothers that their picky eaters were getting all the nutrition they needed, had been suffering from the same worries where Dani was concerned. The boy's all-time favorite meal was white rice. Period. Where was the nutrition in that?

"You sure you don't want another bite of baby carrot and new potato?" Sam remained hopeful Dani might want to show off for his new friend Andrea, but Dani shook his head vigorously, lips sealed tight.

Andrea scooted her chair closer to Dani in his booster seat. She picked up his fork and put a small mouthful of food on it, then made a buzzing sound and moved the fork around like an airplane. She lifted it upward, and Dani followed it with his one good eye, then to the right and the left. Dani might not be sure what was going on but she definitely kept his attention.

"Open wide for the landing," she said, buzzing and moving the fork in concentric circles toward his face.

Amazingly, Dani opened his mouth and let her place the food inside.

"You're good at that," she said, grinning. "Can you do it yourself?" Without waiting for his answer, she speared another small bite of dinner with his fork, but this time handed it over to Dani. "Bzzzzz," she began, and Dani moved his fork up then down, then around and round and right into his mouth. He laughed, mouth full of food and all, and Andrea clapped.

"You really are good at that. Want to do it again?" she said, sitting pertly on the edge of the chair in her layered tank tops of orange and blue, looking as colorful as one of her paintings.

Dani agreed to a third bite, but after that he was through, and she didn't push him. Good for her. She glanced at Sam and he nodded at her secret message. Yup, that was three more bites eaten that neither of them—them being him or Dani—had expected. Evidently, with the satisfied smile perched on that lovely mouth of hers, she'd never had a doubt it wouldn't work.

Sam had no sooner subtracted points from Andrea's scoreboard for not being a cook than he added some back for helping Dani eat, and several more for being so damn sweet about it. Not to mention the bonus points for being so easy on the eyes and the fact she was a damn good kisser. Sam stood to clear the table, and hopefully clear his head. Andrea had him all mixed up.

"Let me do that," she said, hopping up and taking the dishes from his hands. "It's the least I can do to thank you."

He stopped himself from making a wisecrack about not having a stool for her to stand on at the sink, choosing instead to enjoy having a woman like Andrea in his home, bringing such warmth and fun along with her. "Okay, if you insist."

She tossed him a sassy glance. "I do." Then she moseyed off to the kitchen sink, swaying her jeans-clad hips in an exaggerated manner. He and Dani weren't the only ones having a good time. The thought squeezed his heart the slightest bit. Was it a good idea to let Dani fall for her right along with him?

"Well, in that case, come on, Dani, are you ready for your bath?" He helped his son down from the booster seat and Dani ran straight for the hall.

"Yay, bath!"

"Be careful, remember the bookcase," Sam couldn't stop himself from warning Dani about the furniture, since they were still working on his loss of vision on the left.

Dani pretended to run into the wall, then made a big deal about faking falling down.

"You character," Sam said, grinning.

The boy got up again, squealed with delight and, having clearly gotten his dad's approval, ran into the opposite wall on purpose.

"You're a silly, silly guy, you know that?" Sam said, laughing and playing along with Dani all the way toward the bathroom. Realizing that his son most likely did it to impress Andrea, Sam shook his head. *Guys, even little guys, can't resist showing off for pretty ladies.* That moment of understanding, that Dani was a little guy who would one day become a man and who deserved all the fun stuff in life, just like anyone else, circled Sam's chest with warmth.

That clench of the heart from earlier squeezed about ten times harder. No matter how many times Sam had doubted himself about adopting Dani, the boy always proved what a perfect decision it had been. Adoption was just like a marriage vow, in sickness and in health. They were on this road together, and Sam never intended to let him down. The same way Mom Murphy had thought about him and the other foster kids she'd brought into her home. Damn, he missed her.

As he walked down the hall, just before he reached the bathroom he glanced back toward the kitchen. A whistling and singing-under-her-breath picture of beauty, Andrea stood at the sink as she organized the dishes and ran steamy, soapy water. Then he applauded himself for making another spot-on decision—asking her over for dinner tonight.

And God help him if he was setting himself up for another fall.

CHAPTER FOUR

ANDREA WORKED DILIGENTLY, polishing the clear acrylic replica of Dani's eye shape, taken from the mold in her office workshop. The sooner he was fitted, the sooner she'd know if the prosthetic was comfortable and therefore functional for a healthy and active growing child. The month-long adjustment period was probably the most important step in the process.

Then she'd begin delicately painting the subtle characteristics of his individual iris. The series of photographs she'd taken the other night were posted on her computer screen for her to zoom in on and examine. Everything from color patterns, striations and flecks would be replicated in Dani's final prosthesis. Even now red embroidery string had been draped in the configuration of minute red vessels on the white blob that would soon become Dani's sclera.

Sure, there was a new push for digitized replications for prosthetic eyes, but her grandmother was strictly old-school, and that'd made Andrea, even at the age of twenty-eight, an old-school diehard, too. Though she admitted to being interested in the new process popping up around the country. If it meant getting more high-quality eyes to more people in an efficient manner, it might be worth looking into.

When she hooked up the acrylic to a muslin-mopped buffing machine, her mind wandered.

A shiver snaked down her spine as she remembered the time-stopping kiss she'd shared with Sam on Saturday night. They'd been spending a lot of time kissing over the past few days. He was a good kisser. While they'd lingered in their lip-lock she'd explored the strength of his shoulders and chest, resisting the urge to continue on down his frame to his butt. That was definitely territory she hoped to check out in the near future. If she played her cards right...

A countertop pressure cooker dinged. An eye her grandmother had been working on had cured to rubbery toughness, so she took it out. With Andrea's thoughts securely back on the business of prosthetics and Dani, warmth opened and spread like a big floppy flower in her chest as she thought about her growing crush on the boy. He was so trusting and sweet and, well, she'd gone and let him steal her heart. A smile, urged on by tender thoughts, spread across her face until she thought about Sam and jitters replaced that warm fuzzy feeling. Would it be wise to fall for a highly driven doctor, like her father? She knew firsthand the consequences of stepping into that situation. What about Dani? Would he grow up feeling the way she had all her life, second best to his father's profession?

She thought about how caring Sam was with Dani, how attentive and alert to his needs he'd been that night. And after putting Dani to bed, how attentive he'd been to her. Another shiver shot down her spine. No. He was nothing like her father. That guy she'd met the first day here in the office had been an aberration. His son had just had surgery! He'd been stressed to his limit, and she hadn't helped the situation one iota. Of course they'd gotten off on the wrong foot.

Sam was *nothing* like Jerome Rimmer.

Her office desk phone rang.

"Hey," Sam said on the other end.

"Hi!" *I was just thinking about you.*

"I had a minute and wanted to call."

Because he was thinking about her, too? "I'm glad you did. I'm working on Dani's acrylic and need to fit him again."

"I'll ask Cat to bring him in, if that's okay."

"Of course. You've got a busy schedule."

"And it just got busier. Have you read the newspaper today?"

"Haven't had a chance yet." It wasn't a part of her routine because national news always depressed her.

"I'm part of a medical mission group, that's how I met Dani, and we try to set up clinics at least once a year wherever we're needed. I just got an email that our scheduled trip got postponed because of the drug cartel activity in Mexico, and they want to discuss it at a last-minute meeting tonight. I've been so busy with Dani I'd forgotten all about it. Anyway, I'm going to have to go to a meeting tonight." He went quiet.

She caught on to where he was going with the conversation. "And you need me to watch Dani?"

"As a matter of fact…"

After all the swooning thoughts she'd had about the boy, not to mention Sam, she didn't need to think. "I'd be happy to. That means I get to see Dani." *And maybe kiss you again.*

"Thank you so much." She heard pure relief in his voice.

On the verge of saying "Anytime," she stopped herself. She'd already just jumped right in and offered to babysit without giving it a second thought. She didn't want to be taken for granted. "You're welcome."

"Is six-thirty okay? I'll try to have him bathed and ready for bed by then."

Again, she stopped herself from saying "No problem, I can do it" and instead went the efficient route. "That works for me."

"Can you stick around afterward?" His tone had gone quiet. Sexy. "Let's take that rain check on wine and…" Hadn't they already done that on Saturday night? But who was counting? She'd gladly keep rain checking over and over.

"Ah, sweetening the pot, I see. Now I'm all in." How was a living, breathing woman supposed to resist that kind of invitation and not play along?

His low, sexy-as-hell rumble of a laugh nearly had her hanging up the phone and marching upstairs to Pediatrics so she could plant one major, sloppy kiss on him right then and there to seal their deal.

"I'll see you later, then," he said. "I've got to run now."

"Okay, see you later." After hanging up, she quickly returned to her senses.

Sure, she liked Dani and Sam but things needed to proceed naturally and at their own pace. Plus she didn't want to come off like a welcome mat for Sam to take advantage of. She'd known the guy for a week and was already volunteering to be his babysitter. Sheesh. If she was going to get into a relationship with Sam, it should be for all the right reasons, not because of convenience.

She needed to stay focused and realistic.

Truth was, any night spent with Sam or babysitting Dani was a night away from painting. Since they'd bumped her up to five days a week instead of four in the O&A department, that left the weekends plus weeknights for painting, and she had minimal time for art as it was. Plus she worried about Sam always being taken away from his son. A medical mission meant travel. Who'd take care of Dani? Then it hit her.

Was Sam setting her up for that, too? If not her, how often did Sam expect to ship Dani off to his aunt Cat's? Little Dani had had no say in the adoption, but she was quite sure that wasn't what he'd bargained for. Kids needed their parents around as much as possible. That's how they felt loved. Again, she knew that from personal experience.

Hating how her relationship with her father shadowed her thoughts about Sam, but admitting she had some real concerns about him not being around enough for the boy, she refocused and went back to work on the prosthesis. But this time the job wasn't accompanied by dreamy thoughts or a wistful smile.

The next week...

Dani arrived at Andrea's office for the fine-tuning of the clear acrylic the boy had been wearing in preparation for his permanent prosthetic eye. They'd arranged for an end-of-shift appointment, so once Cat delivered the boy, Andrea could take Dani to Sam after his pediatric clinic ended. They'd also agreed to all have dinner out afterward, nothing fancy or exotic this time, just good old American food for Dani's sake.

Andrea replaced Dani's eye patch and patted his arm. "You're getting used to it?"

The boy shrugged his narrow shoulders.

"Does it bother you?"

"Don't know." He looked at his lap. She realized he didn't understand her questions.

"Does it hurt? Do you want to rub it?" She demonstrated rubbing her eye and made a face as if her eye hurt.

He stared at her with his one beautiful brown eye and slowly shook his head.

"That's good, then I did a good job." She smiled and he smiled back. "Want to go see your dad?"

His face brightened as he nodded exuberantly. After saying goodbye to her grandmother, off they went toward the elevator, Andrea feeling protective of Dani when people noticed his eye patch and reacted with sad pouts or sorry faces. She'd come to know the boy quickly in the past couple of weeks, and already she was attached to him, always eager to see him whenever she saw Sam. She also was beginning to understand Sam's deep concerns, not wanting Dani to see himself as inferior or pitied by others.

After they got out of the elevator on the pediatric clinic floor, they used the back entrance to reach Sam's office. Surprisingly, Sam was sitting at his desk.

He looked up and grinned. "My two favorite people!" he said diplomatically. Andrea knew, hands down, if it came to making a choice Dani would win, but it felt good to be included in Sam's world. With each kiss they seemed to be getting closer to crossing the line to making love. She wondered how that would change the dynamic, between not only her and Sam but her and Dani.

Dani rushed to his dad for a hug and the sight released bubble-like warmth in her chest, all floaty and happy feeling. Sam stood. "How'd the fitting go?"

"I only needed to make tiny adjustments and polish the acrylic. Things are going great. I should be finished with his prosthetic by next week, and after another week we'll replace this one for the real thing." She grinned at Dani. "Then you won't have to wear the patch anymore. Yay."

Dani clapped. After smiling at her tiny patient, her gaze drifted toward Sam. He must have really liked what she'd said because he bore a look that mixed practical appreciation with nothing less than smoldering desire. What a combo! It set off a sparkling cascade across her shoulders and breasts, and she knew for a fact her peaked breasts pointed against the thin material of her blouse. It didn't go unnoticed. He stepped toward her, put his hand behind her neck and gently brought her within kissing range. His eyes flickered with pure desire just before their lips met.

It may have been a clinical office kiss but, wow, it thrummed right through her center straight down to her nearly curling toes. There they lingered on the outskirts of heaven until Dani tugged on both of their slacks and put a swift end to the moment, but not before Andrea saw a promise for much, much more…later. And she was definitely ready for that next step. Had been almost since the first night they'd kissed. Sam was a man she wanted to know completely, big scary doctor or not.

"I just finished my last appointment…" There was that post-kiss huskiness in his voice she'd come to love.

"Dr. Sammy!" A nurse appeared at his door. "There's a little girl having an acute asthma attack in the waiting room."

He instantly snapped out of their promising romantic moment. "Bring her to my exam room."

Andrea stepped aside and gathered Dani to her legs as "Dr. Sammy" strode out the door.

Down the hall, another nurse rushed in, with a panic-stricken mother following behind holding a limp child with her head on her mother's shoulder. "The urgent care triage nurse said she didn't hear any wheezing, so I left, but this happened before we got to the car."

Sam knew that wasn't always a good sign. The urgent care nurse may have heard a "quiet chest" but for all the wrong reasons. If the child had been suffering from a prolonged asthma attack, it may have turned into status asthmaticus, where the lungs had shut down, which could lead to imminent respiratory failure and, if not treated, cardiac arrest.

He strode to the exam room and saw a cyanotic toddler being propped up in a sitting position by her mother. The little girl used the accessory muscles of her upper chest, trying to breathe. When he had the mother remove the child's shirt, retraction was obvious between her ribs. The child was in acute respiratory distress. He instructed his nurse to measure the pulse oximetry, then put oxygen on the patient immediately.

"Mom, has she had a virus recently?" He pulled out his stethoscope, preparing to listen to the child's lungs. "Had to use inhalers more often? Been treated with steroids lately?"

"Yes," the stressed mother said, sounding as breathy as her child. "Last week. I knew I had to bring her to you, Dr. Marcus, but your appointments were full."

He shook his head, wishing for more time in the day and more appointment slots for kids like this, but also in disappointment over the UC triage missing the bigger picture than lungs without noticeable wheezing. They were supposed to be the safety net for situations like these, but today they'd let a patient and her mother down.

The pulse oximeter indicated a hypoxic patient with a loud alarm. Sam sighed at the reading. "Get a mask on her at eight liters. Start a line," he said to his nurse Leslie. "I'm going to give her a pop of adrenaline. Mom, how much does she weigh?"

The mother told him and he made quick mental calculations and drew up the drug, hoping to buy time before they set up a nebulizer treatment. He delivered the intramuscular injection, then stuck his head out of the examination room door. "Sharon? We need more hands in here." From the corner of his eye, he saw movement and turned toward Andrea and Dani. Concern covered her face.

"I'm going to take Dani home with me," she said, her brow furrowed.

He gave a grateful nod, trying to offer reassurance, but honestly he hadn't a clue how things would turn out for the little girl. "I'll come later as soon as I can. Thanks."

They left the department just before the tiny asthmatic took another step for the worse.

"Let's nebulize some adrenaline, try to open her up, then start the bronchodilator—oh, and add some ipratropium bromide, too." Why did he have the feeling he was running a precode? He studied the limp child. "Got that line in yet, Leslie?" His major hope was that her veins hadn't collapsed.

The nurse had just finished opening the tubing and the fluid flowed into the vein in the child's antecubital fossa. "Let's titrate terbutaline." He did quick mental math for kilograms of weight, then gave the amount for the piggyback to the IV. "Call the pharmacy, tell them we need methylprednisolone IV for a thirty-five-pound child, stat.

"Sharon, have someone call Respiratory, get someone up here pronto for blood gases." So far none of their efforts had increased the child's O2 sat, and if things continued on this trajectory they might soon be dealing with a code blue. "We'll keep the respiratory therapist around in case we need to intubate."

And so it went…

Andrea drove Dani slowly to her house, worried about not having a car seat for him and making him sit in the backseat of her car with the seat belt buckled tight. What would Sam have done if she hadn't been there? That wasn't all she worried about. Every time she'd seen him over the past three weeks, with each kiss she'd felt herself slip closer and closer to falling for him. Just now, seeing Sam spring into action like a hero for a child in need helped her understand how dedicated he was to his profession. It also helped her put her own situation into perspective.

Seeing his unwavering commitment forced her to take a good long look at herself, and how unsure she still was about her own professional path. She seemed to be standing with one foot in ancillary medicine and the other in the creative arts. And the truth was she loved both! Straddling the line hadn't paid off with her painting, she hadn't completed a picture in months, and it kept her anxious and unsatisfied when she worked her forty hours a week in the O&A department. She should never have agreed to add that extra day.

Add in starting to fall for a guy with a demanding job and an adorable kid who needed attention, and she nearly panicked, feeling completely out of control of her own situation. How had she let this happen? Sam had a way of taking over, just like her father, even when it wasn't obvious. Was that how it had all started with her mother? Little by little, because her mother hadn't figured out where she wanted to be in life, Jerome had taken over until there seemed nothing left of her mother. Until she'd practically disappeared!

Could the same happen to *her*?

"I'm hungry," Dani said from the backseat.

Thank goodness he'd broken her negative train of thought. "Want a hamburger?"

He clapped. "Yes!"

At least some decisions were still easy to make.

Fortunately, Cat had delivered Dani's day bag with him when she'd brought him by that afternoon. Andrea found pajamas and a pair of clean underpants plus some kids' books inside and so much more. Even Ribbit, the stuffed frog she'd given him. She'd been able to bathe him and read a book that apparently was his favorite, *Goodnight California*.

The author used the *Goodnight Moon* setup to say

good-night in travelogue style to all the beautiful places in the state. Dani sat rapt, holding Ribbit, snuggled under her arm on the sofa, listening to every word as if he'd never heard them before, and pointing to his favorite pictures. The redwoods, Yosemite, the beach. Ah, the beach probably reminded him of home in the Philippines. She wondered if Sam had taken Dani to the beach yet.

Dani's day bag even had a toothbrush, so after one last glass of milk, where Andrea opened up Dani's world to the graham cracker experience of dipping them into the milk, she brushed his teeth and put him to bed, along with Ribbit, in her studio, which had a daybed and trundle bed combo left over from her childhood. Nowadays she used it to flounce onto when she needed to think about what she'd just painted and where to go next, or, as was often the case, to nap on when she'd painted so long she couldn't even bring herself to walk down the hall to her own room. When she'd been a girl, before her mother had gotten really depressed and hadn't allowed her to have friends over, her sleepover guests had got the trundle bed section, and she felt Dani, who had special toddler bed rails at home, would be safe there.

She kissed him good-night and started to tiptoe out of the room.

"Do I live here now?" he asked, just before she shut the door, having left a night-light on in the far corner.

Was that how orphans thought? "No, honey. You're just visiting, like when you go to Aunt Cat's house. Your daddy will come and get you later. But he needed to save a little girl at the hospital first."

"Okay."

It struck like a baseball bat how similar her explanation was to what her mother's used to be on countless nights when her father hadn't made it home in time for dinner or to kiss her good-night. The tender feelings she carried for Dani puffed up and made her eyes prickle.

It was scary to care so much for a little person.

Within a couple of hours of putting Dani to bed, a quiet knock on her door drew her from the art magazine she'd been reading in her living room. She opened the small peephole on the door. It was Sam, looking exactly the way a guy should after having a long, stressful day where lives had been at stake and family responsibilities had had to be put on the back burner. There was a combination of fatigue, guilt and gratefulness she read in his powerful blue gaze.

She invited him in with a quick kiss, pointed to the nearest chair with an ottoman for his feet and offered him a drink of his choice.

"Seems like the perfect time for that rain check on the wine," he said. His shirt collar was unbuttoned and the sight of his throat looked sexy as hell. But, then, she found every little thing about Sam Marcus sexy, she may as well admit it. And she loved the way they'd made an ongoing gag about every glass of wine they shared being a rain check.

"Red or white?"

He closed his eyes on a slow inhalation, as if making one more decision was beyond his grasp, so she solved his problem.

"I've got a fabulous triple red wine open. How does that sound?"

Again, that grateful blue gaze, standing out all the more thanks to the after-five stubble on his cheeks and chin, nearly bowled her over. She turned to fetch the wine when a thought occurred to her. "Have you eaten?"

"No." He didn't need to think long about that.

"I told you I don't cook but I *can* make a pretty good omelet. Would that work?"

"Sounds perfect."

She understood he could probably eat cardboard if he had to by now, as it was almost ten.

"Dani in bed?"

"Yes," she said, as she got down two wineglasses and reached for the bottle on the counter. "Fell right to sleep in my old trundle bed. What a sweetheart he is."

"Okay if I take a peek?"

It was his kid, why did he need to ask? "You're not seriously asking me permission, are you?"

She imagined that Sam Marcus smile she'd come to know and adore spreading across his boyish but all-male face as she poured the wine and he padded down the hall. "Which door?" he asked with a loud whisper.

"First one on the left." She put his glass on the kitchen table and got busy gathering the things she'd need to make her one good dish. Sad but true, her cooking skills didn't go beyond sandwiches and eggs. But she was determined to make the best damn omelet of her life for Sam. She took a quick sip of liquid confidence from the wineglass and went to work.

After a couple of minutes Sam stepped into the kitchen, standing right behind her as she whipped the eggs. He put his hands on her hips, bent and kissed the back of her neck. She nearly dropped the whisk, it felt so heavenly. One touch from Sam. One kiss in the perfect spot, and she was covered in tingles. She stopped what she was doing, leaned back, giving him full access to the side of her neck, and enjoyed every second of this gift as he gently nuzzled and kissed her.

"Thank you," he whispered over the shell of her ear.

More sensations fanned across her scalp, down her neck and over her chest. "Anytime." Whoops, had she just given him permission to leave Dani with her anytime? "I should get this omelet going before you starve to death. Oh, and your wine's on the table."

He let go of her hips and stepped away, and she had dueling thoughts. She was either nuts to let him stop or smart not to let him take advantage of her right there in the kitchen. She took another sip of wine. Yeah, she was probably nuts.

"Good wine," he said.

"I thought you'd like it. How's the little girl?" Listen to them, a regular couple discussing the day and the kids. The thought almost made her smile, but the subject of the little girl fighting for her life kept Andrea serious.

A kitchen chair skidded along the tile as he pulled it out and sat, then took another drink and propped his feet on an adjacent chair. "She's alive, but not in great shape."

Something in Andrea's chest withered with the news as she heated the skillet and oil and when it reached the perfect temperature she poured in the eggs, listening to every word Sam said, giving him time to share as much or as little as he cared to.

"She coded shortly after you left. We intubated her, got her to the ICU in time for a second code." He sighed, and she glanced over her shoulder and saw him rub his temples with his thumb and middle finger. "She's on a ventilator right now, and hopefully the drugs will kick in tonight so we can get her off it as soon as possible."

"Oh, the poor baby." Andrea's insides twisted over the thought of a child fighting for her life. "If her mother hadn't brought her to you, she might be dead."

He nodded deeply and took another drink of wine.

"You look beat. Why don't you go make yourself comfortable on the couch, put your feet up, and I'll bring your dinner as soon as it's done."

He didn't argue, just took his wineglass and left the room. "Good idea."

She flipped the omelet, added grated cheese to the lightly browned side, waited a minute or two for the toast to pop and the eggs to set, then folded the omelet in half and put everything on a plate, then walked to the living room to find Sam asleep on her couch, her everyday hero breathing deep, peaceful breaths that did more for her libido than those butterfly kisses on her neck a few moments ago.

His long, sturdy legs stretched the length of her sofa. He'd kicked off his shoes, his sock-covered feet crossed at the ankles, arms folded over his trim middle, head tilted chin to chest. All he needed was a cowboy hat to complete the picture. He was a fine-looking man, and she could hardly believe he kept coming round. A quick fantasy of crawling like a cat over him and kissing the lips she'd come to long for started a deep yearning to be skin to skin with him. What would it be like?

Truth was she hadn't wanted a man this much since college. The complete opposite of the artsy fellow students she'd dated back then, Sam managed to turn her on wearing, as it happened today, a gray business suit. He hadn't bothered to take off the jacket, so she had to settle for looking at his naked throat and the top of his white undershirt as he slept. *Gimme, gimme.*

She glanced at the plate, steam rising from the best omelet she'd ever concocted especially for Sam, sighed, then took a bite to prove it really was as light and fluffy as it looked. She savored the egg and Cheddar cheese taste and the sight of the man she'd fallen head over heels for in record time passed out from exhaustion on her couch, then made a snap decision.

Tonight was the night.

She tiptoed to the kitchen, found a notepad and scrib-

bled Sam an invitation. Then, making sure to leave one
light on so he'd see it, she propped the note against his
wineglass.

If you want to stay over, I'm keeping the bed warm
for you. My room is at the end of the hall.

CHAPTER FIVE

SAM WOKE UP, a crick in his neck from the awkward position in which he'd fallen asleep on the not-so-soft modern couch. It took a moment to realize where he was. Andrea's cozy triplex apartment. He scrubbed his face to help him wake up. Dani was asleep in her guest bed. Right. No way would he disturb his son at this hour.

He took out his phone and scrolled with blurry vision for any messages from the hospital. He'd signed off with the on-call ICU doc and knew they'd only call with extremely bad news, so he gave a sigh of relief over the lack of "missed call" notices, texts or email.

In the dim light, his gaze drifted to the uneaten omelet on the glass coffee table. It touched him, knowing Andrea was a devout non-cook yet she'd offered to make the one thing she could, especially for him. He felt bad he'd fallen asleep before he could enjoy the fruit of her efforts.

From being so bristly at first, she'd turned out to be the sweetest lady he'd met since Mom Murphy. He thought about reheating the omelet in the microwave and eating it, so her work wouldn't go to waste, plus he really was hungry, but first his vision landed on the wineglass with a propped-up note. He didn't need to pick it up to read: *If you want to stay over, I'm keeping the bed warm for you. My room is at the end of the hall.*

She'd sketched a perfectly sexy eye in mid-wink at the end.

Suddenly wide-awake, Sam gulped down the rest of the red wine, the thought of making love with Andrea foremost on his mind. Hell, yeah, he wanted to. Had since the night he'd first kissed her, right here in her living room, and he remembered every second of that goodbye. Somehow, since then, their make-out sessions had never gotten beyond hot kisses and lots of groping and grabbing.

Why? Not because he hadn't wanted to. No. It was because he'd always sensed Andrea wasn't ready for that. Sure, she'd jump right into making out with him, he never doubted she wanted to. But something about their frantic kisses and fully clothed body sex had always ended with him backing off. Because of one message that always cut through the sexy haze. At some point she'd always tense up and there was no way, no matter how desperate he'd been to have her naked and to be inside her, he would force the next step—getting naked.

Maybe she'd sensed he was the kind of guy who kept his distance. Intimacy, trust, hell, how did a man make heads or tails of that when his own mother had ignored him and let him get taken away? Not to mention Katie leaving when he'd finally felt ready to commit to her.

But there was no doubt about the invitation from Andrea tonight. She was keeping the bed warm for him. It said so right there in her near perfect cursive. An ironic half smile lifted the corner of his mouth. She was an artist, of course she'd have beautiful handwriting, and the artistic winking eye was a great touch. He stuffed the note in his shirt pocket as a reminder. She wanted him.

The thought of her asleep yet waiting for him, her skin warm to his touch, relaxed and completely open, drove a spear of desire straight through him. Fatigued, who? It may have been a long and exhausting day, but he'd had a nap now, and he was fueled by pure desire for Andrea. More than ever he was ready to have his way with his artist.

He stood, took off his jacket, began unbuttoning his shirt and padded in his socked feet straight to her bedroom and the one woman he wanted right now. She'd even left the door open a crack. Once inside, he stripped, leaving a pile of clothes beside her bed before he crawled under the covers.

A blanket of heat and strength spooned behind Andrea as she stirred from her light sleep. Arms enveloped her, pulling her close, igniting excitement and, being honest, fear. She took a trembling breath when Sam kissed the side of her neck, his breathing steady, hot over her ear. She wanted him, God knew she did, so why was she so nervous about making love with him?

Because having sex was a big deal to her, it always had been. She'd tried her share of free and easy dates during college and had always limped away feeling somehow used, or like a user. Need had been a strong stimulant for the "right now" back then, but try as she might she'd always wanted much more. Could she ever actually say she'd loved someone? The truth? Not so far.

She turned toward Sam's chest, letting him capture her mouth with deep kisses as their bodies stretched along each other's. He felt great, every inch of him. Of course she'd gone to bed naked. She couldn't very well leave such a bold-faced invitation and not be ready when or if he took her up on it. She'd even left a condom on the bedside table.

Thankfully, he had followed through, because right now she felt the obvious length of him along her thigh, and the heat radiating from his body was lapping away at her every worry. His hands wandered everywhere, touching, testing, exciting her. Oh, how she wanted him.

She understood sex for sex's sake and wanted to be with Sam no matter what his desire was right this instant. There wasn't a single doubt in her mind that she wanted sex with Sam. Yet their coming together, wrapping, entangling, growing closer and closer still, seemed very different in comparison with others.

Sam rolled her, his weight pressing her down. She rocked against his strong thighs as he held her arms above her head with one hand and devoured her breasts with his mouth and tongue. Fireworks seemed to skip across her chest and burrow deep toward her core. She needed him. Soon, completely under his spell, she was lost to any thoughts beyond flesh and sensations, and the burning desire for him and him alone. With every cell in her body ignited from his touch, she bucked against him, opening, nearly begging for him to put an end to her frustration. She needed him inside. Needed to connect in the deepest way possible with him.

She held on to his hips, felt the muscular bulge of his ass as he followed her lead to the bedside table, sheathed himself, then slowly entered her. He'd already worked her into a frenzy and her moisture made their introduction smooth and, if possible, even more stimulating. The fresh sensations zinging throughout her pelvis made her gasp.

"Are you okay?" he quickly responded.

"Oh, God, yes. Don't stop."

He did stop, just long enough to deliver a broad, I'm-in-control smile. A shaft of moonlight caught that wicked twinkle in his eyes as he planted one big hand on her hip and began thrusting and withdrawing, never breaking their staring match. Wanting to close her eyes and crawl inside, to curl up with all the amazing feelings coursing through her body, she forced her gaze to stay locked with his, mainly because he willed it. And it both frightened and excited her to see the near wild look of passion on

his face. He'd given in totally to their one point of connection—him being inside her—and his obvious desire
to satisfy her.

Did it feel as astonishing to him as it did to her? His
long, smooth thrusts seemed to pass over every single
nerve ending. He treated her to minutes and minutes and
more minutes at this heightened, sensitive place. Some-
day she would have to thank him profusely, but not now.
Right now all she could do was experience everything he
gave her. Her arms tensed, hands grasping the bedsheets,
and she screwed her eyes tight as her mind drifted toward bliss. Then he pushed faster. Harder. The sensations
tensing, tangling and balling up, building deeper, wider,
threatening to overwhelm her. She held on to him with all
of her might. Her gasps came quicker. She clamped her
thighs tighter around his hips and lifted her pelvis just so,
adding pressure and, oh, yes, yes, yes, pleasure, pleasure
beyond her wildest hopes.

"Don't stop." Her voice sounded strangely disconnected
from her body. Their body. Because they were a single
unit now.

Sam didn't stop. He built and built and finally came at
her with everything he had.

She sucked in air, held it, and as he drove at record
speed into the center of her universe she caught fire one
spark at a time. A twitch, a rush of tingles breaking out
from the hot gathering knot that grew and demanded release. Soon. Soon deep, breathtaking spasms exploded inside her, overtaking her, shooting down her legs and up to
her breasts, holding her in suspension of time and mind.
Out of control, her back and neck arched as he continued
to push into her, prolonging her rush of blinding feelings.

Everything burst apart, flattening her, as a low, distant
groan grew, building somewhere out there in the world
she'd just left behind. Somehow, Sam moved even harder

and his groan changed to a grunting as he thrust and pumped on and on until he joined her on the other side of their bliss.

Like rag dolls they landed in a clump of body parts on her mattress, sated and stunned by each other. Snuggling into the crook of his strong and inviting arm, feeling as she never had before, safe and completely claimed, she sighed and shut her eyes. No words needed to be said.

With only the occasional croak of a frog on the lawn, she drank in the contentment and silence, and the faint yet steady stroke of Sam's fingers along her arm. Then, knowing for this single moment all was perfect in her world, and as if she was having an out-of-body experience, she gently floated off to sleep.

Morning came entirely too quickly. Andrea cracked open one eye to find Sam blissfully asleep beside her. She began the slow process of stretching and slowly rejoining the living when crying woke her up. Dani!

She'd completely forgotten about the boy.

She shook Sam awake. "Dani's crying. Maybe you should get him."

Without a word, the once big puddle of flesh beside her came right to attention. Though he didn't look in the least bit sure of where he was just yet. He jumped out of the bed, searched for his clothes and hopped into first one leg then the other of his suit slacks, then strode out of the room, from the looks of him not anywhere near awake. "Coming, Dani. Hold on."

Being a single father, he'd probably gotten down the routine of waking up at a moment's notice to a science.

Andrea smiled. She lay there, drinking in the morning and the lovely body aches from last night's gymnastics with Sam, and the delicious lingering sensations between her thighs, thinking how lucky she was to have met him. Then one negative thought grabbed her by the throat.

Having him meant having Dani. How could she have forgotten about Dani so easily? Which made her wonder if she was ready to be a girlfriend to a guy who was still getting used to being a single father. Was that even what he wanted from her? If they got involved, would she be a girlfriend or a mother figure for Dani? What was Sam looking for?

The complications made her head spin, so she got out of bed to help ignore them, and made a quick bathroom stop before reporting for breakfast duty.

Sam helped Dani get dressed, then took the boy to the bathroom. Sitting him on the small tiled vanity counter, he washed his face.

"Why I sleep here, Dad?"

"I had to work late, so Andrea let you sleep over."

"I like *my* bed."

Point taken! "I know, Dani, and tonight you'll sleep there. Are you hungry?"

The boy nodded.

"Then let's see what we can rustle up for breakfast." He held Dani's hand and they walked down the short hall to the kitchen. Already he could smell coffee brewing and toast. The thought of seeing Andrea in the daylight, after ravishing her last night, excited him, yet he wondered how she'd receive him now. He hoped she wouldn't go shy or make things awkward, because from his standpoint things were going great. "Hey, good morning." He went the casual, oh-yeah-I-sleep-over-with-my-son-all-the-time routine.

"Hi!" Her eyes, without a trace of makeup, looked younger, oddly enough, bigger and browner, too. He'd noticed last night in the moonlight she hadn't had makeup on, but he'd been too distracted to comment. Very distracted, and gratefully so. "You two hungry?"

"Yeah!" said Dani.

"I've got plenty of eggs. Why not omelets?"

"I want cereal," Dani said.

"I think I have some of that," she said, opening a cupboard and pulling out a box. Sam could plainly see she was ready to cook more eggs.

"If you don't mind, I'll take you up on those eggs," he said.

"Done." She glanced over her shoulder and when their gazes connected a zing through his center served as a great wake-up call.

He could easily get used to looking at her in the morning. "Sorry I fell asleep too soon to enjoy your cheese omelet last night."

She found a small bowl and poured in a big helping of multigrain cereal for Dani. "I'll consider last night my practice session," she said, the double entendre making Andrea and Sam lock eyes again in a totally adult way. If what they'd shared had been practice, he couldn't wait for the dress rehearsal. "So you want more?"

Oh, yes, he wanted more of her. Hopefully soon. "Loaded question." She gave a quick, breathy laugh. "Yes. Definitely. I'll have—" he placed his hand around her upper arm and squeezed it the tiniest bit "—more."

She gave a coy smile as she looked up at him, and he bent and kissed her good morning. "Thank you," he whispered. "For a thousand things."

Her eyes widened the tiniest bit. "You're welcome, and thank you, too," she said, her gaze shifting downward and her cheeks turning pink before she got back to the business of pouring milk over Dani's cereal and whipping eggs for Sam's fresh omelet.

What did all this mean? He'd found a woman he liked.

A lot. Had finally had sex with her. Which had been great. Beyond great. Of course he wanted to see her again. Often. But he was a busy doctor, a new and adjusting father. Were there hours enough in the day for all the time she deserved, too? Or was he already thinking up reasons to keep a distance between them? The safe route?

His phone rang. He quickly checked to see if it was the ICU. No. It was Bob Brinker, the lead on his missions team. "Do you mind if I get this?"

She puckered that sexy mouth of hers and shook her head, distracted and busy with making the omelet.

He'd missed the call but Bob had left a long message. They'd rescheduled the meeting Sam had missed last week for tonight. Did it work for him?

Hell, did it? He'd missed putting Dani to bed last night. Then Sam read the last sentence. *It's the only night all of us are available.* How could he refuse?

He scrunched up his face and looked at Andrea. "I hate to ask you this, but could you possibly watch Dani for me at my place tonight? They've rescheduled the missions meeting. It's the only night that works for the rest of them."

She glanced cautiously toward Dani, then back at him. "If you don't have a choice but to go, then okay."

Did he have a choice? He really needed to rethink his priorities. He'd committed to this mission long before Dani's adoption had become final. Hell, if it hadn't been for his medical mission trips, he'd never have met Dani in the first place.

But things were different now. He was a father with a son who needed him as much as possible, and he'd just met Andrea, was already crazy about her and wanted to know her more. Juggling his job, fatherhood plus a new romance was complicated. Maybe Katie had been right— he wanted too much.

He looked at Dani. No way had Katie been right about

not adopting. Dani was the best part of his life. Then he glanced at Andrea, putting a perfectly fluffy cheese omelet onto a plate especially for him. A lady who didn't cook had just given him the best she had, not to mention what she'd given him last night, and that meant something.

Who knew where the best of Andrea Rimmer might lead? One thing was sure, if they were going to pursue this "thing" going on between them, she deserved the best of him, too.

He pushed Dial on his phone. "Hey, Bob? Yeah, I got hung up in ICU last night. Never made it home. So, listen, I'm going to have to ask you to fill me in on whatever goes on tonight. I need to be home with my boy tonight."

A subtle smile crossed Andrea's lips as she handed him his breakfast, then their eyes met when she gave him a fork, and he knew he'd made the right decision.

A week later...

It was a big day. Sam had cut short his afternoon appointment schedule by two so he could personally take Dani to get his official prosthetic eye. Andrea had made a big deal about not showing it to him until it was inside the boy's eye socket, and who was he to argue?

They'd spent a couple more nights together over the past week, one planned and one, unfortunately, another last-minute "Can you watch Dani for me so I can attend the early morning staff meeting?" Turned out having someone to be there for Dani in the morning for breakfast and to get him ready for Aunt Cat's was a win-win situation. Andrea had opted to sleep over the night before, rather than get up at the crack of dawn and fight the traffic over to his house.

Any night making love with Andrea was a win-win,

even though he felt tension mounting over the fact he'd yet to be completely honest with her.

He guided Dani toward the elevator. "After this appointment, you won't have to wear that darned patch anymore."

"Yay." Dani clapped his pudgy hands.

Sam's stomach felt a little queasy as he worried about how the prosthetic would fit and, almost more important, look. Would it be obvious that it was a fake eye? What if he didn't like Andrea's version of Dani's iris?

He took a deep breath and got into the elevator, choosing to focus on more positive things, like how incredibly great it was to make love with Andrea, and to spend time with her. But where did they go from here? If he wanted an honest relationship, he'd have to come clean. He'd let her think he was from a big family—which theoretically he was in one sense—when he was actually the kid of a young single mother who hadn't had a clue how to be a mom or how to support both of them with the few skills she'd learned with only a high school education. She'd had to work two jobs, and Sam had had to spend nights alone in a shabby apartment, afraid and vulnerable, until he was ten and the courts had taken him away from his mother. And she'd let him go.

Soon enough they were in the basement, and knowing the routine Dani ran ahead. "Hey, hold on there, buddy, you don't want to wind up in the wrong place." He avoided saying "In the morgue."

"I want to see Andrea!" Dani eagerly kept going, knowing the way from all his prior appointments, so Sam picked up his pace to catch up.

"Okay, but let's go in together." He took his hand just in time to open the O&A department door, wondering why the dark, dingy hallway and office in the corner didn't creep out the kid.

Judith Rimmer met them in the display room, wearing the headgear getup and smiling. "It's your big day, Dani. Let me get Andrea," she said to Sam.

Almost immediately, Andrea emerged from the workshop, wearing a lab coat and a huge smile. "I wanted to give your eye one last polish," she said to Dani, as if preparing to give the boy a special gem. "Want to watch?"

Andrea had explained the entire process to Sam, and the final step was to cover the prosthetic in clear resin, and to polish the living daylights out of the new eye.

Being only three, Sam wasn't sure how much Dani understood about everything that was going on, but the kid couldn't look any more excited or expectant than if it was his birthday. "Yes!" Dani ran to follow Andrea into the back and the workshop. Sam chatted with Judith to pass the time. Soon enough Dani and Andrea reappeared.

Andrea helped Dani sit on a chair with a booster seat near the eye display counter. "Let's take off this patch." She gently removed it, and Dani watched and smiled the whole time. So trusting.

She checked the alignment of his new eye, had him open and close his eyes several times. She even checked for natural secretions and anatomical function before giving it her final seal of approval. Dani sat perfectly still like a little soldier the whole time.

Truth was, Andrea was a natural with his son. Her gentle touch, her care and concern for Dani, the way he trusted her. All systems seemed to say go, yet his lousy experience with Katie held him back from taking things further between them. Hadn't that proved he didn't know how to really love someone? He'd been completely convinced Katie had been the one for him, had been for all the years they'd dated, yet when he'd finally got around to asking her to marry him, her career had suddenly come first. How wrong could a guy be? What did it say for his judgment where women were concerned? Now he had a son who needed to come first. Sam knew firsthand that the less drama in life, the better stability for the kid. Wasn't that what the person who had really become his mother, not just a foster caregiver, had taught him? Since Mom Murphy had died, the person he'd trusted more than anyone, he'd struggled to let anyone get close. Hell, Katie could attest to that. Did Andrea deserve the same treatment?

Plus Andrea had been candid with Sam in one of their post-lovemaking talks. She longed to be the artist she'd set out to be at university, and felt for the past four years her dreams had been on hold while she'd apprenticed in ocularistry. Yet she obviously loved her clients at the hospital and enjoyed the work—Dani being a case in point—which proved she was as confused as he was. But had she been trying to warn him? Was she still holding out for her big break, the same way Katie had been?

He stepped out of his thoughts in time to see Dani turning around with his prosthetic eye in place. Sam had to do a double take to remember which eye was real and which was fake. Holy cow, she'd replicated his real eye perfectly. A mirror image. So much so, it brought a lump to his throat. "That looks fantastic, buddy." His grateful gaze met Andrea's. She looked relieved.

But Dani seemed puzzled, and usually when he did he asked Sam a question. This time, though, he turned to Andrea. "I can't see." He covered his good eye to make sure.

Sam's throat lump doubled. How the hell was he supposed to explain the truth?

Andrea went down on her knees to be at eye level with Dani. She cupped his shoulders and gave the sincerest look he'd ever seen. "Honey, the eyes we make here can't see. You'll always have to rely on this one." She touched him above his right eye. "This one will be good enough for both your eyes. This one—" she touched his brow above the new prosthetic "—is just to look pretty, so you don't have to wear that patch. Is that all right?"

Dani nodded solemnly. "I guess so."

Sam stepped closer, first giving Andrea an appreciative glance and nod, then studying his son's new eye up close. "It's amazing how perfectly matched this is to his own eye." He hugged Dani and looked at Andrea. "I can't thank you enough for making the most incredible prosthetic. Only a true artist could duplicate his iris so perfectly. My God, I'm shocked at how great it is." Maybe he was laying it on too thick, but he meant every word and gratitude got the better of him. "You really are a great artist."

"Now I think you're going overboard."

He touched her arm. "No. I'm not. This is fantastic. No one will know this isn't his real eye without looking really closely. You've just given him an amazing gift."

"It's my job."

"And you were made for it." From the other side of the room, Judith spoke up.

Sam could see a flash of rebellion in Andrea's reaction over the reminder from her grandmother of that continual war between practical day job and the artist itching to take flight. She chose not to say anything just then.

Dani jumped down from his chair and walked to a mirror, studying his image really closely. He made monkey faces and joked around, but Sam knew he liked what he saw. As for Sam, he couldn't be happier. His son wouldn't need to ever feel inferior, wearing a perfect eye like this one.

Andrea stepped up behind Dani, placed her fingertips on his narrow shoulders and spoke to him in the mirror. "You shouldn't fiddle with your new eye or treat it like a toy. If it bothers you or feels uncomfortable, you ask Daddy to bring you to me so we can polish it." She turned to Sam, her expression clouding with something unnamed, and she avoided making eye contact, instead seeming to look at his shoulder. "You'll need to clean it a couple times a day at first so it doesn't get gummy. Until his eye socket gets used to it."

"Will do. Are you all right?"

Her lower lip quivered the tiniest bit. "Yeah." She nodded, tried to brush off the emotions obviously building inside, doing anything rather than look him straight on.

Judith, as though sensing something was up, took Dani by the hand. "Would you like to see where I make eyes?" she said, leading the boy toward the workshop.

"Is that a hat?" Dani commented about her headgear, then took her hand, eager to follow her to the "eye" room.

"It makes things look really big. Want to look through it?"

"Yes!"

Once they were gone, Sam reached for Andrea and kissed her. "What's wrong?" He held her close, biting back his own mixed-up feelings, reliving all the reasons Dani had needed the prosthetic in the first place.

She shook her head against his shoulder. "Remember that first night I came to your house and you told me your biggest fear was the thought of Dani losing his other eye?"

He held her closer, kissed the top of her head. "Yes. It still is."

"I worry about that, too. I've fallen in love with your son and I can't stand the thought of him suffering or losing any more than he already has."

The lump in Sam's throat became too big to swallow so he couldn't speak. But he held on to Andrea with all his strength, hoping that maybe the two of them together could will away any future problems for Dani, even while knowing they were powerless. Life happened. It just did. There was no good-luck charm to ward off bad events or illnesses, or parents letting their kids go into foster care, no way to skip around the messy parts. What would be would be for Dani, and they'd have to deal with whatever played out. Andrea's support meant the world to him, helped him think he could get through whatever lay ahead.

As they stood holding each other it hit Sam how, without even realizing it, they'd become a kind of family where Dani was concerned. Yet he hadn't even gotten up the guts to tell Andrea the truth, and if he couldn't do that, how could he ever love her? Did he love her? Wasn't that how he'd started off with Katie, jumping right in up to his neck, deciding she was the perfect girl for him, only to find out several years later she had been anything but that girl. Even if he did think he might love Andrea, being a reasonable man he still couldn't believe that was possible yet, so was he ready to tell her something he wasn't even sure he was capable of?

Plus he had Dani now. There would be two broken hearts if things didn't work out. Yet Dani had fallen for Andrea right off, and kids were usually pretty good judges of character. Which brought his thoughts full circle back to Andrea, the woman in his arms who'd gone all weepy worrying about his son. Yeah, they'd become a modern-day melded family, whether they were ready for it or not.

Those astounding thoughts had him squeezing her even tighter, mostly for support. How had this happened so quickly, and was it even possible?

CHAPTER SIX

SAM HAD TALKED Andrea into joining him and Dani at the park closest to St. Francis of the Valley Hospital after the appointment. Still being spring, the sun was far from setting at 6:00 p.m. "Let's celebrate Dani's new eye," Sam had said.

Since she'd made it, how could she refuse?

Earlier Andrea had been hit with a world of worries about Dani. Sam had spoken of his fear the first night she'd gone to his house—that his son might lose his other eye. The thought made her feel queasy. It was also a sure sign she'd fallen for the kid. And his dad. How could her life get tipped on its ear in a month?

Maybe she should have put more thought into dating a man with a kid, a man with a huge family photo on his wall and a framed parable about saving starfish one at a time. None of which she could relate to and, honestly, was afraid she'd never be able to. But it was too late now to worry about "getting it" where Sam and his dreams and desires were concerned. She was already crazy about both of them.

Sam sat beside her on the bench in his work suit, a beige one with an Easter-egg-yellow shirt and, in typical Dr. Sammy style, a SpongeBob tie for the kids at the hospital. His legs were extended and crossed at the ankles, arms stretched wide along the back of the bench. Confident and relaxed. Instead of relaxing, like him, she perched on the edge of the bench, ready to run after Dani at a moment's notice in case he needed her on the kiddie slide or mini jungle gym. Sam was all about giving the kid independence. She was about keeping him safe.

A grin stretched across Dani's bright face. He teetered, then stood at the bottom of the slide before he galloped for the swings. Andrea hopped up and met him just in time to set him inside the toddler bucket-styled swing. That grin disappeared and he shook his head, pointing to the standard swings, the big-kid swings, down the line on the thick metal play set frame.

Andrea glanced at Sam, who was already up and heading their way. With a kind smile he lifted his son like a sack of potatoes over his hip, which Dani loved, then walked him down to an empty regular swing seat and put him in the center.

"You've got to hold on really tight," he said, making sure the boy's hands held the swing chain securely on both sides. Dani gave a solemn nod, as if realizing this was a big step in his playground life. A step worthy of his new eye.

She'd made plenty of eyes for patients during her nearly four-year apprenticeship, and she'd witnessed firsthand how life-changing that could be for them, which was incredibly satisfying. But with Dani—she patted one forearm, then the other—never before had the gratification been so intense that it raised the hair on her arms.

A few moments went by with only the sound of Dani's delighted squeals while Sam gently pushed him on the swing. Andrea stood enjoying the view and the light evening breeze, warmth pulsing in her heart. Beyond the huge sandbox area with all the playground apparatus, the grass was fragrant, freshly mown, spring green and dotted with young myrtles and ash trees. In a decade they'd offer shade in this newly opened park. For now, they were simply new and pretty to look at.

The vision inspired her, making her want to capture the essence of this moment with bright colors on a canvas. Thoughts swirled through her brain. Creative sparks made her come alive in a way she hadn't for months. On the verge of telling Sam she had to get right home, he looked up with an earnest expression, a man completely content pushing his kid on a swing, as if something had just occurred to him, too.

He started talking, but she was so lost in her thoughts she didn't hear him until she picked up at the point of new shoes. "What?"

"I said, when my mom used to take all of us for new shoes the week before school started, when we got home we'd all try them on and parade around for Dad. And Dad would say, 'It's a good day. All my kids have new shoes. Let's go have ice cream.'" He looked at her nostalgically over Dani on the swing, capturing her gaze. "Well, it's not just a good day today, it's a great day. Thanks to you, my boy has a beautiful new eye. What do you say we go get ice cream?"

Dani cheered, and there was no way right then Andrea could make an excuse to go home to paint.

That night, right after they'd put Dani to bed, they made love, then cuddled in Sam's huge bed. Sam surprised Andrea and opened up, telling her the entire story of how he'd come to be Dani's father. He shared every detail, including the heartbreak of Katie walking away over his decision, and it brought tears to Andrea's eyes.

Their relationship had grown so quickly, it seemed, and his willingness to share feelings normally left close to the heart was part of the reason. She thought how they'd both tiptoed into this new relationship, and she didn't want to upset the fragile foundation forming between them with one ongoing concern that he might want to be with her only because he needed a mother for his son. So she kept it to herself and they made love again.

Now stretched out side by side, they held hands and stared at the ceiling, letting the flush of fresh lovemaking spend its remaining moments covering them before dissolving into the dark.

Earlier Sam had asked her if she could watch Dani on Thursday night while he filled in for another doctor friend who needed to attend his son's sports banquet. After sidestepping the subject with sex, she couldn't, in the name of honesty, avoid any longer telling him what was on her mind.

Andrea first snuggled against his chest, which was lightly dusted with crinkly brown hair, thinking she'd never get tired of how sturdy he felt or his natural guy scent, and wondering over the difference in their skin tones. Then she broached the tough topic by sitting up and engaging Sam's full attention. Except his attention settled solely on her breasts, so she wrapped the sheet around her chest.

"You know how I love Dani," she said. He nodded. "And frankly you've given me lots of chances to get to know him. The thing is, I've been putting off painting a lot lately and I'm beginning to panic about it."

That got his full attention. He seemed uncomfortable, realizing he was keeping her from her passion. "The last thing I want to do is stand in the way of your painting."

She leaned forward. "I believe you, and I have to admit it's always fun to watch Dani, but…"

He went up on his elbow. "Well, that's something, then, right? Because he loves you so much, and I trust you, I always know he's in good hands with you. And that means a lot to me."

"I'm glad you trust me, but it's clear you're the center of that boy's universe. He loves you so much and wants to be with *you*."

"Thanks. I know, but you two are really great together, too. You've got a very special friendship going on."

"So much so I'm beginning to wonder if this is what motherhood feels like, which scares the daylights out of me." She'd decided to tiptoe into the conversation.

He grabbed her and pulled her close. "Aw, you're just being a scaredy-cat about kids." Sounding like a typical pediatrician. "You're a natural."

A natural? Being raised by a deeply depressed mother and an oblivious father probably made her the furthest thing from that.

"Don't get me wrong," she said, glancing up at his chin, memorizing the fine stubble there. "I adore Dani, but he's your son and you need to be there for him as much as you possibly can."

"I am there for him, every day. I get him up every morning and put him to bed most nights. He knows I'm his dad, and I love being his dad." He squeezed her shoulder. "I even hope to have more children, too. I guess I should be up front with you about that, right?"

Now he tells her? She sat up again. "Yes, you definitely should."

Why did his hope for a big family make her immediately wonder where she'd fit in? He wanted more children? What exactly did he have in mind?

"Sam, you're a great dad, Dani is thriving living with you. But lately I feel like I'm doing as much, if not more, of the caregiving as you." She wouldn't dare mention that it also felt like being second best to his job, just as it'd always felt with her father. But it did!

"My job will always keep me busy, it's the nature of the beast. I *will*, however, get a babysitter before the end of this week. I promise." He looked sincere as all get-out, and she felt obligated to believe him.

"Thank you." It wasn't a perfect solution, but at least Dani could go to sleep in his own bed and she wouldn't be the one always putting him there. They kissed more, but she couldn't get into it. "You seriously want more kids?"

"Yes, but not, like, tomorrow. I come from a big family and I want the same. I've told you that."

Something about his answer didn't ring true, but she couldn't quite put her finger on it. Where did his need and desire to have a big family leave her? If they were together, would she have a say in the matter? This conversation was making her feel like a helpless child all over again. "But doesn't it take two?" Actually, he'd already gotten around that loophole by adopting. Would he do it again? Her head throbbed with questions.

"I'm not rushing things," he said. "I'm just being honest."

This obviously meant he was serious about her, and on so many levels she was crazy about him, too, but she couldn't discount her ambivalence about his desire for a big family. Not with her background.

Maybe he deserved to hear her side of the story. She owed it to him. "I know how it feels, as a kid, to always want my dad home, because he never was. That's probably why I'm so sensitive to that for Dani. But unlike you with Dani, when my dad was home he'd be completely distracted with work. I'd be, like, 'Daddy, look what I drew,' and he'd glance up from his paperwork and say, 'Not now.' Sometimes I'd be quiet like a good little girl and wait for him, but I felt as though he didn't even know I was in the same room."

Sam pulled her closer, wrapping her in his arms. "You deserved better than that." He kissed the top of her head.

"I'm not asking for sympathy, I'm just saying that kind of experience doesn't make for 'natural' skills in parenting, like you've experienced."

He went still for a heartbeat, then sighed. "Trust me, if I can do it, you can do it."

Maybe she should be flattered that he felt open enough to tell her his plans, but she had plans, too. And she needed to think about those plans as well, but he pulled her back toward him. They snuggled down again and kissed a few more times. Her mind drifted to other points of anxiety in her life—ignoring her art, her love-hate relationship with her job, loving the patients but not the administrative part and feeling pushed to run a department. She stopped the kiss in the middle.

"My grandmother's retirement is getting closer and closer and soon, if I don't figure something out, they'll expect me to be the head of the department, which means administrative meetings and more responsibility. Where will that leave my painting? Honestly, I'm feeling trapped."

"Is this your father's or grandmother's idea?"

"Both, but mostly my father's."

"Then tell him you don't want that responsibility. Tell him you want to go back to working part-time so you can still pursue your painting."

It sounded so logical, but Sam didn't know her father as she knew her father. "It's not that easy."

He didn't push her on the topic. Maybe he sensed what she knew firsthand, that there was no saying no to Jerome Rimmer.

He went quiet for a second. "Do I make you feel trapped?"

"No." She lifted her head to make eye contact. "No.

But I can't be your babysitter, Sam, or a stand-in parent for Dani."

"That's the last thing I want."

"If we become a couple, I don't want to feel second in line to your job, because that's how I always felt with my dad. Nor do I ever want Dani to feel that way."

"I understand. That's the last thing in the world I'd want, either. And I really don't want to interfere with your art." He held her close, ran his fingers over her hair. "We'll work something out. I just need some time to think about this."

Right, men were task-oriented problem solvers. But this wasn't an easy-to-solve situation. She didn't have a clue what he'd come up with, but right now she was exhausted and couldn't summon a thought about what she should do, so she let him hold her, satisfied she'd said her piece. She'd let him know her fears, and why she was the way she was, totally ambivalent about his big family plans, and he'd accepted her concerns. But the most important thing of all was that they'd come closer as a couple tonight.

They'd taken their worries and fears and acted on them with caveman sex just now, the one thing they seemed to do best together. At least from Sam's view it was the least complicated part of their relationship. Plus it fit right in with his lifelong habit of trying to prove himself worth keeping. He knew how to make her lose it, and did it as often as he could.

He wasn't using her. He respected her completely, and he loved how she got along with his son. He could see a future for them, but they'd only started dating. Maybe it had been a boneheaded idea to announce how he wanted a big family. He was lucky she hadn't run for the hills.

It was his time-to-be-honest moment, and since Andrea had drifted off to sleep, he couldn't avoid thinking about it. He wanted to be around her as much as possible. They both led complicated lives, and he felt guilty keeping her from her painting. He understood her inner battle about always having to create time for her passion, as if it didn't mean as much as the more practical job of making a decent living while helping others. Maybe he could come up with a way that she could do both?

What if he asked her to move in with them?

If she did, she could paint every evening if she wanted to. He admired her talent, wanted nothing more than for her to feel fulfilled. He and Dani would learn to respect and honor her need to paint and stay out of her way when she did. He had a perfectly available spare bedroom he could turn into a studio for her, too.

Okay, his solution sounded more practical than romantic, and also scared the daylights out of him. Maybe he should think more about this first before he brought it up. But he had to be honest with himself.

I want her here. I see a future with her. I... I think I love her.

He shook his head, suddenly needing to take an extra breath. He did. He loved her. But she was all tangled up with job changes and a demanding father, not a great time for a woman to fall in love. And how could he tell her he loved her when he hadn't been completely honest with her about his family, and how he'd been the foster kid left alone until the Murphys had taken him in? When would he quit feeling unworthy of being loved because his mother had walked away from him? Wasn't he in charge of his life now? So why couldn't he come clean with Andrea and tell her he'd been an only child like her, and in two completely different ways they had both been abandoned.

Because it still hurt too much, and he didn't want her sympathy. He'd proved himself by becoming a successful doctor, yet why did he still feel unworthy of a woman's love?

It hurt too much to let the old pushed-down feelings out, so he focused back on Andrea and her issues. She needed to figure out how to deal with her father. It would be a shame if his overbearing attitude chased Andrea out of the profession. The way she'd painted Dani's iris was uncanny. No digital computer program could duplicate what she'd captured with her artistic eye. What she'd done for Dani was nothing short of a miracle. Just like that eye peeking through the keyhole painting. People were her canvases, and didn't the saying go that the eye was the mirror to the soul? What she did on the job was nothing short of art. Andrea had a gift that needed to be shared with the world, whether on canvas or with glass eyes and silicone ears.

There had to be some way he could help her. Should he confront her father for her? No, that was her business, but it ticked him off that Jerome made Andrea's life so difficult.

Now his head was spinning a mile a minute. He wanted to solve her problem because he truly cared about her. He knew he couldn't resolve her issues, that it was totally up to her to work it out with her father. But wasn't the hospital redoing the lobby? Wouldn't they be looking for new artwork once they remodeled?

Those big splashy paintings on the walls at her house would be the perfect style for a modern hospital. Who did he need to talk to about that?

Then the one painting in particular that stood out from all the others at her house came to mind, the single eye peeking through a door keyhole. In his opinion, it was a masterpiece, and no doubt featured the skill she'd developed in her apprenticeship as an ocularist. The iris. The mirror to the soul. And the world was filled with billions of people with their own individual versions.

She'd never run out of subjects to paint.

Sleep would probably never come tonight. He'd at least diverted his thoughts from old painful ones to Andrea's concerns. He smiled with satisfaction into the dark because he'd found a way for Andrea to share her talent with the world. At the hospital. Genius!

Now all he had to do was convince her to face her father and tell him to back off, to let her do her job the way she wanted, the way things were right now. Being a department head might hold prestige for Dr. Rimmer, but Andrea was a modern woman, why couldn't she have it all on her terms? Not everyone was meant to be a department administrator. She had an artist's soul.

CHAPTER SEVEN

TELEVISION NEWS WAS playing the minute Sam and Andrea hit the hospital lobby the next morning. The huge flat screen on the farthest wall ran pictures of death and destruction in Mexico, with captions. A drug cartel had bombed several places, one being the village where one of the drug traffickers who'd cooperated with the police lived. As usual, the innocents had paid the price.

The explosions and subsequent fires had taken hundreds of lives and caused countless injuries across the countryside, leaving only rubble and near total devastation in one quiet border village between Mexico and the United States. The hospitals were overflowing and emergency personnel stretched beyond their limits. The area needed help, and even the Red Cross didn't seem to be enough.

Andrea stood with her mouth open, reading the horrible story. Sam put his arm around her for comfort and it occurred to him that was the first time he'd made a public display of his affection for her at the hospital. Despite the horrible news, the comforting part felt good.

"Hey, Dr. Marcus," a passing young resident said. "Terrible stuff, right?"

"Unbelievable. So senseless," he replied, still trying to get his head around the incident.

"A few of us are making plans to head down to Mexicali this weekend to help out. Someone needs to triage those patients in Cuernavaca. Is your passport up to date?"

"Of course."

"Why don't you come, too?"

Sam glanced at Andrea, who wore an uncertain expression, and he held off accepting, saying he'd think about it.

The resident seemed gung ho on helping, and recognizing Andrea he continued, "Aren't you from the anaplastology department? You should go, too," he said to her. "The explosion and fire probably left a lot of people with facial injuries. There might be all kinds of ways you could help."

This young, long-haired resident's enthusiasm was almost palpable, and compelling, and it was quickly rubbing off on Sam.

"I, uh…" Andrea seemed stumped by his challenge.

Sam stepped in. "We'll definitely think about it and get back to you, Anthony. When are you planning to leave?"

"Tomorrow, 6:00 a.m. The sooner we get there, the better. The border town is only about four hours away—we've already arranged for four free vans from the local car dealership." He said that part to Andrea, as if it might help her make up her mind. "And we plan to come back late Sunday. We're trying to get the hospital to donate supplies, too. We're still working out the details, but I'll definitely get back to you later."

As it was Friday morning, the new doctor had a lot to work out in a very short time, but judging by his exuberance, and seeing a little bit of himself in the guy, Sam had no doubt all would be arranged in record time.

"Yeah, give me a call," Sam said, putting his hand at the small of the back of the mildly stunned lady beside him to guide her toward the elevator. They didn't say a thing about the medical mission plans as they walked. Once at the elevators, where he needed to go up and she down, he pecked her on the cheek, liking the freedom of letting the world know—well, the hospital, anyway—that he and Andrea were a definite item.

"I'll see you later," he said, enjoying the subtle twinkle in her eyes after the kiss. She must've liked his public display of affection, too. "Oh, by the way, *is* your passport up to date?" he asked, just before stepping into a nearly full elevator.

Her eyes widened and she gave a closed-mouth huff in reply.

If Sam expected her to drop everything, pack up and head south at a moment's notice, he'd better think again. Though she had to admit that for one split second she'd found the offer intriguing. Frustrated about being put on the spot, she got in the next elevator going down.

What about Dani? Sam might not be married, but he wasn't a single guy anymore. He couldn't just drop everything and travel to parts unknown. He had a son to think of. If she did go, and there was a big "if" about that, who'd look after Dani? The mere fact that Dani was always her first concern made her stop and think. She was already in over her head with the Marcus men.

The elevator door closed. She was the only person heading to the basement.

More truth, who was she to judge how Sam and Cat bartered time and money? The lady cared deeply for Dani. Andrea had seen it with her own eyes whenever Cat had brought Dani in for his appointments, and she probably loved having him around her boys, as well. He was such a sweetie.

She got out of the elevator and headed down the dreary green and beige linoleum hallway toward her department.

Andrea had to admit, until she decided whether to go or

stay, whatever Sam worked out in order to take this last-minute medical mission trip was between Cat and Sam.

What she needed to do was search her soul about whether to go or not. The thought made a band tighten around her head.

Andrea opened the door, checking her watch. Her first appointment was in ten minutes and she needed to get the custom prosthesis ready for attachment. She rushed around, gathering everything she'd need when the patient entered the department.

From his records she knew he was a veteran who'd survived two tours in Afghanistan, only to return home and get his ear bitten off by a neighbor's Rottweiler. From personal experience, he was an affable guy who just wanted to look normal again. Surgical reconstruction had been ruled out because the damage was too great, so he'd been coming to Andrea for custom prosthetic restoration. He'd decided against surgical magnet placement and instead had undergone a small but important bone anchor procedure, which allowed her to create a bar-clip attachment for the perfectly duplicated mirror-image ear, if she did say so herself.

Greg smiled widely, his ball cap tilting low over what was left of his right ear, hiding the fact he didn't have one. She greeted him, and after a little small talk about how his surgery had gone, she revealed the silicone ear she'd made to match his skin tone and the existing ear.

"Wow, this looks weird but great," he said. "I'll be two-eared again." He chuckled.

"You won't be lopsided anymore," she said, motioning for him to sit as she adjusted the lights for best visibility. She'd spent several hours replicating his other ear first with sketches, then in a mold, then touching it up to be a nearly perfect mirror-image match to the other side, but in silicone. "That's new." She always got a kick out of his tattoo sleeves, noticing he'd added a new colorful section just above his wrist on one forearm.

"Yeah, I saw the porpoise and thought it'd be cool there."

While they chitchatted she removed the large flat bandage covering the implanted bar and easily clipped the new ear in place, adjusting the tilt to match the other side. "See how easy this is? Now you try." She removed the ear and handed it to him.

Under her tutelage, he attached his new ear, then sat and stared at himself in the mirror for several seconds, turning first this way, then that. "Wow. It looks real."

"Of course it looks real." She couldn't deny the pride she always felt when clients were happy with what she'd made for them. "It should help your hearing by twenty percent, too. Those auricles are there for a reason, you know."

"Look at this!" He put his ball cap back on his short-cropped military-style hair, and it was now perfectly balanced between two ears.

"You look great." Her smile was genuine and heartfelt. "But, to be honest, I kind of like the tilted cap look, too."

"Thanks, Andrea." The sincerity pouring out of his gaze nearly melted her.

"You're welcome, Greg. Come back anytime you think you need an adjustment, okay?"

"You got it."

Next she had an appointment in the hospital to measure a young woman who'd lost most of her nose to cancer. Andrea had been studying the woman's photographs and wondered, since now was a perfect opportunity, if the patient might want a sexy new nose, or if she'd rather stick with a replica of what she'd been born with. It could be a touchy subject, and Andrea was working out in her head how she wanted to broach the topic when a text message came through.

Lunch?

She knew exactly who it was and texted back.

What time?

After she'd finished her bedside appointment, having discovered that the young lady would indeed love a new nose, specifically one like Reese Witherspoon's—which put a smile on Andrea's face—she met up with Sam in the hospital cafeteria, excited about her next project but even more excited about seeing him.

Then she ran into her father. "Andrea, you're just the person I wanted to see."

"Hi, Dad." Why did she always go on alert whenever he spoke to her? "You know Sam Marcus, right?"

Her father glanced distractedly at Sam, only acknowledging him with a quick nod. Sam had put out his hand for a shake, but when Jerome made no attempt to do the same, he withdrew it.

"Your grandmother tells me you still haven't filled out the job application."

"That's right. I've been pretty busy."

"Too busy to apply for the biggest job of your life? If they don't get applicants from inside—and let's be honest, you're the only person suited for the job at this hospital—they'll send the posting out to the public."

"Maybe that would be a good thing."

"You're talking nonsense and you know it," he scolded. The man never cared who was within hearing range when he berated her or when he was on a mission. "I'll expect to hear you've applied for the job before the end of the day."

With that, he walked away, leaving Andrea feeling humiliated and angry with him, like so many other times in her life. Did he still think she was ten? She stood and watched her father leave the cafeteria, then mumbled under her breath, "Jerk."

Sam bit his lip, watching her, probably realizing her old man treated everyone the same, including his only daughter. "You okay?"

She nodded. "Let's eat." Determined not to let on how upset she was, she led the way, taking some pleasure in the fact that Sam looked as if he wanted to deck her father.

They headed toward the line, filling their trays with the day's special soup-and-sandwich combo, tomato bisque and turkey deli. She'd been busy and hadn't realized how hungry she was, but now she'd lost her appetite, so with little thought she picked the sandwich combo. They found a table off in the corner of the cafeteria.

"You want to talk about what just happened?" Sam asked shortly after sitting.

"Absolutely not."

"Okay. Moving right along… I've been thinking about last night."

Even though she was still furious with her father, a naughty thought about their triple header last night crossed Andrea's mind and warmth trickled up her neck, spreading across her cheeks. Grateful for the respite from the tense encounter with her father, she couldn't hide her response.

"Not that, you bad girl," Sam said, lightly pinching her arm, playing along, embers igniting in those steel blue eyes.

She laughed, relieved she was back to her life as normal with the guy she was crazy about, especially those sexy eyes of his. "You don't know what I'm thinking." Yes, he did!

They shared a special smoldering gaze and smile that proved he knew exactly what she was thinking, and which set off a stream of liquid heat traveling through her navel and meandering southward. Wow, no guy had ever had such power over her that she could instantaneously forget yet another lousy meeting with her demanding father. Sam reached across the table and squeezed her hand, letting her know he felt exactly the same way. This, the sexual sparks between them, they both understood without a doubt or a single word.

She was in way over her head, with everything moving too fast, but there didn't seem to be anything she could do to stop it other than break things off. Which was the last thing she wanted to do.

He took in a slow breath and let go of her hand. They'd come to the cafeteria to eat after all. "So, anyway, what I was saying about last night refers to our conversation about your feeling like Dani's babysitter."

She'd just taken a bite of her deli turkey sandwich so she just nodded deeply and lifted her brows. Yeah, she remembered that tense conversation very well. As she recalled, she'd started it.

"I don't want you to feel like I'm using you to watch my kid, or that you are somehow considered second best in my life. Anyway, I've devised a plan to make sure you won't feel that way about this weekend."

She hadn't yet swallowed, but she did so quickly in order to ask her question. "What are you talking about?"

He took a quick spoonful of soup and continued. "I've decided to go to Mexico this weekend and I want you to come with me."

She nearly choked on what was left of her next bite of sandwich. "You're going?"

He nodded, lips tight in a straight line, the quintessential look of determination.

Just like Dad. "Just like that?"

"Cat's agreed to watch Dani so we can go with the hospital team. Medical missions are life-changing. I can't wait to share it with you."

"But, Sam, I haven't made up my mind yet." She still hadn't painted one stroke from that inspirational moment at the swings in the playground. Was he planning on taking over her life and interfering just as her father did? She tensed.

"We could have a romantic weekend away in Mexico." There went his hand again, reaching for hers and grasping her fingers.

"With the drug cartels?"

"I get it. You don't have to go if you don't want to," he said. "But I was hoping you'd go with me. I want to share it with you, have you there so you can see why I feel so committed to these trips."

"But don't you worry about Dani losing more time with you while you follow that passion for medicine and missions?"

"I know that's a touchy subject with you these days but, Andrea, as much as I love Dani, sometimes he'll have to understand that my job comes first. Not always. And certainly not because I put him second. Just that sometimes things come up that I feel called to do. This is one of them."

Why did the guy have to make such sense? "I need more time to think about this."

"You've got all afternoon and night. Those people could use your help just as much as they need mine. I can guarantee it." He shoved what was left of the half sandwich he'd been eating into his mouth and watched her.

She'd been in plenty of these positions with her father her entire life. Her back figuratively against the wall, but the words being used sounding like anything but an ultimatum. *Do this, it'll be good for you.* Part of her wanted to believe he was using one of her father's subversive techniques. But the other part, the part that knew this man was nothing like her father, nor could he ever be, understood he simply wanted to share his passion for medicine with her. This trip was special to him.

But having just come away from another tense encounter with her father, she wasn't in the proper frame of mind to give in so easily.

She sat spine straight, chin up, hands folded on her lap, not about to let him win this round, even while hating that a hospital mission to help the needy was at the center of the argument. What did that say about her? But she had to stand firm for now. "And I'd like to use all of that time to make my decision. On my terms. *If* I decide to go, it will be on *my* terms."

The man must be good at poker, because he didn't give away a single reaction to her holding out for more time. "That's perfectly understandable and reasonable." He spooned more soup into his mouth.

"Damn right it's reasonable," she mumbled. Okay, so she didn't sound quite as reasonable as he did, but maybe because she still felt as if she was talking more to her father than to Sam.

The way he lifted the corner of his mouth in a near smile proved she hadn't offended him. Did he think everything she did was cute?

When he'd finished his soup he wiped his mouth, stood, then bent to kiss her cheek. "If you make up your mind, we're leaving from the south parking lot at 6:00 a.m." He started to go but turned back. "Oh, and don't forget your passport." Then he left.

She shoved the rest of her sandwich into her mouth and chomped, irritated that Sam might be taking her for granted but also very curious about what a medical mission to Mexico would be like.

Sam was on the verge of feeling disappointed in the woman he was pretty sure he loved when he saw her beat-up champagne-colored sedan pull into the hospital parking lot at five forty-five the next morning. He'd purposely left her alone to make up her mind last night, though he'd thought about calling her any number of times. Relieved, he grinned all the way to opening the car door for her.

She tossed him a conciliatory glance as she got out. He hugged her, and she was receptive. "Glad to see you. Where's your bag?"

"In the trunk."

He found her duffel bag and several fishing-tackle boxes, but having had her make a home visit to Dani he understood that was how she carried her O&A supplies. From the backseat of the car he saw her remove a large over-the-shoulder portfolio bag. "Planning on painting?"

"Maybe. Actually, as crazy as it may sound, if time allows, it might be a way to help the kids deal with stress. We'll see."

That was exactly why he loved this lady, she was thoughtful and caring and knew how to use art for therapy. What more could he ask?

He helped her carry everything to the van he'd been assigned, making room for her belongings despite the overflowing medical supplies. With very few words but a heartfelt kiss before they left, they set out on a nearly four-hour drive across the border to Mexicali.

It had been a long and, even though it was early morning, warm drive to Baja California, then on to Mexicali and the village on the outskirts of the city of Cuernavaca. The landscape looked much like the high desert in California and long flat vistas similar to the San Fernando Valley except without all the buildings, and it struck Andrea how similar the two states were. Though poverty was more apparent here. Slowly the roads got smaller and the towns grew poorer until they were on the farthest outskirts of

Cuernavaca in a village decimated by a bomb and fire, thanks to a drug cartel.

The nearest hospital was small and overflowing, and though most of the severely injured patients had been taken there, many wounded and in need of care remained in the nearby area. Plus, as was always the case with these kinds of missions, word traveled fast and people who'd been dealing with medical issues for any number of reasons came pouring out of the countryside, looking for help.

The medical mission had been instructed to set up their makeshift clinic at the local school. They'd discussed it on the drive down and planned to divide classrooms into triage areas, patient education, easy procedures and exams, and more complex issues. A long line of people was already waiting to be seen when they arrived.

The vans were emptied of volunteers and supplies in record time and by noon the clinic was in full swing. Andrea glimpsed the dedication Sam had for helping those in need. He jumped right in and over the next several hours worked tirelessly to see and treat as many people as he could, along with the handful of other doctors, residents and nurses.

It was inspiring, and Andrea admitted she was glad she was there, even if she was nervous and felt a bit out of place. She saw her first patient with half an ear missing, made her mold of the other ear and took several pictures of what was left of the damaged side for fitting the prosthetic, then took all the information on where to mail the final product. Once again word got out and parents seemed to come crawling out of the woodwork with their kids. Some children were in need of prosthetics due to trauma and some due to a condition known as microtia. These injuries and conditions had nothing to do with the bombing, but Andrea was glad to help the community in any way she could. It turned out auricular prostheses were in high demand. Who knew?

By the end of the first day she'd seen no less than a dozen patients who needed everything from eyes to a portion of the nose and several who needed ears. She could do this, and what a joy to help little children look and feel normal again, not to mention the handful of adults who presented with missing facial parts. The only drawback was them having to wait until she went home to her workshop to make all the prosthetics and mail them back. And the prosthetic eyes wouldn't be custom-made or fitted as usual, but anything would be an improvement over an empty eye socket.

The gratitude was overwhelming, and because she didn't speak Spanish she'd smiled and nodded so much all day that by the afternoon her cheeks nearly cramped and her neck was sore.

During the evening she invited the young patients who were able to move around to come and draw pictures with her. She'd set up a little art clinic so they could dabble in just about any medium they wanted. Most stuck with pencil and drawing paper, but a few ventured into watercolors and one lone and talented teenager asked to try his hand at acrylics on canvas. She was thrilled to see them come out of their shells as they reached inside to their creative muses and worked out their fears and concerns through art. She knew firsthand the power of art and loved sharing it.

Sam caught up with her and grinned to see how engaged she'd become with the locals.

"Anyone ever tell you that you look like a canvas?"

She didn't get what he was saying until he took a rag and wiped away paint smudges from her cheeks. She laughed. "I do get messy when I'm in the zone with painting. I guess that's a good sign."

He hugged her, and after they'd shared a kiss she could see the passion for her and all things medical in his gaze, even though he looked exhausted from the long hours he'd put in. He belonged here. People in the world needed doctors like him, and a pang of guilt over her wanting him to stay home with his son made her stand straighter, and feel confused. As he'd said, sometimes Dani would have to understand that his job came first. So would she.

Life was complicated. Always would be.

"Have you got a minute?" he asked.

She looked at the group of kids deeply involved in their various projects. "Will you guys be okay without me?" She asked the one little girl who knew English to interpret for her. She repeated Andrea's question and everyone nodded and agreed they'd be fine without her for a little while. Andrea looked at the oldest boy working diligently on his small canvas. "Will you look after everyone for me?"

The little girl interpreted again, and the boy, named Rigoberto, nodded. *"Sí, sí."*

Sam took her hand and led her to a separate tent with a few cots inside. "Earlier I participated in surgically cleaning up a below-the-knee amputation. I want to check on Fernando."

"My God, you did major surgery here?" She glanced around at what was essentially a camping excursion setup, not a hospital.

"Actually, the bomb took care of that. The kid's leg was blown to smithereens. Good thing we brought a surgeon along. We debrided the flesh and cauterized the veins. Hopefully he didn't have too much nerve damage. For now he's stable and on pain meds and antibiotics." He went straight to a cot where a young black-haired boy slept deeply. He didn't look more than five or six.

Sam placed a gentle hand on his forehead and studied the kid, and Andrea's heart nearly broke over the compassion she saw in the man. He had so much to give, was heroic even, and didn't need to think twice about coming here once the opportunity had arisen. Unlike her. Plus he had to be an amazing doctor to do what he'd done for this young boy today.

What wasn't to like, or love, about Sam Marcus?

An IV flowed into one arm with a large fluid bag and several smaller ones, no doubt antibiotics to fight off infection in his mangled leg. In the other arm, blood was being given through the second IV. A nurse Andrea recognized from the hospital kept close vigil over the boy, who'd obviously been given something for pain.

"How's he doing, Gina?"

"Pretty good. No fever. Vitals are stable."

"Great."

A quarter of his tiny right leg was missing and heavily bandaged. "He's small for his age," Sam said to Andrea. "He's seven, and both of his parents were killed in the explosion. His uncle was the informant and they all lived together. Tomorrow we'll have to transfer him to the main hospital in Mexicali to wait for real surgery with excess bone removal and most likely skin grafts. Then after that he'll probably be put in an orphanage." He glanced up at Andrea, empathy coloring those blue eyes with concern. "Who knows what will happen to him after that."

Sam looked so sad. She understood the boy's future didn't look bright, and the ache in her chest made the backs of her eyes prick momentarily.

Sam noticed, and being the benevolent healer he was he put his arm around her. "The good news is with a below-the-knee amputation a modern prosthetic could let him walk and run almost like normal."

After one last check of the boy, Sam led her outside. "The bad news is he'll probably never get a prosthetic in an orphanage, or it will be some clunky outdated version, and he'll have to spend the rest of his life on crutches, feeling like a cripple."

"But you'll find a way to help with that, right?" If anyone could, Sam would.

He nodded, determination turning his blue eyes darker. She hugged him, thinking she loved how he couldn't walk away from children without helping in some way. He could make a difference for this one, just like the starfish parable. It was the mark of a good, good man. He had a near saint of a mother and a big family to thank for that. They stood for several moments comforting each other and Andrea considering the bad fortune in life.

Then it hit her. She didn't have the special gift Sam did, the compassion and love in his heart. She'd been left emotionally flawed because of her childhood, and it held her back in life. Her wounds weren't obvious, like Dani's or Fernando's, but they were nevertheless there. Her eyes burned and while holding Sam she let some tears flow, let him think it was because of the moving experience of the boy with the missing leg on this medical mission. Not because she felt broken inside.

Later, they slept near each other on the ground in sleeping bags, holding hands, and somehow it seemed as romantic as staying in a tropical B and B. Her world had opened up in ways she'd never dreamed of since meeting Sam. Maybe he could help heal her, too.

He'd been right about the medical mission. It had not only been life-changing, it had opened her eyes. The hard part was that she didn't like what she saw about herself.

Late Sunday afternoon they headed home. Andrea had seen how special Sam was with the sick children and finally understood without a doubt that he'd found his true calling. He was willing to make sacrifices for it, too. Though she'd been deeply moved by interacting with her share of patients, she, on the other hand, was heading home feeling a bit overwhelmed. She had a dozen or so prosthetics she'd promised to make for children and adults in the village, plus her regular work lined up at the hospital. How would she find time to do everything? Not to mention to paint that landscape she'd had on her mind since the evening at the playground.

How did Sam do it?

Why did she have to feel pulled in two directions, one practical and one artistic? Could she be a whole person if she gave up her art in order to help needy patients full-time? Wasn't there a place for art in life? Didn't it bring joy and beauty to people? She'd seen the sparkles in those kids' eyes as they'd drawn and painted, and shouldn't that be valued as much as the practical things? But she also knew she'd miss her patients. She loved helping people as much as painting.

Maybe she wasn't as emotionally deficient as she'd thought.

She forced herself to stop analyzing and worrying and once she weeded away those negative confusing feelings she realized she'd changed by coming on this mission trip. The experience had moved her deeply, she felt happy, and it had fed her creative muse in a way she hadn't experienced since college. It also made her determined to prove her father wrong. She could hold her head high and be both an ocularist and an artist, and she didn't need to run a department to prove her worth.

Now all she had to do was figure out how to make every single day longer. She'd have to get up earlier and put in time in her studio before work. She'd also have to stay late at the hospital to do the pro bono projects she'd agreed to for the people in the village. They deserved no less. She'd have to cut back on time spent with Sam and Dani, which pained her, but if she wanted to do it all, and she really did, there had to be sacrifices. A sick feeling dashed around her stomach and circled her heart. Sam would understand, but would Dani?

"How're you feeling?" Sam asked, taking her hand in his.

"Exhausted. Elated. Overwhelmed." She glanced at him through newly wise eyes and he still looked gorgeous. "Surprisingly, pretty good."

"Are you glad you came?"

"You know I am. Seeing you with the children, especially with Fernando, made me realize what a gift you have. It made me realize how lucky Dani is to have you as his father. But it also made me face myself. Your childhood turned you into the person you are and so did mine. But, unlike you, I don't think I'll ever have what it takes to be a parent."

"What are you talking about? You're great with Dani."

"Because I'm not his parent. I'm not responsible for him. You are."

Sam gave her a skeptical glance. "Something tells me there's more going on than meets the eye here. Are you okay?"

"To be honest, no. I'm not okay. This weekend I realized how messed up I am. You can open your heart and reach out to help people when I want to run scared. Loving others means something totally different to you than it does to me. My mother loves my father and it has nearly destroyed her."

"You talk as though your father is a monster."

"Not obviously so, but you saw how he was with me in the cafeteria. He still talks to me like I'm ten. He has zero respect for me or my mother. He was the kind of dad who'd demand I get straight As in school, then not bother to show up at the awards assembly. I'd be the only kid there without a parent in the room, because my mother was too timid to ever learn how to drive."

Andrea hated sounding so lost and needy, but she and Sam had been raised completely differently. He had the confidence to do whatever he felt he should, completely independent, interestingly enough, not needing anyone. Or anyone's approval. Sam needed to know why she was mistrusting and hesitant.

"My dad would holler and carry on if things weren't perfect at home, then rarely ever be there. I never felt love from him. All I ever felt was lonely and miserable, and I'm afraid I don't know how to feel or show love because of him."

Sam drew her near and snuggled her close. "You're not anything like your father. Don't try to fool yourself."

Bitter thoughts and intense sadness made her eyes prickle. Sam believed in her. He saw something worthwhile in her. He wanted to encourage her to branch out and experience a different kind of life. A different kind of love?

He put his arm around her on the van bench and pulled her near. "This probably isn't the ideal time to say it, but I thought you should know—" he kissed her cheek "—that I love you."

CHAPTER EIGHT

SAM HELD ANDREA close in the hospital parking lot. He cupped her face and kissed her as if they hadn't seen each other in weeks, even though they'd just spent two full days together. She let him kiss her, not caring what anyone thought. The man had already taken her breath away when he'd told her he loved her a few short moments ago, and she wanted to make sure he knew how happy that'd made her.

Especially after she'd just confessed how messed up her family was, and how it had affected her, and the man had still said it. She kissed him hard. Everyone was busy unloading the vans; they'd probably never even notice what she and Sam were up to.

Was she really worth loving? In Sam's world, yes. He had the capacity to love as she'd never experienced.

She wrapped her arms around his neck and leaned into his kiss with everything she had, and had never felt more beautiful in her life. Except for the fact they were both fairly grungy after a weekend of hard work without a shower, and her short hair, except for a few spikes, was nearly matted flat to her head. Yet she still felt beautiful... because Sam had said he loved her.

They'd made it back to St. Francis of the Valley Hospital parking lot by 8:00 p.m. There was much to be done, but his lips and the cascade of thrills they caused were the center of her world at the moment. She'd never been kissed by a man who loved her before. Wow, even her toes inside her practical cross-trainers curled from this most special of all kisses.

"Can we get a hand here, lovebirds?" said Anthony, the shaggy-haired, bearded resident who'd initiated the medical mission, standing over by one of the vans.

Nearly dizzy from the kiss, Andrea parted her lips from Sam's and looked into his eyes. She'd never seen such a dreamy gaze from him before and she savored the moment. Could she really do that to him? Well, it was a big deal when a guy told a woman he loved her. It had to be the honest-to-God truth or it meant nothing. Everything seemed surreal and it took a couple of seconds to check back in with the real world. She crawled out from the lingering love-hazed moment with him, not wanting it to end but knowing she needed to help with the unpacking.

"Welcome home," Sam said, sending a million possibilities through her brain for a meaning to that phrase.

"Thank you for inviting me," she said, heartfelt. The weekend had been inspiring on a dozen levels. Now that she realized how emotionally mixed up she was, she could work on fixing it. She could change if she tried. Sam would help her.

Sam tossed a look over his shoulder. "Theoretically, Anthony's the one who invited you."

"Yeah," Anthony broke in, "and I'm the one who needs your help unpacking now. Please, guys?"

Grinning, they got busy chipping in with the business of emptying and cleaning out the vans. Before long, when everything had been completed, Sam was at her side again.

"I've got to take off to pick up Dani. I promised him he'd sleep in his own bed tonight."

"I understand. Give him a hug for me."

"You're not coming over?" Surprise tented his eyebrows.

"We've just spent nearly forty-eight hours together. I love you, Sam Marcus, but right now I really need a shower and a good night's sleep."

She'd driven her own car over and had—despite the novelty of having a man tell her he loved her and her believing him—decided to go home tonight, leaving Dani and Sam time together. They needed father-son time, having been parted the whole weekend. Besides, she needed to get serious about a new routine, painting early in the morning before going to work. That special picture was fighting to get put on canvas.

He kissed her again, more a peck of understanding than a real kiss. "Okay. I'll see you in the morning, then."

"Lunch?"

"You're on."

She stood for a few moments, watching the man she loved walk away, wondering over the sudden change in her relationship status. She looked down at her feet to make sure they were still touching the ground. Maybe happiness was finally within her reach. The thought started a whole new tumble of chills.

Then she saw the text from her father.

We need to talk. ASAP. Come for dinner tomorrow night.

It wasn't an invitation so much as a summons.

The thought about falling in love and walking on air dissolved. Look what falling in love and marrying the man of her dreams had done for her mother. She'd often tried to make up for their being alone by telling Andrea about the wonderfully amazing man he'd been when they'd dated. Her mother's love for her father had turned out to be a deeply destructive emotion that had escorted her mother into a dark chamber, left her alone, moody and often withdrawn. Love had eaten her alive.

If she wasn't careful, could the same happen to her?

Andrea asked Sam and Dani to accompany her to her parents' house on Monday night as backup, but not before checking with her mother to see if it would be okay. Plus she needed to feel Mom out, see how her new meds were working. Was her depression under control? Was she really up for a dinner party, no matter how casual? They'd had a great time a couple of weeks ago, eating, talking, but that had been just the two of them. Adding Dad into the mix was always a gamble.

Barbara had promised she was in good spirits and would love to meet Sam and Dani, so Andrea had invited them along. It wasn't fair to use Sam as a buffer, but Andrea had something on her mind she wanted to be firm about, and having Sam there would give her more confidence.

Rather than knock on the door at the huge Rimmer family home in the heart of the Los Feliz hills above Los Angeles, she used her old house key and let them all in.

"Hello? We're here! Mom?"

"Come on in," Mom said, appearing at the kitchen door, wiping her hands on her half apron.

Andrea rushed to her mother and gave her a hug, grateful she had a spark of life in her brown eyes today. "Mom, this is Sam and Dani."

Perhaps overreacting a tad, Barbara put her hands on her cheeks and beamed. "It's so wonderful to meet you," she said to Sam, taking his hand and shaking it enthusiastically. Then she bent forward to greet Dani. "Well, hello, young man. Aren't you a handsome boy."

Dani blushed and hid behind Sam's leg. "Sorry, he's a bit shy," Sam stepped in.

"We'll have plenty of time to get to know each other, won't we, young man?"

Still hiding, Dani peeked around Sam's leg to take another look at the new woman.

Barbara's voice actually sounded cheery, but Andrea didn't trust it. She'd had too much experience with her mother's mood swings over the years. She tensed, hoping for the best, but part of her was waiting cautiously.

Her mother twisted her wedding ring round and round her finger, a sign that underneath the cheery exterior she was nervous. "Why don't we go into the other room."

The Rimmer house was a grand old 1920s-style home with every room fairly small and neatly partitioned off, with a tendency toward being dark and dreary because of it. A perfect setting for her depressed mother. Andrea had forgotten how claustrophobic the house could feel at times. They walked through the living room section, with furniture that probably hadn't been sat on for months, and into the wood-paneled den that connected to the dining room.

"Can we help with anything, Mom?"

"You can get everyone drinks and set the table if you'd like."

Andrea and Sam pitched in and got everything ready at the table, letting Dani have a glass of lemonade while they did so.

In the dining room, Sam reached for Andrea's arm and squeezed it. "Everything will be okay." She'd filled Sam in on her mother's condition on the ride over, and he already knew firsthand the blustery personality of her father. "I'm here for you."

"Thanks." She believed him and it reassured her.

The front door opened and a cool draft entered the house, traveling all the way to the den. Her father was home, and the loose knot that had been forming in her stomach over the family dinner tightened.

"Good evening," Jerome said, making his appearance wearing a dark blue work suit and still acting all business.

Dani went back into hiding behind Sam's leg. Barbara appeared from the kitchen, still twisting the ring on her finger but this time even faster, a new anxious expression on her face. Jerome went to her and kissed her cheek. "Barbara, something smells good."

Poof, tension disappeared from her eyes, and the ring-twisting stopped. "It's your favorite, Jerry, Santa Barbara–styled tri tip with onions and bell peppers."

Turning his attention to Andrea, Jerome ignored Barbara's reply. "I have a bone to pick with you, young lady." He said it as if she'd been truant from school.

Andrea squared her shoulders. "If it's about the job application for department administrator, I'm going to be honest. I don't want the job."

"You don't want the job? Do you know how many people would die for that job? The benefits, the stability, the future?"

"I like the job I have."

His jaw clamped down and his eyes went steely. Rather than wither, as she might have as a child, Andrea stood her ground.

"Do you honestly think I got you that apprenticeship so you could settle for working part-time?"

"Frankly, Father, I don't care why you forced me to take the apprenticeship. I've done what you wanted, will get my credential within the year, and after that I can do anything I want with it."

If steam could come out of a person's ears, it would have right then and there from Jerome.

"Why don't we all take a break from this conversation and have dinner," Barbara spoke up, sounding firmer than

Andrea expected, which surprised and pleased her. Since when had Mom become a mediator? Out of respect for her mother, and little Dani, she'd bite back all the words she'd truly love to sling at her father right then.

As everyone prepared to sit at the dining table, Jerome cast a sideways glance at Andrea. "We're not through with this conversation."

Andrea pressed her lips together and passed her father an oh-yes-we-are stare, just long enough to get her point across.

The new medications for depression seemed to be doing wonders for Barbara. She sat at the dining table, head held high, making light conversation with Sam and teasing Dani to coax him to eat. Surprisingly, even Jerome settled in to a more welcoming mood as the family and guests enjoyed the grilled beef, fingerling potatoes and a vegetable medley casserole. Maybe he'd finally understood that his daughter could be as strong-willed as he was.

With Sam at her side, ready to back her up, Andrea had found confidence enough to make her point. It was her life. She'd make all the decisions from here on. Thank you very much, *Daddy*.

Things were going great for the next couple of weeks. Andrea kept to her schedule of painting every morning before work and only spending the weekends with Sam and Dani. They might say they loved each other, but she still longed for independence, and he needed special father-son time. Plus not going over to his house during the week made Sam all the happier to see her when she spent Friday nights through Sunday evenings with him and Dani. Even then, Sam respected her need to paint in the mornings. And after the boy went to bed they definitely made up for those lost nights together.

With this schedule, the picture that had been impatiently waiting inside her head seemed to pour out onto the canvas, as if it had commandeered the brushes and all she had to do was let her arms do the grunt work. She hadn't been this inspired in ages, and whether it was from being in a solid relationship with a good man whom she loved or from going to Mexico and helping out people in need, she figured her life had definitely taken a turn for the better.

Soon that painting would be done, and she'd already finished a couple of the prosthetics she'd promised to the children in Mexico, too. And, as if her positive message was circulating in the universe, a long-ago friend from art school had contacted her about a few of her earlier paintings. A new café wanted to display art on their walls in the Gas Light District of San Diego. It would be a huge help in getting her noticed, and Andrea was so excited she wanted to personally deliver the paintings and spend a weekend catching up with her old friend. Sam understood and completely supported her going.

It seemed amazing what a woman could accomplish when she was in love.

Even more amazing, Sam had found a second babysitter. The teenager of one of his colleagues from the hospital needed extra money for a big school trip in the fall. Ally was more than willing to babysit on weeknights if or whenever Sam needed her, and, most important, Dani liked her. Yes, all seemed right with the world.

On the eve of her trip to San Diego, a full two weeks from the night she'd lost sleep making her decision to take Sam and the young resident up on their offer to go along on the medical mission, she found herself in a very different situation. She was definitely losing sleep, but this time for a far more exciting reason.

Sam held her hips as she straddled him and rocked his world, doing a fantastic job of rocking her world, too. Quite sure there was no way her breasts could get any tighter or more tingly, he surprised her by rising up on an elbow and taking one into his mouth. She stopped briefly to savor the thrumming throughout her body, but soon craving more she lifted and curved over his length, with him solid and bucking up into her. The benefits of being on top and positioning him just so fanned the heat building between her thighs to a near inferno.

With early signs that there'd be no turning back, tension coiled behind her navel, knotting and threading down, spiraling deeper into her core. The small of her back buzzed with sensations. Every cell seemed awake and vibrating thanks to him. Sam's mouth soon found her other breast as she leaned over him, and he held her hips in place when he drove up into her again and again. Nearly helpless against his thrusts, all she could do was hold steady, willing her arms not to give out.

Rhythmical currents rushed along every nerve ending as he came at her over and over, licking at her mounting fuse, pushing and prodding harder, then faster, sustaining the thrill, and suspending time in that sublime state. He kept on until he set off a deep implosion in her. A guttural sound escaped her mouth, she trembled over him, the sweeping sensations annihilating every thought as her body tumbled and rolled through bliss.

Relentless, he carried on, pulling every last shudder and quiver out of her. Then, reading her perfectly, knowing she was basking in the afterglow, he rolled her onto her back. Determined and lost inside her, on his knees he came at her from the top, hitching her legs over his shoulders, grasping her pelvis tightly over him, holding her in place, bearing down on her. Deeper and faster still he came at her; hard and unyielding, he reawakened her center, then drove her passion so she soon needed him again like breath itself. His undivided attention lifted her, making her soar with inward spiraling sensations, then quickly dropping her into freefall in the nick of time to join him in his earth-shaking climax.

They crumpled together in a heap on the sheets, panting, their skin glowing with moisture as if they'd just run a two-hundred-meter dash. They clung to each other, Andrea never more grateful for knowing a man in her life. He laid a wet and wild final kiss on her and they moaned in mutual satisfaction. Damn, he was good.

She curled into him and they cuddled for several ecstatic minutes in the dark, their sweet love scenting the room. His fingers lightly dancing over her arm and backside, he drew her nearer and placed a kiss on her neck.

As she slowly emerged from her sexual stupor, something niggled at the back of her mind. Sam had seemed preoccupied throughout dinner. Was he worried about her going away? More than once she'd wanted to ask if something was bothering him, but in all honesty was afraid to find out it might be her. Or them. Or the new relationship they were forging.

The only example of love she'd had growing up had been her domineering father and her deeply depressed mother. It had definitely affected her ability to trust in love. But Sam had proved he was completely different from her father, and she was no longer afraid to hold back, to let herself trust and love him with everything she had. She was on the verge of feeling she'd found the right man, that she finally belonged somewhere, with him, and didn't want to upset her cart of dreams.

So she kept her concerns to herself about his earlier quiet demeanor. When he'd made it known that he wanted her after putting Dani to bed, she gave herself to him completely. It had quickly become second nature, almost like an addiction. Now, languishing in his embrace, she didn't want to be anywhere else.

He cleared his throat. Her ears perked up.

"I've been doing a lot of thinking," he said, his arm tightening around her as he spoke.

She hadn't been wrong about something being on his mind. She barely breathed for fear of missing what he was about to say. "Yes?"

"I've been thinking about Fernando in Mexico."

The weight of the universe seemed to come crashing down on her. Stunned, she couldn't take a complete breath. As thoroughly relaxed as she'd been a single moment before, she was now a ball of tension. "You're not saying you want to adopt him, too, are you?"

"I'm seriously thinking about it, and I want to know your opinion."

She sat up, because in her confusion she couldn't bring herself to lie beside him right now, and she needed to see his face. "You want my opinion?"

His lower lip rolled tightly inward; he bit it. "I'm saying I can't get Fernando out of my mind. I swear the ghost of my mother is prodding me to get that boy, somehow, someway."

How could she be honest about her feelings and not come off as selfish when at the core was a noble desire? Sam's compassion seemed to be endless. Regardless, she owed it to him to tell him her thoughts. "You're setting this up to make me look and feel like a horrible person if I don't clap my hands and say 'Gee, that's great. Do it. Right now.' But if we're going to be a couple, you owe it to me to consult me on this kind of thing." Wasn't the decision to adopt a kid monumentally important?

He rubbed his hand along her shoulder and arm in an appeasing manner, and it irritated her. "Which is exactly what I'm doing."

She shook her head, refusing to make eye contact, reverting right back to not trusting him, to thinking he was just like her father. Old habits died hard.

"Life doesn't give us courtesy pauses, Andrea. You saw him. That kid needs a shot at a decent life."

Did this go beyond compassion to a savior complex? "Do you plan to save the whole world? Because the supply of kids who deserve chances is endless."

She may have hit hard and careless, but she stood by her comments. Stoic, he stared at the bedspread. Had he honestly thought she'd be overjoyed?

"You're a doctor, you help children stay healthy, isn't that enough?" He probably hated her right now, thinking she was callous and self-centered. Unworthy of his love.

She should have known the kind of person he was the instant she'd seen the Legend of the Starfish framed and hanging on his family room wall. In perfect calligraphy on parchment paper, the moral of the story came through loud and clear, that though one person can't save every single starfish stranded on the beach... *I can make a difference to that one, and that one, and...*

"I just can't get Fernando out of my head."

He was a true believer in the philosophy, thanks to his mother, a good, almost mythical woman she would never be able to measure up to. Who'd quite possibly died young from working herself to the bone with so many kids.

She hated letting her emotions take over, but feeling defeated before they'd ever even gotten started her eyes prickled and watered. No sooner had she fallen in love, finally giving herself permission for the new and amazing feeling, she'd had it ripped away by a guy who couldn't live with himself unless he adopted children in need.

"Aren't there ways to help him without adopting him? You could arrange for one of those high-tech prosthetic legs for him. Donate money to the orphanage where he'll live."

"You're right, but I'm just saying I can't get him out of my mind. It hurts."

There had to be more to the pain he mentioned than Sam's need to rescue kids. "Where does it come from?" His eyes darted away from hers but she couldn't let him drop the subject, especially with her going away in the morning. "This compulsion of yours, where does it come from?"

He looked back at her and his eyes, thanks to the dim moonlight, looked opaque and pleaded with her. "I haven't been completely honest with you."

A foreboding brick-like weight settled on her chest. Oh, God, he hadn't already planned to adopt the kid and lied when he'd said he wanted her opinion, had he?

He reached for her hand and squeezed it. "There's something I haven't told you."

In fear, but needing to know the truth above all else, she held his hand with both of hers and engaged his eyes. "Tell me, Sam. What?" He didn't respond immediately, as if it was the hardest thing in the world to tell her, so her wild imagination took root. He really had already made plans to adopt this boy. The impact on their new relationship would be more than she could take. Hadn't he learned anything with Katie? "Look, I'm not your mother. I'm sorry for not being a saint. I'm just getting used to Dani, and to be honest so are you. It's too soon for me. I'm not even sure if I could be a decent parent to Dani. Don't you see?"

One eyebrow crimped upward. His look of disappointment may as well have been a dagger to her chest. The fairy tale of love with a wonderful guy evaporated into thin air. Hadn't she learned her lesson from her mother about how destructive love could be? Did he love her for herself, or did he just see her as someone he could mold into a version of his bighearted mother? Maybe he was like her father after all, wanting to change her and dictate her life. Would she only be a way for Sam to have that big family he planned to get by any means necessary? Her brain whirled with questions. None of them good. The thought of him giving her an ultimatum made her feel queasy. The words *the end* came to mind.

"That's not it. I promise I haven't gone behind your back and already made plans for Fernando." He squeezed her fingers, and she felt relieved. "I haven't been honest about my family."

Her mind went suddenly still, waiting, worrying, not having a clue what he was about to say. Sam had always come on like a steamroller, wanting that big family just like the one he'd grown up in, on his timeline and terms. Andrea had stood her ground, being honest no matter how unappealing that may have come across to Sam. One adopted son per single father was more than enough. But there was something about his family he needed to come clean about, and she suspected adoption had nothing to do with it.

"I've let you think I'd come from one big happy family, and in a way I did. But it wasn't my family."

She canted her head, holding her breath over what he might say next.

"That picture out there..." He gestured to his living room. "It's my foster family. *I* was the kid who got taken in by them. The Murphys." A blank stare overtook his face, as if a deeply sad memory fought to take control. "I was ten. I was taken away from my mother for being left alone at night. She was young and single and had to work two jobs to keep us from being homeless. It had been going on off and on since I was eight. She'd been warned on a couple of occasions, and finally one of the neighbors called the authorities. The Murphy family took me in and when my mother never tried to get me back, they kept me until I was eighteen. I've pretended to be something I'm not. I'm sorry. Truth is I'm an only child, just like you."

Love, sadness, anger, compassion and a dozen other

emotions swirled around Andrea. How must a young child feel, being left alone night after night? Talk about feeling abandoned. No wonder he wanted to rescue kids. The hair on her arms stood on end over his revelation. She wrapped her arms around him, holding him tight, loving him more than she could bear to feel. "I'm so sorry, and so grateful to that family." She looked at him. He seemed to be in shock at reliving the toughest moments of his life.

"I wanted to be a part of a family more than anything, and they let me. When I was eighteen, my foster mom helped me look for my birth mother. She'd gotten married, started a new family, and when she could have tried to get me back, she hadn't." His face contorted on the last phrase, but only for an instant before he wrestled back control.

Andrea held him tighter, her heart aching for him.

"My own mother didn't want me, but Mom Murphy did. They accepted me as part of the family, and Cat, too. She was one of the other foster kids. Foster kids came and went, but the Murphys kept Cat and me. We bonded like sister and brother, right along with the other Murphy kids. I was lucky. I guess you could say blessed."

"Oh, Sam." She didn't know what to say. All she knew was that he was a special man. He'd received the grace of a strong woman after being left behind by his struggling mother. He'd had a second chance, like those starfish. No wonder that story meant so much to him. His foster mom had made a difference in his life, but Andrea suspected that even that wasn't enough to erase the pain of having his mother let him go and never try to get him back, even when she could have.

Andrea kissed the man she loved, in that moment knowing he could never be anything like her father. He knew what it was like to feel completely alone, to be frightened, to be saved. Because of that, she suspected she had a lot of making up to do for the women in his life who'd walked away from him, starting with his mother and ending with Katie. At some deep level would Sam always mistrust *her*? Would she have to prove herself over and over to him?

They held each other for several long moments, soothing, reassuring, loving, then found themselves back in bed, *showing* exactly how much they cared.

Late Sunday afternoon Sam jumped to answer the phone when he saw Andrea's number on the screen. He'd given her space by not calling her all weekend. Hell, after what he'd laid on her he was afraid to find out what she thought, because he loved her so much. He'd figured that out for sure over the past two days.

"Hi!" she said breathlessly. "I'm just walking into the house. You won't believe what happened in San Diego."

Wanting more than anything to see her, to hold her in his arms, he jumped in. "Why don't you come over for dinner and tell me all about it."

An hour later, she rushed through his door and into his arms, her excitement obvious.

He kissed her and she eagerly kissed him back. "I sold a painting yesterday! And another couple commissioned me to paint a modern art version of their cat!" She laughed. "It's absurd, I know, but I've already got an idea for it."

"That's fantastic," he said, meaning it. He was thrilled for her.

"For the first time since art school I see the possibility of making some decent money, painting and selling my art without selling out, you know?"

"Sounds like it's a good start." He measured his tone, not wanting to sound like the voice of caution, but part of him worried she'd take this bit of success and blow it out of proportion.

"I know! I'm ecstatic." Her eyes glimmered and her

cheeks were flushed, and seeing her so animated and having missed her so deeply after she'd left early on Saturday morning, the only thing he wanted to do was kiss her again.

Of course he wanted to help her in any way possible to achieve success, had probably already overstepped his bounds by talking to hospital administration about her paintings. Coming from her background, with a manipulative and overbearing father, she needed to prove to herself she was in control.

Man, she's going to hit the roof if she finds out I put in a good word for her at St. Francis's.

They kissed more. He let his concerns go and focused back on showing how happy he was to see her. If Dani hadn't wandered out from his room and tugged on both of their jeans, they probably would have wound up having sex on the couch.

Oh, wait, right, since he'd become a father, those days were over…until later after he put Dani to bed, anyway.

Monday morning, after spending the night at Sam's, having incredible I-missed-you-for-one-whole-day-and-a-half sex, Andrea still managed to get up extra early with her alarm. She headed home, took a quick shower and put in an hour painting her favorite project. The enormous canvas as seen through a modern art lens, complete with a kid on a swing and a long-legged faceless dad pushing him, was really shaping up. The fact that the boy held a starfish in his hand was a new, surprising addition and tickled her.

She arrived at work to see a construction crew tearing down part of the hospital lobby. Was it an omen? She remembered getting the memo about the remodeling project scheduled for this month, but had thought nothing about it until right now. Remodeling meant redecorating. Those tired old print excuses for art on the faded walls needed to come down and never be seen again. She had a damn good suggestion for their replacements, too.

As she headed toward the elevator she wondered who she needed to talk to about her own paintings. The display in the trendy café in San Diego had been a huge hit. Maybe the hospital might consider doing something similar here? Showcase local starving artists? Heck, she knew several artists in the area who'd give their eyeteeth to show their work in a busy place like the lobby of St. Francis of the Valley, including her!

She opened the O&A department with her mind spinning over the possibilities, then saw an envelope from Administration that had been slipped under the door. Once she read the contents, she rushed to call the one person she wanted to share every part of her life with—Sam.

"You won't believe this!" She didn't give Sam a chance to say hello, but he had a sneaky suspicion what she was referring to, since he'd started the ball rolling. "The hospital wants to discuss my art. They've gone to my website and seen my work, they're especially interested in my eye and keyhole painting, and they're interested in seeing more samples of my work in person! I've got an appointment with them on Wednesday. The note says, if they get approval, they'd put my pictures in the lobby entrance."

Since Andrea had finally stopped to take a breath, Sam jumped in while he could. "That's fantastic!" A twinge of guilt and a pang of anxiety gnawed at his conscience. Had he screwed up? What if she asked who had given them her name? Should he tell her first?

"I know! Nothing is definite but, wow, maybe with a few more sales and opportunities like this, I can actually support myself painting!"

What? Why should she immediately start talking about walking away from everything she'd worked toward over the past four years of her apprenticeship? That possibility had never occurred to him because of the great relationships she had with her patients. Shaken, he wasn't sure what to say. It seemed his great idea might have backfired on multiple levels.

"I mean, I may be getting ahead of myself but, really, Sam, do you see what I'm talking about?"

"I do. The hospital lobby display would be a huge opportunity."

"Oh, man, I never thought I'd see the day."

Still shaken, he wanted to ask, *Has it been that bad? Is it so terrible to use your gifts to help people replace missing ears and eyes?* Would he come off as a wet rag over her flame if he brought that up now? Or, worse yet, would he seem totally selfish and overbearing, just like her father, expecting her to stay in a job that she, apparently, could walk away from at the drop of a hat?

Perhaps his biggest offense—now that he understood how important it was for Andrea to step out from under her father's overreaching grasp—had been going behind the scenes and manipulating the outcome. Would she be furious with him for making that appointment for her in the first place if she found out?

Ah, so much for his big ideas.

CHAPTER NINE

SAM EXAMINED THE five-year-old Hispanic girl. His first observation made him think of Andrea. The child had been born with microtia, a condition where the pinna or auricle was underdeveloped. In this case, the right outer ear was extremely undersized compared to the normal left one. He hadn't seen this condition for a few years, even though the statistical incidence was one in six to twelve thousand births.

According to the chart, not only was the patient new to him, it was the first visit on record at St. Francis of the Valley. A small notation at the bottom referred to the family being new immigrants and first-time medically insured in the United States.

"The good news," he said, wanting to help the young mother's concerned expression, "is that the ear canal seems perfectly normal. I'll order a hearing test to make sure of that. Okay?"

The mother nodded eagerly.

"More good news," he continued. "There is surgery for this if you are interested."

Again, her eyes grew wide with interest.

"But Letitia needs to grow a little more first." He emphasized the fact by tickling the child, making her giggle. "You need to eat your vegetables, kiddo." The child laughed more. He turned to the mother. "You may want to think long and hard about the surgery. It involves using rib cartilage to make a graft and the surgery goes in stages, so there will be three different procedures over a period of time. We recommend the surgery the summer before Letitia begins school, and we have an excellent pediatric surgeon on staff who specializes in this."

"Three surgeries?" Worry lining her forehead like a pyramid, she shook her head.

"Another option is to have an ear prosthetic made. We have one of the best departments in the country right here. They can match your daughter's other ear with a silicone lookalike."

"She doesn't have to wait? No surgery?"

"There is need for one small procedure to create a way to attach the prosthetic ear, unless you want to use adhesive tape every day."

"One procedure?"

He nodded. "But Letitia would have to take the ear off every night. If she got sunburned, her ear wouldn't. That sort of thing. But I can guarantee that with our expert anaplastologists you'll have to look extra close to tell the difference from her natural ear."

"I have much to think about," Letitia's mother said.

"Yes. And I haven't even begun the actual physical. Let's get started, okay?"

Armed with options, the child's mother appeared more confident as Sam began the otherwise well-child routine physical examination of Letitia.

He understood that sometimes little kids made fun of anyone who didn't look like them. He'd thought long and hard about it regarding Dani. And as Letitia might start kindergarten soon, her mother would be worried about her, though the child's long thick hair did a good job of covering much of the tiny, underdeveloped ear.

He also suspected, from the mother's acne scars, that she may have been on a medication in early pregnancy that was known to cause the condition. The last thing he wanted to do was to make the mother feel responsible for a condition that really couldn't be pinpointed to any one thing she may or may not have done during pregnancy. So he kept his thoughts to himself. His job was to give a physical and maybe help the child look and feel more like the other kids in school, and that he could definitely do.

Andrea had been on his mind nonstop since her trip to San Diego, and especially since she'd hinted about trying to make a go of her artistic career. Did it mean she'd want to give up the one here at the hospital? Wasn't helping people, and especially children like little Letitia here, to feel good about themselves a noble job, too? Of course he'd support her in any decision she made because he loved her and wanted her to be happy, but he knew she had so much to offer St. Francis Hospital.

"Dr. Marcus." Sam's nurse tapped on the examination room door. "Dr. Begozian needs to talk to you."

Sam had just finished the PE. "Can you give Mrs. Juarez the instructions to the lab and Audiology?"

The nurse nodded, so he said goodbye and slipped out of the room to take the call. "Let me know what you decide," he said when he reached the door.

"I will, Doctor."

Sam headed to his office and the phone with the blinking light.

"I need a huge favor, Sam," said Greg Begozian, a young and bright resident whom Sam had taken under his wing.

"What's up?"

"I'm supposed to work the ER tonight, but I just got word my father's had a heart attack, and I need to catch a plane to Sacramento ASAP. But all the other residents are tied up."

"I'm sorry to hear about your father. Is he stable?"

"For now. Looks like he needs a bypass graft. I don't have the full story just yet."

"Hey, don't worry about tonight. I've got you covered."

"Thanks, Sam. You never let me down."

Sam hung up, thinking he'd be letting Dani down tonight, though, by having someone else read him his bedtime story and tucking him in. Ever since Andrea had brought up the touchy topic he'd thought a lot about it. But he was a doctor, and he felt responsible for his residents. At least he had an extra babysitter these days, one who would come to his house so Dani could go to sleep in his own bed. And Andrea didn't necessarily need to even know about tonight, did she?

Unfortunately, as it turned out an hour later, Andrea would need to know about tonight, because Ally wasn't available and Cat had other plans, so he needed to ask her to watch Dani. He hated making the call because he knew how seriously she was taking her painting now. Plus she had the appointment scheduled with hospital admin on Wednesday.

Fifteen minutes later…

"Uh, Andrea, I hate to interfere with any plans you have for tonight, but Ally has a volleyball playoff game and Cat has parent-teacher conferences, and one of my residents has a family emergency, so I'll need to cover for him."

"And?" Ever since seeing Sam in action in Mexico, she understood the demands of Sam's job and the pressure he was under, but before then she'd really given him a hard time about not being around enough for Dani. She understood the hesitation in his voice right now, but the guy had a serious problem with admitting he needed her.

"And I need someone to watch Dani."

"Was that so hard to ask?"

"I know you've got a lot of projects in the works now…"

"I'll bring my sketch pad and work after I put Dani to bed." Determination to make both her relationship with Sam and her personal achievements work was her new goal.

"You'll do it?"

Did he need to sound so surprised? "Yes. Since I'm your last resort, I'll do it."

"It's time to sleep, my love, my love…" Andrea whisper-read to Dani from an especially pretty book, as he settled comfortably into the crook of her arm. She'd personally chosen the children's book because of the beautiful pictures painted by the author. Each page seemed worth framing. But only after reading the truck book with all the bright pictures and hands-on activities. Reading this one, the time-to-sleep book, was her favorite way to calm the boy down.

Dani yawned wide and long after she'd read only a few pages of dreamy places with unusual animals and sleeping children. He rubbed his eyes.

"Are you ready for bed, sweetie?"

He nodded. She'd helped him brush his teeth already, and they'd had a fun game of hide-and-seek before that. To be honest, she loved being with Dani and when she was with him and Sam, her painting rarely entered her mind. That worried her. Wasn't art supposed to be first and foremost to a serious artist?

She walked him to his bed and helped him in, then tucked the sheets around him. "How's that?"

He nodded, smiling. "I like you to put me to bed." His speech had grown by leaps and bounds, too.

"I like putting you to bed." She kissed his forehead,

savoring the preciousness of the little person and his fresh bath smell.

"I wish you lived with us."

She'd started to reach to turn out the lamp but stopped midway. How was she supposed to respond to that? Even wondered if Sam might have put his kid up to it. That made her smile, knowing how absurd the thought was. She decided to take the change-the-subject route. "You're a lucky boy to have your daddy."

"He works."

Too much. She didn't need to finish the sentence for Dani; she knew exactly what he'd meant. "Because he loves you and wants to take good care of you."

"I like you to put me to bed."

"That makes me happy, Dani. Thank you." *And sad for Sam. Oh, man, things are getting more complicated and downright awkward.*

"Will you hug me?" he asked in his usual shy manner.

How could she not hug this sweet, sweet boy? She wrapped her arms around Dani and held him until he gave a signal that he was ready to let go. "Sweet dreams, my little man."

Just as she got to the door he whispered, "I love you."

No doubt he'd heard it hundreds of times from his dad. What could she say? "I love you, too." It was true. She loved Dani with everything she had. She'd fallen hard for him the first night she'd met him. Now both of the Marcus men had declared their love for her. She gazed at Dani snuggled into his pillow, looking so small in his twin bed.

The poor kid had lost his parents before he could remember them, but he instinctively knew he wanted a family. Sam had been a blessing to the boy, just as the Murphys had been a blessing to him, and Andrea felt honored to be a part of his life. But Dani obviously wanted them together, like a real family. Which put both Sam and Andrea in a tough position.

After Dani had gone to sleep Andrea sketched some preliminary drawings, using the photograph of the cat from the couple who'd commissioned her to paint it. It was hard to concentrate, knowing that she had to tell Sam what she'd discovered tonight, but soon enough she got lost in drawing. It was almost eleven when he got home.

His eyes looked weary and his posture imperceptibly stooped, but enough for her to notice. Whenever she saw him her heart felt full, and that had never happened with anyone else. She walked toward him, and they hugged. He felt so good to hold.

"How'd things go?" he asked after she kissed him hello.

"Good. Dani's the sweetest kid I've ever met. But you already know that." She didn't mean to let emotion take over, but her voice had caught on *ever* and now there was stinging behind her eyelids.

It didn't get past Sam. "You okay?"

"Yeah. Can I make you a sandwich or anything?" She tried to recover fast, but moisture gathered at the sides of her eyes.

"To hell with the sandwich." His posture straightened, concern tinting his eyes. "Did something happen here tonight?" He came closer, looked into her face.

She swallowed against a sudden thickening in her throat. *Dani told me he loved me.* "Your son misses you so much, Sam."

A snap of emotion changed the concern in his eyes to irritation. She'd obviously hit a sensitive spot. "Look, a resident's father had a heart attack. He couldn't find anyone to replace him, so I agreed to work tonight."

"I get it. I know you have a demanding job. I'm just saying he misses you." *And now he's foolishly decided to love me, and I'm not ready for that responsibility.*

"And sometimes he'll have to understand that working late comes with the territory."

"But he's so young." She couldn't allow herself to get sidetracked. Dani's sad little-boy confession that his father worked a lot had set off bad memories. "Do you have any idea what it was like, never seeing my dad? Wondering if he cared?"

"You think you're the only one who ever wondered that? It's a fact of life. Being a foster kid with loads of brothers and sisters ensures you never get as much attention as a kid wants." He went quiet, turning inward.

How quickly she'd forgotten how frightening the first ten years of his life must have been. She needed to hear and understand his side of the story. "What's going on?"

"I was just thinking that, even though I didn't get the attention I may have wanted from Mom Murphy, I at least had my foster siblings to fill in the gap." He went still, and she filled in the blank… *Who did you have?*

No one.

Her lips tightened, fighting back the old hurt, confusion and anger, willing the first words to stay stuck in her throat. *I was so lonely. So was my depressed mother. Having each other wasn't enough.* Was that all she could promise sweet little Dani?

"Look," he said, obviously reading her expression of withdrawal, "I know you're still upset about my bringing up Fernando."

That was a fact also, but she had new concerns on her mind, which protected her from the ancient feelings threatening to make her break down right then. "Sam, I'm more upset with this Superman complex you seem to have. That you don't understand you can't do everything by yourself."

Sam and Dani's situation was too damn similar to the always-absent father setup when she'd been growing up. Because her father had been doing good things to help other people, she had never been allowed to express her true feelings of loneliness and longing for attention and his love. Nice little girls weren't selfish. Look where it had gotten her mother.

Though Sam was a completely different person than her father, she kept getting tripped up projecting those old awful feelings onto him. And now Dani wanted her to put him to bed every night. He'd told her he loved her. The kid needed a mother, and that was the last thing she thought she could be.

"Dani misses you, that's all I'll say."

He ground his molars and rubbed his temples. "Look, I've just had to tell a mom who brought her four-year-old into the ER last week, thinking he only had a bad flu, that he has leukemia. I had to admit him and get him started on chemotherapy. It's not a Superman complex, it's a job. Now, if you'll excuse me, I need to go give my son a hug."

That did it. *That poor mother.* The dammed-up feelings burst free and Andrea cried. Oh, could she ever have the emotional stamina to be a parent? Sam had seen it all as a pediatrician, he'd spent most of his life in a huge family with rotating foster kids, and though she tried to insist he was being selfish by even thinking about another adoption, the truth was he was anything but. The hard part would be trying to explain all of that to Dani.

She was the emotionally deficient one. She was the one who was selfish. Broken.

They hugged and kissed and comforted each other as no one else could. He wiped away her tears, even as she tried to smile through them. She told him she loved him and he did the same, then she left him for her house, so he could peek in on his boy and give that hug he so desperately needed just then.

Being a parent had to be a killer job. She'd never be able to do it.

* * *

The next night Sam was getting ready to put Dani to bed. The boy had been moody at dinner and throughout his bath. Maybe he was coming down with something. He felt his forehead, looked into his eye, and everything seemed fine, but Dani squirmed and resisted his intrusion.

"Ready for your bedtime story?"

Dani shook his head.

"What? No *Goodnight California* tonight? What about the truck book?"

Dani pouted and folded his arms. "I want Andrea."

To read to him? "She's at her house tonight."

"I want her to put me to bed." That was possibly the longest sentence Sam had ever heard come out of his son's mouth and, boy, had it packed a wallop.

Was his kid mad at him for not being around enough, as Andrea worried about? Or had the boy done the same thing he'd done, fallen in love with Andrea and wanted her there 24/7? Oh, man, this couldn't be good, two guys pining for the same girl. "She'll be back in a couple of days." Fingers crossed that wasn't a lie about the upcoming weekend. "Come on," he said, tickling Dani, hoping to tease him out of his sulking. "Want a bowl of your favorite cereal before I read to you?" No, he wasn't above bribing his kid out of a sour mood.

The offer got immediate consideration. Thank God for children and short attention spans. And endless appetites. "And don't forget you get to see the eye doctor for a recheck day after tomorrow. You need to be big and strong for that, and also get lots of sleep. You don't want the doctor to give you a sleepy eye report, do you?"

The child didn't have a clue what that meant, neither did he, but it definitely got Dani's attention. "No," he said, both his real and prosthetic eye wide.

After Dani had eaten his cereal and magnanimously

allowed Sam to read him a bedtime story and kiss him good-night, he admitted that Dani thought of Andrea as a mother figure. How had he not thought that would happen? Probably unconsciously had wanted it. For a smart guy, sometimes he was a real bonehead. Had he inadvertently set her up to be his competition for his son's affections? That needed to change, unless she was interested in marrying him. The thought sent a little shock down his spine.

He finally got around to eating that sandwich, since the bowl of cereal before with his son had hardly helped quench his appetite. As he chowed down tuna salad on toast, he reran in his mind the entire conversation from earlier with Andrea. She understood loneliness and worried about Dani. She loved his kid as much as he did. Didn't have to say it, it was very apparent. And he himself loved her for a hundred different reasons.

He had proof that she'd wanted him once upon a time, too, since he still carried around the note she'd written him the first night she'd invited him to her bed, sketched winking eye and all. Yeah, he'd folded up that letter the next morning after they'd first made love and tucked it away in his sock drawer for times like these. When he got ready for bed later, he'd pull it out and take a well-needed look.

Seemed as if there was only one way to settle the issue.

Maybe it was time to make their relationship full-time?

The last bite nearly stuck in his throat. Was he ready to risk asking the big question of another woman finding her way back to her artistic passion? Proposing had totally backfired with Katie. But looking back, he realized all the obvious signs with her. Things were completely different with Andrea. He loved her. Trusted her. Wanted to make a life with her. He was pretty sure she'd want the same with him. But, still, maybe they should take things one step at a time.

* * *

Wednesday morning, Sam barreled into the ocularistry and anaplastology department to talk to Andrea about moving in together, not out of convenience but as a definite step forward in their relationship, with the intention of making it permanent not far down the line.

He found Judith, wearing her usual eye magnifier headgear, talking to a young man with scraggly blond hair. The guy moved confidently around the room, making clicking noises.

"I'm pretending to shop," he said, with a wry smile, immediately aware of Sam's entrance.

Pretending? Sam stopped and had to think for a second to realize that the twentysomething man must be blind. If so, his prosthetics were phenomenal. "Don't let me interfere."

"This is Ned," Judith said, smiling. "He's a longtime customer." She stood off to the side, like a proud parent.

Ned clicked more, then turned and nodded to Sam, uncannily nailing where he stood in the room.

"Ned rode his bike over to tell me he wants to change the color of his eyes," Judith said, pride brightening her face.

He rode a bicycle?

"I want to go blue. Tired of brown. Oh, hey, what if I get one blue and one green?" His wide, youthful smile was contagious, if not confusing.

Sam needed to clarify something. "You rode a bike over?"

"Yeah, been riding bikes my whole life."

"He's taught himself something called echolocation," Judith said. "Kind of like a sixth sense for the blind. Too bad not many use it or even know about it."

So the clicking sounds helped him find his way around? Kind of like bats using sonar navigation, bouncing sound waves off objects and pinpointing the location? His interest was definitely piqued. "If your technique works, why don't more use it?"

"Socially annoying," Ned spoke up. "Some folks don't want to hang out with a guy who's always making clicking noises. I call it BurstSonor, by the way. Sometimes it even drives my sighted girlfriend crazy." He laughed. "But she loves me anyway."

Sam couldn't get past the original statement. "You seriously rode your bike to the hospital?"

"Woodman Avenue is mostly a straight shot. I only live a mile away but, yeah, I even do off-road bicycling. Why hold myself back?"

"Ned is a great example of a totally independent sightless person. Lives by himself and does everything the rest of us do," Judith said.

"That's commendable," Sam said, stepping forward to shake his hand. "It's an honor to meet you."

He took his hand as if he'd seen it. "I'm a pretty damn good cook, too, if I do say so myself. Nice to meet you, too."

Amazed at what this guy had accomplished without sight, Sam shook his head.

"Ned is an outspoken advocate for independence of the blind, much to the chagrin of many who think of echolocation as annoying or disgraceful, even. Many of them are other blind people, too."

"Seriously?" Sam thought about Dani, and the horrible potential for him to lose his other eye. Wouldn't he want his son to know freedom and independence like this guy if he became blind?

"Yeah, some of my staunchest adversaries are blind people who think echolocation is offputting." Ned laughed, having said the last phrase as though it had tasted bad. "Like the whole point of life is not to bother other people.

Unfortunately, that's what most blind people learn. That they're an inconvenience. That they are destined to spend their lives dependent on the kindness of strangers, the government and blind organizations looking out for them."

"It's a radical concept," Judith chimed in. "Ned has even started his own coalition to raise money and teach independence to the blind through his technique."

"This is fascinating, and, for the record, I think you should go with one green and one blue. Or get a pair of each and change eye color anytime you feel like it."

"That's a great idea." Ned smiled, as if really considering the suggestion. "Maybe I'll go violet."

They all laughed, but Sam suspected Ned might become Judith's first violet prosthetic-eyed customer.

"Well, it's been great talking to you," Sam said, suddenly eager to get back on track to why he'd come down here. "Judith, is Andrea around?"

"She took the rest of the day off after her appointment with Admin this morning," Judith said, unfazed, gazing happily at Ned. "She's painting. The hospital lobby needs new paintings, fast."

"I see." Sam winced over that expression with Ned in the room.

"And I don't," Ned said, not missing a beat. "But, you know, I've always wanted to try my hand at painting."

The quick levity may have gotten a chuckle out of Sam, but it didn't help the uneasy feeling crawling over his skin. Andrea had made connections and had found a way for her talent to be showcased. He certainly didn't begrudge her success, was happy about the hospital lobby deal, but she'd skipped work today because of it. Maybe it was her way of pushing back at her father?

She had paintings to paint, and a part-time job to hold down. Hell, he'd opened the door for her to showcase her work in the St. Francis Hospital lobby after the remodel.

He should consider himself responsible for her taking the day off. If her art took off, lack of time might force her to make a decision about working at the hospital and helping guys like Ned look sighted, or going full speed ahead with her painting…and kissing this place, and him, goodbye?

His history with the women walking away who meant most to him still managed to step in and keep him insecure and off balance. He needed to get hold of himself. Stop the negative, insecure thoughts. But it was the first thing to pop into his head.

Of course he wanted the best for Andrea, wanted to support her every step of the way, whatever made her happiest.

Sam had big plans he wanted, no, needed to bring up with her today. But she wasn't here. She was home, painting. Having to postpone what he wanted to ask her made his stomach knot and kept the knot tight. Women didn't stick around for him. But what if he showed up at her house with the perfect secret weapon?

CHAPTER TEN

It had been an amazingly productive day. Andrea's arms ached from the nearly nonstop painting. The bright sun had helped make her small workroom ideal during the morning, but by afternoon she had to move outside to her postage-stamp-sized patio for the best light. That had never been a problem before because her painting schedule had been so irregular. Now, however, with a couple of commissioned paintings and, in one case, a cash advance, she needed to paint more and consistently.

Maybe it was time to consider renting space in a real studio. She knew artists who did that, shared studio space to make the rent more reasonable, and once she'd cleaned up she planned to make a call or two.

Someone knocked at her door. She glanced at the clock on the wall—it was six-thirty. Wow, she'd really lost track of time this afternoon. She looked a mess wearing a baggy T-shirt and the oldest, holiest jeans in her wardrobe, probably had as much paint on her face, arms, hands and her clothes as on the canvas, but there wasn't time to clean up before answering the door.

Not bothering to check the peephole on the old thick wooden door, she pulled it open a few inches and peeked around the corner.

"Surprise!" Dani blurted, tickled with himself and clapping.

"Hi!" She dropped to her knees, genuinely happy to see him, put her hands on his shoulders and kissed his chubby cheek.

"You look silly," he said.

"I know, I've been painting." Slowly she shifted her vision from the toddler to the long jeans-clad legs behind him, lifting her gaze until she saw Sam's handsome face looking a little more worn than usual. He'd combed his brown hair neatly, and his piercing blue eyes promised this was a no-nonsense visit. Her pulse fluttered at the sight of him, as it always did. "Hi."

"Hi. You get a lot of work done today?"

"Yes. Come in!"

"Don't know if you've eaten, but I brought you some of that take-out chicken you like with black beans and a side salad."

"How thoughtful of you. Thanks. I'd totally lost track of the time." She stood and hugged him hello.

They all went into the kitchen. "Share?" she said.

"We've already eaten. Thanks."

It felt so formal, and not at all the usual casual, comfortable routine between them. Something was up. She opened the bag and took out a chicken leg seasoned with the usual lime and pineapple juice, oregano, garlic and chili pepper—it smelled so good—and took a big bite. Loving the taste, the tenderness, she lifted her eyes to the ceiling, then, also loving the thoughtfulness from the man she loved, she smiled at him and took another bite.

But he wasn't smiling.

"I was surprised to find out you weren't at work today," he said.

Why did she feel the sudden need to explain, to account for her actions, as if he were her father? She shuddered inwardly at the reference, feeling uncomfortably like her own mother. "I've been keeping up on everything, all the orders at work. I sent off the prosthetics I promised to the people in Cuernavaca last week. Even supplied a year's worth of special adhesive for the ears. I needed to get the cat in the bag, no pun intended, so I could get started on my next project. Hey, guess what, I've been commissioned for some paintings for the new hospital lobby."

"I heard that from your grandmother. Fantastic. I'm so happy for you."

"Thanks. I'm a little nervous."

"It'll be a big break for you, that's for sure."

"So you saw Grandma today?"

"Yeah, I stopped by the department, looking for you."

"Did I miss something?"

"A guy who clicks his way around the world."

"Ned! Isn't he an inspiration?"

"Sure is."

She could instantly tell Sam was done with small talk. He'd come here on a mission, and it was obvious he had something he wanted to get off his chest.

She wanted to love Sam and felt he wanted to love her, too, but regardless of their best intentions their pasts seemed to keep tripping them up, him always keeping a safe buffer zone, and her waiting for him to magically turn into her father. Would they ever get past that?

But the truth was she'd also missed him in twenty-four short hours, and that was a fact. Having finished the small chicken leg, she couldn't bring herself to eat another bite, as something besides hunger crowded out her stomach. Anxiety?

"Dani," she said, "would you like to play with the building blocks?" She'd gotten involved enough with Sam that she'd actually picked up a toy here and there for Dani to keep at her house. Remembering how much he liked his building blocks at his house, she'd bought a set for him to play with here.

He rushed at the chance, and soon sat contentedly in the corner of her living room, building a tower, knocking it down, then building another.

Andrea wiped her hands on a napkin, then glanced at Sam, who was still tense. "What's on your mind?"

"I've been doing a lot of thinking," he said, stepping closer, running his index finger along the curve of her jaw. "Anyone ever tell you that you look sexy with paint on your face?"

She gave a breathy short laugh, but tension took hold in her stomach as she waited for what he'd say next. Though the mere touch of his finger nearly made her lose track of her thoughts. How did he do that?

"I think we both know we love each other." He cupped her entire jaw, leaned in and delivered a delicate kiss to prove his point. Kissing always felt so right with him. "If your feelings haven't changed about me, I'm thinking we should join forces, you know, move in together."

Just move in. Like that.

Disappointed, she stared at him, eyes wide, not knowing how to respond. It certainly wasn't the most romantic proposal—in fact, the more she considered it the more she thought it was far too practical. But the man *was* a problem-solver after all. She had to be honest about what it made her think. "Shacking up out of convenience?" *How unromantic.*

He pulled in his chin, his eyebrows knitted. "No. Not at all."

If this was his idea of solving their problems, it made her angry. "Are you sure you're not just looking for a child-care provider with privileges?" she whispered, so Dani couldn't hear.

He grimaced, reacting to her low blow. "I thought you'd be in a good mood after painting all day."

Was he really that clueless? "I am in a good mood, but you seem to think about love as a business deal. You want what you want and I, well, the same. I love you, but a girl likes a little romance along the way."

He held her upper arms, looked deeply into her eyes. "Are you saying you're not interested in moving in?"

"Look, I do love you, and I love Dani so much I can hardly believe it. But I need to know you want me for me, not just to make your plans work out, but because you *need* me. Sort of like breathing."

"That's a bit dramatic, isn't it?" His comment fell flat, he knew it from the expression she tossed at him. So he tried again. "My plans involve making a life with you."

"Are you sure this isn't about putting all your ducks in a row for adopting more kids?" She narrowed her eyes for emphasis.

"Now who's being unromantic? I came here to ask you to move in, a huge step for us. You may not know it yet but we belong together."

Did they belong together? Him holding on to his secrets, giving the impression he was totally into the relationship but somehow always holding back some deep part of himself. She got it that his behavior was in no small part thanks to his childhood and feeling rejected by his mother, but nevertheless. Her with fears of becoming like her mother, giving up, giving in, lost and lonely on child duty while her husband pursued his profession and ignored the relationship.

Dani had stopped playing with the blocks, Andrea couldn't help but notice. "Dani, would you like a graham cracker and some milk?" Besides, she needed something to change the heavy atmosphere.

"Okay."

She led him into the kitchen and set him at the table with his snack. Then she went back to Sam, who was standing exactly where she'd left him, appearing dumbfounded, as if he already knew how things might work out. She pressed her hands together and placed them by her mouth, as if praying, as she approached.

"I do love you, Sam. I'm flattered beyond belief that you want us to live together, but maybe we're rushing things. The thing is, I need to know that it's me you want, and *need*, that I'm not merely a missing piece to fill that big puzzle you've created in your mind about the kind of life you want." She pleaded with her eyes for him to understand, to not be hurt by her honesty. "Don't get me wrong, it's a great idea. I'm just not sure about right now." Realizing she might have just hurt him deeply, she begged with a stare for his understanding. "We've got to be completely honest and open with each other, right?"

"I've been more honest with you than anyone else in my life."

"And I'm so grateful for that." *Was she so messed up that that wasn't enough?* "But you and your big compassionate heart scare me. I'm worried I'll never measure up to your standards. I don't know if I have the same capacity you seem to for reaching out to all those kids in need." Ironically, she worried he didn't need her anywhere near as much as he needed those kids.

Bewilderment filled Sam's eyes. "But you just said you love Dani."

"Yes, I do, and you, too. But I'm afraid I'll lose myself in your busy life, and I've only just started to find me." She pleaded for understanding with her gaze, her body tense and her feet bolted to the floor.

"How can you worry about losing yourself with me when I want success for you, too? I know how talented you are, hell, who do you think suggested you for the hospital remodel project?"

What? He'd set that up? It hadn't been her dazzling talent that'd gotten their attention? Roiling emotions made her face grow hot. Stupid her for thinking Sam was nothing like her father. He'd gone and done something behind her back, manipulating her life without her approval. *Jerome Rimmer strikes again.*

She nearly stomped her foot. Angry darts shot from her gaze, aiming to hurt. Because it ached to realize he'd misused her trust. "You just said how honest you've been with me, yet you listened on the phone when I crowed about how excited I was about the appointment. You never said a word that you'd set it up." He must have felt so proud of himself, not having a clue how much she'd *needed* to win that one for herself.

She wanted to run away to her studio and slam the door, rather than face the man she thought she loved. The man who'd just halfheartedly tried to fix their problems with an offer that they move in together, and to fix her professional problems by stepping in where he didn't belong. But she couldn't stand the thought of leaving Dani in the kitchen confused or worried. She forced herself to move and went to him. "Dani, honey, I think it's time for you to have your bath and get ready for bed."

"Will you read to me?"

"Not tonight, sweetie, but I promise I will soon. Maybe you can come here and spend the night with me sometime?" She tried to hide the slight tremble in her voice. Tried to keep it from breaking.

Sam cleared his throat at the kitchen entrance. She glanced up and saw total defeat on his face. Hell, he'd just asked her to move in with him and she'd essentially turned him down because she felt his big idea was for all the wrong reasons. He'd taken a risk and she'd shot him down.

"She's right, Dani, it's time to go." Sam said it kindly, but with a hint of dejection. The boy dutifully got down from the chair, having finished his milk and cracker, and took his father's hand. The pressure in her chest seemed to squeeze harder with each beat of her pulse.

Andrea rushed to Dani and kissed him good-night. "Have some fun dreams for me, okay?" He nodded. Then she stood, her heart feeling stretched to near tearing, took a deep breath and looked into Sam's tortured gaze. Words failed her.

He nodded his goodbye, skipped the kiss, turned and took his boy home, giving her the impression he totally didn't understand but knew when it was time to go.

She crumpled to the floor, never more tormented and mixed up in her life. How could she let a good man, a man who loved her and wanted to make a life with her, walk away? She'd sent him away!

Why did everything have to lead back to her childhood and her overbearing father planning every aspect of her life but never bothering to be around as she'd lived that life he'd prescribed? And her withdrawn mother letting her father run roughshod over her and never speaking up for her daughter or herself. Would it be the same with Sam? Why couldn't she believe him when he said he loved her and wanted to live with her, and not assume there was a big catch, that he only wanted her for his purposes, not simply because he loved her?

Because there *was* a catch, a huge one. He wanted her and he wanted that big family that he'd never felt he quite belonged in, and he wanted her to be like his saintly foster mother to make his world right again. Mother Murphy had died, the cruelest form of abandonment. Those were huge shoes to fit into.

Andrea felt she was barely ready for anything beyond loving Sam and Dani. But Sam expected so much more.

She trembled with anger over his foolish and insensitive mistake, but more so with fear that deep down she just didn't have what it took to be Sam Marcus's woman.

Things couldn't have backfired any worse. Sam helped Dani into his car seat, even though his hands trembled. Pain, disbelief and a stew of other emotions kept him from thinking straight. He'd asked Andrea to move in, laid it all out there, and she'd brushed it off. Was that all he meant to her? He'd said he loved her. What did she want from him? Had her father messed her up so much that she couldn't trust his honest feelings? Maybe he should have asked her to marry him, but they obviously weren't ready for that!

Why did he feel so numb? Why had he run to her with a last-ditch plan to keep them together when they hadn't really even broken up, and now it felt as if maybe they were on the verge of ending everything they'd barely started.

Why did he never feel good enough?

Did he really expect her to give up everything she held dear for the kind of life he wanted? He honestly didn't think so, but that was evidently how she saw it. If he could only figure out what she wanted from him, he'd do it. If she'd just given him a clue.

Did she really think she'd lose herself in his life? What about building a life *together*? He wanted what she wanted for herself. Hell, he'd spent twenty minutes talking to hospital administration about the new lobby remodel, encouraging them to brighten things up with pieces of art. Not cheap prints but real art from local artists.

As dumb as Andrea seemed to think it was, he'd given the executive secretary to the hospital CEO her website address to search for samples of her colorful artworks. He'd left the meeting with a grin on his face, and it had been for Andrea. All for Andrea. Now she had a commission for paintings.

But that had totally backfired. Man, had it ever. Did a guy who wanted to take over a lady's life do stuff like that?

Oh, man! That was exactly like something her father would do! Jerome Rimmer would go behind her back and set things up, as if she was a little puppet. No wonder she'd gone ballistic.

He'd screwed up royally just now on just about every level and didn't know how to begin to fix things.

Maybe he just needed to get his son home, to go through their nightly routine, then life would feel right again. But without Andrea he doubted life would ever be the same.

He hoped she wouldn't give up on them—he sure as hell wouldn't. He loved her too much. There had to be a way to work this out. But there wasn't enough time tonight.

As he drove into the garage at his home an image of her face appeared to him. "Maybe, instead of losing yourself with me, you'll come to *find* yourself in a life with me," he whispered. "And maybe I'll finally find myself, too."

CHAPTER ELEVEN

THE NEXT MORNING at the medical appointment, the doctor dilated Dani's eye, made a thorough examination, then had his nurse take him into a dark room to play while the eye medication wore off. Sam sat across from the desk in the office, waiting for the doctor.

The doctor looked grim, and Sam's instinct caused his entire body to tense.

The salt-and-pepper-haired ophthalmologist sat with a loud thump on his chair cushion, like a two-hundred-pound sack of potatoes, and sighed. A sound of defeat. "There are early signs of retinoblastoma in the right eye."

Stunned, Sam may as well have been hit with a two-by-four. He couldn't manage to breathe, his heart stuttered, and gut-wrenching pain for his son filled every part of him. He'd gone through this before, yet this time it felt twice as bad. Was that even possible? His head dropped into his hand, the burden of holding it up suddenly beyond his ability.

"We've caught it earlier this time, Dr. Marcus. We'll get a CT scan and an MRI, go through the staging process and see what our options are."

Sam couldn't think straight. Couldn't begin to string words together.

"Since you don't have any medical history on Danilo—I believe you said his parents are deceased?"

It took every last bit of strength Sam possessed to hold himself together. A simple nod seemed beyond his capability at the moment, but he managed to grunt a reply.

"I can tell you that *bilateral* retinoblastomas are always inherited, and therefore one of Danilo's deceased parents had to have been blind from the same cancer." The doctor continued as if Sam had agreed. "And with hereditary retinoblastoma, we must also be on the lookout for pineal tumors in his brain."

The mounting information tore at every nerve ending in Sam's body. Surely this was how it felt to have his heart ripped out of his chest.

"We have options this time around that we didn't with the last tumor because of the size. Even though before, without his family medical history, we didn't know he possessed a genetic mutation, and we hoped it might only affect one side, we might have handled things differently right off if we had known, but all is not lost. Once I gather the staging information, I'll know for sure if it's small enough to consider chemoreduction."

Sam glanced up at the doctor.

"The chemotherapy will be placed directly into the eye to reduce the size of the tumor. Then we can use laser light coagulation, also known as photocoagulation, to destroy any blood vessels leading to the tumor, starve it and destroy it."

"What about his vision?" Sam finally found his voice by focusing on the doctor's treatment plan.

"We might be able to save his sight."

He'd tossed Sam one tiny ray of hope.

"Our goal in shrinking the small tumor and essentially cutting off its blood supply is to save his remaining vision. All we can do is hope for the best and move forward from here."

"Thank you." They might be able to save Dani's sight. That was what he'd hold on to. That would help him through this horror show.

"We'll line up those tests ASAP and move forward as fast as we can," the stocky doctor said.

"I'm counting on it."

Sam left the doctor's office, seeing Dani playing contentedly in the dim room, and nearly lost it again. He inhaled, forcing himself to keep it together for his son. He walked down the hall, out of voice range, and fished out his cell phone with an unsteady hand.

His first thought was to call Andrea. But they'd had that nasty fight and she'd kicked him out of her apartment last night. And truth was he didn't know how he'd get the words out without breaking down. He needed to stay strong right now. For Dani's sake.

He dialed another number instead.

"This is Dr. Marcus. I need to clear my schedule for the next couple of weeks," he told the administrative nurse for his department. "I have a family emergency."

After a couple of days off, and without a word from Sam, Andrea returned to work, hoping she hadn't blown the best thing in her life. Selling her art only brought so much happiness. In fact, without someone to share the milestone with, it felt pretty damn empty. Paintings couldn't compare to a living, breathing man. Nothing could compare to Sam. She'd missed him and Dani terribly and had also missed being in the hospital, working on her projects for patients. By late last night she'd admitted she'd overindulged in painting for the past couple of days and the results on canvas were disappointing, to say the least.

It was time for a change, a breather from creativity, and ocularistry was the answer. Plus she'd be closer to Sam in the hospital.

Feeling fortunate she had choices in life, she entered the department humming.

Her grandmother met her at the door to the workroom. "I thought you'd forgotten you had a job."

"Not for a second. But I did have some banked personal time off and decided to use it."

Before her grandmother could answer, her father strode through the department door. Andrea went on alert.

"Well, I thought you both should know they've hired an administrative assistant from inside to take over this department. Now, Mom, you'll only need to concentrate on O&A. Hell, you can work part-time, just like this one." He pointed to Andrea. "If that's what you want."

"Well, that's good news, but won't I have to train this administrative assistant?" Judith was all about business before pleasure, probably where Andrea's father had gotten it.

"Of course." Andrea's father looked at her, narrowing his eyes, though seeming far less imposing than usual. "I still can't for the life of me understand why you wouldn't take the job."

"You're the head of cardiac surgery, Dad, you don't have to understand what goes on in this department." *Or inside my head.* She knew her vague answer irked the heck out of him, and she thoroughly enjoyed it.

"You're right about that. I'll probably live a lot longer if I quit trying to figure you out." At last, a feeling they shared. His response wasn't to bristle, as it usually was. It actually seemed as if he just shook it off. Wow. That was a first. "But that's not the reason I came down here." He handed his mother a letter. "This came through Administration, and I thought your grandmother might like to read it to you."

Judith opened the letter and read it out loud.

Dear St. Francis of the Valley Hospital,
The community of Cuernavaca, Mexicali, wishes to thank you and your mission members for helping us in our time of need. You saved lives and helped us get back on our feet.

We are especially happy about the recent packages received by many families with new eyes, ears and even noses. These gifts seem like miracles for so many children. The parents of Jesus Garcia cannot thank you enough for giving him back a normal face.

We hope these pictures say what we cannot in words.

Forever grateful.

Moved by the heartfelt letter, Andrea stepped forward. "May I see the pictures?"

Smiling, Judith dug inside the envelope and found a photo, then handed it to Andrea. It was a grainy group shot of all the children she'd helped. Immediate fond memories, recognizing face after face, made her grin. A second picture remained inside the envelope. Judith took it out, studied it, then gave it to her. It was of a young boy that Andrea remembered well, beaming with pride as he now had both ears and a tip for his nose, and it seemed impossible to tell which ear was his and which had been made by Andrea. Though she knew it was the left one.

"This, my dear father, is why I need to be here in the lab, making eyes and noses, and not becoming one of the suits, running things."

Her father glanced at the pictures, then studied them more closely. "Nice work."

Had he just paid her a compliment? Had Mom started sharing her new medication with him? "Thank you. Now, if you don't mind, I need to show this letter to Sam."

"He's off on a family emergency," Jerome said.

Concern shivered through her. "How do you know that?"

"I just came from the monthly administration meeting, remember? He's been off since yesterday."

Anxiety sliced through Andrea over what the reason was for Sam taking family time off. Part of her plan for coming back to work today had been to invite him for lunch and admit she'd discovered that not only did she love him but she *needed* him in her life. And if his offer was still on the table…

Something must be wrong with Dani for him to take off so suddenly. She reached for her cell phone and dialed his number, walking into a secluded part of the department to talk to him, leaving her father and grandmother to chat.

"Sam? Is everything okay?"

"Oh, hi. Um, yeah. Dani's had a couple of tests and we're just keeping things low-key."

"What kind of tests?"

"A CT and an MRI."

He wasn't exactly forthcoming with information about why Dani had needed those tests. "Is he sick?"

Sam cleared his throat. "The cancer has come back in the other eye."

She gasped, couldn't help it, and spontaneous tears flowed. "I'm coming over right now."

"No. You don't have to. We're working through this. We just need some peace and quiet."

Shaken and taken aback that he'd dismissed her so matter-of-factly, she wasn't sure how to respond. "Uh, okay."

"Okay. Thanks for calling."

Still stunned over the horrible news for Dani, and feeling dismissed by a zombie version of Sam, she let him disconnect and stood staring for a few seconds, wiping the tears from her eyes, her fingers trembling. He didn't want her there.

Hurt wrapped her up and nearly squeezed the air from her lungs. She stood, stuck to the spot, thinking rather than panicking.

She'd spent a lot of time thinking while painting the past couple of days, too, and had figured a few things out. Sam kept her at a distance, even when he'd asked her to move in, by making it seem like a practical decision, having nothing to do with love or longing or—her new favorite word—*needing*. Because that was the missing ingredient she'd discovered while painting. Need.

That was how he'd learned to deal with his personal pain of having a mother who'd left him alone and vulnerable, who'd had to give him up and who had never tried to get him back into her life. He'd grown up feeling an outsider in a big family, always afraid he'd get sent away, pretending to be part of one big happy family but always keeping his distance, watching, waiting for the day to come. His relationship with Katie had proved he wasn't capable of committing until it was too late and the relationship was over.

From where she stood, Sam was repeating history with her. He'd asked her to move in in a halfhearted way, not to get married, and had probably used her "no" as a reason to shut her out now.

Well, he wasn't going to get away with it this time because, unlike Katie, *she* loved him enough to fight for him. For Dani, too. *Oh, God, poor Dani!*

Rather than stand there and bawl helplessly, she grabbed her shoulder bag and marched toward the department door. Her father had left, and Andrea spoke to her grandmother on her way out. "I've got some personal business to take care of. I promise I'll be back tomorrow."

Judith raised her palms. "Like I could stop you? Do what you've got to do. Your job's safe with me—that is, until the new administrator takes over." She winked and smiled, as only a grandmother could.

"Thanks, Grandma."

Thirty minutes later Andrea knocked on the white front door of the boxy mid-century modern home in the hills above Glendale. It seemed she'd first stood at this door a lifetime ago. Sam's house. She'd been nervous then, but right now nothing could compare to the butterflies winging throughout her entire body—even her palms tingled. And her heart, it pounded hard enough to break a rib. She'd never taken a bigger risk in her life, but Sam and Dani were worth it.

Sam opened the door looking haggard and pale. He wore sweats and a ratty old T-shirt. His hair hadn't been combed in a while. "Andrea, I said you didn't have to come over."

"And you thought I'd listen? Sam Marcus, you'd better let me in or I'll roll right over you." Yes, it might seem absurd for a woman barely five feet tall to talk tough like that to a six-foot-tall guy, but right now she believed with all her might that she was capable of taking him down if he gave her any grief.

He didn't crack a smile but he stepped aside, letting her enter. "Dani's taking a nap." At first Sam avoided her eyes, but then those tired blues connected with hers and held on. There was so much pain there it made her ache inside. "Look, Dani and I will work through this together, just like we did the last time."

"How can you look me in the face and say that? Don't I mean anything to you?"

"Of course you do, but things have changed since the other night."

"You mean life got tougher, so you shut out the people you need most?" She'd play hardball if she had to. But, honestly, why hadn't his first phone call been to her?

"Didn't you kick me out of your house the other night?"

"I did, because you were being a bonehead. You asked me to move in—gee, how romantic. And you still don't think you need me. Or anyone, for that matter. You won't let yourself need anyone. But over the last couple of days I've done nothing but think about you and us and our situation.

"Now, are you going to let me sit down and get me some water or do I have to do that myself?"

She wasn't sure where this wild warrior woman had come from, but right now Sam needed someone to tell him what to do, and she was more than happy to do it. She trudged on into the living room and sat down. He brought her a glass of water, and one for himself, and she couldn't help but notice his hand trembled when he set the glass down. Her heart grieved for him in that moment, but she needed to say her spiel and get him to realize a few things before she could let out her true emotions over Dani's heartbreaking situation.

She took a sip for strength. "I say this as one only child to another. You've always felt like an outsider and kept your distance, even from me. Your foster mother loved you unconditionally, but you never believed it because it would hurt too much if she sent you back into the program, like some of the other kids that passed through her house."

"What's this got to do with anything?" He was definitely short on patience, and could she blame him?

"It has everything to do with us. Don't you see? You've always felt like you needed to prove yourself in order to be loved. Dani was abandoned. You knew how that felt. You could help him and return the favor your foster mother did for you. Loving a vulnerable kid is easy compared to a complicated grown-up like me."

She took a long drink to gather the confidence to bring up the next part. The part about her. "Then there's me, a girl who always felt rejected by her father. I didn't have a clue how to trust a guy, and you wanted to keep a safe distance, but the problem was that we had the hots for each other. We were crazy about each other's bodies. So we got in over our heads and tried to be grown-ups doing grown-up things, like falling in love." She'd been looking around the living room instead of at him because what she had to say was hard, but now she zeroed in on him. She had to, to make sure he was following her line of thinking.

"But we still weren't ready for that, even though we're both adults. Then there was the third ingredient of *us*, Dani. He needed both of us because he lost both of his parents. And like I said, you and I really got along great in bed, and we thought we loved each other. Which is fine. We should love each other. But, Sam, there was still something missing. *Need.* We had to need each other, and not just for practical purposes."

She stood, walked to him and knelt down in front of him, placing her palms on his knees. "After you left the other night, after you made the most unimpressive suggestion about moving in together, I had a lightbulb moment. You didn't need me in that deep-down, I-can't-live-without-you way every girl dreams about. It felt almost as if you could take me or leave me. Safe. You know?"

He didn't react in an obvious way, but she was quite sure there was a glint of something in his gaze, except she was too afraid to read it just then. What if he really didn't need her? "I had time to think and I realized I truly *needed* you in my life, whether you were ready for me or not. You made me come together. All my mixed-up parts finally came together. I needed you for that. Now I'm here because *you* need *me*. Because the little boy we both love is sick and *needs us* to come together and be there as a family unit for him. And you're right, that might not be any more sexy or romantic than your offer to shack up, but I'll settle for that right now. For Dani's sake."

She glanced up and saw a hint of gratitude in his gaze. "You need me because you don't have the strength on your own to go through this alone again." She squeezed his kneecaps. "You need me, Sam. And because of that I want to be here for you. For Dani." Her eyes prickled, her vision blurred. She'd gotten to the hard part, the part she'd promised herself on the ride over she'd beg for if she had to, and so far it looked as if she might have to. "I'll be your rock, I won't abandon you if things get too tough, I'll be your safe haven, I'll comfort you, I'll love you with everything I've got, because I love and *need* you, Sam." The tears came and she couldn't hold them back. "Can you admit you *need* me?" Her voice fluttered.

The invisible mask that held Sam's face together dissolved. His chin quivered and his eyes squinted tightly, forcing tears out the sides. He grabbed Andrea's hands, squeezing them like a man afraid to let go. "I thought I'd lost you forever when you asked me to leave. I might be the kind of screwed-up guy who asks a woman to move in because it's the practical thing to do, but underneath I meant it with all my heart, and I was too damn afraid to ask you to marry me."

She squeezed his hands. "Say it, Sam."

"Propose?"

She shook her head. "You know what I want to hear."

"I love you, Andrea."

"And I love you. But I *need* you even more. Now say it. Please?"

He grew very serious and stared down at her. "Honey, I need you. I can't face life without you."

She sighed as chills covered her shoulders and back. He reached for her and she climbed onto his lap, wrapping her arms around his neck and kissing his wet cheek. "Baby, I'm all yours."

Later, when Dani woke up, Sam made a simple dinner for the three of them, and afterward they played blocks and trucks and pretended that Dani's life hadn't been turned on its head again, until it was time to put him to bed. They'd take it one day at a time from here on.

"May I do the honors?" Andrea asked.

A week ago Sam had felt threatened by the fact that Dani had wanted Andrea to put him to bed instead of him. Tonight the request seemed like a godsend. How had he been so lucky to find a woman as strong and unyielding as Andrea?

"Give me a kiss," he said to Dani. The scrawny kid's arms circled his neck and tiny soft lips brushed his cheek, giving Sam a little taste of heaven, yet he ached inside. "I love you."

"I love you, too," Dani repeated, oblivious to what the near future would bring, as he trotted off to Andrea's waiting hand. She beamed at the boy who'd soon be facing the battle of his life, but for now he was suspended in sweet grace, surrounded by the two people who loved him most.

As Andrea and Dani walked down the hall Sam couldn't help but overhear his son's question. "Are you going to be my mommy now?"

Andrea laughed. "That's up to your daddy."

Sam grinned, the first time he'd done so since he'd gotten the dreadful diagnosis for Dani's remaining eye. Then he called out, "You can count on that, son."

EPILOGUE

One and a half years later...

DANI JUMPED ONTO the grass from the new wood swing set in the backyard. His independence always put Andrea on edge. He quickly utilized his newly learned skill of clicking to find his way back to the seat and climb on again. He'd been taking lessons from Ned, learning the art of echolocation and future independence, right along with Braille. They hadn't been able to save his vision but had successfully killed the cancer.

At first the blow from the news about Dani having retinoblastoma in his remaining eye had seemed insurmountable. But Andrea and Sam, together, had given each other strength and support so they could be the rock their boy had needed while he'd gone through the process of going blind.

They'd also, as the tight-knit family unit they'd become, agreed not to coddle Danilo unnecessarily. Their goal was to make a stable home for the boys, something they could depend on and trust, and that was now especially important for Dani. That's where the lessons with Ned came in, and the increase in Dani's confidence as a result brought joy to both Andrea and Sam.

With his prosthetic eye in place, and his sightless eye

looking exactly like the prosthetic, from this distance no one would ever notice he was blind. Dani jumped from the swing again, this time landing on his butt and laughing. Fernando may have a prosthetic leg, thanks to the drug cartel blowing up his village, but he ran like the wind, thanks to the latest high-tech prosthetics, and he swooped in to give his little brother a hand. Nando's determination never ceased to amaze Andrea, and he always touched her heart with his gentle spirit. She couldn't imagine a life without either of her sons.

Once Andrea had married Sam, she'd seen how much Sam had helped the orphanage in Mexicali and that he'd always stayed in touch with Fernando's caregivers. Opening her heart to loving and needing Sam had opened her mind, too. She'd been the one to suggest they go through with the adoption. It had taken over a year, but here he was, a great addition to their ever-growing family.

Nando tripped on a tree root as he rushed to aid Dani again, but she didn't run to him. These days it was too hard for her to get up. She and Sam had made a pact that the boys would be as independent as any other kids their age. She and Sam were determined not to let their sons' special challenges hold them back in life. That's why they'd let Nando try out for the junior soccer team in grade school, and he'd been accepted. He knew how to get back up, and he wasn't hurt from tripping just now, so she stayed put in the Adirondack chair.

In the meantime, Dani had found his way to the slide and, squealing with joy and hands held high in the air, he slid down a little too fast, and at the bottom he tumbled head over heels onto the grass. After a long motherly sigh, Andrea watched with interest to see how he'd handle things. He started to stand, but not before his big brother had offered him a hand and pulled him up.

"Thanks!" Dani said. "Did you see that?"

"Pretty cool," Fernando said, with a proud brotherly smile showing the gap from his newly missing front tooth.

Dani soon rushed back to his favorite outdoor pastime, the swing set and jungle gym complete with tree house, clicking all the way to the ladder for the slide. Back up he climbed.

Being eight and a half months pregnant made it almost impossible for Andrea to keep getting up and down. By the time she stood up, Fernando and Dani would have already worked out their problems, and wasn't that the way to raise two independent boys? So she just sat there and observed the fun, praying for the best.

"Dinner's ready!" Sam called from inside their new extra-large home. They'd found the perfect older house farther up the hills of Glendale, bordering La Crescenta, with four bedrooms, an add-on in the basement doubling as an art studio and prosthetics lab, including patient and/or client waiting area. So Andrea could work out of the house part-time for the hospital and part-time for herself. Judith had trained the replacement for herself and was now happily retired, but still working two to three days a week. The new house also had a rumpus room and a huge backyard! How could they raise two boys and their soon-to-be little sister without those essentials? And Grandma Barbara was a frequent guest, especially if Andrea had work or painting to do and Sam was at the hospital. Having grandchildren seemed to make her mother happier than Andrea had ever seen her.

Sam strolled toward Andrea, love openly twinkling in his eyes, and helped her up from the chair, then kissed her gently. She never grew tired of her husband's simple displays of affection. She'd made the smartest decision of her life in marrying him. Once she'd convinced him of how much they needed each other, old emotional walls had come tumbling down and they'd never looked back. Neither had they ever been happier.

"Eww," Nando teased.

"What happened?" Dani asked.

"They kissed. Again."

"Yucky."

The boys giggled, then rushed toward their parents.

"When are you guys going to get used to it?" Sam said, smiling, herding his sons along toward the house, Dani clicking all the way. "Wash your hands!" he called out when they overtook him, beating him to the back door, then he turned back to Andrea. "You coming?"

"In a second." She'd had a Braxton Hicks contraction when she'd been getting up and wanted to wait for it to subside. Using the time to gaze around, she grinned at nothing in particular and everything in general. The yard. The huge oak tree. The beautiful old house. The sky the exact color of her husband's eyes. The family that had just rushed inside for dinner. Her family. The people she loved with all her heart.

To some the life she'd chosen might seem super complicated, and it was, but the strangest thing had happened— she'd managed to find herself in the middle of that chaos. To Andrea the challenge of becoming Sam Marcus's wife had turned out to be the greatest adventure of her life.

* * * * *

WANTED:
WHITE WEDDING

NATASHA OAKLEY

To Jenny, my editor. Without your support and belief in me this book would never have been written. Thank you.

CHAPTER ONE

FREYA bit down hard on the expletive hovering on the tip of her tongue and called again, her eyes raking the rows of old sofas and chests of drawers. 'Hello?'

There was still no answer. No sound of anything in the cavernous building except the clip of her heels on the concrete floor. 'Mr Ramsay? Anyone? Anyone at all?' She came to a stop and looked back across the auction house.

She sucked in her breath and spun round to look again at the long line of caged cupboards piled high with knick-knacks. Where was everyone? The entire place was deserted.

Freya tucked her hands further into the depths of her sheepskin jacket and stamped her feet to get warmth back into her frozen toes. This was such a crazy way of doing business. There had to be someone whose job it was to speak to people like her. A porter? Wasn't that the way it worked?

She hadn't expected anything like Sotheby's or Christie's in a place like Fellingham, but this was plain ridiculous. Left to herself, she'd walk straight back out of here—and a casual trawl through the telephone directory would, no doubt, produce any number of more promising alternatives.

Except…

Her almost habitual frown snapped into place. Except Daniel

Ramsay had somehow managed to convince her grandmother he was all things wonderful. *Damn him!*

Twelve years' hard experience had taught her that anyone who gave the appearance of being 'too good to be true' was usually exactly that. The trouble was it would take something approaching the impact of World War Three to shift the elderly woman from her opinion of him now.

Freya pulled her hand out of her pocket and glanced down at her wristwatch. Where was he? She really wanted to see Daniel Ramsay for herself, gauge what kind of man he was, and preferably without her grandmother being there to witness it.

She stepped back, and her leg jagged against a box of china on the floor behind her. She swore softly and bent down to brush the dust off the fine black wool of her trousers.

What kind of place was he running here? Whatever the reality of Daniel Ramsay turned out to be, he was no business-man. His auction house was full of junk. Row upon row of it.

Freya looked round, her nose wrinkled against the musty smell. He couldn't be doing more than scratching a living here…

She frowned. No doubt that was why he'd gone out of his way to befriend her grandmother. Stopping to chat and eat lemon drizzle cake whenever he had an hour free.

He'd certainly managed to inveigle himself very success-fully. According to her grandmother, his prowess extended from the removal of mice to changing a lightbulb. And, of course, antiques. Apparently Daniel Ramsay knew *everything* there was to know about antiques…

Freya stamped her foot again as the cold bit at her toes. Looking at the sad specimens around her, she seriously doubted that. In her opinion his 'gift', such as it was, was in correctly reading an elderly woman who wanted shot of things she didn't much value but which he knew would earn him a hefty commission.

Her eyes fixed on the green painted door with the small

'Office' sign on it. She gave her wristwatch another swift glance and then sidestepped the box, pushing her way passed a battered rocking horse.

This was a stupid waste of her time. If the office door was unlocked she'd leave a note, asking him to call this afternoon.

Not perfect. Not what she'd hoped for. But better than nothing. And it was always possible she was worrying needlessly anyway. Perhaps Daniel Ramsay genuinely liked spending time with her grandmother and had no ulterior motive at all?

Only....

Freya's eyes narrowed as her normal scepticism rose to the surface. Only that wasn't very likely. Not in the least likely. She rapped with her knuckles on the closed office door, scarcely pausing before pushing it open. 'Mr Rams…?'

His name died on her lips as she took in the threadbare rug and the muddle of…stuff. There was no other word to describe the eclectic mix of furniture and paintings. All of which would have been better consigned to a skip rather than an auction house.

What was going on here? Was this some kind of 'lost and found'? Or a modern-day 'rag and bone' business?

She picked her way across the floor and stopped by the heavy oak desk, one part of her mind speculating how anyone could work in such disorder while the other questioned whether the elusive Daniel Ramsay would even be able to find a note left for him in the mess.

Freya let out her breath on a slow, steady stream and pulled her handbag from her shoulder. She set it on the desk, starting slightly as the telephone on the other side of it started to ring. Conditioned as she was to take all her calls within a few seconds, it set her teeth on edge to hear it echo off into the distance via a crude tannoy system.

She reached across to pull a pen from a colourful mug, starting as the office door banged violently against the wall.

'Get that, will you?'

'I'm—'

'The phone. Take a message,' a disembodied male voice shouted, followed by a grunt. 'I'll be through in a minute.'

'I—'

'Phone! Just answer the phone!'

For a brief second she wondered whether she'd inadvertently stepped into a farce, and then Freya shrugged, stepping over a pile of vinyl records and an old gramophone to reach the other side of the desk. What did it matter? And at least it would stop that infernal noise ricocheting about.

'Ramsay Auctioneers,' she said into the receiver, her eyes on the closed door.

'Daniel? Is that you?'

Hardly. She rubbed a hand across her eyes, the humour of the situation finally reaching her. 'I'm sorry, Mr Ramsay isn't available at the moment. May I take a message?'

'Can you tell him Tom Hamber called, love?'

Her right eyebrow flicked up and she reached over the scattered papers for a pad of fluorescent sticky notes. In her real life she'd have paused to tell Tom Hamber she wasn't his 'love'. She might even have told him that while she *could* pass on a message, she was by no means certain she would…

'Have you got that? You won't forget?'

'Tom Hamber called,' she said dryly, drawing a box around the words she'd written. 'I think I'll manage to remember.'

'Tell him I need to speak to him before midday.'

Freya added the words 'before midday' to the note, then turned at the sound of a loud crash. 'I'll leave him a note,' she said into the receiver. Whether he actually found it really wasn't her problem.

'That's it, love.'

She set the receiver back on its cradle, ripping the top note off the pile. One thing she was certain of: there was no way on earth she was going to let her grandmother sell anything valuable through this crazy set-up. She looked at the confusion on the desk and stuck the note firmly on the telephone.

'Thanks for that.'

Freya turned and found she was looking up into a pair of brown eyes. Very definitely up. At five feet ten—more in heels—it wasn't often she had to do that.

Why did that feel so good? Some deep Freudian something was probably at the root of it. He had to be at least six foot two. Quite possibly more. And those eyes... Dark, *dark* brown, and sexy beyond belief.

'I was holding up one end of a table and couldn't let go.'

Freya pulled her eyes away from his and wrapped her sheepskin jacket closely around her. 'Right.'

'Did you get a message?'

'Yes. Y-yes, I did. Yes.' The corner of his mouth quirked and she stumbled on, feeling as foolish as if she'd been caught drooling. 'It was a Tom Hamber.'

'Ah.'

'He wants to speak to Daniel Ramsay before midday.'

'I can do that.'

The most horrible suspicion darted into her head.

'I'm Daniel Ramsay.' He smiled, and Freya felt as though the floor had disappeared beneath her.

This couldn't be Daniel Ramsay. From her grandmother's conversation she'd conjured up a very different picture. Someone altogether more parochial. More...

Well...less, if she were honest. Much less. Truthfully, this Daniel Ramsay looked like the kind of man you'd quite like to wake up with on a lazy Sunday morning. A little bit rumpled and a whole lot sexy.

'You're a little late.' Then he smiled again, wiping his hands

on the back of dark blue denim jeans, and the effect was intensified. 'Not to worry. I get here about eight thirty, but I told the
agency nine-thirty was fine.'

He held out a hand, and she automatically held out her own.
His wedding ring flashed. *Of course* a man who looked like
this one would be taken. They always were—even if they pretended not to be.

A familiar sense of dissatisfaction speared her. It was amazing how many men said they were separated when the only
thing keeping them apart from their significant other was temporary geographical distance.

She was so tired of that. Tired of the game-playing.

Daniel bent down and pulled open the bottom drawer of his
desk. 'I've got the key to the inner office here. I'll show you
where everything is, and then I've got to drive out to the Penry-
James farm.'

'I'm not—'

He stood straight. 'Which part didn't you get?'

'I understood you perfectly, but I'm not from any agency.'

'You're not?'

'Merely a potential customer.'

His hand raked through his dark hair. 'Hell, I'm so sorry!
I thought—'

'I was someone else.' It didn't take the mental agility of
Einstein to figure that one out. It was vaguely reassuring to
know he didn't actively intend to run his business in such a hap-
hazard way.

Sudden laughter lit his eyes, and she fought against the curl
of attraction deep in her abdomen.

'So you're not the cavalry after all? Perhaps we'd better
start over?'

'Perhaps,' she murmured, feeling unaccountably strange as his
hand wrapped round hers for the second time. He had nice hands,

she registered. Strong, with neatly cut nails. And a voice that made her feel as though she'd stepped into a vat of chocolate.

But *taken*, the logical part of her brain reminded her. And apparently the kind of man who, if he wasn't actually preying on her grandmother, was certainly making the most of an opportunity.

'You must have thought I was mad. Did Tom say what he wanted?'

'No, he didn't.'

'I expect it's about the quiz night next month.' His smile widened and her stomach flipped over. Helplessly. 'So, if you're not from the agency, what can I do for you?'

'Not me. My grandmother,' she said, her voice unnecessarily clipped as she struggled to regain her usual control.

She took a deep breath and exhaled in one slow, steady stream, watching the droplets hang in the frosty air. 'Is it always this cold in here?'

'Not in summer.' He moved away and bent to switch on a fan heater. 'Then it can get quite unpleasant—'

'It's unpleasant now!'

He looked up, his brown eyes glinting with sexy laughter. 'Because the window in here doesn't open,' he continued, as though she hadn't spoken, completely unfazed. 'It's been painted over too many times.'

She bit back the observation that getting a window to open was something which could be easily fixed. Something that most certainly would be in any sensibly run business.

'I suppose I ought to sort that.'

'I would.'

He gave a bark of laughter. Startled, Freya looked at him. It had been a long, long time since anyone had dared laugh at her. She took in the faint amber flecks in his laughing eyes and swallowed, desperately willing her throat to work normally.

He was so entirely unexpected. She'd got one image of him

entrenched so firmly in her imagination that this incarnation was difficult to adjust to. She tucked a strand of hair behind her left ear and felt the back of her hand brush against her crystal earring. It started swinging and jagged against the collar of her jacket.

'How can I help your grandmother?'

Freya blinked. 'She has a few items she's interested in selling, and I'd like to have a professional evaluation of them.'

'Can you bring them in?'

'Not easily. There's a chiffonier, a dining table—'

'Then I'll come out to her.' He moved effortlessly past the piled boxes and sat behind his heavy desk, taking a pen from the same chipped mug she had.

'Today, if possible.'

He nodded, his pen poised. 'And you are?'

Freya hesitated. She wasn't quite ready to tell him that. Not exactly, anyway. Three days in Fellingham and she'd already had more than enough of people's reaction to her name. From the way their eyebrows shot up into their scalp she could only assume she'd gone down in local folklore as all things depraved.

It shouldn't matter. Didn't. But somewhere not so deeply buried her anger about that was still there. Nibbling away at her, despite all the success which had followed.

'My grandmother's Margaret Anthony. Mrs Margaret Anthony.'

His sexy eyes narrowed slightly. If she hadn't been so attuned to people's reaction to her she'd probably have missed it. Possibly even the beat of silence which followed. 'Then that would make you Freya Anthony.'

'That's right.'

His strong fingers opened a large black diary and he wrote her grandmother's name at the end of a long list. 'It looks like it'll have to be near five. I'm a little choked up today.'

'That's fine.'

He looked up and his eyes were no longer laughing. Something inside her withered a little more. He was a stranger to her, an 'incomer' to the area, and yet he'd already formed a poor opinion of her.

But then of course he had. What was she thinking? She knew Fellingham's vicious network had gone into overdrive, and it didn't take much imagination to guess what he must have heard about her.

'Has she thought any more about selling her vases?'

'She's thought about it.'

'And?'

Freya held his gaze, meaning to intimidate. She could do that. She'd always been able to do that. 'I'm going to make sure she gets the best possible price for them. I understand an undamaged pair can be quite valuable.'

'Can be. You just need two collectors who badly want to own them.' Daniel stood up. 'I think she could confidently expect to get a thousand for them.'

'And in London?'

He shrugged, completely unfazed by the question she'd shot at him. 'Possibly more. But the internet is narrowing the gap. Dedicated collectors search online.'

'I wasn't aware you had much of a website here.'

'It's in development.'

'But very early stages,' she said dismissively. 'So not much use yet.' Freya lifted her jacket collar and snuggled down into the warmth.

It didn't matter what he thought of her. The only thing that mattered was her grandmother, and she was going to do anything and everything to see she wasn't hurt or cheated. Not by him or anyone. 'I'll tell my grandmother to expect you.'

Daniel nodded. 'As near to five as I can make it.'

'We'll both be there.' She gave him a swift smile, one that didn't quite reach her eyes, before picking up her bag and walking out of the office.

CHAPTER TWO

SO THAT was the notorious Ms Anthony. Daniel watched the swing of her hips as she left…because he couldn't help it. She had the longest legs. The kind that would wrap around you twice. Then he listened to the sound of her ridiculous heels clipping on the concrete floor until it faded to nothing. He shoved his hands deep in his jeans pockets.

Not exactly what he'd been expecting Fellingham's very own bad girl to be like. *Interesting.*

He carelessly tossed his pen back into the orange and red mug. Freya was a great name for her, though. If he'd ever taken a moment to think about it, he'd have thought someone who was named after the Scandinavian goddess of love and beauty ought to look pretty much like she did.

Daniel fingered the tag on the Gabrielle cream plush Paddington Bear that was destined for the twentieth century sale later in the month. Margaret Stone's wayward granddaughter would need to be beautiful to have lived one fraction of the life village gossip attributed to her.

He hadn't expected her to so obviously exude class, though. Hell only knew why not. He'd known all about her Audi Roadster within minutes of it driving into the village. He shouldn't have been surprised by the skilfully highlighted blond hair and the designer clothes.

'Dan?'

He turned.

'We've got a problem.' His porter rested his hand on the doorframe. 'The blonde bombshell wants Pete's van moved. It's blocking her car in.'

'Damn!'

'She's being quite vocal about it.'

'I just bet.'

The porter gave a rare grin. 'I told her the driver had gone for breakfast and wouldn't be back for twenty minutes or so but she's not having none of that. Says my time might be worth less but hers isn't. She wants it moved right now.'

Somehow he didn't find it difficult to accept that Freya Anthony expected things to happen when and where she wanted. One imperious click of her manicured fingers and Daniel had no doubt the world habitually fell where she wanted it to.

'I'll talk to her.'

'You'll have to. She's spitting fair to blow.'

Daniel smiled. The image Bob was creating was all too indicative of what he expected Ms Anthony would do when the world didn't bend to her will.

'She's one that likes things to happen yesterday, I reckon.'

'Okay, I'll sort it.' Daniel glanced down at his watch and grimaced. There couldn't be much more that could go wrong today. He seemed to have been running behind from the minute he'd opened his eyes this morning.

'Nice looking woman, though, ain't she?'

Yes—if you liked the kind of woman who would eat you up and spit you out.

He stepped out onto the forecourt, pausing for a minute to gauge how blocked-in her car was. The faint hope he'd had that it might be possible to guide her past faded as he took in how far Pete had driven the van in.

Daniel walked towards her. 'I'm sorry about this.'

'Just get it moved.'

He looked back at Bob. 'See if you can find Pete and get the
eys—'

'You don't have a spare set?'

'Why would I? It's not my van,' he replied calmly, taking in
he angry flash of her blue eyes. Then he turned back to Bob.
I think you'll find him in Carlo's. If not he'll have gone on to
hat place in the arcade for one of their all-day breakfasts.'

The older man nodded and ambled off towards Silver Street.
Beside him, Freya made a small guttural sound of pure irritation.

'It shouldn't be too long,' Daniel offered. 'Would you like
o wait inside?'

'What's the difference? It's as cold in there as out here.'

'You're welcome to use the phone if you need to call someone,' he added seamlessly.

'I've got a mobile.'

Quite deliberately he let the silence stretch out between
hem. She could be as difficult as she liked, but she wasn't going
o get a reaction out of him. After a moment it seemed she made
a conscious decision to relax. Though by other people's standards she was still as tense as a bowstring.

Spoilt, he thought, watching the small frown disappear from
he centre of her forehead. A woman who'd had her own way
far too often and easily. She spun round on her ice-pick-thin
heels and walked over to perch half a buttock on the low brick
wall behind her car.

His eyes travelled to the sleek grey Audi he'd heard so much
about. 'Nice car.'

'I like it.'

Daniel smiled. It was a 'statement' car, not one chosen
simply to get you from A to B. It was a car which would always
be noticed. Would inspire envy. She had to know that. Would

surely have anticipated the reaction it would produce when she drove it into the village. Even in Fellingham, which had its fair share of London money.

It made him wonder whether this was all some kind of game to her. Did she like the idea of wafting back to her old stamping ground and giving the gossips something to talk about?

Because they *were* talking. Everything she did and said would be dissected. Everywhere she went...

Did she even care?

Daniel took in the dark smudges under her eyes and the tight hold to her mouth. She cared. He had no idea how he knew that so certainly. 'How long are you planning on staying?'

'I've not decided.'

'Nice to have the freedom to choose.' Daniel sat down on the wall beside her, perversely determined to make her speak. 'Is Margaret still planning on moving to a warden-controlled place?'

He was aware of the slight hunch to her shoulders and the short delay before she replied. 'Quite possibly.' Then, 'You know, you really don't need to wait with me.'

'It's not a problem.'

'I'm sure—' She broke off with a swift frown. '*Bob*, was it?'

Daniel nodded.

'Well, I'm sure Bob will manage to find the driver of that thing,' she said, pointing at the white van, 'and get it moved some time before lunch. You go on doing whatever it is you need to do.'

Daniel stretched out his legs. 'Pete's on his break, so you're going to need me to reverse it. Unless...you're happy to do it yourself?'

'I've no problem with that.'

He fought down an unexpected desire to laugh. She'd do it. A vehicle she didn't know, and a tight bend out on to a narrow road...

He'd kind of like to see that. It was a shame Bob would re-use to hand over the keys. Pete would have him lynched if there was even the slightest scratch put on his baby.

'Pete might have a problem with it. That's his pride and joy.'

'Then why make the suggestion?'

Fair question. Why had he? Daniel studied her face for a moment.

Because he liked to see the challenging tilt of her chin, the determination in a face that otherwise looked as if it could be the model for a porcelain doll…

Freya Anthony had the darkest lashes of any woman he'd ever seen. Though maybe they looked like that because her skin was so fair. Purple smudges beneath blue eyes. Intelligent eyes. Guarded.

Hurt.

He recognised that because he'd felt it. There was always an unspoken connection between people who knew what it was to suffer.

Daniel shook his head. An affinity between two souls who knew life wasn't perfect. Could never be perfect. And for some reason he knew this carefully packaged blonde understood that. She knew it with the same bone-deep certainty he did.

'If we're going to be sitting here a while, shall I bring us out a couple of coffees?'

'No.' Then, as though some semblance of politeness was dragged out of her, 'I'm not thirsty, but that's no reason for you not to go and get one for yourself if you're determined to babysit me.' She stood up and tapped her foot against the tarmac.

Daniel's eyes travelled to the caramel suede of her boot, the impatient movement of her foot. 'No problem. I'll just sit here and wait with you.'

'How long have you known my grandmother?'

The question surprised him. Or rather the antagonistic tone of it did. He shrugged. 'A few years—'

'How come?'

His eyes moved back up to her face, taking in the pinched look. Daniel sat back as far as the wall would allow. *What exactly was her problem?* Something had really got under her skin. And that something appeared to be him.

Maybe she was the possessive sort? Perhaps she wasn't happy to discover Margaret had filled the void left by her family, if not well at least adequately?

'Margaret takes an interest in other people's lives,' he said slowly. 'People like her for it.' He watched her process that—make some kind of judgement. Her foot moved again, and she spun round so he couldn't see her face.

'How much longer is this Bob going to be? This is completely stupid.'

'That'll depend on how difficult Pete's been to find.'

Her head snapped round, her long earrings swinging. 'I've got things I need to be doing.'

Daniel felt a smile twitch at the side of his mouth. Unreasonable and spoilt was the only way to describe Freya Anthony's behaviour.

Very similar, in fact, to the way his daughter behaved when he vetoed something or other 'everyone else' was doing. Only Mia was fifteen, and had considerably more excuse for behaving like a brat than a woman in her late twenties…however beautiful.

Oh, hell! The thought of his daughter had him reaching inside his coat pocket for his phone. He'd forgotten to turn it back on, which meant her school wouldn't have been able to contact him if…

What did he mean *if* they tried to call? Given the morning they'd had, it was an inevitability. It was a little over three years since Anna had died, and he'd never missed his wife as much as he did right now.

Anna would have known what to do. She'd have had one of those mother/daughter chats the 'How to Deal with your Teenager' books suggested.

But Mia might not have been behaving the way she was if Anna hadn't died... Daniel closed his eyes against the thought. Things were the way they were. They just had to be got through in the best way possible.

It wasn't what he'd have chosen. None of it was as he'd chosen—

A bleep alerted him to a missed call. Damn it!

He looked up, and Freya waved an impatient hand towards him. A fatalistic sense of foreboding settled on him as he pushed the button that would let him hear the message. It was brief, and very much to the point. Daniel pulled a hand across the back of his neck.

'Trouble?'

He turned. 'I need to make a call.' Cold wind whipped at the fine blonde hair she'd loosely clipped up. He shouldn't really leave her sitting here alone, waiting for goodness only knew how long. Daniel hesitated before his priorities slipped into their habitual pattern. 'I'm sorry, I really do—'

'It's fine.'

His hand bounced his phone. 'It's my daughter's school—'

'It's fine,' she repeated, and for the first time her eyes lost their hard, combative edge.

It was so dramatic a change that it cut through his preoccupation.

'If I have to wait for Pete to finish his break, then that's what I'll have to do.'

Daniel studied her eyes, looking for some kind of explanation for such an abrupt change of manner. 'I'll—'

'See you at five,' she finished for him, returning to sit uncomfortably on the wall.

'Thank you. I really appreciate that.'

Freya climbed into the driver's seat and leant across to reach into the glove compartment of her car, pulling out some lip balm.

She hadn't done that well. Any of it. Not only had she not really been able to gauge what sort of man Daniel Ramsay was, she'd probably done more harm than good. After witnessing her behaviour today, he probably thought her grandmother needed protection from *her*.

Nothing about this visit was going as she'd planned. She unclipped the twisted silver barrette, throwing it on the passenger seat, and ran her fingers through her hair. What exactly was she so cross about anyway?

For all she knew Daniel Ramsay was a genuinely kind man, trying to make a go of a small country auction house. He'd seemed kind. After all, how many men in her London circle would drop everything to go running when their daughter's school rang?

That didn't take very much thinking about. None. She didn't know anyone like that.

She shut the glove compartment with a hard shove. It was the fault of this wretched place. She couldn't seem to stop herself from behaving badly. Maybe because that was what everyone was expecting from her? Who knew what the psychology was? Whatever it was, she was certainly living down to their expectations.

Steve, the driver of the white van, walked past her car, sparing her only the briefest of glances. No doubt this morning's performance would be added to the canon of her supposed misdemeanours. Only in this case she was more than a little guilty.

Freya bit her lip. Why had she ever thought coming back here was a good idea? Okay, so she'd thought her physical presence might deter her dad more effectively than the knowledge she was watching from a distance, but there was more to it than that.

So many complex reasons bound up together. The fact was, this whole approaching thirty thing had taken on a life of itself. It felt almost like a life crisis. At least it would if she didn't hope to live considerably longer than sixty years.

Now she had something to prove—to herself if no one else. She *would not* run back to London like a dog with its tail between its legs simply because other people didn't like her. Been there, done that, had the battle scars to prove it.

But being back in Fellingham did make her feel as judged as before. And after twelve years she honestly hadn't expected it to feel like that. She could feel everything unravelling. All her hard-won peace of mind.

Statements like *It's so important to feel no residual anger towards anyone or anything* no longer seemed to make sense. What did it mean when you actually unpicked it?

She was angry—*really* angry. How about *One's past must not be allowed to determine one's future*? Wasn't that what her therapist had said?

It was all total rubbish. Freya turned the key in the ignition. Clearly Dr Stefanie Coxan had no first-hand knowledge of what it was like to live in a gossipy little place like Fellingham.

Of *course* one's past shaped one's future. Even if you managed to draw a black line under the grotty bits, pieces of it still steeped through and stained whatever came after.

She reversed out into the narrow country lane and, without stopping to analyse why, turned her car towards Kilbury. Post-war bungalows still lined the entrance to the village, followed by a rash of 1930s semis, many carefully extended beyond recognition.

She took the left-hand turn towards Church Lane, the second right into Wood End Road, and bit down a wave of pure loathing as Kilbury Comprehensive School appeared from behind a row of Leylandi.

Squat. Ugly. Built of breeze blocks some time in the 1970s, when it had seemed a good idea to make everything square and functional. She slowed her car down to a stop as large droplets of rain spotted the windscreen.

There'd been nowhere on earth she'd been more unhappy. Nothing to do with the school, of course. Now, with hindsight, she could see that. Everything that had tortured her had been from within. But at the time it had been just another thing to kick against. Something else to resent.

Freya glanced down at her watch and restarted the engine. There was no point in sitting here remembering how unhappy she'd been. If she'd hoped seeing it again would lay some ghosts to rest she'd been kidding herself. If anything it felt as if she'd stirred a few up.

Freya turned the car round in a lay-by and headed back along the main road towards Fellingham. She set her windscreen wipers going and flicked on her headlights to compensate for the overall gloom.

It was strange to be driving along this road. It was all so familiar, and yet not. The red telephone box had been replaced by one of those see-through boxes. The pub at the end of the lane had changed from the Pheasant to the Plough.

But most things were the same.

Presumably the school bus still took this route. Still left at 7:25 a.m. from the bus stop opposite the garage, still took a lengthy detour through Westbury and Levingham before looping round to Kilbury.

She slowed at the crossroads and glanced over at the brick-built bus shelter which had been her escape route. It hadn't taken too much ingenuity to slip out through the changing rooms, cross behind the bike sheds and then walk down the main road to this bus stop. From there it had been a twenty-minute ride into Olban and all the diversions of a big town.

And it seemed times hadn't changed much. Out of the corner of her eye she caught sight of a teenage girl in school uniform, turning away from the wind to light a cigarette.

As she pulled away from Pelham Forest it crossed her mind to wonder whether she should have stopped. But then what would she have done? Or said?

You couldn't just pick up stray adolescents. There were laws against that type of thing. And if that girl was anything like she'd been at the same age she'd have given her a mouthful for interfering in what didn't concern her.

But...

Freya glanced in her rearview mirror, softly biting her lip. *Maybe she ought to ring the school?* She debated with herself for all of thirty seconds. She couldn't do it. It would feel like a betrayal. *Honour among thieves, and all that.*

From the distance she heard the slow rumble of thunder. Moments later there was a crack of lightning.

Freya glanced again in her rearview mirror but she'd driven on too far to be able to see what the teenager's reaction to the storm was. It was one hell of a day to have picked to bunk off school.

It was all too easy for her to imagine how that girl must be feeling. And how cold. Freya swore softly and steeled herself to go back and check the teenager was at least okay.

At the next junction she performed an illegal U-turn and drove back up the other way. It was one thing not to want to deliberately get someone into trouble, quite another to drive off leaving them wet and miserable.

The light from her headlights picked up the rain, now coming down like stair-rods. Despite it, the girl stepped straight out and lifted her thumb—which certainly made it all much easier. Freya gave quiet thanks that she didn't have to get out of the car. She slowed and came to a stop.

'You in trouble?' she asked, opening the window with the push of a button.

'The bus is late and I've got an appointment in Olban.' The girl took a drag on her cigarette. 'Are you going that way? I could use a lift.'

Rain slipped in through the opened window, darkening the suede of Freya's jacket. One glance at the teenager showed she was faring much worse. Her khaki coat was sodden, and her hair, dragged back in a tight ponytail, hung limply down the back of her neck.

'What time's your appointment?' Freya asked, mentally reviewing her options. Now she was here she wasn't at all sure what she was going to do.

'Twelve-fifteen. I'm meeting my mum at McDonalds.'

And she believed that just about as much as she wanted a hole in the head. 'Can I ring her? To check she doesn't mind me giving you a lift?'

'She won't mind.'

'I'd like to ring her anyway.'

'My phone's died,' she said, with a jut to her chin, then brushed a long strand of sodden hair off her cheek.

'We can use mine.'

'I can't remember her number.'

Freya's hands moved over the steering wheel. *Hell,* this kind of thing never happened to her in London. For one thing she was always too busy to notice if anyone was out of place.

Damn it! She really should have just rung the school. They could have checked their records and she could have driven back to Fellingham guilt free.

'Are you going to take me?' The girl took another drag on

her cigarette and then dropped it to the ground, twisting the ball of her foot on it. 'I won't smoke in your car. And I've got a plastic bag in here,' she said, lifting her schoolbag forward. 'I can lay it across the seat if you're worried about your leather.'

Freya fought the smile that tugged at the corner of her mouth. This girl was only a beginner in delinquency. Way back when, she wouldn't have said anything like that. She'd have been more inclined to smoke if she thought it would shock, and the idea of protecting a car seat just wouldn't have occurred to her.

'I can give you a lift, but I need to ring your school and ask them to contact your mum. I need her permission.'

'Don't bother.' The girl turned back towards the shelter, her shoulders braced against the wind.

'You know hitch-hiking is dangerous,' Freya offered, wincing at words she knew would achieve nothing. 'I might be anyone.'

The girl looked over her shoulder. 'But you're not. You're Freya Anthony. I've seen you before.'

'Have you?'

'And everyone's talking about you.'

Ah. Why did that still have the power to surprise her? 'Do I get to know *your* name?'

'Do I get a lift?' she countered.

It was a little like looking into a mirror. Albeit one that had the ability to turn back time. There was something else, too. Some sense that she'd seen this girl somewhere before. Maybe it was nothing more than the ghosts of her youth haunting her. Reminding her.

'It's pouring down out here, and I'm wet.'

'I…' Freya was momentarily distracted by a bright light shining in her rearview mirror. She looked up and then over her shoulder as a silver estate car bore done on her.

The girl swore, and Freya turned in time to see her duck out of sight. *What the—?*

The lights were switched off and a car door slammed behind her. Freya swung round in her seat and she watched, amazed, as Daniel Ramsay stormed over towards the shelter.

Oh...my...goodness. She made the connection surprisingly slowly. Somehow it had never occurred to her that a man the age of Daniel Ramsay would have a daughter as old as this one. But that had to be it. Every line of his body screamed his anger.

His dark eyes met hers briefly, but his attention was on the belligerent teenager. Fascinated, she watched the confident, mouthy girl turn into a sulky, quiet one. Freya deliberately looked away, and carefully re-zipped the inner pocket of her handbag.

She felt a strange pang of envy watching the two of them. No one had ever come looking for her. Certainly not her dad. Not ever. It would have meant a lot if he had. If just once he'd put her first. Freya brushed an irritated hand across her eyes. It had been such a long time since she'd allowed herself to be so affected by thoughts like that. It didn't matter.

Not any more.

Her parents were her parents. They'd done the best they could and that was that. One's worth must come from inside oneself. She only wished she could believe that...on some level other than a cerebral one.

'Ms Anthony?'

Freya looked up.

'Is that yours or hers?' he asked abruptly, his voice edged with anger and his eyes on the cigarette butt on the kerb.

'I'm sorry?'

'The cigarette?'

His voice was like steel...and she instinctively reacted against it. *Who did he think he was, to be talking to her like that?* She glanced at his daughter, standing sullenly behind him, and caught the appeal for help in her eyes. It was fleeting.

Barely there before it was gone. And Freya couldn't do anything but respond to the sense of kinship she felt.

'You have a problem with that?'

His brown eyes narrowed infinitesimally. 'Actually, plenty. But if you want to sabotage your chances of living into old age so be it.' He turned his head. 'Mia, get in the car. Now. I said *now*!'

The teenager allowed herself a quick glance of gratitude towards Freya before doing as she was told. It was amazing how much 'attitude' she still managed to exude. Even the slam of the door spoke volumes.

Freya turned back to look at Mia's father, feeling a little guilty.

He took a moment, seemingly trying to gain some control. 'That wasn't helpful. I don't know what you think you're playing at, but—'

'I—'

'—if she'd actually got into your car I'd have seriously considered charging you with abduction.'

'I—'

'I suggest, in future, you mind your own business,' he said, stepping back from her car and heading towards his own.

Freya sat, a little stunned at his attack. She felt as though she'd been verbally cut off at the knees. And people said *she* had a tongue dipped in vitriol.

She wouldn't care to be in Mia's shoes right now, she thought as she caught a glimpse of Daniel's expression as he drove past. There was a price to being loved, it seemed. Because she didn't doubt he was motivated by that.

Even so...he'd had no business talking to her like that. Slowly she reached down for the ignition to start the engine.

Surely it had been a tad disproportionate? She'd known from his reaction to her name earlier that he'd heard something of her history, but what exactly did he think she'd want with a truanting teenager? Did he honestly imagine she went around the country finding disaffected girls to turn into mini versions of her?

After starting the engine, Freya pulled away from the kerb. The sooner she got out of this spiteful little place the happier she'd be.

CHAPTER THREE

'IS YOUR granddaughter here?' Daniel asked, shaking the rain from his coat. 'I'd like a word with her if I may?'

'Through there.' Margaret nodded towards the door to the dining room. 'I don't think you're Freya's favourite person right now.'

'I don't imagine I am. May I—?'

'Go through,' she said with a smile, giving every appearance of thoroughly enjoying herself. 'I'll put on the kettle. Call if you need rescuing.'

Daniel walked down the hallway, but he didn't venture further than the doorway. Freya was there. Wrapping china and seemingly absorbed in her task.

He stood with one hand on the doorjamb, searching for the words he knew he needed to say—and trying to whip up some anger towards Mia for having placed him in this embarrassing situation.

But he knew this was about him. He'd spent long enough over the past few months talking about personal responsibility to know he'd no one to blame but himself for the way he'd spoken to Freya.

He'd done it because he could, he supposed. Because he'd needed someone to blame. Someone to take out his anger and frustration on.

Only…

Only—and this was the damnable part—he'd seen the slight widening of her blue eyes and caught the hurt in them. A fleeting expression. Swiftly controlled. But he'd seen it—and it felt as he imagined he would feel if he kicked a puppy.

There were enough people round and about who were ready to stick the knife into Freya Anthony, and he didn't intend to be one of them. She was here now. That was wonderful, as far as Margaret was concerned, and if she was happy he had no business making it hard for her granddaughter to stay.

Which meant he had to put things right.

Try to. This wasn't going to be easy. The slight tilt of her head told him Freya knew he was there, but that she'd no intention of meeting him halfway.

And why should she? He thrust his right hand deep in his jeans pocket. 'I owe you an apology.'

Freya looked up momentarily from the bubble-wrap she was cutting. 'Yes, you do.' She reached for the top saucer from a pile to her left and placed it carefully in the centre of the bubble-wrap.

'What I said to you…'

One perfectly shaped eyebrow flicked upwards.

'…was…was out of line, and I apologise. I was unfair…and…'

'Rude?' she offered, her voice like a shiver.

Yes, damn it! He'd been rude. Completely unreasonable. Daniel pulled his hand out of his pocket and thrust it through his hair. 'I took my anger out on you and I'm sorry. I had no right to do that.'

He'd done it. Made his apology. The best he could do without going into his relationship with his daughter.

'No.'

His mind stuttered. No, his apology wasn't accepted? Or no—

'No right,' she clarified, her fingers moving for a second saucer. 'Would you pass me the sticky tape, please?'

Daniel walked further into the room and picked it up from the far end of the dining table. Stepping closer to her, he caught the waft of her perfume, light and citrus. Saw the pulse beating at the base of her neck…

And suddenly it mattered, really mattered, that she should believe him. He'd hurt her, and he had the uncanny sense that far too many people had done that.

He kept hold of the sticky tape as she reached for it and forced her to look up at him. 'I'd like to have shouted at Mia, and since I couldn't I took out my anger on you. Made you my whipping boy, if you like.' His mouth twisted into a wry smile as he saw the flicker of understanding. 'I really am sorry for the way I spoke to you.'

There was a moment's hesitation, then, 'I know that.'

Just three words, but her voice had lost its hard edge, and the underlying huskiness of it seemed to hold him frozen. A small tug on the roll of sticky tape pulled him back to the present. He swallowed, watching as she ripped off a few centimetres and taped it across the top of the pile.

'I can understand why you were angry. I just don't think I deserved—'

'No, you didn't.' *She really didn't.*

She moistened her lips. 'What happened to…Mia? Did you get her back to school?'

Freya's concern merely added to his confusion about her. People asked about his daughter all the time, but none of them managed to imbue it with real concern. Why would she care? By all accounts empathy wasn't one of her strong suits, and she'd not been anywhere near Margaret all the time he'd lived in Fellingham. She had to know her grandmother had desperately wanted her to.

'Do you mind my asking?'

'No. No, not at all. I drove her straight there.' Daniel watched as Freya carefully folded over the end of the Sellotape and replaced it on the dining table.

He'd love to know what had made Freya visit now. She didn't look like someone who'd want to spend days on end packing up someone else's possessions. Maybe Sophy was right in thinking she had nowhere else to go?

Her hands moved to cocoon another teacup in bubble-wrap. She made even that mundane task seem faintly exotic. As was her dress ring. Whilst the thumb ring she wore was more bohemian. And she had tiny wrists that reminded him of Anna's.

But that was where the similarities stopped. He looked up at Freya's oval face, with her perfectly shaped eyebrows and carefully accentuated lip colour. The two women couldn't have been more different.

His Anna had been a woman without artifice, whereas Freya couldn't have exerted more care over her appearance. She was beautiful, but he fancied she'd look more beautiful first thing in the morning—before she'd hidden herself away behind her make-up.

He stopped. Maybe she *was* hiding. Maybe that was *exactly* what she was doing. Maybe Freya Anthony was less spoiled and more scared.

God only knew why that bothered him so much. She was nothing to him. But…

There'd been something unpleasant about the gossip swirling around the village over the last few days. Something in it he didn't like.

'The school picked up on her absence very quickly,' Freya remarked, placing the saucers into a cardboard box by the wall. 'That was good.'

Daniel put his hands deep in his jeans pockets and determinedly focused on her question. 'They register her at the start of each lesson.' She glanced up at him and he added, 'Unusual,

I know, but Mia skips off so often we've got a fairly established routine going now.'

'Is she being bullied?'

'Nothing like that.' *If only it were that simple.* 'There's no real reason. At least not one she's prepared to tell us about. We've got an excellent Educational Welfare Officer assigned to us now, but nothing anyone says to Mia seems to make any difference. She can't see the point of school and that's that.'

'Tea?' Margaret said, coming in behind him with a tray.

Daniel turned to take the tray from her, and she sat herself down in the nearest chair with something like a sigh. 'My hip… The sooner I get that operation the better.'

'If you'd go private,' Freya said, rolling the bubble-wrap back on the roll and standing it in the corner, 'you wouldn't have to wait. I keep telling you that.'

'I'm not paying.'

'You wouldn't have to. I would.'

Daniel set the tray on the table as another preconception bit the dust. From everything he'd heard he hadn't expected there to be any kind of emotional connection between Margaret and her granddaughter…but there undoubtedly was.

How come? Freya Anthony had shaken the Fellingham dust from her shoes a long time ago, and hadn't looked back. Before that she'd been nothing but trouble. But what he was watching wasn't a new reconciliation. There was familiarity in the way they talked to each other. Love.

'I've paid into the National Health Service for nearly fifty years, and I don't see why I should have to pay extra now.'

Freya sat down opposite Margaret, but her blue eyes flicked over in his direction as she picked up the milk jug. 'I assume you take milk?'

'I do. Thank you.'

She poured some in the bone china teacup, and then lifted

the matching teapot, steadying the lid with her finger. 'We've been arguing about this for months, and I don't think we're ever going to agree.'

'No, we aren't!'

'It's crazy to go on in pain when there's an alternative.' She passed across her grandmother's tea. 'Just think—when you've had your operation you might not feel the same need to move from here—'

'No one will want this place after I'm gone,' Margaret said, setting the cup down in front of her and reaching for the sugar bowl. 'This is a family home. I should have sold it a long time ago.'

'I don't see why.'

'Let someone else worry about the garden, for one thing. And your dad is quite right in saying I need to take steps now to avoid paying inheritance tax.'

'*You* wouldn't be paying it! Dad would. It would come out of your estate.'

'But I don't want my money going to the government.' Margaret set her spoon down in the saucer and turned her attention to him. 'Daniel, what have you done with Mia? There was no need for you to rush here this evening. I hope you didn't feel you couldn't cancel?'

Actually, it hadn't occurred to him. His sole thought had been to apologise to Freya.

'She's in the car.' He brushed a hand across his face, reluctant to confess even that much. He'd got a fifteen-year-old daughter he didn't trust to leave at home even for half an hour. What did that say about him?

His life was a mess. Other parents seemed to be turning out well-balanced young people, whereas he was heading towards a fully-fledged delinquent. What did Freya make of that?

Of him? For reasons he couldn't fathom he was suddenly interested in that. There was something particularly astute about the expression in her eyes when she looked at him. It made him feel she was weighing everything he said. Making a judgement. Probably finding him wanting.

'Oh, Daniel, bring her in. It's too cold for her to be sitting out there, even if she's got her...whatever that thing is they all seem to be plugged into.'

Opposite, Freya smiled, her blue eyes holding a sudden sparkle. 'I suspect you mean an MP3 player.'

'Something like that,' Margaret agreed. 'Freya, be a darling and go and get her a glass of diet cola. She must be so fed up, sitting out there.'

'She's—'

'She's going to be frozen, Daniel. Just bring her in.'

Freya smiled and pushed her chair away from the table. She'd heard that tone in her grandmother's voice many times before, and it really did brook no argument. Even her dad had done as he was told when faced with that voice.

It was a shame she hadn't used it more often. If she'd been able to stay longer than that one summer holiday perhaps she'd have made different choices. Passed some exams.

For the umpteenth time that day she wondered what was motivating Mia. Her relationship with her dad was clearly fractured, but that didn't necessarily mean it was all his fault.

'*A nice man doing his best.*' That was what her grandmother had said when she'd recounted the incident earlier.

And she honestly hadn't expected him to apologise. At least not in any sincere way. That changed things. Maybe she really had stumbled on a man with integrity?

She found a two-litre bottle of diet cola on the floor of the larder and poured some into a tall glass, carrying it back to the dining room. 'I found it.'

'Good. We can't leave Mia sitting out there. She'll be texting someone she shouldn't.'

'A little like me, then,' Freya said, setting it down on the tray.

'Except there wasn't texting when you were her age. You made your trouble in other ways.'

She'd certainly done that. But she'd had her reasons. When a person deliberately set out to push the self-destruct button there usually were reasons for it. *So what were Mia's?*

Freya turned her head as she heard father and daughter returning, taking in his bleak expression and her sulky one.

'Come and have a drink,' Margaret said as soon as they appeared.

Dry, Mia really was a very attractive girl. Her hair, which had looked a dirty honey shade earlier, was a dramatic strawberry blonde colour. She'd have been quite stunning if she'd smiled.

In case they didn't already know she was here under sufferance, Mia scarcely acknowledged that Margaret had spoken to her. Daniel ripped an exasperated hand through his hair and frowned at his daughter.

From this side of the fence it was almost comical to watch. Almost. It would never be quite that, because Freya knew what it felt like to carry a hard knot of anger inside. To feel lonely and frightened and so angry you didn't know what to do with yourself.

'Have you finished your tea?' Margaret asked.

Freya looked down at her empty cup. 'Yes.'

'Perhaps you'd take Daniel to look at the chiffonier and the table? I'll sit here and keep Mia company.'

'They're in the morning room,' Freya said, standing up.

Daniel quickly drained the last of his tea and set the cup back in the saucer. He glanced at his daughter. 'I won't be long.'

Mia hunched a shoulder and picked up her cola. This time Freya couldn't stop the tiny smile, then turned to look at Daniel and caught the quick flash of anger in his eyes. If Mia was looking to provoke a reaction from her father she'd succeeded.

A second glance at his daughter confirmed that she was com-
letely aware of that. Whether or not Daniel was the root cause
f Mia's anger, he was certainly the focus of it. 'If you want any
nore cola, I've left the bottle on the side in the kitchen.'

'Thank you.' Daniel spoke for her.

Freya turned her head and smiled. 'I assume you know
where you're going?'

He nodded, and walked in the direction she'd pointed.
'reya glanced back. With her dad out of the room Mia's whole
elligerent air had vanished. She just looked sad. And quite a
it younger.

Margaret smiled at Freya across the top Mia's head. A look
f complete understanding passed between them.

'Would you mind pouring me a second cup of tea, Mia?'
Margaret asked. 'This hip of mine makes it difficult to get out
f the chair.'

Freya followed Daniel out into the Minton-tiled hallway,
with its stunning mahogany staircase sweeping upwards. She
lanced across at him, wondering what had happened in their
elationship to make it so strained. It might be arrogant, but she
omehow felt that if she just had half an hour with Mia she
night be able to help.

But it was none of her business. And Daniel was at least
working on it. He lifted his hand to rub his temple, and Freya
aught sight of his wedding ring.

Where was Mia's mother in all this? Her grandma hadn't
nentioned her and she hadn't liked to ask. Just *'a nice man
doing his best'*. That was all she'd said.

'Margaret's really good with her,' Daniel observed.

'With Mia?'

He nodded. 'This is one of the few places I can bring her.'

'Well, one way or another she's had practice.'

'You?'

Freya walked past him into the morning room. 'Don't tel
me you weren't thinking that. I imagine you've heard at leas
five versions of my youthful misdemeanours.'

'One or two.'

It shouldn't hurt to hear what she already knew. But it did
Nevertheless, she liked him better for not lying to her. 'That'
the trouble with Fellingham,' she said breezily. 'Nothing eve
happens here, so they have to re-hash old stories. You'd think
they might have found something else to talk about after this
much time.'

'Your arrival re-sparked interest.'

'I just bet. Let me know if I'm under suspicion for murder.
Or whether it's just abduction of minors—'

'I've apologised for that!'

Freya brushed an irritated hand across her face. 'True. My
turn to apologise.'

'You can't have been much older than Mia when you left here.'

She took her hand away and caught the full force of his expression. Daniel really had the most incredible eyes. They
seemed to offer a warmth and an acceptance she hadn't seen
in the longest time.

'How old were you when you left?'

'Seventeen.'

Daniel nodded. 'Mia's fifteen. Not so very different in
age, then.'

'Two years is a long time when you're a teenager,' Freya said
quickly, wanting to make it absolutely clear that she didn't
think Mia's life was on the same trajectory as hers had been.
'Fifteen to seventeen weren't good years for me, and I didn't
make it easy for anyone to like me.'

Funny how you could encapsulate so much angst into a
simple sentence. Thinking back now, she could see how she'd
managed to antagonise pretty much everyone.

The consequence was that they weren't pleased to see her back. Everywhere she went she felt the whispers, the looks, and the constant speculation about what she wanted in coming back.

'Margaret's really glad you're here,' he said, as though he was able to read her mind.

She looked up at him and found he was watching her. For some inexplicable reason she wanted to cry. She bit on the side of her mouth in an effort to control the prickle of tears behind her eyes.

How did he know what she'd been thinking? If she wasn't careful she'd be pouring out every secret she'd ever had. Maybe she didn't have to. Maybe those dark brown eyes could see into her soul and read them all for himself?

'Half your trouble is because of that. Margaret was so excited when she knew you were coming that she mentioned it to one or two people…' He let his words taper off.

Freya's breath caught on an unexpected laugh. 'Yes, I know.' She hadn't quite believed she'd arrive until she'd actually stood on the doorstep.

'And you need to remember you're not seventeen any more,' he said, his voice soothing like velvet.

No, she wasn't. Right now she didn't feel seventeen at all. Whatever it was Daniel Ramsay had, he should bottle it. It would make him a fortune. Even a cynic like her was dissolving at his feet in a pool of hormones.

God help his poor wife. Daniel would have more opportunity than most to stray. Maybe he did. Maybe that went some way to explaining Mia's anger?

Only that couldn't be right.

His hand moved to touch the chiffonier. 'Margaret wants to sell this?'

Freya nodded.

'Honestly, she'd do better to hang on to it for a few years.

Dark wood isn't as popular as it was a few years back. It's all fashion. It'll have its time again.'

Daniel couldn't be that kind of man. If he was, her grandma would hardly describe him as 'doing his best'. And he was still wearing his wedding ring.

Freya pulled her eyes away from the unexpectedly sensual movement of his fingers running along the wood grain. 'It won't fit where she wants to go, so she doesn't have much of a choice.'

He pulled a face. 'I can't see sheltered housing suiting her.'

'Neither can I. But now they're building some in the village she's become quite keen…and I suppose it makes sense long-term. I don't mind, if it's what she really wants.'

He nodded and turned back to the chiffonier. 'This isn't going to make much more than five hundred. It's early nineteenth century, not particularly unusual, and big. Most houses just can't take a piece of furniture like this.'

'And it's ugly.' Freya moved away to stand nearer the door. She felt better with more space between them. One thing she'd learnt was that danger was best avoided. And, with a finely tuned instinct for survival, she knew Daniel Ramsay was dangerous.

'The barleytwist side columns are nice, but that's really all it's got going for it. I'd put a reserve of about four hundred on it but, I don't think it'll go much higher than that.'

'Anywhere?'

His eyes narrowed infinitesimally. 'If I thought she would get more elsewhere I'd tell her. Margaret's a friend, and my auction house isn't particularly looking for things to sell. With all the antiques programmes on TV recently, business is booming.'

'I didn't mean—'

'Yes, you did.' Daniel cut her off, and his eyes held hers. He didn't even blink.

There was a beat of silence. *He really was a mind-reader.* 'Actually—yes, I probably did.'

Daniel thrust his hands deep into his jeans pockets. 'Is there any particular reason you think I'd do something underhand? Was it something I said or just a chemical reaction?'

'I don't know anything about you,' she said quickly.

'But you don't like me?'

Freya moved across to the dining table, pushed up into the corner of the room, and started to lift down the boxes stacked on it. 'I don't have to like you. I just need to be certain my grandmother isn't being taken for a ride.'

'And you think I'd do that?'

'I think your business needs a good injection of capital, and I think you want quality pieces passing through your auction house even if the owners would get a better price elsewhere.'

The silence was longer this time. 'You don't take any prisoners, do you?'

She shrugged. 'What's the point? The sooner we get finished here, the sooner you can take Mia home. What do you think of this?'

Daniel moved back to look at the bulbous legs of the table. 'Do you have the extra leaves?'

She nodded, feeling unexpectedly mean. 'Three. Behind the door over there.'

'What does it measure when fully extended?'

'Three hundred and ten centimetres.' Daniel crossed over to look at the other pieces of the table and she added, 'There's a scratch on one of the leaves. I can't remember which one now. I think the back one.'

He looked for a moment. 'It's quite deep, but that won't affect the value much. This will most likely go to a dealer who'll be able to sort that.' Daniel turned back to her. 'I'd no idea Margaret had this. It's lovely. Why doesn't she use it?'

'She did. When I was younger. We used to have big Sunday lunches.'

Daniel's eyes softened again, making her want to run away and hide. What did he imagine he was seeing when he looked at her? There was no way on earth he could know how much she'd loved those Sundays. Loved the huge knickerbocker glorys her grandma had made especially for her.

'She's not used it for years, so there's no point hanging on to it,' she said brusquely.

He nodded. 'It's worth something in the region of three thousand pounds. I'd certainly want to see a reserve of at least two thousand on it. Is there anything else you want me to look at while I'm here?'

'There's a clock in the hallway. She doesn't really want to sell that, but if she does end up in Cymbeline Court it'll never fit.' Freya led the way back into the hall and stood in front of it. 'I quite like this, actually.'

'It's lovely.'

Freya looked over her shoulder. 'Don't you need to look at it more closely?'

'It's a New Jersey Federal mahogany longcase clock, and it's a gem. I've looked at it before.' Daniel gave a wry smile. 'Every time I come here. Honesty compels me to admit this might be something you'd do well to sell elsewhere. We haven't had a clock of this quality in our saleroom for months. I'll look into it.'

'So how much is it worth?'

'Conservatively, about twenty thousand.'

'Why so much more than the table? There seem to be loads of clocks about.'

He walked forward and stroked his fingers down the side of the case, as though he were touching something precious. 'This one is attributable to a known cabinet maker. William Dawes worked in Elizabethtown into the first decade of the 1800s. This clock was probably made at the turn of the century.'

'So it's American? How the heck do you know that?'

Daniel smiled. 'Look.' He pointed up at the clock face. 'In a European clock you'd expect to see a brass dial, but metal was hard to come by in America so they used iron and painted it white.'

'Ah. So, how do you know it's by this William Dawes?'

'It's got "William Dawes, Hackensack" on the face. That's a good clue.'

He was laughing at her. Again. A sexy glint lighting his dark brown eyes. It made her feel flustered.

What was the matter with her today? Her whole survival plan was based around control. Control was everything.

But there was something about his brown eyes which ripped through her defences. Made her wish...

Damn it!

She turned away. He was *married*. And she wasn't interested in a man who was prepared to lie to someone they'd promised to love.

'Are you done?' Margaret called from the dining room.

'Are we?'

Freya turned back to him. 'Everything else is small. I can bring them to you when we're more organised. The bigger things we're going to need to have collected.'

He nodded. 'That's a flat fee, and we'll take it out of the profits after the sale. Just let me know what you want to do.'

'It's not my decision.'

His smile was slow in coming, but all the more sexy for that. Her stomach flipped over in a way she couldn't control. 'Somehow I doubt that,' he said, walking past her. 'All finished. I'll put my valuations in writing, and pop them through your door in the next couple of days.'

'Lovely.'

Freya hovered in the doorway, much as he had done earlier. He was wrong. If it *were* her decision her grandma would sell

absolutely nothing and leave her entire estate to her favourite charity.

But her grandma was determined to sell. And she would
probably give her son a large chunk of the profits, because she still
couldn't bring herself to say no to him. And she'd use Daniel's
auction house, whatever anyone said, because she liked him.

Freya looked over at Mia, who had finished her drink and
was already standing up. It couldn't be much fun for her, being
dragged round to valuations. But that could only be because
Daniel didn't trust her to stay at home.

Did Mum work late, then? She was rabidly curious to know
what kind of woman Daniel was married to. Someone small and
fluffy, she reckoned. Or, she thought, looking at Mia, some
elegant redhead who saved lives.

'We'd better go. Don't get up,' he said to Margaret, who predictably ignored him.

Freya stood back to let them pass. She caught Mia's eye
and winked.

Mia smiled. 'Thanks for the cola.'

'Any time.'

Daniel placed a hand on his daughter's shoulders and steered
her towards the door.

'Bye,' Margaret said with a wave, shutting the door behind
them as Daniel's car drove away. 'Did you like him any better?'

The speculative gleam in her grandmother's eyes had Freya
walking briskly back through to the dining room. 'He knows
more about antiques than I thought he would, which is a start,'
she said casually, stacking the cups on the tray. 'Though I still
think you'd do better finding a larger auction house.'

'I told you earlier—I'd rather do business with someone I like.'

'Most people at least settle for competence in their chosen
profession.' Freya shuffled the saucers to one side to make space
for the teapot. 'I don't think I've ever seen an office like his.'

'I doubt it's like that all the time. He's making do with temporary help at the moment, and that's never going to be as good as a permanent person, is it?'

Freya snorted. 'I'm surprised he's ever had a permanent person. His office is like a sorting office, and every bit as dirty. If you spent much time in there you'd have to be fumigated when you came out.'

'Then, of course, there's Mia,' Margaret offered, as she watched her granddaughter with intense amusement. 'She must take up a lot of his time.'

Freya smiled. 'Which is a dig at me, I suppose?' she said, picking up the tray.

'I can't honestly say my son ever put off anything because of your antics. Daniel's a very different kind of father.'

'I like Mia.'

'So do I. She's a bright thing, but unless she's careful she'll waste it.'

Freya stopped at the doorway. 'I didn't.'

'You were unusually driven. I don't think Mia's the same,' Margaret said, following behind her. 'Unless I've missed my mark, I reckon that girl is floundering. It's no time for a girl to be without her mother.'

'Is she?' Any number of possible scenarios waltzed through Freya's head. Perhaps she'd had an affair and left Mia behind? But then *why* would Daniel still be wearing his ring?

Margaret cut through her thoughts. 'You remember Anna Jameson, as was?'

'Yes. I think. Vaguely. Sophia Jameson's elder sister—?' Freya stopped. 'You're telling me Mia Ramsay is *Anna Jameson's* daughter? I don't believe it!'

Her memories of Anna were sketchy. She was a few years older but—she frowned—from what she recalled Anna had been long, thin, and very, very good.

How in heck had Anna managed to attract a man as sexy as Daniel Ramsay?

'Anna died…' Margaret hesitated, pulling the necessary information together in her head. 'Oh, it must be three years ago last October. Not so very long before Christmas anyway.'

Died. 'Anna's dead?'

Her grandmother nodded. 'Horribly young. She was only in her early thirties, as I remember. I could work it out exactly if I sat down and thought about it.'

'That's awful. I—I hadn't heard that.'

'There's no reason why you should have,' Margaret replied, clutching at the doorjamb, her face convulsing in a sudden sharp pain. 'It's not as though you kept up with Sophia. You didn't like her much, did you?'

She hadn't liked either of them, if she were honest. Sophia had been a real thorn in the flesh. One of those catty girls who seemed to fool everyone into believing they were all sweetness and light.

Anna had been the middle-class embodiment of perfection. Freya hadn't really known her—just about her. Anna had been the best cellist in the school. She'd been a straight 'A' grade student. She'd had the kind of hair that stayed beautifully plaited all day. Red hair.

Hair exactly the colour of Mia's. Hell, but she was stupid. Freya frowned as a new thought popped into her head. 'Anna can't have been very old when she had Mia, can she?'

Margaret's mouth twisted into a wry smile. 'No.'

'So, how old was she?'

'All I know—and it's not much—is that Anna had to drop out of university when she found out she was pregnant. Andrew and Lorna were mortified, of course.'

'Couldn't she have carried on at uni? Gone back after the birth or something?'

'I don't know. You don't imagine anyone ever speaks about it, do you?' her grandmother said in mock horror. 'We all go about pretending we can't do our maths.'

That fitted snugly with everything she'd ever known about the Jamesons. *But Daniel?* That wasn't such an easy fit.

Why would he have got involved with someone like Anna Jameson? Had he loved her? Or just been trapped by circumstances?

He was still wearing her ring three years after her death. He must have loved her. Must still love her.

Freya stepped down in the kitchen and set the tray down on the side. But any man who'd think about getting involved with any member of the Jameson family needed his head examined. And to move here, to be near them…

'Why the frown?' Margaret asked, coming in behind her.

'If Mia's fifteen, I was still here when she was born. How come I didn't know anything about it?'

'Anna didn't come back here. I think she went to stay with some friends of her mother's sister.'

'Until after the baby was born?'

'I really don't know the details, Freya. The official line was that Anna was married, had had a baby and was living very happily in London. The next thing we heard was that Anna had been diagnosed with cancer. Presumably she wanted to be near her family, because they moved back here about six or seven months after that. All very difficult for Daniel, I imagine, as they're not the easiest of families. And Anna was dead inside of a year.'

CHAPTER FOUR

FREYA knew Mrs Runton had been talking about her the minute she walked into the trendy farm shop. She knew it from the sudden awkward hiatus in the conversation, and the way neither she nor the girl at the till would meet her eyes.

She took in a deep breath and made a show of looking at the jars of jams and chutneys, refusing to follow her instinct and walk back out.

'How's Margaret?' Mrs Runton asked. 'I've been meaning to call.'

Freya looked up. It was weird to think the nosy old biddy must be possessed of a first name. But if she was she'd never heard it. Mrs Runton, in her cheap anorak and sensible boots, had always been a disapproving figure.

'She's well, thank you.'

'And your mother?'

Freya turned back to the rows of preserves and selected a champagne and strawberry jam.

'I haven't liked to ask Margaret since the divorce,' Mrs Runton continued. 'I don't suppose they're on particularly good terms now.'

With calm deliberation Freya selected two different chutneys. 'She's well. Just finished renovating her first two *gîtes*.'

'Already!' she exclaimed, as though she'd already known all about the château in Normandy and her mother's plans.

Freya found herself smiling. For the first time since she'd arrived in Fellingham she found it all slightly ridiculous, rather than painful.

'And your father's remarried...?'

Not only had he remarried, he'd done it eight years ago—which only went to show how truly meaningless this conversation was.

'Very happily, yes.' To the perfect trophy wife, if she really wanted to know.

Freya's head whipped round at the sound of the shop bell.

'Freya!'

Daniel looked almost as shocked to see her as she was him. Though, when she took a second to think about it, it wasn't so very surprising. They'd been bound to run into each other again eventually. Only she didn't feel quite ready to yet. She hadn't even begun to process the information that he was Anna Jameson's widower. *That he was single.*

'I didn't spot your car.'

'I hope it's still there.'

'You should be all right. Fellingham's car crime figures are fairly low.' He smiled, but it looked like hard work somehow. In fact, he looked tired. Not surprising, since he'd gone home with a very angry teenager.

'I'm here to pick up a quick lunch.'

'I've been sent to get "essentials",' she said, holding out her basket.

Mrs Runton leant between them to pick up a jar of marmalade. 'Your father settled in Beadnell, didn't he, Freya? I'm sure I heard that.'

'That's right.'

'I was saying to Mary Davidson just yesterday...'

Freya settled some elderflower cordial into her basket and

added a box of six fresh eggs, letting Mrs Runton's voice hum away in the background.

'...we haven't had a doctor in the village like him since he left. He was a wonderful man.'

Daniel moved across to the chiller section, and Freya's eyes followed him. She'd have loved to know what kind of evening he'd had with Mia—but she couldn't really ask. She'd also have liked to ask whether he was still actively mourning Mia's mother. And whether that was why he was still wearing her ring.

Anna Jameson. He'd been married to Anna Jameson.

That was just so difficult to accept. In fact, the concept of Anna Jameson being overwhelmed by any kind of sexual activity to the extent that she forgot to use contraception was unbelievable.

'You remember Muriel, I assume?' Mrs Runton continued inexorably. 'Her daughter Jenny was in your year at school. The same year as Anna's younger sister,' she said, pulling Daniel into the conversation. 'Sophia was in Jenny's year, wasn't she?'

'I don't think I know, Pamela,' he answered, a cheese and pickle sandwich in hand. 'Anna never mentioned her.'

Pamela Runton, Freya registered with a sense of satisfaction. It was nice to have a mystery solved—though Mrs suited her better. Pamela seemed too human.

'You've met our Daniel already, then, Freya?' Her small dark eyes looked curiously from one to the other.

Freya risked a fleeting glance in his direction, wondering how he liked being tarred by association.

'Yesterday.'

'Oh?' the elderly woman said, pausing hopefully, in case either one of them would voluntarily add any more. 'Sophia didn't mention that earlier. And I saw her not half an hour ago...'

Something snapped inside Freya. Her new-found sense of freedom evaporated as quickly as it had come. *They'd been talking about her.* Mrs Runton and Sophia *bloody* Jameson. If she *was* still a Jameson. Of *course* they had. It was all anyone in this closed-off, narrow-minded village had to do.

Freya fought against the sudden spurt of anger. Sophia probably still managed to spread poison with that butter-wouldn't-melt kind of smile on her face. Still managed to stick the knife in with supercilious graciousness and that kind of 'who me?' expression if anyone ever challenged her on it.

She just wanted to scream at the claustrophobia of it all.

'If you've finished your shopping, Freya,' Daniel said, coming to stand beside her, 'perhaps we could grab a coffee and discuss which sale Margaret wants to put her furniture in? I've got twenty minutes or so before I need to be back at the saleroom.'

He was rescuing her. Rescuing himself, too, maybe. Freya looked up and caught the expression in his eyes, which clearly said he didn't want to be left to the mercy of Mrs Runton, either.

'I know Margaret wants it all settled as quickly as possible…'

Freya set her basket on the low shelf at the till point. 'I've got a few minutes.'

The girl behind the till slowly scanned each item.

Mrs Runton came to stand beside her. 'Oh, is Margaret going to sell up?'

'She's thinking about it.' Freya placed her credit card in the machine. 'Nothing's absolutely decided yet.'

'I suppose that's why you're here…?'

Freya ignored the hopeful way she left the question hanging.

'Tell Margaret I'll be round next Monday with the flowers from church, to hear all about her plans.'

Freya almost managed a smile. Her mouth tilted, even if there was no softness in her eyes. 'I'll pack these away in the car,' she said, looking over at Daniel. 'And meet you outside in a few minutes.'

'Great.'

She gathered up the last of her things. Inside her head she was screaming. Living in this village was like living in a gold-fish bowl.

Freya pushed open the door and escaped into the chill of the January morning. She took in a couple of huge gulps of air before walking towards her car. She hated this place. Everyone was going round and round, doing the same things they'd always done, watching and sniping at everyone else.

She tucked her bags into the footwell of the passenger seat and slammed the door shut. How could her grandmother bear to be a part of it? Everyone sniffing about in her business. Everyone thinking they knew exactly what was going on behind closed doors when they most certainly did not.

'Are you all right?' Daniel said, coming up quietly behind her. His hand reached out, and then fell back by his side without touching her.

Freya twisted a stray lock of hair behind her ear. 'Just angry. I can't even pick up bread and milk without running into some-one who thinks—'

She broke off abruptly and pulled a hand across her eyes. 'I'm sorry.'

'What?'

'I don't mean to let it get to me. Sorry. It doesn't matter.'

He didn't believe her. One glance at his face told her that, but he let it go.

'Look, do you want that coffee or not?'

Did she? She wasn't sure what she wanted. He wasn't married, but he was a potential complication she just didn't need right now. A year out, a year free of men, was what she'd promised herself.

'Or would you rather make your escape while Pamela is still marvelling that she knows someone who's renovated a couple of *gîtes*?'

She looked up into his dark eyes, wickedly laughing, and felt much of her anger evaporate. 'Is that what she's doing?'

'Oh, yes. Though she's not at all surprised because "Christine always did like her foreign holidays",' he said, in a passable imitation of Mrs Runton.

Freya's chuckle caught at the back of her throat. She pulled up the collar of her jacket, saying, 'She's a horrid woman.'

'Not so much. Just a bored one.' He placed his hands deep in his pockets. 'Come and have a coffee. Take some deep breaths and forget all about her.'

It was tempting—but probably not wise *because* it was so tempting.

Not wise at all. Then a new thought popped into her head. Unless his sister-in-law's character had changed beyond recognition, Daniel couldn't have heard a single good thing about her—so why was he bothering? He must *really* want to sell her grandma's things.

'Are you sure your reputation will survive being seen in public with the scarlet woman of Fellingham?'

'It might even go up a notch.' His smile twisted. 'You might not like what people are saying about you, but I'm more than a little weary of my own reputation,' Daniel said, bringing his hands out of his pockets. 'Go on—tell me I've not been described to you as a "good boy" or words to that effect.'

'Apparently, you're *nice.*'

'Nice?' Daniel hung his head.

'Uh-huh.'

'Not exciting, is it?' he said, and she began to laugh. Maybe those glinting eyes were more of an indicator of his character than his choice of wife.

'Come on—have a coffee. I owe you anyway, for having been so unreasonable yesterday. Let's call this a peace offering.'

'I didn't behave particularly well myself.'

He shrugged. 'If you think I've been manipulating Margaret then it's understandable. I like you better for looking out for her. She's kind of special.'

'Yes, she is.' Freya looked up into those dark eyes and made a snap decision. *It was just coffee.* And they did have business to discuss. Of a sort. 'Where do we go to get this drink?'

'Annabelle's.' He pointed back towards the courtyard. 'Best teacakes in the business.'

'Great.'

They started across the courtyard and Daniel glanced across at her. 'You know, I've got no hidden agenda as regards Margaret. I just like her. You always know exactly where you are with her. And she's got a good heart.'

'She's equally complimentary about you.'

He smiled. 'You still don't like it, though, do you? A natural sceptic.'

Life had made her like that. It didn't sound so wonderful, though. Scepticism wasn't a character trait people generally aspired to.

'I'm not sure what I think.' Freya glanced up at him. Truth be told, she wanted to believe him. Tall, dark, clever, handsome. Surely there had to be a catch somewhere? 'You drop round for cups of tea, change her fuses, dispose of wandering rodents...'

The glint in his brown eyes intensified. 'Guilty.'

'Why would you do that?'

'She's a friend.'

She shrugged. That was the bit she had trouble accepting. 'I suppose I don't believe anyone does anything without some kind of agenda.'

'But then I'm *nice,*' he shot back quickly.

Freya felt a smile start in her chest and work out from there. *God, he was good.*

She looked over her shoulder. 'I'm reserving judgement on that one.'

His laugh was a bark. Sexy. Staggeringly sexy. What would his reaction be if she told him she'd just sold her business for two and a half million? Would he be intimidated by it? Unable to look at her without seeing figures stamped across her forehead?

She weaved her way through the oak tables and settled herself at one with a clear view of the courtyard. 'What are these?' she asked, turning in her seat to look at the oak chairs with a shelf at the back. 'Are they from a church?'

'Annabelle bought a job lot at the auction. St Andrew's Church over in Kilbury ripped out all its pews eighteen months ago and turned itself into a community centre. We sold everything. Even the pulpit.'

Freya spun back and picked up the menu. 'That's a shame.'

'Why? I'd have guessed you were all for progress.'

'Some things should stay the same.' Like her grandma's house, she realised with a pang.

How unreasonable, considering she'd not visited in more than a decade. But it was comforting to know it was all going on the same. That there was still a walnut tree in the centre of what would otherwise have been a perfect croquet lawn. Still a blue patchwork quilt on the bed in the guest room. Still a small blue dish on the kitchen windowsill, where her grandmother put her rings when she was washing up.

'I'm all for that,' he said, smiling across at her.

'Have St Mark's done the same?'

Daniel shook his head. 'Nothing's changed there. The pews are still being lovingly polished every Friday night, and there's a team of flower arrangers who descend the following Saturday.'

'Good.' Freya smiled and looked down at the menu. 'I used to love St Mark's.'

'You did?'

She understood his surprise—but then, like pretty much everyone else, he didn't know just how many arguments there had been at home. The old vicar had got used to her coming over, and he'd let her sit and read quietly. One of the few who hadn't been blinded by her parents' sham of a marriage.

'Wouldn't that shock Mrs Runton?' Freya said flippantly, turning as the door chimed. An elderly couple struggled to manage the step and lift their shopping basket in. Daniel was on his feet in a moment.

'Thanks, Dan.' The man smiled and nodded across at her.

'I'm sorry I didn't make it out to the farm yesterday.'

'Don't give that a thought. I'm just glad you found your girl before she got herself into any trouble.'

'I'll give you a call later on today and we can reschedule.'

'Righto.' The elderly man nodded. 'There's no mad hurry.'

Freya moved her chair out of the way to make it easier for the couple to manoeuvre the shopping trolley further into the tearoom. She scooted it back in when they'd passed. 'Did you miss many appointments yesterday?'

'One or two.' Daniel sat down and rubbed a hand across the back of his neck. 'It was a long and very difficult day.' He looked up. 'Incidentally, why did you lie about that cigarette?'

'I didn't.' He raised one eyebrow and she smiled. 'Not exactly. I very carefully asked if you had a problem with it being mine.'

'Yes, I got that. But why?'

'Honestly?'

Daniel nodded.

Freya slipped her sheepskin jacket off her shoulders and let it fall on the back of her chair. 'Mia looked at me for help. And,' she said watching for his reaction, 'I thought she was dead meat already.'

The muscle in the side of his cheek twitched. 'True enough, I suppose.'

'I like her.'

He looked up, seemingly surprised. 'I like her, too. But some of the things she's doing at the moment…' He pulled the wooden table number towards him and rotated it between his long fingers. 'I hate her smoking. She must think I'm an idiot if she thinks I can't smell it on her breath.'

'I don't suppose she thinks that.' Freya looked out of the window, distracted by a glimpse of Mrs Runton's red anorak. 'I suspect she wants you to know. On some level. She's just pushing against the boundaries. Working out where they are.'

'It certainly feels that way.' Daniel sat up straighter and smiled. 'So, what are we having?'

'I think I'd like a filter coffee to go with my toasted teacake.'

'Sounds good.' The merest nod in the direction of the waitress brought her over. 'Filter coffee and toasted teacake, twice. Thank you.' He waited until she'd written down their order and then asked, 'How's Annabelle feeling?'

'I think she'll be back tomorrow.'

'What's the matter with Annabelle?' Freya asked, as the waitress disappeared behind a half-door.

'Flu. It decimated most of Fellingham over Christmas. Margaret had it, too. Did she tell you?'

Freya turned back. 'Yes.'

'Is that why you're here?'

'Partly.'

'And partly not?' His lips twitched as she said nothing. 'But you don't intend to tell me?'

'I haven't decided if you're nice yet. I like to make my own judgements.'

His eyes glinted. 'Fair enough.'

The waitress returned with the two coffees and a small jug of cream. Brown sugar crystals sat in a small bowl in the centre of the table.

It was quaint. A real touch of Ye Olde England. If the waitress had been wearing a starched white apron over a long black dress she wouldn't have looked out of place. Freya let her eyes wander up to the exposed beams and felt herself relax. This was lovely.

She looked back and caught Daniel watching her. Something about his expression made her feel as though heat was rushing up from her toes. His thumb moved against his gold wedding band, twisting it round.

She ought to be careful. Daniel might be officially single, but he still chose to wear his wedding band. Men who were looking for a new relationship didn't do that.

Which was probably just as well. She wasn't looking, either.

Freya smiled and forced her mind to think of something else. 'You know, when I left Fellingham the farm shop was basically a lock-up and the barns were just that. This whole Craft Village idea is amazing.'

'It's better in summer, when there are tables out across the courtyard. Some weekends there's a string quartet playing. A couple of times I've heard a jazz band here.'

Freya looked out of the window and imagined the hanging baskets full of lobelia and busy Lizzies.

'Though Christmas is kind of magical, with all the lights. And over there,' he said, pointing to a corner near the bead shop, 'is home to Santa's Grotto.'

'Santa's Grotto?' she repeated.

'In aid of the local hospice. It's been there every year for the past three years.'

'And who gets to be Father Christmas?'

The waitress returned for a second time with their teacakes, and butter freshly curled into two round dishes. Having spent most of the last few years religiously counting every calorie, Freya made the decision to simply indulge. The butter oozed across the top of the teacake and dripped down onto her plate.

'We have a rota.'

Freya looked up. 'For…?'

'Father Christmas.'

'Oh.' And then, as she caught up with the conversation, 'You're telling me *you've* been Father Christmas?'

'Obviously not *the* Father Christmas. He's too busy to come. But I think I'm quite good at it.'

'Being nice?' He wasn't just *nice*, he was chocolate coated. His eyes glinted, and the effect was rather like balsamic vinegar cutting through a sweet dish. Not too nice. Daniel had hidden depths. And when they were combined with the niceness the effect was lethal.

'Exactly. Though I'm never quite sure why parents bring their children to sit on the knee of a complete stranger.'

Laughter hovered at the edge of her mouth. 'Is there much knee-sitting involved these days?'

'Not so much.'

'There you go, then.' She took a bite of her teacake. 'I've not had one of these in years.'

'Why?'

'I haven't had time to sit in coffee shops. Far too busy.'

Daniel lifted the cream jug and let it hover above her cup. 'Please.'

He swirled in the cream, and then poured some on top of his own coffee. 'And too busy to come to Fellingham?'

She looked up, searching for some kind of criticism in his question—but there was none. Only interest.

'That's what Margaret told me when I asked about her family once.'

'I've been abroad a lot.' Freya knew she was trying to justify what was really unjustifiable.

Of course it would have been possible to come to Fellingham before. It was a mere fifty minutes down the motorway from

London. The truth was she hadn't wanted to. They'd spoken on the telephone. Met at her dad's. Her grandma had also come up to London—though that hadn't happened for a good two years.

'And now?'

And now that didn't seem like such a good excuse. Her grandma's hip was significantly worse than she'd ever let on, and her dad was becoming more and more persistent in his efforts to get a chunk of his inheritance early.

Freya's fingers played on the handle of her coffee cup. 'Now I'm between jobs. I'm taking a year out to travel.'

'Anywhere in particular?'

'I'd like to spend some time in Australia. I've got friends who've just returned to Melbourne from London. I'd like to see them.'

'Melbourne's great.' He lifted his cup and sipped. 'Anna and I spent some time there in…' He frowned. 'I can't remember. Years ago. We went during the summer break of Anna's first year at uni.' There was a small beat of silence before he added, 'Brunswick Street. You ought to go there. It's…fun.'

Fun. She couldn't imagine Anna Jameson ever having fun. But Daniel had chosen to marry her. *And he still wore her ring—even though she was dead.* That part really fascinated her. Half the 'happily' married men she knew slipped their rings off on a fairly regular basis.

Perhaps that was just the men she knew. Daniel appeared to still want to wear a symbol that tied him to his late wife.

'I only heard yesterday that your wife had died. I'm so sorry.'

'You didn't know before?'

She shook her head.

'I'm surprised.' Daniel lifted the spoon in the sugar bowl and twisted it about, then carefully patted the sides so that it made a kind of desert dune scene. 'It's usually the first thing anyone says about me.'

'Well, my only source is my grandma—and she's not really ne for gossip.'

'No, she isn't.' He smiled and sat back in his chair. 'She asn't told me a great deal about you, either.'

'So you only know what you've heard in the village?'

'That's about it.' He smiled again. 'And I only believe about alf of it.'

Freya laughed and looked down at her teacake. She loved he way he smiled. The lines at the corner of his eyes. Why did row's feet look so darn sexy on men?

'You wouldn't tell me yesterday, but how long are you lanning on staying in Fellingham?'

'I really don't know. This was going to be a flying visit.'

'But?' he prompted.

'But my grandma's hip is much worse than she told me. I uppose I'd like to see her have the operation before I disap-ear out of the country.'

'Which could be a while if she insists on waiting for the NHS.'

'I know,' Freya said, with a grimace.

'She'd love it if you stayed.' He hesitated. 'If you're between obs, and want to stay in the village for a bit without eating into our reserves, you could always come and work for me.'

'Pardon?'

'Why not?' His fingers still played with the sugar spoon. You're out of work, and I'm in desperate need for some kind f administrative help.'

'You don't know anything about me.'

'I know you can string two words together, and you can nswer the telephone. If it turns out you can type with more than wo fingers you'll be an improvement on what I'm being sent.'

Freya laughed—mainly from shock. She couldn't quite elieve she was being offered a job as a kind of Girl Friday— r that a significant part of her thought it might be fun to accept.

'What did you do before?'

'It was…computer based.'

That was true enough. She'd infinitely prefer it if people in Fellingham remained unaware that she'd built up a successful dot com business, selling natural beauty products worldwide.

'Can you do websites?'

'Actually, I can.' In fact, that was how it had all begun.

'In that case,' Daniel said, sitting back in his chair, 'I'm begging.'

Freya hid her smile behind her coffee cup. 'But I don't want to work for you.'

'Is that a straight no?'

'Pretty much.'

He laughed. 'It was worth a try. Who knows? Perhaps the next person I get might be the answer to my prayers.'

Freya looked at him curiously. 'Can't you contact a different agency if you're not happy with the service the one you're using is giving you?'

He shook his head. 'There are only two agencies in this neck of the woods, and both say there's a dearth of good temps at the moment. Last year there was a glut. But not this year.'

'The good ones will be going somewhere else,' Freya remarked, finishing her teacake. 'Be a bit demanding—'

'You would?'

'I would! If it were my business.'

His eyes were laughing again. She wasn't sure how he managed to do that. His face was completely passive, but his eyes were…dancing. She felt herself melting from the inside out. She was such a sucker for men with eyes like that. It was definitely her Achilles' heel.

'Temporary staff are expensive—'

'Don't I know it.'

'—and I like to get value for money,' she said, picking up her cup.

'Maybe I should just get *you* to phone the agency? See if you can get them to magic up someone who's actually employable.'

'I bet I could. I'm a good manager of people, I think.'

'You *think*?'

'Well, it's not rocket science.'

His eyes were sparkling with laughter. *So sexy.*

'I just state what I want very clearly, and then I make sure it gets done.'

'Doesn't work if the person you're speaking to isn't capable of doing the job.'

'I suppose not,' Freya agreed, looking at him curiously. But then she hadn't ever employed anyone who wasn't.

She'd never employed anyone on a whim, either. And she wouldn't have had a window painted shut in her office. And she most certainly would have been difficult enough to make any agency think twice about putting her to the bottom of their 'to keep happy' list.

But then she wasn't nice.

Freya picked up her handbag. 'I really should get back. Did you want me to say anything to my grandma about different sales, or was that a ruse?'

'Definitely a ruse. There's no question Margaret's items should go into our monthly Antiques and Collectables sale.'

'As opposed to…?'

'The weekly general sale,' he said, with a glance across at the waitress, who came over with the bill on a china saucer. Daniel took his wallet out of the inside pocket of his jacket and placed down a crisp twenty-pound note.

For the first time in a very long time Freya wasn't sure what she should do. She might know a lot about how to run a business, but she was out of her depth when it came to the simple social things. It was the part of her life she'd neglected. 'How much do I owe you?'

'My treat.'

'I—'

'You can pay next time.' The expression in his eyes let loose a million butterflies in her stomach.

No doubt he didn't mean that the way it sounded.

But what if he did?

She fingered her earring self-consciously. 'Thank you.'

The waitress came back with the change. Daniel slid his wallet back into his pocket. 'I'll contact Margaret to arrange a sensible time to collect her furniture, but it won't be until after this month's sale.'

'When is that?' Freya asked, standing up.

'Friday week. The Antiques and Collectables sale is held on the last Friday of every month. I'll drop you round the catalogue for the one up-and-coming, and then you'll probably feel happier about the whole thing.'

'I just want to know she's getting the best possible price. That house is her life's work.'

His eyes smiled. She swore they did. A slow lilting smile that began at the centre and worked out. The butterflies in her stomach changed to something which felt more akin to a million and one ants marching around in concentric circles.

'I know. That wasn't a criticism. I'll drop round the valuations as soon as I possibly can—only I'm without office help at the moment.'

She laughed, picking up her jacket. 'Get on to that agency again. Thanks for the coffee.'

'Any time.'

Daniel watched as she ran across the courtyard, the edges of her short skirt flipping round her thighs.

She really did have longest of long legs. And the sexiest purple high-heeled boots he thought he'd ever seen.

He pulled a hand across his face and let out a breath in one steady stream. Considering everything, it would be better if he didn't focus too much on Freya Anthony's unquestionable sex appeal. He'd got a daughter to parent, and that was going to take every bit of his energy for the foreseeable future.

'Where did she get that jacket?'

Daniel turned his head to look at the waitress, suddenly conscious they'd both been standing looking out of the window. London, I imagine.'

'It must have cost the earth,' Hannah said, placing a teapot on her tray. 'It's just like the ones you see in *Vogue* and that.'

Was it? Daniel's eyes wandered back to Freya, moments before she disappeared round the corner. Probably. It was a timely reminder. Freya Anthony was high maintenance. Too rich for his blood even if he had the time to pursue anything—which he hadn't.

Just as well she thought the idea of working for him—even temporarily—was a bad idea, because the temptation might just have been too much.

'Is it true she's going out with a rock star?'

Daniel pulled on his jacket. 'I've no idea.'

But privately he doubted it. There was such nonsense being talked about her. The rock star boyfriend was just one of many possible explanations floating around to account for her expensive car.

There'd been no mention of any boyfriend in her travel plans. Perhaps Sophy was closest, with her 'between relationships' theory. His eyes helplessly followed as her sleek car disappeared from view.

She seemed like someone who was at a bit of a loss for direction—and a complete contradiction. Confident and yet vulnerable.

He shook his head. He ought to be getting back to work, no
speculating about the personality traits of a stunning blonde
who would ultimately leave Fellingham as fast as her designer
boots would take her.

'Thanks, Hannah. Say hi to Annabelle.' Daniel stepped out
into the windy morning, shutting the door of the teashop behind
him. He lifted the collar of his jacket against the rain.

He liked her. Simple as that. He hadn't expected to, but he
did. With her, he felt like a person. Not Anna's poor husband
Mia's unfortunate father. Professor Jameson's bereaved son-in-
law. Nor in any of the other pigeonholes people were all too
ready to put him in.

And he liked the fact Freya didn't seem inclined to believe
she ought to fill the space in his life created by Anna's death
That made a change.

Why did women so often feel that about widowers? It was
almost as though you hit the eighteen-month mark and it flicked
some kind of switch that sent out a subliminal message across
a fifty-mile radius.

He wasn't ready for that. Still wasn't, after three years. True
enough, the raw ache of the early days had gone—but he wasn't
ready to put another woman into his life. Mia really did need
to be the centre of his world.

The phone in his pocket beeped and he pulled it out of his
pocket, barely needing to glance at the familiar number of
Kilbury Comprehensive to know it was his daughter's school.
The familiar sense of foreboding and sheer exhaustion spread
through him. 'Ramsay.'

The voice at the other end belonged to one of the reception-
ists. He could even pinpoint which one. Carol. Grey bobbed
hair. Extremely controlled. 'Mr Ramsay?'

'Yes.'

'The head has asked me to contact you to say there's been

an incident this morning, involving Mia and another girl in her year. They're both safe, but he'd like you to come in to discuss what we do next.'

It took every ounce of control he had not to swear, long and loud. Even so, it wasn't entirely unexpected—considering the mood Mia had woken up in. She'd been ripe for trouble. Again. He closed his eyes against the images the word 'incident' conjured up. 'Do I need to come now?'

'Preferably some time this morning.'

Daniel glanced at his wristwatch. 'I've got an appointment in fifteen minutes, which should last half an hour or so. I'll come straight after that.'

'Thank you. I'll let Mr Oxendale know.'

He had to ask. 'What kind of incident?'

The well-modulated voice at the other end of the phone hesitated. 'Would you like to speak to Mr Oxendale now? I can see if he's available.'

Daniel could almost sense Carol's finger hovering over the call transfer button, and he rushed to answer. 'There's no need. I'll be in within the hour.'

He ended the call and slipped the phone back into his pocket. He could wait to speak to the head. For now it was enough to know Mia was physically safe. Whatever bad news was coming, he'd prefer to hear it with his daughter sitting in the same room and hearing every word. This was getting serious. If she'd reached the end of the road as far as Kilbury Comprehensive was concerned, what then?

CHAPTER FIVE

FREYA put the last of the china in the box. 'You're absolutely sure you want this to go in the general sale?'

Margaret looked up from her position, comfortably surrounded by old recipe books. 'Just get it out of the way. I've never particularly liked that set, and it'll be one less box to fall over.'

Freya stretched masking tape across the top and smoothed it out. 'If you're *absolutely* sure, I'll take it down with the other two.'

'Good.'

'I won't be long.'

'Be nice to Daniel if you see him.'

Freya let that comment slide past, but she thought about it as she was carrying the boxes out to the car. Her grandmother really did like Daniel. And she'd missed him not coming by the house.

Because of her? Was *she* the reason he hadn't dropped by in over a week? She reversed out of the narrow parking space. Maybe she was being over-sensitive and he was simply busy sorting out his business. Or his daughter? Either one needed lots of attention. But perhaps she *was* the reason.

The valuation had arrived as promised. Badly typed. Pushed through the letterbox when he could easily have rung the doorbell.

She took the final corner and drove straight onto the auction house forecourt, as close to the central doors as possible, in case she needed to carry the boxes in by herself.

Daniel's daughter was sitting on the wall, her shoulders hunched against the cold, and she had the kind of vacant expression that suggested she wasn't thinking of anything much.

Freya reached forward and turned off the engine. It was *Tuesday* morning. Surely Mia was skipping school, and yet sitting on a wall where her father would see her? Which meant what?

She picked her handbag off the passenger seat and opened the driver's door. A icy January wind blew across the forecourt and she paused to button up her coat, aware that Mia's eyes had turned to watch her, almost as though she wanted to talk.

After the briefest hesitation, Freya walked towards her. 'Hi again.'

Mia hunched a shoulder in recognition.

'Aren't you cold, sitting out here?'

'No.'

And then she shivered, which made Freya want to smile. 'It's freezing. Mind, last time I was here I thought it was as cold inside as out.'

A spark of interest lit Mia's tawny eyes. 'Dad said you said that.' And then, 'He's put a heater in the office now.'

Had he? Freya tucked a rogue strand of hair behind her ear. 'Has he forced that window open by any chance?'

Mia almost smiled. Almost, but not quite. 'He took a penknife to it.'

'Excellent! Did it work?'

'Yes, but he broke the penknife.'

Freya laughed.

Mia fingers worked at the frayed cord of her coat. 'You haven't asked why I'm not at school.'

'Why would I? It's none of my business.'

Mia looked up, the expression on her face hovering some-where between surprise and defiance. 'Everyone does.'

'Oh.'

'I've been expelled. For slapping another girl and swearing at a teacher,' she added, when her first statement didn't elicit the response she'd wanted.

'That would do it.' Freya watched confusion flicker across Mia's eyes. She'd have said she wasn't particularly good with teenagers—she didn't have much experience of them—but she understood this one. However brash Mia sounded, what-ever she said, Freya knew she wasn't feeling very 'big' on the inside.

'Dad's really angry.'

She could imagine. 'That's his job.'

There was a sudden spark of laughter in Mia's eyes. They were so like Daniel's when they did that it was a little startling. 'He said that.' The laughter faded and her fingers resumed their picking. 'He says I've ruined my life.'

'What do you think?'

Mia shrugged, and Freya waited. It was the weirdest sensa-tion to know so clearly what was going on in someone else's mind. Or at least to think she did. She could see the fear and hear the need for reassurance in the teenager's voice. 'I don't think it matters.'

'If you've ruined your life?'

Mia shrugged again. 'There are no jobs anyway. You're better off on benefits.'

'You think?' There must have been something in her voice, because Mia looked up curiously. 'It's hard to manage on benefits, you know. Boring when you can't afford to go out. Can't afford to buy the clothes you want. Difficult to find a place to live…' She let the thought hang between them for a moment or two.

'School's more boring.'

Freya looked up at the grey clouds moving towards them. 'Whatever your dad said, you've not ruined your life. He knows that. You've just made it more difficult for yourself.' She smiled. 'And he knows that, too. It's probably why he's so angry. Is he here?'

'Somewhere.' Mia nodded towards the building behind her. 'Probably the office.'

'I'd better go and find him. Are you coming in?'

She shook her head. 'He told me to wait out here for my tutor to arrive.' Then, as Freya started to move away, 'Were you expelled ever?'

She'd been waiting for that question. Freya shook her head, inwardly smiling as she saw the teenager's disappointment. 'I wasn't there often enough.'

'You skived?'

'Waited at the same bus stop you were at the other day and took myself to Olban.'

Mia's mouth quirked. 'Aunt Sophy said you were always in trouble.'

Did she? Well, there was no surprise there. Freya fought back a stinging reply. Sophia Jameson was Mia's aunt, and she'd respect that.

'Not so much. I was more on a mission to self-destruct. I didn't like school.'

'I hate it.'

'I didn't like my home much, either,' Freya said, watching for a reaction. 'I was really angry. Lonely. I suppose I kind of wanted everyone around me to feel as badly as I was, but I didn't physically hurt anyone. Swore a bit. Drank too much.'

For a moment she thought Mia was about to reply, and then something pulled her gaze away. Freya turned to see Daniel walking towards them. He looked tired, which wasn't so very surprising. With Mia having been expelled, he must have had one hell of a week.

'I'm still here, if you're checking on me,' Mia said, her voice belligerent.

Freya looked back. The change in the teenager was dramatic. Her body was hunched, and the life she'd coaxed out of her had vanished completely.

Daniel wisely ignored the challenge in his daughter's voice and came to a stop beside them. 'Hello.'

'Hi.' *Was it her voice sounding so breathy?* 'I've brought some things down for the general sale. China, mainly. And some old enamelware.'

'Okay.'

Freya moistened her dry lips with the tip of her tongue. This felt so embarrassing. Though goodness only knew why. This was an auction house, and she'd brought something to sell. Nothing embarrassing about that. And yet…it was. Really was. That kind of toe-curling embarrassment she remembered from her adolescence.

It felt a whole lot like the way she'd felt when she'd just happened to be outside the Army Cadet hut at twenty past nine each Thursday night, when Calum Dane was leaving.

Only she wasn't fifteen any more; she was nearly thirty. And Daniel Ramsay was no Calum Dane. Even tired, with deep, deep frown lines at the centre of his forehead, he was entirely too gorgeous for a place like Fellingham.

'It's in the car.' Freya moved across to open the passenger door of her car, and went to lift out the box nearest to her.

'Let me see,' Daniel said.

She stood back and watched as he pulled a penknife—presumably a new one—from his pocket, and scored down the tape she'd placed across the top. 'It's china. Pretty horrible, really.'

He lifted out one of the coffee cups wedged in at the side

and carefully unwrapped it. 'That's not horrible. It's Royal Doulton—'

'It says that on the bottom,' Freya cut in. 'I looked.'

Daniel smiled across at her, and her stomach reacted by doing a kind of belly flop. She glanced over at Mia, wondering if the teenager had noticed that one smile from her dad had her hyperventilating.

Since Matt—the male half of her last serious relationship— had packed his bags and left, she'd struggled to summon up much enthusiasm even to date. So what was this? Maybe it was the total abstinence decision which was making Daniel so particularly attractive? The 'you want what you can't have' syndrome?

'It's a nice-quality set. How much of it is there?'

'I've no idea. I didn't count. Sorry. There are teaplates, and a teapot…'

His smile broadened, and she fought against inanely smiling back. He had a great smile. It changed his face completely. Incredibly sexy.

'Let's get it inside, then, and find out. Bob, can you manage the other two?' he asked, calling across to the porter she'd met on her last visit, who'd come to stand in the open doorway.

The older man disappeared for a moment, and then ambled over with a trolley. 'Shall I take that one?'

'No need—I've got it.' Daniel shifted the box in his arms and then started towards the building. 'Mia, give it another five minutes and then you come back in.'

For all the notice his daughter took he might not have spoken. A surreptitious glance in his direction showed he felt it. All signs of laughter had vanished.

Freya helped Bob put the boxes on the trolley, and then paused to lock the door of her car. 'See you later,' she said, looking over at Mia.

She gave a small nod of recognition. Not much, but it was

so much more than she'd given her father. Freya pulled her handbag high onto her shoulder and walked slowly inside.

Her grandmother's box of china was already set out on one of the trestle tables, and Daniel had begun to unwrap some of the pieces.

'There's a lot here,' Daniel said as she approached.

'She bought it all in one of the knick-knack places on Beadnell High Street a few years ago, and it's sat in a cupboard unused ever since.'

'Not that surprising,' Daniel said, putting down one of the small coffee cups. 'Almost everyone prefers the convenience of a mug these days. That'll be the trouble with selling this. How much did she pay for it?'

'I've no idea. I'm not sure she even remembers.' Freya watched his long fingers tap against the side of the box.

'I'm happy to sell it for her, but it won't bring as much as you might expect. It's the same with all those wonderful bone-handled cutlery sets. No one wants them any more. They don't fit our twenty-first-century dishwasher lifestyle.'

Freya tucked a strand of blonde hair behind her ear. 'She's got a couple of sets of those, too. Actually, no,' she corrected herself. 'She's got three sets, but one's so tiny it must be for children.'

'That'll be a dessert set,' Daniel said. 'They're difficult to sell, too. The days of cutting up our bananas with a knife and fork have gone.'

He drew his penknife across the tape that shut the second box. 'This'll be more popular,' he said, lifting out an old enamel flour bin. 'It's not going to make big money, but it's the kind of thing people like in a country kitchen.'

'She really does just want shot of it all.'

Daniel flipped the lid shut. 'Fair enough. We can do that for her. Come through to the office and fill out the paperwork for this lot.'

He really did seem like a man under pressure. Freya slipped her hands into the pockets of her coat and followed him through to his office.

It still had a dank, cold smell about it, but, as Mia had said, it had a heater pumping out hot air. Her eyes wandered up to the grimy window, and she noticed the flaked paint chipped off at the edges.

She looked back and caught Daniel watching her. Faint colour stained his cheekbones, as though he knew what she was thinking.

'Mia said you tried to open it.'

'I thought I'd better see if I could get some ventilation in here, since we're using the fire.'

'Good idea, if Mia's got to work with her tutor in here.'

His eyes narrowed speculatively, and then he turned away. 'I'll just get you a form to fill in.'

Freya watched as he took a grey box file down from a shelf and walked back with it to the desk. 'How long has Mia been expelled for?'

His hands hesitated before he flipped open the front cover. 'Is that what she said? That she'd been expelled?'

'Yes.'

'She told you?'

Freya nodded. 'Shouldn't she have?'

He turned and pulled a hand across the back of his neck, as though that would ease some of his tension. He exhaled slowly. 'She seems almost proud of it.'

'I don't think that.'

'It's not official yet,' he said quietly. 'At least not in the sense that it's still got to be rubber-stamped by the governing body.'

'Will they?'

'Yes.' Daniel took out a new pad of paper and flicked over the first page. 'Oh, yes. We've got a meeting next Tuesday, to discuss the way forward, but, to be honest, there really isn't one.'

Freya said nothing, just watched the expressions passing over his face. His voice was resigned, but she didn't believe he felt like that for a moment.

'It's possible she might be offered a place in a PRU, but she says she won't go.' He reached for a pen. 'That's a Pupil Referral Unit.'

Freya nodded.

'God only knows what she thinks she's going to do now.'

'Maybe she'll be better for a break. At least…' She stopped, searching for the words. 'It's possible that once she sees there aren't a lot of options without exam results she'll want to go back to school.'

'Is that what happened to you?' The question shot from his mouth and pooled in the silence. 'I'm sorry—that's none of my business. I—'

'Of sorts.' Freya bit her lip. She wanted to help. Both of them. She did. But what could she say? Her path wasn't a pre-scribed one. She'd worked incredibly hard, seen an opportunity and made the most of it, but she'd been lucky.

If she ever had a daughter she wouldn't want her to make the same choices. She'd want what Daniel probably wanted for his daughter—safe choices.

'My sister-in-law told me you left before your exams. I just wondered if—' He spoke into the silence and then stopped abruptly. 'I'm sorry—that was rude question, and also absolutely none of my business.'

For days she'd been dodging questions about what she'd done since she'd left Fellingham, and it was no one's business but her own. But Daniel's motivation for asking was different.

'I did,' she said calmly. 'Well, I left when I was seventeen. But I hadn't turned up for most of my exams the year before, and I dropped out of my retakes.'

'Did you go back later?'

'If I'd needed to I would have. When I had to find some-where to live, food to eat, everything made more sense to me.'

She watched a muscle pulse in his cheek. Freya searched for words that would describe the...*drive* she'd found to succeed. 'I was lucky, but if I hadn't been I know I'd have enrolled myself at college and started over. Mia's too clever not to do the same.'

He pulled a hand across his face.

'I know it's not what you want for her, but she'll surprise you in the end.'

'Did she tell you why she's been expelled?' he asked, hand-ing her the pen.

'She said she slapped a girl.'

'And she would have done a whole lot more if a teacher hadn't been there to pull her off. Completely unprovoked.'

Freya frowned. She doubted that. Mia didn't come across as someone who was naturally violent. At least not violent without provocation.

In her first squat she'd known a girl who'd had a chip on her shoulder that meant she despised the whole world. She'd been violent simply because of the turmoil going on inside. But that wasn't Mia. She was sure of it.

Freya accepted the pen. 'Did Mia tell you that?'

'Hardly. She doesn't talk. Her mouth was wired together about two months after she turned fourteen.'

Then how did he know what she'd intended? He might love his daughter, but he was a good deal too ready to accept other people's evaluation of her.

'Difficult to help her if she won't tell me what the problem is.'

Impossible. But...he was her dad, and it was his job to try and work out what was eating Mia alive. And, if he wanted her opinion, she'd begin with the death of her mother. It was a screamingly obvious place to start.

But he was unlikely to want her opinion. He rubbed at his

right temple, as though there were a sharp pain there, and Freya experienced an overwhelming sadness—for him and his daughter.

'You need to fill in one of these,' Daniel said, indicating the form on the desk. 'Basically your name and address at the top there. Then a brief description of what you're selling. And whether you'd like us to post a cheque or come in to collect your money.'

'I may as well collect it.'

'Or I can drop it in when I'm passing,' he suggested. He paused while she looked at the form. 'How's Margaret?'

'Sad not to have seen you.'

'I've been busy with Mia.'

Freya looked up. 'Yes.' *Of course he had*. 'Other than that, she's still determinedly packing. We must have filled fifteen or so boxes over the past few days.'

'All destined for here?'

'Mostly. A couple are full of books. I'm not sure what to do with them.' Freya tried to write her surname in the first space, and then drew a couple of circles on the top of the page. 'I'm sorry—I don't think this works.'

Daniel took the pen and aimed it at the wastebin, scoring a direct hit. 'Try this one,' he said, reaching for another pen.

'Thanks.' Freya bent over the desk and filled in details for the first two boxes. 'I'm assuming you want me to put my name in here?'

'It has to be your name if you're going to sign the form. There's a place towards the bottom to say you're bringing in the goods for a third party and want the money to be released to them.'

Freya nodded, and continued on down the form.

'You're welcome to sit down.'

'This won't take a minute,' she said, trying to remember whether the postcode ended with a B or an F. She settled on F.

Beside her, Daniel shut the box file and returned it to the

shelf. Freya glanced over, noting the way his denim jeans clung to his beautiful male bottom.

Whatever had made her think that? Freya sucked in a breath with lungs that suddenly seemed less effective, and looked back down at the form. Honestly, if Daniel lived in London she'd have been seriously tempted to break her 'no men' resolution.

'Done it,' she said, moments later. 'At least I think I have. I've just put "floral tea service".'

Daniel came closer, and she caught a waft of soap. And the smell of damp cotton hanging about his clothes. It was bizarrely sexy. His arm brushed against hers, and her breath caught as though on cobwebs. She brushed her hair out of her eyes and tried to smile.

This was just the strangest experience. It was a little like walking along a sandy beach and having the tide tug at your toes. Every time she looked at him she felt as though she were sinking a little deeper, becoming more trapped.

Freya blinked hard and stepped back a couple of paces, ready to leave as soon as she possibly could.

'That's great.' He quickly added 'Royal Doulton' next to her description, and then said, 'You just need to sign at the bottom.'

What did Daniel think about her? She just couldn't tell. There were moments when she thought there might be *something*, but most of the time he appeared oblivious. Which was good.

Probably.

Freya took two steps back towards the table.

'Just here,' he said, pointing.

She bent over the table and put her signature on the dotted line.

'That's everything. I'll put the cheque through the door some time.' The door banged behind him and he turned, leaving Freya to return the pen to the chipped mug.

The porter was there, holding on to the handle. 'Chris Lewis has come to deliver that office furniture. Do you want me to tell him to bring his van right in?'

Daniel looked at her, his brown eyes holding a glint of unexpected laughter. 'Do you need to get out first?'

Her stomach reacted predictably. 'Probably.'

'Tell him to hang on a minute. I'll—' He broke off as his phone rang. 'I'm sorry—I have to get this.'

She nodded. 'Ramsay Auctioneers.' A short pause and then, 'Jack!'

Freya looked across at the porter. She ought to go while he was busy. Run while she had the chance. Go back and continue with the packing. 'Is that everything I need to do?'

'You've filled out the sheet, have you, love?'

She nodded and pointed down at the table. 'All done.'

'That's it, then,' he said, coming into the room and letting the door bang shut behind him.

Freya looked across at Daniel, meaning to point at the door as a kind of farewell gesture, but he was looking down at his watch.

'I can't do anything before midday. Mia's got a tutor coming today, and there has to be a responsible adult present.'

Daniel stepped back and his elbow caught a large pile of papers, which scattered over the floor. Freya crouched down and automatically started to pick them up.

He mouthed his thanks and spoke into the phone. 'The agency couldn't send anyone again today. And even if they could I don't think I could leave Mia with them. That's not exactly in the job description.'

Freya looked up as she placed a brown manila file on the desk. Her eyes met his and he gave something approaching a shrug, as though he could guess what she was thinking about the chaos of his life.

She smiled, and gathered together a loose selection of papers. It did look hellish—but that wasn't what she was thinking. In her entire life she'd never felt this kind of connection to someone, a feeling that their problems mattered to her simply because they were theirs. If that made any sense.

There was absolutely no reason for her to be concerned about his relationship with his daughter. Or the way he ran his business. Or the fact he didn't have enough hours in the day to be in all the places he needed to be.

Except she liked him.

How scary was that? She could cope with finding a man sexually attractive. That was a biological response. But to *like* someone was something else entirely. It suggested an emotional connection—and that terrified her.

Freya settled the last of the papers on the desk and then turned as she felt a waft of cold air. A woman, conservatively dressed, with neatly bobbed hair, walked confidently into the office with Mia beside her. The door banged shut.

'I'm Susan Phillips. Mia's home tutor.'

Freya glanced back at Daniel. He pulled a hand across the back of his neck and she fought the desire to walk over and hold him. He looked like a man who needed a hug. 'You'll need to have a word with Mia's dad. He won't be a minute.'

'Look, I'm going to have to go,' Daniel said into the receiver. 'I'll call you back in five minutes.' There was a pause, during which he raked the same hand through his hair. 'I know. I'm sorry, but it can't be helped. Right. Yes. Bye.' He put the phone down and immediately turned his attention to the tutor. 'I'm so sorry.'

'Daniel Ramsay?'

'Yes.'

'I'm Susan Phillips.'

'Hello. Yes, we were expecting you.'

Freya was pushed back against the table as the door opened again and a large man stood in the gap. The already over-filled office seemed to shrink a few feet more. 'Do I get to bring the van in? It's blocking the road.'

It was chaos. A type that would have been unimaginable in her tightly controlled offices.

Daniel spared her the briefest of glances, and then turned towards the man in the doorway. 'Hang on. I'll be with you in a minute—'

'Don't worry,' Freya said quietly. 'It's fine. I'll wait until you've finished unloading.' That part was easy. 'I've got nothing I need to rush off to today,' she said by way of explanation as Daniel turned to look at her.

She wasn't at all sure whether it was part of the home tutor's remit to report back on the home situation, but if it was then this wasn't the best of starts. Mia looked sulky, and entirely disengaged from the whole proceedings. Daniel looked like someone who was being pushed further than he could manage.

'Okee-dokee,' the porter said cheerfully. He ushered the larger man out of the room. 'I'll get a couple of lads to help you with the desks and such.'

Daniel waited until the door had swung shut behind them before turning back to his daughter's tutor. 'A delivery of office furniture has arrived. A little earlier than we'd anticipated.'

Ms Phillips didn't seem remotely interested, merely unbuttoning the top button of her coat. 'We ought to get started. Is there a quiet place we can work?'

Freya hung back. *She could help him.* It would be so easy. She just had to offer. It didn't have to mean anything. And it wouldn't be for long.

'I thought here,' Daniel said, looking at the desk in the corner.

The tutor's mouth pursed slightly. 'We will need quiet in order to concentrate.'

It wasn't so much what she said as the way that she said it. Freya felt her own ire rising at the aggressive stance she'd adopted.

'There's a small kitchenette and a table through there,' Daniel said, pointing at a door in the far left-hand corner, 'but I honestly think you'd be better off in here. Mia and I cleared a space earlier this morning.'

Susan Phillips slipped of her coat. 'We can try,' she said, sounding as though she'd offered a great concession. 'I assume there'll be a responsible adult staying throughout?'

Daniel hesitated. The first time since Susan Phillips had blown into the auction house.

Freya stopped agonising and just acted. 'That would be me.'

Daniel's head swung round in complete disbelief, his eyes unreadable. All of a sudden she wanted to laugh. Freya tossed her hair and set her bag down on the table. 'I'm staying to chaperon.'

CHAPTER SIX

WHAT the—? Daniel raked a hand through his hair. What was Freya doing now? He caught the edge of her smile before she turned back to Mia's tutor.

'Mia's father has an unexpected appointment this morning, so I'm staying in his place.'

'I see.'

Beside him Freya slipped off her jacket and reached out a hand to take the tutor's grey-coloured raincoat. 'Where shall I hang these?' she asked, turning to him.

This was like stepping into an alternate universe. Better than the one he'd inhabited up to now, but certainly different. He'd decided Freya Anthony was a temptation best avoided. For all kinds of reasons. All good. But here she was, offering him a lifeline he couldn't exactly refuse.

But why was she doing it?

'Daniel?' she prompted.

He must look like an idiot. 'Just here,' he said, moving past her and shutting the door to reveal a row of four hooks.

'Have you got a hanger?'

'No.'

One beautifully shaped eyebrow flicked up, and he knew exactly what she was thinking. *She'd* have several hangers. A

indow that opened. Ergonomically designed office furniture
rranged on feng shui principles.

Despite everything, he felt like laughing. She walked over and
arefully slid the loop of the tutor's dark coat over the first hook.

'What are you doing?' he murmured quietly.

She looked up, and he almost forgot what he'd asked. Wide
lue eyes met his. 'Helping.'

Daniel took her jacket from her hands and slid the loop over
he next hook along, taking the opportunity to say quietly, 'This
; going to be at least an hour.'

'That's fine.'

Fine? This was the woman who, less than two weeks ago,
adn't been prepared to wait twenty minutes. So why…? What…?

If she were the kind of woman Sophy thought her, then he was
ardly an obvious target for her attention. He'd got no money to
peak of, and responsibilities coming out of every pore.

'Freya?' he breathed, as she was about to turn away.

She glanced over her shoulder, her incredible eyes full of
iischief. 'Yes?'

With Mia's tutor standing so close he couldn't have the con-
ersation he wanted with her—and she knew it, and was enjoying
very second. He pulled a hand through his hair and watched
elplessly as she walked back into the centre of the room.

'Can I get you a coffee or tea before you start work?'

'Coffee would be lovely. Thank you.' The tutor managed
omething approaching a smile, but it was still fairly tight-
ipped. 'White, no sugar.'

'Perhaps Mia and I could get that?' Freya suggested, looking
t his daughter. 'You could show me where everything is, and
our dad could check with Ms Phillips that she has everything
he needs.'

Mia didn't answer, but she slid down from the low sideboard
n which she'd been perched and walked towards the kitchen-

ette. Considering she'd been fairly vocal earlier about not wanting to do any kind of schoolwork, this was a major step forward.

'I'm not sure this room will be suitable long-term, M Ramsay,' the tutor said, pulling his attention back to her. 'In fact I've got reservations about trying to teach here at all. If we have too many distractions today we'll have to have a major rethink.

The door to the kitchenette clicked shut, and he felt more able to concentrate on what the older woman was saying. 'Of course.

'Is there no one at home who could chaperon?'

'Not since my wife died. No.'

Usually people fell over themselves to offer their sympathy but Ms Phillips was made of sterner stuff. A frown snapped across her forehead. 'Perhaps it would be possible for your re ceptionist to go there…?'

'Freya's not my receptionist. She's a friend of a friend who has offered to help out on this occasion.'

'I see.'

She didn't, because he didn't, either. *Was Freya doing this for him?* It didn't make any sense. Unless she was doing it for Mia

That was possible. But he didn't like the idea as much as he preferred the one which put *him* centre stage.

Susan swung round and looked at the desk he'd carefully cleared earlier. 'I think that will probably be best for our purposes.

'Right.'

'And perhaps your friend would sit in the room off here? I'd prefer it if we had this room to ourselves. I find the students concentrate more if they don't have anyone else to play to. But of course we'll need to leave the door ajar.'

What she said made sense, but his thoughts immediately went to the windowless kitchenette Freya would have to sit in

Susan Phillips settled herself in the chair to one side of the desk looking up at him with a slightly irritated expression and a swift glance at the wall clock. 'As soon as Mia's ready we'll get started.'

'I'll fetch her.' Daniel walked over to the door and opened it.

He wasn't sure what he'd expected to find. From what he ould tell Mia had decided she liked Freya, but whether she had nough 'pull' to get her to co-operate with schoolwork was nother matter.

'Ms Phillips would like to get started,' he said, watching as is daughter poured milk into the two cups on the table. *How as it everything had gone so wrong?*

Freya stood up and took the milk carton from Mia's hand. I'll put this away. The sooner you get started, the sooner you'll e done.' She walked over to the fridge and opened the door.

His daughter pulled a face, but she picked up the mug and glass of water for herself.

'Don't blow this,' he said, unable to stop himself, and winced s she let the door slam shut behind her. *Damn!* He didn't need he flick of Freya's expressive eyebrows to tell him that hadn't een clever. 'I know. Stupid to say it.'

'She won't blow it.'

'You reckon?'

Freya just smiled, but she hadn't been around to see the chances Mia had already thrown away. He glanced down at his watch.

'Are you sure about this? If you want to back out now—'

'It's not for long.' She returned to the other side of the table nd sat down, cradling one of Anna's hand-thrown mugs in her ands. One of the early ones, made during the time she'd been xperimenting with glazes. 'Do I stay in here?'

Daniel nodded. 'I'm sorry.'

'I offered. Actually—' her smile widened '—I didn't give ou much choice.'

'Why?'

'Because I can. Because it's a nice thing to do. Because if I ;o home and say I didn't my life won't be worth living.'

That reason coaxed a smile out of him.

'And you know I'm right.' Freya sipped her coffee, her eye
watchful above the rim.

'If you're sure…?'

'Are you always this difficult to help? Make your call, do
what you need to do, and come back when you've finished. Thi
is a piece of nothing.'

Just like that. For the first time since he'd met her he could
see something of Margaret in her. That same determined tilt o
the chin, and the same laughter hidden deep in the dark blue o
her eyes. She knew he was finding it hard to accept help, and
there was a part of her that was really enjoying that.

Truth be told, he'd have been a darn sight more comfortable
with the whole thing if it were Margaret sitting there. Freya came
with baggage, for want of a better word. Certainly a poor reputa
tion—and, while he preferred to take as he found, he wasn't at al
sure he wanted too much interaction between her and his daughter

But what choice had he? Daniel pulled his hand through his
hair, easing his fingers across the sharp pain at the base of his
skull. 'I'll pay you for your time.'

The twinkle in her eyes deepened. 'Just go. We can talk
about that later.'

'Thank you.'

'Go!'

Daniel pulled his mobile from his pocket. 'I've got this
switched on if you need me.'

Freya nodded.

'Mia knows the number.'

She laughed.

Daniel felt the tension ease from his shoulders. 'Okay
I'm going.'

Daniel swung his estate car into the auction forecourt, half
expecting to see Freya's car gone. Two hours was too long.

Damn it! He should have phoned. No, actually, he should have ust come back to coincide with the end of the tutoring session. If 'reya was madly tapping her foot he'd only have himself to blame.

And goodness only knew what kind of mood Mia would be 1. He'd promised to take her up to Stotfold Farm so she could o riding with Sophy this afternoon…

He slammed the door of his car. The fact he'd discovered a eritable treasure trove shouldn't have been a factor.

'Mia? Freya?' Daniel called. He pushed open the door of the ffice and immediately saw the two of them laughing, sur-ounded by box files and half opened boxes. He took a moment o take it all in. The reality was completely different from nything he'd been imagining.

His daughter looked up. 'We're sorting through the archives.'

'So I see.'

'Freya can't stand mess.'

Daniel looked across at Freya, with the sleeves of her ashmere jumper pushed up and her blonde hair pulled back in loose ponytail, soft fronds falling about her face. She looked s if she thought she might have been caught doing something he shouldn't.

'Guilty as charged. Do you mind?'

So much younger than she'd looked the first time he'd met er. Less intimidating, if he was honest. Enchanting. He wasn't ure where *that* thought came from, but it slid into his brain and ettled there.

And Mia was happy. Sophy might think she'd be a disastrous nfluence, but all indications were to the contrary. And since vhen had he ever rated Sophy's judgement highly?

'Don't let me stop you.'

His daughter stood up and reached for a pad on the table. We've taken all the messages. There are a couple of important ines.' He reached out for the pad, but his eyes were on Freya.

Somehow she'd worked a little miracle and he was *beggare.* if he knew how.

'Thanks.' He cleared his throat. 'I'm sorry I'm so much late than I thought.'

'We phoned Margaret so she wouldn't worry,' Mia said 'And Aunt Sophy to say I'd be late for riding. Freya says peopl get less irritated if they know what's happening.'

Daniel winced. 'I should have phoned you.'

'We had your number if we wanted to call you. We were fine Warm,' Freya said, in a voice full of soft laughter.

His daughter brushed dust off her jodhpurs. 'This place i really dirty, though.'

'When we've cleared the floor you can mop it.'

Mia held out a pair of grubby hands. 'Cool.'

A real miracle. Daniel watched as the miracle-worker close a wallet folder and set it on the pile to her left. As though sh felt his gaze, she looked up—and then she smiled.

There was a whole movie industry built around the powe of that kind of smile. It was just a smile, and yet it wasn't. Sud den wanting swept through him. He hardly knew her—kne there were a thousand and one reasons why it was better thing stayed that way—but for the first time in years he felt— Jus that. *Felt.* Something. Anything.

He'd spent years now in a kind of limbo. A kind of nothing ness. He woke up, he went to bed, and in the middle he got or with things. But in the space of a moment he knew he wante more than that. He wanted her.

He pulled his gaze away and transferred it to his daughter. Tha was where his attention should be focused. All the time. On Mia

Anna would expect that. He'd promised her he'd take car of their daughter. *Promised her.* And that promise didn't includ taking time out to get involved with a woman she probabl hadn't liked.

'I can take you up to the farm now. I'll get Bob to listen out or the phone.'

'But we've not finished,' Mia said, her eyes travelling over he controlled chaos.

Whilst he was thrilled to see this embryonic sense of respon-ibility, he really wanted to be gone. He wanted to shut the door n all this and think about what was happening to him. Some-ow, in the space of a few minutes, everything had shifted for im—and he really didn't like it. 'It'll all still be here later.'

'But it's sorted. It just needs putting away.'

He hadn't seen Mia so engaged in anything for the longest ime. Daniel put his hands deep into his long wax coat and traightened his spine a fraction. He was out of his depth here, nd entirely uncertain what he should do.

In his peripheral vision he saw Freya get up from her knees. he straightened her wrap-around jumper across her breasts and moothed out her black trousers.

What had Anna thought of her twelve years ago? What vould she have thought now?

'How would it be if I stayed to make sure we don't go back-vards and you go off riding?' Freya smiled over at Mia.

'There's no need—' he began, but the lift of an eyebrow ilenced him. He was beginning to sound like a broken record ven in his own ears. What possible excuse could he give that vouldn't sound lame? She was offering to sort out his paper-vork, not move into his home and fill it with cupcakes.

He smoothed out the tension in the back of his neck. 'Are ou sure Margaret can manage without you?'

'She's out at the Women's Institute fundraiser. I'm better off ere.'

Fellingham's very own 'bad girl'—and he was falling for her ook, line and sinker. Did Freya know that? And, if she did, how lid she feel about it?

Mia reached for her jumper, which had been draped over the back of a chair, and pulled it over her head. 'As long as we don' have to start from the beginning again, I'm cool. It's taken way too long.' She looked at Freya. 'Shall we finish this tomorrow?'

Freya looked across at Daniel, a slight question now in those beautiful dark-lashed eyes. It said, *What do you want?*

And he didn't know. If it were just the offer of some reliable office help that would be easy—but it wasn't. Not for him, ever if it were for her.

'Freya's here to help Margaret,' he said lamely.

'I can manage a couple of hours a day,' Freya said, looking directly at him. 'If it'll help? Perhaps we could combine it with Mia's tutor's visits, and that'll free you up too?'

Two hours every day. He'd see her every day. And then one day she'd leave. She'd go back to her glamorous London life. The kind that required soft suede jackets the colour of clotted cream and high suede boots.

How would he feel then?

And what about the alternative? What if she stayed? In Anna's house? With Anna's daughter? *With him?*

Daniel pulled his car keys from his pocket. 'If you're going riding, I'd better take you up to Sophy's now. There's no need to stay if you need to get away,' he said, risking a look at Freya. 'Bob'll mind the phones.'

Her smile dimmed, and he immediately felt awful. Her eyelids hid the expression in her eyes, but he knew he'd hurt her. His hands balled into fists by his sides.

He was making a mess of this. Something else he was making a mess of.

'I'm feeling really awkward about all this.' He pulled the words out. 'I'm completely wrecking your day. Your stay with Margaret…'

'Actually, I love doing things like this.'

She smiled, and he felt his chest grow tight. Was she really trying to convince him he was doing her the favour? Daniel forced his fingers to relax.

'My plans are really fluid, but I'm going to be here another couple of weeks at least.'

Two weeks wasn't long. He wasn't sure whether that was a good thing or a bad thing. From the hard ache in the centre of his chest he was inclined to think it fell more on the side of 'bad thing'.

'Are we going, then?'

Daniel turned his head to look at Mia. 'Have you got everything you need?'

'I left my stuff up at Aunt Sophy's.'

'Okay, then. Let's go.'

'See you tomorrow, Freya,' Mia said, opening the door.

Two weeks of Freya Anthony in his life. How did he feel about that?

CHAPTER SEVEN

FREYA slipped an invoice for January into its proper place and shut the file. She loved this. She really did. Creating order out of chaos was balm to her soul. Right from a little girl, she'd loved setting everything to rights.

More unexpected was that she genuinely liked being in this place. She liked the steady tick of the old station clock on the wall by the door, the smell of… She sniffed. She wasn't exactly sure what the smell was. It was a kind of mustiness, but not quite and not unpleasant.

She lifted the box file and went to put it back on the high shelf she'd assigned to it. She liked knowing she was being useful, too. Without even thinking about it she could find things to do which would keep her busy for months.

Two weeks she'd told Daniel—and that was about right. Long enough to do some good. Short enough to do no harm.

Freya picked up a second box file to return it to the shelf and then hesitated as she heard voices some way in the distance. She set the box on the shelf and turned in time to see the door open.

'You're still here.'

'I've just got those to put up here,' she said, indicating the eight box files on the floor, 'and then I think I'm done for today.'

Who was she kidding? Two weeks was plenty of time to

wreak havoc. Seeing him was like being kicked in the solar-plexus. And it was so unexpected. Daniel looked like a living personification of *Country Living* magazine—wax jacket, snug jeans, hair crisply curling from the damp air outside.

Up to now she'd thought she was a city girl through and through, but there was something incredibly seducing about it all. Sexy.

But then with or without the wax jacket Daniel was sexy. Something about his eyes, she reckoned. The crinkle at the corner which made her want to smile back. Or maybe it was the frown at the centre of his forehead that made her want to smooth the lines out with her finger.

He shrugged out of his jacket and threw it over the newly cleared desk. 'This looks amazing. You've done a great job.'

For someone who'd created a successful business from tiny beginnings that shouldn't have meant as much to her as it did. It's going to look better than this.'

His eyes narrowed, then he thrust his hands deep into the pockets of jeans. 'I thought you didn't want this job.'

'I don't,' she said quickly. 'Not as a job.'

'Then why do this?'

She drew a shallow breath. *Because you need my help. Because I like you. Because I can.* The answers were easy to find, less easy to say. 'Why not?'

The frown lines above the bridge of his nose deepened. 'If it clashes with anything else you've got planned you need to say.'

'Of course.'

Daniel picked up a couple of the box files and carried them over to her. 'I could pay you what I do the agency. That way it'll be a bit above the going rate.'

'You don't—'

'This is a deal-breaker.' He turned to look at her. 'The fact you're prepared to chaperon Mia if needed is worth a lot.

Obviously I'll try and be here, but…' He shrugged. 'A safety net would be great. I'd appreciate that.'

Was this the moment she ought to tell him just how much she didn't need his money? The words hovered on the tip of her tongue and then she swallowed them back down.

If she did it would change things, and she didn't want that. Since Matt had left all the men she'd dated had only dollar and pound signs when they looked at her. Matt hadn't been able to cope with her success. Wealth, she'd discovered, was something of a poisoned chalice. A bit disheartening when it had been her *raison d'être* for a decade.

Freya walked back and picked up another file. He might not even like to feel she was helping because she felt sorry for him. And, actually, she didn't. He wasn't the kind of man you could feel pity for. She just felt an overwhelming sadness for the circumstances in which he found himself.

'Okay,' she said slowly. 'I'll keep some kind of timesheet. That way we can be a bit flexible about it all.' There was a small pause. 'So we have a deal?'

'I think we do.'

Somewhere, not so far to the back of her mind, alarm bells were screeching as he held out his hand. This wasn't wise. She liked him. She might even be falling in love with him. And everything about Daniel was wrong for her.

She stretched out her own hand and let his fingers close round hers. For once she didn't think about whether her hand was on top or beneath. It didn't enter her head to take the dominant position or control the length of the handshake.

His hand felt good round hers. Warm and strong. Her eyes flew up to his face—anywhere to avoid looking at the contrast of her pale skin and his darker hand.

But his eyes were the wrong place to look. The air between them crackled with something she didn't understand and hadn't experienced before. Her breath came in painful gasps and her head felt as if a tight iron band had been wrapped round it. It was a lot like she imagined jumping off a cliff would feel. Exhilarating. Scary.

And she wanted him to kiss her. Every single fibre of her being wanted him to pull her closer. She wanted to know what it would be like to have those hands slide down her back. Her eyes flicked to his lips. She wanted to kiss him. *Really wanted that.*

And for a girl who usually just reached out and took whatever she wanted it was a bizarre feeling to let him release her and turn away. Freya bit down hard on her bottom lip until she could taste blood.

'I ought to be getting back.'

His head turned. She watched the movement of his throat as he swallowed. 'I thought Margaret was at the Women's Institute fundraiser this afternoon?'

'She is. Until three-ish.'

'Then come and get some lunch.'

With him?

'I'm going to grab a baguette or something similar at the Wheatsheaf.'

Freya moistened her lips with the tip of her tongue in a nervous gesture. He made it sound like the most casual of all invitations. Heaven help her, she was entirely out of her depth. She wasn't good at this type of thing. Hopelessly out of practice at reading the subtext.

It was probably only a handful of seconds, but it felt longer. 'Okay.'

Daniel walked over to the door. 'Bob, keep an ear out for the phone, will you? I'm on the mobile if you need to get me.'

She hung back while he picked up his coat, pulling the band from her hair and running her fingers through the tousled curls.

'I won't be long,' he said as Bob stuck his head round the door. 'Forty minutes, maybe.'

The older man nodded. Freya deliberately turned away and busied herself by looking in her handbag for her credit card. She felt…self-conscious. There was no other way to describe how she was feeling.

Out of her depth and self-conscious—and she'd barely even started to think what it would be like to walk into a pub right in the centre of Fellingham. Had he thought at all about what people would think when they saw them together?

'Okay?' Daniel turned to smile at her, leading the way across the auction house floor and out. 'It's literally round the corner.'

'Yes, I know.' The wind swiped across the forecourt and Freya caught her breath as it blew directly into her face. 'It feels cold enough to snow,' she said, huddling down into the warmth of the sheepskin.

'Possibly.'

Freya nervously filled the silence. 'I'm glad you managed to do something about putting a fire into that office. I think Ms Phillips might have been seen running in the opposite direction if you hadn't.'

'She wasn't that keen to work there anyway.'

Freya struggled to keep pace with his long stride. 'She seemed happy enough in the end.'

'Was she?'

'Well, she didn't mumble anything too negative at the end. Just said she'd be back on Friday.'

'We were certainly on trial.' He modified his step, suddenly becoming aware that she was almost running. 'Sorry. Mia's always telling me I walk too fast.'

His eyes wandered down to Freya's feet, and the high heels she'd been tripping along beside him in. Real city girl shoes.

The kind that were designed to go from penthouse to car to restaurant and back.

Soft mizzle began to fall from the grey sky. Daniel looked up. 'Looks like we're going to be just in time. Perhaps Mia's not going to get her ride after all.'

'Where does she go?'

'Stotfold. The hamlet between Paxton and—'

'Yardley. I know it.'

'Her aunt lives there and has a couple of horses.'

'Sophia?'

'Yes.' You couldn't tell from Freya's voice what she thought of his sister-in-law. Was their dislike mutual? It surely must be.

'She and her ex-husband bought Stotfold Farm.'

'Arthur Cambell's old place?'

'I don't remember. They bought about four acres of the original farm.'

They walked past the newsagents and crossed the road towards the Wheatsheaf. Freya's pace slowed. 'The car park is full.'

'It always is.'

'Really?'

'Always,' he confirmed, looking down at her, suddenly sensing how nervous she was. 'It'll be fine.'

Her blue eyes met his. For a moment he thought she was going to deny feeling any kind of unease, but then her mouth twisted into a half-smile.

'You can't stay hidden away for ever. And you have every right to be here.'

She stamped her foot, as though she were trying to bring life back into cold toes. 'Easy for you to say.'

'Your call.' And then he waited.

She visibly straightened her spine and flicked back her blonde hair. 'I think I'm tired of letting other people control what I do.'

'Then let's do it.'

'The last time I was here I was under-age.'

'Was this a regular haunt?' he asked, stepping up under the porch.

'I didn't come here often. If I wanted to indulge in any kind of illegal drinking I didn't try it closer to home than Olban.'

'Ah.'

'I wasn't stupid. At least not in that sense.'

Which meant what? That she regretted the things she'd done? And what exactly were they? The only thing he knew for certain was that she'd left Fellingham with a lad from the local estate. Reports varied as to his name, but all seemed to agree that he'd been several years older and the drummer in a local band.

She pushed the heavy door open and Daniel followed her inside.

'Grief!'

Daniel laughed. 'It's changed a bit. There were one or two complaints when they ripped down the old horse brasses, but pretty much they've managed to keep all of the period features intact and local opinion has come down largely in favour.'

He watched as she scanned the crowded bar area, then took in the careful melding of old and new.

'They've done a good job.' Freya stepped back as a man carrying three pints of beer knocked her arm.

'Sorry, love.'

Instinctively Daniel's hands moved to steady her, coming to rest on her arms. His breath caught as her hair softly brushed against his face, and he was rocked by how protective of her he felt. 'Of course there's a downside to it being popular,' he said, forcing himself to let her go.

The room was humming with conversation, and there were lots of people congregated by the bar, but fortunately there were still some free seats. He made a concerted effort to keep his voice light. 'Any preference as to where we sit?'

'There,' she said, pointing at a couple of sofas tucked into an alcove.

Slightly out of the way. The perfect choice if you wanted to escape too much notice. With real city girl flair Freya cut a swathe across the crowded room and settled herself in the sofa which gave her the best view of the rest of the room.

'If you let me know what you'd like, I'll go and order it at the bar.'

She shrugged out of her jacket and let it fall carelessly beside her on the sofa. Then she crossed her legs, before leaning forward to pick up the creamy coloured menu. 'What are you having?' she asked, looking up.

'I occasionally branch out with a Mexican Chicken baquette, but I've got a bit of an addiction to Spicy Meatball panini.'

Her blue eyes smiled. 'I'll try that, then. And I'd better stay on sparkling water since I've got to drive back.'

'Fine.' Daniel took the menu from her, and then jumped up to place their order.

He'd forgotten how to do this. The casual drink and bar snack. The date that wasn't quite a date, because then there was no pressure and no awkwardness about not doing it again.

This felt awkward. And he'd not considered how difficult Freya might find it coming here. She was on the alert. Jumping each time the door opened, relaxing when it wasn't anyone she knew.

He'd meant what he'd said. She had every right to be here. *Damn it,* she'd been seventeen when she'd left Fellingham. She hadn't committed any crime he knew about. People served less time for murder.

He glanced over his shoulder, fascinated to see that she was biting her nails. Something she couldn't often allow herself to do. One of the first things he'd noticed about her was how beautifully manicured her hands were. He smiled as warmth spread through his chest. Outwardly she was so together, so cool, but that was just a veneer. Underneath there were all kinds of emotions bubbling away, and he really wanted to know what they were.

He turned back to the bar and placed his order with the barman, his mind on anything but. He wanted to know everything about her. Why she'd left Fellingham and, more importantly, what had happened to her since.

What was it that had put the sadness in her eyes? Why was she taking a year out when other women her age were hearing the tick of their biological clock? How was it she was driving such an expensive car? Wearing such expensive clothes? Was any of that important to her?

So many questions and so little time to ask them. Freya wouldn't be staying long in Fellingham. Two weeks and she'd be gone. Maybe a little more if Margaret needed her. Not long.

Drinks in hand, he walked back towards her. 'I let them put in ice. I hope that was okay?'

Freya nodded and accepted the long tall glass. 'That's great.'

He set his beer down on a coaster. 'They'll bring the paninis over in a few minutes. It shouldn't be too long.'

'I'm not the one who has to get back to work.'

'True.' He took off his wax coat and threw it over the back of the sofa before sitting down opposite her.

'Do you like what you do?'

Her voice was full of curiosity, as though it were a question she'd wanted to ask for a while. He supposed it wasn't so surprising, considering the state of his business. She was right when she'd said it needed an injection of capital. But more than that it needed his time.

Daniel picked up his beer glass and took a sip. 'Mostly. But right now I could do with the business being about five years further on.'

'How old is it?'

'Four years. But the whole start-up has been difficult.' His thumb brushed against his wedding ring and he twisted the band of metal round. 'My wife…Anna died in our first year here.'

She should have had more time. The first round of chemo had been successful. Or so they'd thought. But then the disease had swept in for a second time, with a ferocity that had caught them all by surprise.

'She'd been ill for a long time. But the end came quite suddenly. Not so very long after we'd come here.'

'I'm sorry.'

'It was very hard on Mia.'

'Hard on you both,' she countered. 'Did Mia know her mum was dying?'

'Towards the end. At the point at which we were told all her treatment was palliative we told her.' Daniel looked down at the beer in his hand and drew his forefinger up the condensation on his glass. 'It gave Anna time to put some things together for Mia. She kept a video diary, wrote letters. That kind of thing.'

Freya watched him swallow. Pain radiated from him, and it was rather beautiful. He'd really loved his wife.

A new wave of loneliness washed over her. If she became sick, if she died, there'd be no one to mourn her. No one for whom she'd made the world a better place on any kind of personal level.

Daniel managed a smile—the kind people gave when they wanted to pretend everything was just fine. 'She hand-made cards for her birthdays, for her engagement, for her wedding…' He pulled a hand over his face. 'This is a bit of a heavy conversation for a Tuesday lunchtime. I'm sorry.'

'Don't be.' Freya took a sip of her sparkling water. 'Missing her is the best compliment you can pay her.'

He ran his hand down his thigh. 'I wish she was here to deal with Mia. I'm making a bad job of it.'

It was the opening she'd been waiting for, but now it was here she was strangely reluctant to begin. 'Has Mia spoken to anyone about how she feels about her mum's death?'

Daniel shook his head. 'She didn't want to.'

'Then. What about now?'

He smiled and took a sip of his beer. 'Wouldn't that be simple?' he said dryly.

Freya twisted her earring between her forefinger and thumb. Maybe it was arrogant of her to think she had the answers when he must have spent hours thinking about how to help his daughter.

Only...what if she did?

'She's angry.'

'I know that.'

'And she's scared.'

His hand hesitated on the way up to his mouth with the beer glass. 'And you know that how?'

'Because I was scared. I got tagged as trouble but inside I was so frightened.' Freya let her hair fall forwards, so that it hid the deep blush she knew was burning across her face. She was in new territory here. For all she was suggesting Mia talked, *she'd* never talked to anyone about what had happened to her. At least not someone she hadn't been paying to listen.

In a way she was ashamed, because it didn't seem to be so very much. It wasn't as though she'd been beaten, or sexually abused, or any of the terrible things that hit the headlines. She'd just been unhappy. Desperately unhappy.

Daniel put his glass down on the table. The expression on his face had changed from defensive to attentive. She'd begun this, and now he wanted to know what had happened.

'Of what?'

'Life. My life.' She tried to smile, but it slipped. 'What has Sophia said about me?'

He sat back, looking uncomfortable.

'Don't worry—I know she will have talked to you about me.'
She stopped and waited while a group of three women walked
out of earshot. 'And I know she doesn't like me.'

'No, she doesn't.'

Freya mouth twisted into a wry smile. There was no prevari-
cation. No platitude.

'She says you liked to be the centre of attention. That you ma-
nipulated people and events to suit yourself. You spent all your
time smoking and drinking with the lads from the estate—'

'I get the picture.' Maybe Sophia believed what she was saying?
Maybe she'd even felt intimidated by her? Freya herself only remembered feeling isolated and frozen out of her peer group.

'Sophy isn't always a good judge of character.'

'I did what I could to show everyone I didn't care what they
thought of me. I did do that.' It was funny that Sophia thought
she'd wanted to be the centre of attention when all she'd wanted
was *some* attention. Behind her eyes she felt a sharp prick of
tears, which she blinked away.

'Freya—'

She brushed an irritated hand across her face. 'It's okay. It's
why coming to a place like this is difficult. I'm twenty-nine,
and I'm still worried about what other people are thinking
about me. It's so stupid.'

'We can leave.'

Freya shook her head. 'I wanted this year to be a new start.
Maybe I need to really clear away the old stuff before I'm
ready for any new beginnings.'

'We could have gone further afield. I didn't think.'

'Why would you? You're *nice*. I suspect everyone has always
liked you.'

'Apart from the time I got Professor Jameson's daughter
pregnant. I wasn't so very popular then.'

It was weird how close crying and laughter actually were.

One moment she was struggling to keep back the tears and the next she was laughing. 'I imagine that was a fun time.'

Daniel sat back on the sofa. 'Making Mia was fun. Telling Anna's father less so.'

'Why didn't Anna carry on with her university course?'

'She didn't want to.' Daniel took another sip of his beer. 'She'd only gone to uni in the first place because her parents expected it. And she was doing French and Spanish when she'd really wanted to do something art based.'

'Oh?' From the outside Anna Jameson had seemed to have everything. Freya hadn't ever paused to think about the pressure the Professor and his wife had been putting on her. On both their daughters.

Freya looked up as the door opened, helplessly tensing until she saw that the couple who'd walked in were complete strangers to her.

'We can go. Just say the word and we'll leave.'

She shook her head. 'I shouldn't mind so much what people think about me.'

'We all do, to some extent.' There was an edge to his voice which surprised her. His eyes met hers and his mouth twitched into a half smile. Self-deprecating and sexy as hell. 'What do you imagine people are saying about my parenting skills? Every mistake Mia makes they look at me. I hate that.'

He might be surprised. As far as she knew absolutely no one had blamed her parents for any of *her* sins. It had been more a case of 'Poor David and Christine'.

'I know what my grandma thinks.'

Daniel leant forward, resting his elbows on his knees. 'Go on.'

'That you're a nice man, doing the best you can.'

He smiled, but said, 'Not enough, though, is it?' Then he sat back. 'Why were you scared?'

'Because…' She searched for the words. 'Because my hormones had kicked in and everything was changing, and I didn't know how to unpack any of it because I was still a child. I didn't feel like a child. But then I wasn't an adult, either.'

He frowned.

'And because everything I thought was safe had started to shift about.' Freya felt a sudden bubble of grief burst inside her. She'd talked about her parents' marriage before, but Dr Coxan hadn't looked at her with the kind of expression Daniel had. He cared.

'Freya, what happened?'

Unshed tears seemed to be blocking her throat, making it difficult to speak. 'Nothing as dreadful as has happened to Mia. My parents were both alive. Both well.'

Daniel said nothing, but his warm brown eyes never left her face.

'But my dad met someone else. I think he'd always had a "someone else" but this time it was more serious. I came home from school early and found them together, and he threatened me.'

Daniel swore softly.

'I never did tell my mum, but I think she knew. There were huge rows.' Freya smoothed out an imaginary crease in her trousers. 'And my mum's drinking escalated. She used to drink vodka, mainly.'

'Freya…'

He said her name like a caress.

'She crashed the car once and my dad hit her. Just that once. I don't think either of them knew I'd seen, but I was watching from the upstairs landing. Mum told me she'd slipped on the stairs.'

'Did anyone else know?'

Freya blinked hard, her eyelashes heavy with unshed tears. 'My parents were great at pretending. That was more important than anything. Eventually my mum didn't even object to Dad bringing his girlfriends back to the house. We just didn't talk about it. And they still did the social rounds together. Everyone thought they were very charming.'

'What about Margaret? Did she know?'

'I don't know. We've never talked about it. Even now. I suspect on some level she must have known, but my dad is very smooth.'

'And you got into a bad crowd?'

'It was a slow journey. Eventually they were the only people who would accept me.'

Daniel looked down at the leather of his shoes. 'So what do you think is happening to Mia?'

'She probably doesn't know why she's doing what she's doing. Inside she'll just feel frightened and lonely.'

His eyes met hers. 'I can't be a mum to her.'

'Just love her unconditionally. Someone once said to me that the only people in your entire life who will ever love you unconditionally are your parents. If you're lucky.'

He was listening. She knew it. His body language had changed.

'A husband or wife will have certain expectations of you. Your children will. But if you're really lucky your parents will love you whatever you do.'

'I love her.'

Freya swallowed. 'I didn't have that. But it's really important. It's that unconditional love which keeps you upright, whatever life throws at you. It's the core that convinces you that you're worth something.'

'Self-esteem?'

'I don't believe Mia would have gone out of her way to have a fight with anyone. There'll be a reason, but no one seems to have asked her.'

Daniel bit the side of his lip.

'I know I hardly know her, but she seems to me to be testing everyone. Pushing as hard as she can to find out how far she can go before she gets rejected.'

'By me?'

'Mainly you, I think. But I don't know that. I just know that you do reject her you'll have confirmed what she's feared all long. She—' Freya broke off as a waitress brought across their aninis. Both the same, she set them on either side of the table. Thank you.'

Daniel leant forward and set his beer glass down on the ble. 'I do love her.'

'I know you do.'

He smiled sadly. 'But she doesn't think so. You're right bout that.'

Freya picked up her plate and settled it on her knee, gingerly icking up one half of the panini. 'She hopes you do.' *And it's p to you to convince her.* She stopped short of saying that. here was no need.

'Hell.' Daniel pulled a hand across his face. 'You really on't pull your punches, do you?'

Not when it mattered. 'I like her.' *I like you, too.*

She bent her head to take a bite of her panini. He had no idea ow rare it was for her to actually like someone. To let down er defences enough to make trusting anyone a possibility. With sudden clarity, she wondered whether she ever had.

'I probably did neglect her when Anna was ill.'

'That's not so surprising, is it?' Freya said quickly.

'I was working long hours in the City, taking time out to go ith Anna to her oncology appointments. Days off to sit with er while she had chemo.'

Freya wanted to weep for him. The pain of that time was in is voice. Of course he hadn't thought about Mia. He'd robably been so scared.

'And then she went into remission and we decided to change verything. Move here. Start this business because it was what 'd always wanted to do.' He looked across at her. 'Mia cried

because she didn't want to leave her friends in London, but w
did it anyway.'

He took a deep breath, forcing out a little bit more. 'Withi
months of our being here Anna's cancer was back.'

And she'd died.

Freya sat in silence.

'I should have taken more time to explain to Mia what wa
going on.'

Easy to see that now, but at the time Freya was sure it ha
been an impossible balancing act. She knew a great deal abou
setting up a business. She knew the long hours—incredibl
long—she'd put into the first couple of years of her ow
company. Daniel must have been stretched beyond capacit
Both in terms of time and emotional strength.

'God, what a mess.' He thrust a hand through his hair i
sheer exasperation.

He'd paid her the compliment of not offering her mindles
platitudes, and she didn't intend to do that to him, either. It *wa*
a mess. And the way back would be slow. It might even tak
years. People were hard to fix.

'Thank you.'

Freya put her panini back down on her plate. 'For interfering?'

'For caring about Mia enough to try.'

She cared about them both.

He looked down at his uneaten panini. 'I'm not so ver
hungry now.'

'It's nice.'

Daniel picked it up and took a bite. 'As addictions go, it'
not a bad one. So, what about you now? Are you still scared?'

Oh, yes. His voice was low and quiet, and it seemed to re
verberate through her bones. Her yes followed after. She wa
incredibly scared of what she was beginning to want.

She shrugged. 'I'm twenty-nine, not fifteen.' But the fac

was she was still searching for acceptance. Still wanting someone to love her unconditionally and to be proud of everything
she'd achieved. And she was beginning to want that someone
to be Daniel.

'I don't know that age makes much difference if you don't
have that core of self-worth.'

A trio of women came through the archway to the left of
them and stopped while they waited for the rest of their
party. Freya looked up, more because they were standing
close than because she'd remembered to be nervous. There
was something vaguely familiar about one of them, but she
couldn't be sure until the brunette turned and spoke quietly
to her friends.

The slightly plumper of the other two turned to stare directly
at her, and Freya cringed.

'It *is*.'

Then there was laughter, and the stupid and ineffectual effort
they made to suppress it.

'Stacey!'

Their friend came running. 'I'm sorry, I couldn't find—'

As the group started towards the door Freya looked away,
just catching her name as they left.

'Let's go. I've had enough.'

Freya looked across at Daniel, not needing to ask whether
he'd heard. She gave him wry smile. 'I wonder how accurate
her account will be.'

'Probably very inaccurate,' he said, picking up his coat. 'By
the time she's finished she'll probably have you abducting teenagers and running your own pickpocket syndicate. Let's go.'

When Daniel looked at her she felt precious. *Did that make
sense?* No one looked at her the way he did. And it made her
feel beautiful. Cared for.

Daniel held the door open. 'My dad once told me that criticism is only worth listening to if it comes from someone whose opinion you rate.'

'Good advice.'

'Which means I think you can disregard that nonsense. Who the hell do they think they are, anyway?'

She looked back at him and smiled. It didn't matter that the women were still huddled together in the car park as they passed. Or that they would probably be adding two and two and making seventeen. If Daniel didn't care, why should she?

'I'll talk to Mia,' he said as they walked into the auction house forecourt. 'We're going to have more time together over the next little while. Maybe that'll be a good thing that comes out of her being expelled.'

Freya stopped at her car and searched the bottom of her bag for her car keys. 'I'll be here tomorrow and carry on getting your office sorted.'

His hand reached out to touch her arm. Freya looked up.

'Thank you.'

And then he kissed her on the cheek. A gentle touch of his lips on her skin. Freya gripped her keys hard, willing the pain of the metal biting into her soft flesh to prevent her raising a hand to touch where he'd kissed her.

His kiss hadn't been about sex. Or lust. Or any of the things she'd experienced before. It had been liking. It had been gratitude.

And maybe, just maybe, it had been a little about love.

CHAPTER EIGHT

DANIEL hadn't been able to stop thinking about Freya. All morning, just knowing she was there, working away, she'd filled his mind. It was why he'd deliberately come back late. He'd needed to prove to himself he could.

It couldn't be for much longer. The two weeks she'd suggested were already over. He was on borrowed time.

Daniel opened the door to his office, and he could smell her perfume hanging in the air. So faint, but it seemed to surround him. There were traces of Mia, too. Her make-up bag left open on his desk. Some of her GCSE Art work laid out on the desk in the corner.

He walked over and studied it. She'd inherited more than her colouring from Anna. She seemed to be doing something on mermaids. The silhouettes were strong, but the overall effect was rather eerie. Anna would have loved it. She'd have encouraged Mia more than he'd done—or could.

'The girls have gone out,' Bob said, popping his head round the door.

Daniel looked over his shoulder and let the drawing fall back on the desk.

'Freya said to say she'd left you a note. Somewhere by the computer, she said.'

'Here?' He walked over to pick up the folded A4 shee propped up against the screen.

Bob shrugged. 'Don't know. After that tutor woman lef they went out. Said something about a window.' He shrugge again. 'Can't rightly remember.'

Daniel opened the sheet. *Freya's handwriting.* He'd got use to seeing it on scraps of paper. Messages telling him to phon someone or other. Asking him to clarify what some piece of pa perwork she'd found was. More often than not with some kin of curlicue or abstract doodle somewhere.

'They've gone up to St Mark's to look at the stained glas window.'

'That was it.'

Bob left and Daniel sat down at his desk, strangely reluctan to get down to any work. The art nouveau mirror which had com in earlier would normally have had him happily researching t see if he could attribute it to Liberty. He did open his notebook but that was about as far as it went. His mind was elsewhere.

He glanced up at the station clock on the far wall. They' still be there. He might prefer to think he wanted to join then because he needed to work on his relationship with Mia, bu he knew that more than half the pull was Freya.

The woman he'd been thinking about since the moment he'd woken up this morning. The woman he'd thought about yester day. And the day before. And the day before that.

He pushed back his chair and stood up. *Damn it.* There couldn' be any harm in going to join them if Mia was there. Howeve tempted he was, he couldn't kiss her with his daughter watching The thought of kissing her was beginning to be all consuming.

'You off for lunch?' Bob asked as he passed.

Daniel raked a hand through his hair. 'I'll grab a sandwich My mobile is on if—'

'If we need you,' the older man finished. 'I've just accepted whole load of pictures. There's a couple of paintings and some drawings. What do you think?'

'I'll check them out when I get back.' Daniel looked up at a rug which was hanging from a high rail. 'I'm not so sure about that, though.'

'No reserve. We should be able to get it out of here.'

Daniel gave a grunt and then walked back out of the auction house, car keys in hand. He hesitated, and then put them in his coat pocket. If he drove up he might miss them, and St Mark's was barely a mile across the fields.

Daniel followed the hedge round to a narrow stile which marked the entrance to a public right of way. The old church was immediately visible, its grey stone tower dramatic against the stormy skyline. He raised his collar against the sharp wind and lengthened his stride.

He heard Mia before he saw either of them. She was laughing, and he felt a huge weight drop from his shoulders. It was a sound he'd not heard in such a long time. He only hoped she wouldn't freeze up again the minute he appeared.

It didn't matter how often he told himself he had to be the adult in their relationship. That it was better she took her grief and frustration out on him as opposed to other people. It still hurt.

'Dad!'

Freya turned her head to look at him, her hair blowing in the wind. He liked her hair loose and blown about. And he loved it when she smiled. Her sensual mouth curved in a way that sent his libido into the stratosphere.

'You got our note?'

'This window is wicked.'

Daniel looked over at the impressive circular window which had been the object of such devoted fundraising when he'd first arrived in Fellingham. 'Why do you need to look at it?'

'I'm going to draw it. It's going to be a part of a series.' Mia held up her phone. 'I've got some great pictures.'

'Don't forget to take a photo through the arched gate.' Freya said, settling herself on a bench. 'Then we can get back. My ears are frozen.'

Daniel smiled, sitting beside her. 'You need a hat.'

'Too late now. Hurry up, Mia. I've had enough.'

Rather than complain, Mia flicked through the photos she'd already taken and then started off down the path. Daniel watched her until she'd disappeared. 'I didn't know she needed pictures of windows.'

'She didn't. It was something they talked about during today's session, and I remembered this one as being pretty spectacular. Mia's spotted all kinds of other possibilities. She's really good at all this stuff.'

'Like Anna.'

Freya huddled down in her sheepskin jacket, her hands firmly in her pockets. 'In case she forgets to tell you, she needs to get some more charcoal.'

'Right.'

'And some special kind of pencil. An HB-something. But they're all HBs, aren't they?' Freya turned her head and caught him smiling.

'I suppose I don't need to wait for Mia to finish now you're here—'

'Have you seen inside?' he asked, cutting across her.

'Will the church be open? I didn't think to try. I assumed it would be shut up against vandals.'

'No, this one is kept open. The vicar thinks it's important.' He stood up.

'Shouldn't we wait for Mia?'

'I will. You can go in and look around.'

Freya jumped up. It hadn't even occurred to her that the church would be open. Too long living in London, she supposed.

'Nice boots, by the way.'

She glanced down at her sensible walking boots, and then up into his glinting eyes. 'Fellingham's not exactly the right terrain for my Jimmy Choos. I bought these in Olban at the weekend.'

Freya stepped up into the stone porch and moved to take hold of the heavy iron handle. It twisted easily in her hand. 'It *is* open.'

'Didn't you believe me?'

She glanced back into his teasing eyes and her stomach dropped a few hundred feet. Freya stepped down into the church and the smell of polish and fresh flowers met her like a wave. Thick white candles were set in each of the arched windows, and the blue-grey winter sunlight streamed through the stained glass window behind the altar.

Just beautiful. She wasn't much of a churchgoer, but this place had always felt holy. She loved the solid feeling of permanence, and the way the flagstones had been worn down by the hundreds of feet that had walked over them. And she loved the hand-stitched kneelers that were hanging on the back of the pews.

Freya picked up the visitors' book and flicked through it, glancing behind her as the door opened and Daniel stepped inside.

'Mia will come in in a minute.'

'Okay,' she said, turning back to the book in her hand. 'You know, people have come here from Australia and Thailand. And there's quite a few from the States.'

Daniel stood so that he could read over her shoulder. She could feel the warmth of his body. If she turned around she'd almost be in his arms.

'There's a steady stream of tourists who come to trace their family trees. Apparently there was a whole contingent who emigrated from here after industrialisation made life tough in the country.'

Freya traced her finger along 'Randy and Laura Williams' to read their comment. 'They're right about it being a special place. I always thought that.' She shut the book and set it back on the top of the oak table.

Daniel stepped back to allow her to pass. He paused to look along the pews and up towards the altar. 'I've not been here in months.'

'Is Anna buried here?' Freya asked, as the thought occurred to her.

He nodded.

Freya bit her lip, wishing she hadn't asked that question. If she'd paused to think before she spoke she'd have known that it was likely. The Jamesons had always been church, not chapel.

'She was christened here. Confirmed, too.'

And then buried. Freya breathed in the comforting smell of polish. It was so incredibly sad.

'Were you christened here?' he asked.

'Oh, yes. My parents had some kind of big formal do with everyone they knew invited.'

'Nice.'

'Daft. They weren't churchgoers, but they dressed up and made promises which meant absolutely nothing to them. Their only purpose was to get nice glossy pictures.'

Freya turned away and started walking down the centre aisle, looking down each row of pews as she went. 'Here it is.' She pulled one of the kneelers off its hook. 'This was my favourite. I used to use it as a cushion when I came here to read. I've no idea why I liked it so much now. Perhaps because it had flowers on it. I don't know.'

She looked round to see Daniel standing facing the altar. His face looked sad. Freya put the kneeler back in place and walked out to join him. 'Does it make you sad to be here?'

'No, not really.'

She paused, and then asked a little hesitantly, 'Were you thinking about Anna's funeral?'

He looked down at her and smiled. 'Am I that easy to read?'

To her, yes. She was beginning to find it very easy to sense his moods—and, more amazingly, she cared about them.

'I think pretty much everyone came from the village. The church was crammed full of people. I can't honestly remember who was here and who wasn't. They were just a sea of faces.'

Freya remained silent, watching each change of expression.

'It was good, though. Anna would have liked it. If that makes any sense,' he said, looking down at her. 'And in the end it was a relief for it all to be over. I was so tired.'

Daniel brushed a hand across his face and walked back up the aisle towards the font. Freya's eyes followed him. It all made perfect sense to her. Watching someone you loved suffer was desperately hard. She could imagine wanting it to be over, and then feeling guilty when your wish was granted.

Did Daniel feel like that? Did he *still* feel like that? It explained why he'd not spoken to Mia about Anna as much as he should. It was all so sad.

Freya took another deep breath, loving the sense of peace that seemed to permeate every stone, and looked up at the high vaulted ceiling. She'd like to be buried here. Eventually. There was a certain symmetry to the whole thing. Christened. Married. Buried.

She looked back at Daniel, standing by the doorway and thumbing through a hymnbook he'd picked up off the side. 'Did you get married here?' she asked, walking towards him.

He smiled, his eyes suddenly laughing again. 'You're forgetting Anna was already pregnant with Mia. By the time we did the decent thing she was already seven months gone, and her parents couldn't have coped with a wedding in their village.'

'I must have still been living here,' she said, inconsequentially. 'How old was Anna then?'

'Twenty.'

Freya did a rapid calculation. 'Yes, I was. Fifteen. I was Mia's age now.' She smiled up at him. 'Just think—if you'd married here I'd have come to watch. I was a real wedding groupie.'

'Why?' he asked, holding open the door to the church.

'I liked to see the dresses. I used to sit on the wall over there and watch them all.'

His eyes softened as they looked at her. She'd got absolutely no idea what he was thinking, but it sent a warm shiver coursing through her body.

'It seemed like such a fairy tale. I particularly liked the brides who arrived in a horse-drawn carriage. That seemed so romantic to me. Less so when it rained, of course,' she added with a smile.

'Is that what you'd do?'

'If I got married?'

He nodded.

Freya laughed to hide her sudden embarrassment. 'If I ever trusted anyone enough to make that kind of commitment I'd do the whole thing. I'd want the big white dress, and to wear something borrowed and blue.'

'And carry myrtle?'

He was laughing at her. She knew it from the wicked gleam in his eyes, but suddenly she didn't care. She'd spent so many years hiding behind a tough nothing-can-touch-me exterior when actually she really did want the whole fairy tale.

'I'd do it all. Why not? You only do it once.' She wanted a happy-ever-after with a man who kept his promises. *With a man like Daniel.*

'I'd have thought you'd have chosen an up-market London hotel and given it all a minimalist theme.'

'I'd have a veil and orange blossom. And one of those huge three-tier cakes with icing so thick it can't be cut without snapping. And my groom would wear full morning dress.'

'And if he objects?'

'He's marrying the wrong girl. Weddings should be romantic, don't you think? Or why do it?'

He seemed slightly stunned, as though her answer had been the last thing on earth he'd expected her to say.

It probably was. No one would ever have expected that the girl who'd sat drinking cans of lager in the bus shelter was also a girl who'd drawn ball dresses in her notebook.

'What kind of wedding did you have?'

'A quick registry office do in Hillingdon, where we were living.'

'Oh…'

'I know.' He smiled. 'It wasn't at all romantic. To be brutally honest, Anna's parents had ruined any chance of that. They treated her pregnancy like some kind of Greek tragedy.'

'But they love Mia now?'

Daniel hesitated. 'As long as Mia behaves in the way they want. They have very high expectations.' He carefully shut the church door behind him. 'I don't think Anna even had a new dress for our wedding. I can't remember.'

'Daniel!'

He laughed. 'But we did the deed.'

And they'd been happy—until her illness had robbed them of all that.

'Did you stay in Hillingdon?'

'For a few years. Then when I'd started earning better money we moved further into London—to Fulham.'

Freya stopped walking. 'Fulham! That's a *lot* better money. What did you do?'

'I was a trader.'

'On the Stock Exchange?'

'Uh-huh.' Then, his eyes glinting down at her, 'Surprised?'

'Very.' More than surprised. 'That's a hell of a change. City trader to country auctioneer.'

'Huge.' Daniel looked about him. 'No sign of Mia. We'd better go and wait for her back on the bench.'

'Did you always want to be an auctioneer?' Freya asked, following him.

'No. Actually, paintings fascinated me more. If I'd not been quite so money-orientated I'd have headed off for some kind of art-connected thing.'

'Painting?'

He shook his head. 'I'm strictly art appreciation. I've got zero skill when it comes to the creative side. I'd have liked to run my own gallery. Something like that.'

Freya sat down and studied his profile. How *extraordinary*.

'It's how Anna and I got together. We met at an exhibition of Lowry's paintings. They were on loan from the gallery in Manchester—' He stopped. 'What?'

'So where did the auctioneer bit come in?' Freya asked, holding back her hair from the wind.

Daniel crossed his ankles and leant back. 'That was a much later passion. We kitted out our entire first home at an auction, and I just loved it. The smell as much as anything, I think. Mustiness and chip fat. It's a heady combination.'

His sexy eyes invited her to laugh at him, as though he thought it was impossible she'd have any understanding of that.

'I just found it exciting. We'd talked about it, Anna and I. Those kind of "what if" conversations you have.'

No. She'd never had a 'what if' conversation, because she'd never been in any relationship where she'd talked of the future. Planning a couple of months ahead had seemed like a bit of a commitment.

Daniel continued, oblivious. 'Anna fancied moving to the South of France and living a self-sufficient lifestyle.'

Anna! She really hadn't known her at all. The woman Daniel had loved was absolutely nothing like the girl she'd imagined her to be.

'Was that a no?'

'My French is appalling, and it seemed like too much of a hand-to-mouth existence to me, so we compromised on my dream. Sold up, cashed in all our investments, and bought the auction house here.'

'Do you regret it?' Freya asked curiously as Mia appeared round the corner.

'Leaving London? Not in the slightest. I'd only ever seen that as a short-term thing. If I was going to have to work I thought I ought to make some money at it.' Her face must have shown her incredulity, because he laughed out loud. 'You look so shocked.'

'Only because people don't *do* that sort of thing! The odd journalist, perhaps. But I reckon that's only so they can write about it.'

'Aren't *you* downshifting? I thought you were having a major life re-adjustment?'

She was. She was doing just that. She'd sold up her business and was searching about for something she could pour her heart and soul into. 'Yes, but I wouldn't dream of buying an auction house. That's a real learning curve.'

'Except my uncle is an auctioneer down in Brighton and my dad is an antiques dealer in Petworth. It was a lot like returning to the family business. Finished?' he asked Mia as she joined them.

'Yeah. I guess.'

'We can come back,' Daniel said, standing up.

'I need to get some charcoal.' Mia lifted the hood of her jacket.

'Freya said. I'll take you to Olban on Saturday.'

Mia's whole stance changed. 'But I need it *now*! I can't start any of this stuff without it.'

It was rather like watching two stags squaring up to each other. Freya could just sense World War Three about to erupt between father and daughter. Daniel was right. Of course he was. Mia was being unreasonable and rude. But she did need that charcoal, and he probably didn't understand quite how important it was to her.

Freya stood up and adjusted her soft pink scarf. 'Would it help if I ran Mia into Olban this afternoon?'

'Cool.'

'Mia, we can't—'

'*Why?*' Mia turned on him like a volcano exploding. 'You always spoil everything. *Always.*' She flung her arms wide and stalked off down the path.

'Mia!'

Freya bit her lip. 'Sorry.'

'That wasn't your fault.' Daniel turned his head to look at her. 'That was a nice offer, but she's got to learn that people can't just drop everything when she wants something.'

He was right. *But...*

But Mia was really keen to get started on her drawings—and that was a good thing, wasn't it?

'I won't say anything else to Mia, but I'm happy to take her if it'll help.'

He started to shake his head.

'The sooner she gets her charcoal, the sooner she can start. The busier she is, the less time she'll have for Steve.' Freya fiddled with the end of her scarf, aware that Daniel was looking at her curiously.

'She told you about him?'

Freya nodded.

'You're honoured. I'm not supposed to know.' He answered

the unspoken question in her eyes. 'Fellingham isn't a great place to keep secrets. I've been told by at least three or four people. Margaret included. And, yes, I want Mia too busy to go anywhere near him.'

'Is he really bad news?'

'He's nineteen, unemployed, and been in trouble with the police. What do you think? What's he doing with a fifteen-year-old, anyway?'

Fortunately the question was clearly rhetorical, because Freya didn't fancy giving him the answer that leapt to her mind. She'd inadvertently broken one confidence, and she wasn't about to break another, but he had more to worry about than their age difference. *Did Daniel know his daughter wanted a baby?*

Freya had said what she could, focussed on what a huge commitment it was to have a baby, but she didn't flatter herself Mia had changed her mind. She hadn't thought further than the lovely clothes she could buy it, and she hadn't given any consideration to where the money for them would come from.

There was another reason, too. Unexpressed, but Freya was certain Mia wanted a baby because it would be something that was hers to love.

'Back down on the trip to the art shop. We could stock her up on pencils, paper, pastels… She'd love it if you bought her a set of those.' Freya watched indecision pass over his face. 'Tell her I've convinced you I really don't have anything else to do this afternoon.'

'And don't you?'

She pulled out her mobile. 'Nothing that can't be sorted with a phone call.'

'Hell!' His hand ripped through his hair. 'I don't like to—'

Freya reached out and touched his arm. Her fingers closed about the waxy fabric of his jacket. 'I'd like to.'

'I seem to spend a lot of time thanking you.'

'You're welcome.'

His eyes seemed to darken, and Freya knew he was thinking of the time he'd kissed her on the cheek.

'Okay. I'll break the good news to Mia on one condition.'

Freya took her hand off his arm, suddenly shy. 'What?'

'Come to supper with us.'

She hadn't expected that. Freya looked up at him, trying to search out whether he was merely being kind or whether he actually wanted her to accept. Since that kiss he seemed to want to keep his distance. He'd been grateful, stopped to talk, but he'd not repeated his invitation to lunch.

'It's not going to be anything fancy, but you deserve a proper thank-you.'

She'd begun to think he was doing the right thing. Helping out in his office, she'd come to see how much a part of this community he was. He was happy here as she'd never been. And she suspected he was still in love with his dead wife. No one could compete against a ghost.

But…she wasn't strong enough to turn down the chance to spend time with him. *Before she left.* Where would be the harm in that? 'I'd like that. Thanks.'

CHAPTER NINE

FREYA stopped to unlace her walking boots.

'You don't have to bother with that,' Mia said, dropping her coat into a cupboard and pushing the straining door shut with her hip. 'Dad doesn't care.'

Nevertheless, Freya eased her foot out of the second boot and left the pair carefully by the front door. She'd tried hard during the past three hours not to speculate on what kind of place Daniel would call home, but this was pretty much what she'd expected.

Given his love of antiques, she'd guessed at old, but couldn't imagine him in something too cottagey. For one thing he'd have to perpetually duck under the low doorways. But this was perfect. One of the six late-Victorian semis which lined the road out to Kilbury. The ceilings were high and, if the hallway was anything to go by, the decoration was plain and masculine.

She liked it—although it was a world away from her interior-designed penthouse suite overlooking the River Thames. There, everything was arranged according to Feng Shui principles and nothing was allowed to mar the overall harmony.

But this felt more like a home. The pictures which lined the walls were incredibly eclectic. Colourful brash paintings sat side by side with subtle pencil drawings.

'Dad'll be in the kitchen.'

Freya padded along behind her as Daniel called out, 'Mia?'

'Yeah. We're back.'

And then he came round the kink in the hallway, book in hand. Freya felt her stomach lurch at the sight of him. It was instantaneous. Almost like a reflex action. She seemed to have absolutely no control over it.

'Hi.'

Who'd have thought jeans and a loose open-necked shirt could look so sexy? His feet were bare, too. It seemed a strangely intimate thing to have noticed. Domestic.

'Did you get what you wanted?' he asked his daughter.

Mia's words tumbled over themselves. If Daniel had wanted to distract his daughter's attention away from her boyfriend he couldn't have happened upon a more likely way to do it. Mia was passionate about art. She drooled over sticks of pastels like other girls her age lusted after make-up.

'And Freya said you wouldn't mind if I got all twenty-four colours,' she said, holding up a box of pastels. 'I was going to buy them individually, but this was cheaper.'

Above her head Daniel met Freya's eyes. He said thank you as clearly as if he'd spoken. She let her mouth soften with what she hoped said *you're welcome*.

In fact, she'd genuinely enjoyed the afternoon. Mia was good company. A little spiky, but then she'd have been bored if she hadn't been. And Freya had taken the opportunity to talk about Steve. The baby plan didn't seem to be more than an abstract idea. Which was good.

'I'll put them outside,' Mia said, pushing past her dad.

'I've given her Anna's studio.'

'I bet she loves that.' Freya followed Daniel up the hallway. In all her speculation she'd forgotten that this house had been Anna's home, too. Had she chosen the neutral colour walls?

The solid oak floor? Were any of the paintings hers? It didn't seem unlikely that at least one or two would be.

He stepped down into a large family kitchen with hand-painted blue-green cupboards and dark granite worktops. Through a large archway she could see a sitting room which was dominated by an entire wall of books.

It was that kind of house. Large comfortable sofas, kelim rugs, the kind of kitchen that belonged to someone who loved to cook.

'Wine?'

'I can't. I'm driving. Water will be fine.'

Daniel laid the book he'd been reading open on the large wooden table. 'Why don't you leave your car here and collect it tomorrow?'

'I—'

'It's only a fifteen-minute walk to Margaret's, and I'll walk you home later.'

How tempting was that? During the afternoon she'd almost managed to convince herself her feelings for Daniel were entirely altruistic, but an invitation like that blew everything out of the water. She wanted to be with him. Wanted to spend time with him. Even though she knew he wasn't looking for a relationship and that she was unlikely to be his choice even if he were.

Wine glasses were hanging on a wooden rack, and he pulled one off and poured in a large quantity of red wine. 'Red or white? There's white in the fridge, if you prefer that.'

'Red's fine.'

Daniel handed her the glass and pulled another goblet off the rack for himself. The wine was more than fine. It was the kind that had a thousand flavours bursting in your mouth and yet the whole was somehow unified. It was the wine of a connoisseur, and if she hadn't known about his London lifestyle she'd have been surprised.

'This is gorgeous.'

He smiled. 'I'm glad you like it. Have a seat,' he said, gesturing at one of the bar stools.

Freya set her wine glass down on the granite work surface and settled herself on one of the high stools. Her stomach was churning over and over. He made her feel so vulnerable. Nervous.

She felt as if she'd got her nose pressed up against the window, looking inside at a life she wanted. And inside her a voice was saying *Please love me*; *Please want me*.

Her hand closed around the stem of her glass. *Love?* Had she thought that?

Matt had told her she didn't know what love was, and she'd been inclined to believe him. She didn't 'do' love. Ever. It was a cut-off mechanism. The point at which she backed off.

Because deep down she thought love was a con. It was something men said when they wanted to have sex with you. Something her parents had said when they'd wanted to control her behaviour or punish each other.

Twenty-nine years had taught her love was a lie—but Daniel made her want to believe it wasn't. Freya twisted the stem between her fingers.

'You're not a vegetarian, are you?' Daniel asked, his hand on the fridge door.

'No.'

'Good,' he said, pulling out three fillet steaks. 'A bit late to be asking.'

He turned to look at her and she felt her body respond. His eyes seemed to look right into her soul. So often there was that mix of warmth and laughter. He made her feel *liked*.

Not a body. Not a means to an end. Someone he actually enjoyed being with. And she really enjoyed being with him. Could this be what she was looking for? Was this the big life-changing

something she'd sold her business to give herself time to find?
Was Daniel *it*?

Was she in love?

And what about him? What was he really seeing when he
looked at her?

Daniel put the first fillet into the hot pan. 'How do you like
your steak?'

'Rare.'

'Two rare and one cremated.' He put the other steak fillets
into the pan and then leaned over to take a sip of his wine.

Freya sat quietly running the events of the past three weeks
in her head. Was being in love like this? Was it an awful churning
fear of rejection? Was it a feeling of horrendous uncertainty?

It wasn't like that in books. Heroines were supposed to *know*.

Daniel knew what it was like to be in love. He'd loved Anna.
He'd loved her when she'd been tired from the chemo, when
her hair had fallen out, when she'd been too ill to really care
whether he was there.

She wanted that kind of love in her life.

'How much do I owe you?' Daniel asked, with a look over
his shoulder.

'Mia has the receipt.'

He nodded and flipped over the steaks with a palette knife.
'I'll get that off her and settle up.'

'Can I do anything?'

Daniel shook his head. 'It's all done bar the steaks.'

Which left her with nothing to do. Freya took another sip of
wine and then let her eyes wander around the kitchen, searching for little touches she could attribute to Anna. Did he still
surround himself with things that would remind him of her?

The sad truth was it probably didn't matter whether or not
she was in love with Daniel, as he wasn't likely to fall in love
with her.

Sophia would have told him about Jack. About the squat, too. Freya took a small sip of wine and watched as Daniel took a saucepan of new potatoes out of the oven, where he'd been keeping them warm. Sophia knew all about them.

What else had he been told about her? Had he picked up on the suggestion she'd overheard the other day that she was a kind of professional girlfriend? That her car was an ex-boyfriend's present for 'services rendered'?

The truth wasn't so bad, but it wasn't so great, either. She'd had three important relationships with three very different men—the one unifying thing being that they'd all cheated on her. She'd bought the car herself, with money that was hers, but that had wrecked her relationship with Matt.

Why would Daniel want her?

He'd been kind. He'd let her work in his office because he'd thought she'd needed it. Let her grow close to his daughter. Offered her friendship.

But none of that was love.

It was time she left. All the major clearing of her grandma's house had been done. Long done. Even the loft was empty. But she'd stayed.

For Daniel or for Mia she couldn't quite tell. Maybe a little of both. But for how much longer could she let things slide like this?

Maybe what she should take from this experience was that there were nice men out there? And maybe the payment for that knowledge was that she'd been able to do something to help Daniel's relationship with his daughter?

'Penny for them?'

She looked up with a start.

'Your thoughts. You were miles away.' Daniel laid the steaks onto warm plates.

Freya straightened her spine. 'I was. I was thinking about Mia.'

He untwisted a roll of foil and cut slices from chilled butter lavoured with Roquefort cheese, red pepper and black pepper, aying them across the top of the steaks.

'She was brilliant today. Have you heard anything else about vhether she can go back to take her exams at Kilbury?'

'That's not going to happen. And, actually, I think it's probably or the best. It would be hard for her to go back now.' He looked p. 'You were right, you know, when you said there'd be a reason he got into that fight. She'd gone into Art that morning and found ome of her work damaged. Everything snowballed from that.'

'Her poster for *A Midsummer Night's Dream*.'

'She told you?'

Freya nodded.

'Why didn't you tell me?'

'Mia said she was going to. And that's better, isn't it? She leeds to talk to you. I'm not going to be here for ever.'

Daniel stood straight. 'I suppose not,' he said slowly.

He knew that. From the very beginning he'd known Freya lidn't intend to stay in Fellingham. The very fact she'd come t all was a huge surprise. So why did it bother him so much vhen she said it aloud?

He'd made the decision to keep his distance. Certain it was he right thing to do. Nothing had changed. Mia still needed all iis attention. And Anna…

Daniel twisted his wedding ring round. They'd never talked bout this. Through all the appointments, the treatment she'd ndured because she'd so desperately wanted to live, the days n the hospice, they'd never talked about 'after'. He didn't know what Anna would have felt about him remarrying.

He looked across at Freya as a bright light burst inside his iead. Was that the way his mind was working? Was that the eason he wanted to keep his distance?

'This is ready,' he said, moving to pick up the platter with he steaks on it.

'Shall I carry it through?'

'That would be great.'

Freya slid off the stool and walked through into the dining area. He swallowed. His reasons for keeping his distance suddenly didn't seem so clear any more.

'Is it ready?' Mia asked, bursting back into the room.

Daniel lifted the lid off a salad spinner and tipped a selection of salad leaves into a wide bowl. 'On the table. Mia, take the plates across, will you?'

He took the dressing out of the fridge and picked up the bowl of new potatoes.

'Can I have some wine?'

'A little,' Daniel said. 'Get yourself a glass and bring the bottle.'

Freya was standing looking at his bookshelves. 'Is there anything you don't read?' she asked, looking back at him.

He smiled. 'It's probably more of an addiction than Spicy Meatball paninis.'

'That's bad.'

'What about you?' he asked, setting the bowl of new potatoes down on the table. 'Please sit down.'

'Anywhere?'

He nodded. 'To be honest, we rarely eat in here. We usually use the breakfast bar in the kitchen.'

'It's nicer in here,' Mia said. 'How much wine can I have?'

Daniel took the bottle from his daughter's hand and poured her a generous third of a glass. 'Sip it slowly. If you're thirsty you should drink water. In fact, bring a jug of water through, with three glasses.'

He followed Mia back to the kitchen and brought the salad bowl, and the dressing in a separate glass bottle. Freya had settled herself at the table, her hands cradling her wine glass and her eyes sparkling.

'A top chef says you kill your salad within three minutes if you put dressing on it,' Mia said, putting the water jug down in the middle of the table. 'I saw that on the telly yesterday.'

'That's why I've put it in the bottle.'

'Which glasses?' Mia asked, as though he hadn't spoken.

Daniel sat down opposite Freya. 'Use the ones in the top cupboard.'

Mia nodded and went back to fetch them. He couldn't remember the last time Mia had co-operated like this. It was because of Freya. Because she wanted to impress her.

And the truth was he wanted to impress her, too.

He watched as she took another sip of wine. Watched as she let the flavours swirl about her mouth. The tip of her tongue as it licked her bottom lip.

Hell, but he was so out of his depth here. He'd been married for such a long time he didn't know how this was done.

'Do you really read Tolstoy in the original Russian?' Freya asked.

Mia returned with the glasses. 'He does. And Russian poetry.'

'I do.' *Was that really boring?* Daniel looked across the table to see what Freya was making of it all.

'*And* he's never failed an exam.'

Her blue eyes turned on him. 'Never?'

Daniel shook his head. ''Fraid not.'

'What was your degree in?'

'Pure Maths.'

She pulled a face, exactly as he'd known she would. Everyone always did. Unless they happened to be a mathematician and got the same buzz from numbers as he did.

'Okay, so that's all my dirty linen out in the open. What are *your* secret passions?' he asked, putting a steak on her plate.

'They're secret.' Freya reached for the salad.

'That's not playing fair.'

'Okay—well, I think I might have developed a similar addiction to Spicy Meatball paninis, because I had another one today in Olban.' She poured dressing over her salad in one easy movement. 'And I love shoes.'

'How many pairs do you own?' Mia asked.

Freya bit the side of her lip. 'You don't want to know. And I've a bit of a thing for handbags. And perfume. And nice lingerie.'

Please God, she couldn't read his mind. Daniel concentrated on putting dressing on his own salad.

'And stationery,' she continued, adding a few potatoes to her plate. 'There's nothing better then getting a new notebook. Oh, and I love computers.'

Computers didn't seem to fit with the rest of her list.

'She's done a wicked template for your website, Dad.'

'You don't have to use it,' Freya said, with a quick look in his direction. 'I was playing about.'

'It's really cool.'

She shrugged. 'I love that sort of thing. I know it bores everyone else, but I find it really satisfying. It's as much about branding as designing great packaging.'

Daniel sat back and listened. With Mia prompting the conversation he really didn't have much to do but sit there and glean as much as he could about her. He learnt that she'd taken three goes to pass her driving test, that her favourite colour was blue, that she'd wanted to keep a pet mouse but her mum wouldn't let her, and that she knew how to make a honey and oat face mask.

And every now and again she would look at him, her face unreadable.

After white chocolate cheesecake they moved through to the sitting room, with its large and comfortable sofas. Mia settled herself on a leather beanbag and he sat opposite Freya, so he could watch her face.

The truth was he absolutely loved seeing Freya in his home. He'd known he would. On some kind of level somewhere that sixth sense had kicked in and he'd known. She seemed to fit.

He loved the way she swirled her red wine in her glass, as though she knew something about what she was drinking. He loved the way she unconsciously pushed back her hair when she was talking. And the way she'd relaxed into his sofa, tucking one foot beneath her.

Daniel leant forward and studied his own wine, swirling it in his goblet. He'd been in love before. He knew how it felt. There had been that moment when he'd looked at Anna and had known they belonged together. It had all been so easy.

He looked across at Freya, laughing at something Mia had said, and knew he was right at the edge of that moment. Standing on the precipice, deciding whether to jump or not. Because that was what it took. That decision to go for it and hope to God she'd be there to meet you.

Would Freya be there to catch him? It was harder this time. He didn't know how you did the dating thing. When did you take a woman to bed for the first time? His wine swirled all kinds of colours red. Had things changed in sixteen years? Did people really just fall into bed with each other a couple of hours after meeting? If so, he was way behind on his game. He'd wanted to make love to her for days.

What would it be like to slip that crocheted tunic off her shoulder? It was practically there anyway. He wanted to kiss the hollow of her shoulderblade. Peel the white T-shirt off and make love to her.

Did Freya want him? Sometimes when she looked at him he thought…

It should be so easy, but it wasn't. Daniel looked over at his daughter, her face slightly ruddy from the heat of the open fire. He had Mia to think about. He wasn't free to just take what he wanted.

Mia liked Freya. Was that enough?

And what kind of woman was Freya really? He hardly knew her. She glanced over at him and smiled, her hair a blonde halo around a face that was so beautiful it seemed to shine.

He knew her. On some deep, fundamental level he'd always known her. He'd heard the stories, but he *knew* she was as lovely inside as out. As flawed as he was, and sexy beyond belief.

So, did he jump?

Mia uncurled herself from the floor cushion. 'I'm going to get some cola. Do you want any, Freya?' Freya held out her half-full wine glass. 'Dad?'

He shook his head. 'I'm good.' Then he watched as she walked down the step into the kitchen. He could hear the sound of the fridge door, the clunk of her glass against the granite.

Freya took a sip of wine. 'I ought to be getting back.' But she leant back again, against the soft cushions of his sofa. 'Trouble is, it's hard to move after eating so much. Have you always cooked?'

'No.' He could happily spend the rest of his life watching her. She was almost feline in the way she curled herself in front of the fire. She looked sleepy. Relaxed. 'I only started when we moved here.'

'When Anna became ill?'

He liked the way she did that, too. There was no pity in her eyes. No awkwardness. She merely wanted to know. And he found he liked talking about Anna. It didn't mean it changed the way he was feeling about Freya. He shook his head. 'When I stopped working City hours.'

'Oh, yes—the City.' Her sexy blue eyes laughed across at him. 'You don't look like a City trader.'

'Not now.'

'But you did? I should have liked to see that.'

Was that the kind of man Freya was attracted to? Did she crave top London restaurants? The fast cars which made no sense in a city so crowded it had to levy a congestion charge? *The lifestyle he'd rejected?* Was that what she wanted?

'Is there anything you miss about London?' she asked.

'The art galleries. Theatre.' He smiled. 'But even when I lived in London I hardly ever went. I just liked knowing it was so near.'

Freya pulled her top higher on her shoulder, only for it to slip back down. 'I never go, either. Crazy, isn't it?'

'What about you? If you decide to leave London, what will you miss?'

'If I go travelling, you mean?' She uncurled slightly and leant forward to put her wine glass on the low trunk which served as a coffee table. *What would she miss?* It was a hard question.

Freya settled back on the sofa, pulling a cushion onto her knee and hugging it towards her. 'I like the noise outside my bedroom window. Strangely.' She smiled, trying to put words on what she meant. 'Cars. People. The sense of something being about to happen. The buzz of living in a city, I suppose. And I'm very attached to the Starbucks at the end of my road. I like going there for breakfast. And...'

She hadn't got a clue what she'd miss, really. She hadn't allowed herself anything that could genuinely be called a 'lifestyle'. She'd had work. Her *raison d'être*.

She didn't even have the kind of friends who'd be there in times of trouble. Her fault. She'd not made time and space to make any. She'd had colleagues. People whose mortgages depended on her.

And at the end of each long working day she'd known that when she shut the door that was it. She wouldn't speak to another living soul until she went to work the next morning.

'Starbucks?' His voice was incredulous.

She shrugged, her mouth twitching. 'Cappuccino each and every morning. It's my drug of choice.'

'As drugs go, that's not so bad. Have you—?' And then he stopped abruptly.

Daniel didn't ask a lot of questions. He hadn't asked about her time in London as a teenager. Or anything about Jack. He didn't even know what she'd done for a living.

Maybe he wasn't that interested? But she thought he was. His eyes rested on her too long. Hovered on her mouth as though he were thinking what it would be like to kiss her.

'Drugs?'

'I'm sorry. Rude question.'

'Well, I smoked too many cigarettes. Does that count?' she asked. 'Mainly to annoy my parents, but I didn't much like it. You?'

He shook his head. 'Clean-living guy, me.'

'What's your one vice?'

Daniel held up his glass. 'Really, *really* expensive wine. I think I could easily become a complete wine bore. I'll probably end up going on those wine-tasting tours.'

'That's quite a nice vice. Have you never smoked?'

'And ruin my palette?' he said in mock horror.

'Would it?'

'Uh-huh. Never trust a chef who smokes.' He took his last sip of wine. 'My grandparents on my mum's side were wine merchants from way back, and my parents are real wine buffs. Foodies, too. It was just part and parcel of my childhood.'

'Are they still alive?' she asked, watching the way the light from the fire caught the angles of his face.

'Both of them. They're still in Petworth, running their antiques shop. My sister lives nearby in Pulborough, with her four children.'

'Four?'

'And I've got a brother in Hong Kong who's earning the mega-bucks.'

She liked imagining him against the backdrop of his family. 'Do you see much of them?'

'Less than I like. Richard hardly at all. But when we do get together it's like pulling on an old jumper. Claire is hugely busy with her own family. Since Anna died I've tended to take Mia down to Sussex each Christmas, and we spend a week or so in the summer with my mum and dad.' He placed his hands behind his head and stretched back. 'What did you do this Christmas?'

Freya thought of the ready-made meal she'd bought on her way home from work on Christmas Eve. The pile of romantic comedy DVDs she'd borrowed in case there wasn't much on TV she fancied.

'Margaret was with your dad, wasn't she?'

She nodded. Her grandma did that most years. She called it 'keeping the channels of communication open', and said that it was 'just a day—nothing to get too het up about'.

Christmas dinner with her dad and his new wife was more than Freya could handle.

'This year I spent it at home,' she said carefully. 'I watched too many movies, had too much to eat.'

'By yourself?'

'This year. It is just a day.'

Daniel looked thoughtful. His clever dark eyes seemed to reach in and see too much. He had a habit of doing that.

Freya drained the last of her glass, then looked at her wristwatch. 'It's almost eleven!'

'Is it?'

'I ought to be going.' She stood up and straightened out her crotchet top. 'My grandma is probably waiting up until I'm home safely.'

Daniel stood up. 'I'll walk you down.'

'It's—'

'What's going to happen?' he said, in a voice that brooked no arguing. 'If Margaret is going to be waiting up for you then I'm not having my reputation for "niceness" ruined.'

'I don't think I've been walked home since I turned fifteen.'

'But then you picked very bad friends.'

She couldn't deny that.

'Mia,' he said, walking through to the kitchen. 'I'm just walking down into the village with Freya. I'll be back in about half an hour.'

'Cool.'

Freya rubbed at the goosebumps which had inexplicably appeared on her forearms.

Mia appeared in the doorway. 'Are you going to work tomorrow?'

'I think so,' she said, with a glance across at Daniel.

At some point she was going to have to stop this. It was fun to pretend for an evening, but it was ultimately pointless. She was going to wind up hurt.

Daniel paused to put the fireguard in front of the fire. 'I'll sort that out when I get back. I've got my mobile on me if you need me, Mia. Okay?'

'Yeah.'

'I'm sorry it's so late. I didn't notice the time,' said Freya.

Mia drained the last of her cola. 'It's not that late.'

'It is for my grandma. She's a strictly bed at ten o'clock kind of woman. I bet she's a got-to-lock-up-safely kind of one, too.' Freya walked down the hallway and picked up her walking boots, quickly slipping her feet in and lacing them up.

Mia followed, setting her empty glass down on the hall table. 'Here's your jacket.' She pulled back the curtain and swore. 'It's snowing.'

Freya walked over to stand beside her. The ground was more frost than snow, but the sky was full of the kind of soft snowflakes that might settle.

'The forecast was snow,' Daniel remarked, coming up behind them. 'I didn't quite believe it, but they're spot-on.'

She was such a child. Snow would always be magical to her. Freya laced up her book, wrapped her pink scarf round her neck and pulled on the pair of suede leather gloves she kept in the pocket of her sheepskin jacket.

Outside the air was crisp, rather than freezing, and the ground was crunchy beneath her boots. The wind had dropped from earlier, which made it feel far less cold. And the night sky was a clear, dark black and dotted with tiny white stars.

'This kind of weather always makes me feel like I've stepped into a Victorian Christmas card.' Thick heavy snowflakes fell on her hair and quickly mottled her jacket. Freya glanced over at Daniel, walking beside her. 'I suppose *you* think about how difficult it's going to make the roads tomorrow.'

He smiled. 'I am that boring.'

For one moment she wondered whether she'd offended him, but his smile reassured her. 'I hope it settles.'

'I think it will. It's cold enough.'

They turned into Ellis Road and walked on down into Rope Lane. Freya just felt happy. Beneath a sky like this, she felt as though anything were possible.

'I hope my grandma isn't sitting up for me. I shall feel so guilty.'

'I bet she isn't.' Daniel's arm lightly brushed against hers.

They rounded the final bend into the top end of Fellingham's narrow High Street. Her grandma's house was positioned sideways, so it wasn't until they'd scrunched their way into the driveway that Freya could see the sitting room light was off.

'She must have gone to bed,' she said with a glance up at him.

'And left the hall and landing lights on for you?'

'Yes.'

Daniel waited while she searched for her keys. Freya felt unbelievably flustered. Why did keys always fall to the innermost corner of a handbag? She pulled them free and refastened her bag. 'I had a really lovely time with Mia this afternoon.'

'Thank you for taking her.' His eyes were on her lips.

Freya struggled to breathe. Every atom in her body was begging him to kiss her. She moistened her lips with the tip of her tongue. 'And dinner was wonderful, too.'

'You're welcome.'

'I've not had such a nice evening for—'

'Freya.' Her name on his lips was half-ache, half-moan.

Her eyes flicked up to his. She must have communicated something, because he ripped off his gloves and his hands were warm on her cold cheeks. He held her so that he could look deep into her eyes, very gently, and then he moved to kiss her.

That first brush of his lips against hers sent shock waves soaring down her veins. And then his tongue flicked against her bottom lip and her mouth opened to receive him. This was what she'd wanted since the first day she'd met him.

Her chest felt tight and her breath was coming in ragged gasps. This was so much more than any kiss she'd ever received. There was something desperate about it. Almost forbidden. And so entirely perfect.

Daniel drew back and rested his forehead on hers while he steadied his breathing. His hands remained cradling her face, his thumbs moving along her cheekbones.

'I've been thinking about that for such a long time,' he said huskily.

'Me, too.'

He groaned and kissed her again. Hard and fast. 'I need to get back to Mia.'

'Yes.'

His lips moved against hers, his tongue thrusting into her mouth and tangling with her tongue. Freya's hands slipped up his back and held him close. He smelt of night-time air and cold, and he tasted of the wine they'd shared.

'Will you be in tomorrow?'

Freya nodded silently, and he kissed her again.

'I don't want to go,' he said, moving back to look into her eyes.

She didn't want him to. It would have been the easiest, most natural thing in the world to take him upstairs and make love to him—but that wasn't going to happen tonight.

His thumb moved once more against her cheekbone. 'This is crazy.'

'It's going to need thought,' she said, smiling up into eyes that seemed to offer everything she'd ever wanted. He made her feel so safe. So desired. So *loved*.

'Hmm,' he agreed, closing the gap between them for one last kiss. It stretched on for the sexiest length of time. 'You'd better go in. If Margaret is watching from behind the curtains you're going to have some explaining to do.'

Freya gave a gurgle of laughter. 'That'll be your reputation besmirched.' She put her key into the lock and opened the front door. 'Goodnight.'

'Night.' He held onto the pillar of the porch.

Freya walked through to the sitting room, without turning on the light, and watched as Daniel walked slowly away.

He'd kissed her. Really kissed her. She could still taste him on her lips. And that felt absolutely incredible.

CHAPTER TEN

DANIEL'S arms slipped round her waist and she turned in his arms. 'You've had three messages and one wrong number,' Freya said against his mouth as he came close to kiss her.

His face was cold, and his hands even more so, but she forgot that as he kissed her. She let her fingers slide up into his hair and gave it a firm tug. 'Two need you to call back really urgently.'

She could feel him smile against her mouth. 'I'm too busy.'

'Not for a couple of Victorian stuffed bird scenes, surely?'

He stood back, his face everything she'd hoped. 'Really?'

Freya couldn't stop the laughter. 'No, not really. I just know how much you love taxidermy.'

His hands were quick to pull her closer. She loved the way his hands cradled her face. It made her feel as though he were really concentrating on kissing *her*. This time his lips were warm and oh-so-sensuous.

She could feel heat pooling in her abdomen and spreading out like a sunburst. Freya let her hand fist against his shirt as he flicked his tongue between her lips.

Vaguely, very vaguely, she heard voices approaching. 'Daniel.'

He stood straight. 'I hear it.'

Freya hurried round to the other side of the desk and pulled out the notepad where she'd written his messages. Daniel raked a hand through his hair, turning as the office door opened.

From the look on Bob's face they'd probably fooled no one. 'Dan, I've got someone out here who'd like a word.'

'Right,' he said, with a quick glance over his shoulder. 'I'll make those calls in a minute.'

Freya bit her lip to stop the laughter bubbling out uncontrollably. She'd never been this happy. Even when she'd been spending long hours building her own business.

She put the notepad back down on the table and went through to the kitchenette to put on the kettle. She loved him. Trusted him. *Enough to tell him about the money?*

That was more difficult. There'd been a couple of times over the past week when she'd almost told him. It wasn't that she didn't want to—it was more a case of lack of opportunity. She wanted to tell him in the right way.

Freya poured boiling water into a couple of mugs. Matt's voice sat in her head. It was as she'd always thought. You couldn't isolate the present from the past. Even though Daniel was a very different kind of man, she still carried the scars from that relationship into this one.

'Any good?' she asked, as she came back into the office and found him sitting at his desk.

'Could be. He's a Hornby train collector whose wife has decided it's her or it.'

Freya passed him his coffee. 'Your messages are on the first page of that notepad.'

He glanced at them briefly and then looked back up at her. 'They can wait. I want to talk to you.'

His voice had taken on an unfamiliar edge. Freya let her hands slide round the warmth of her mug and held it comfortingly against her lips.

'Don't look like that,' he said, pulling her towards him.

Freya set the mug down on the desk and reached out to smooth back the hair from his forehead. One week in, she didn't feel so very confident. 'What, then?'

'I want you to come with me to a reception at Kilbury Manor next week.'

Her hand stilled.

'Fun though this is, we're going to have to go public some time.'

Fear licked through her. She liked it like this. As soon as they went public the real world would intrude upon them. 'What about Mia?'

'Freya, we can't keep doing this. It feels like something furtive, and there's absolutely no need.' Daniel linked his fingers through hers and pulled her closer. 'You told me you were tired of letting other people judge you for something that happened twelve years ago. Let's lance it. Let's let them get all their gossiping out of the way in one fell swoop.'

His thumb moved against the palm of her hand.

'What's the worst they can do?'

They could spoil this. It was so bright and new she didn't want to let anyone into their relationship yet. Even Mia. She didn't want his daughter to put any doubts about it in his mind. It was too fragile a relationship. Too much pressure and it might snap.

'What happens at Kilbury Manor?'

'It's just a charity fundraiser organised by Lady Harrold in aid of the local hospital. She's done it every year for the last five years.'

Freya chewed the side of her mouth nervously. 'Did you go with Anna?'

'Yes.' Daniel stood up and brushed her hair off her face, looking closely into her eyes. 'I was married to Anna. She's part of who I am.'

'I know that. It's only that people are going to think I'm a poor exchange.'

Daniel let his hands slide across her shoulders and down her arms, gathering her hands loosely in his. 'You're not an exchange. Anna died. And I've found you.'

Which only meant that if Anna had been alive he wouldn't have looked at her. Which, of course, she wanted. If he'd been the kind of man to wander she wouldn't have been interested in him. But...

She couldn't even straighten it all out in her own head, let alone explain it to anyone else. She was just feeling neurotic, that was all. Nervous.

'What happens at the fundraiser?'

'The great and the good of the Downland Villages gather together. It's very formal, slightly dull, but it's the most obvious place to make a statement about you and me.'

You and me.

'When is it?'

'Next Saturday.'

'Can I think about it?'

Daniel shook his head. 'No. We need to get tickets.'

His thumb continued to move against the palm of her hand, but other than that he didn't move. Just waited. *Why* did they have to go public? It was perfect the way it was.

Well, perfect except that they had nowhere they could guarantee they'd be alone. And that they were lying to Mia by omission. The logical part of her brain knew that he was right. This was one of those forks in the road. They could either decide to go forward with this relationship or they were going to have to decide not to.

'Okay.' The single word was wrung from her.

Daniel leant forward and kissed her. 'It'll be fine.'

Fine. Daniel didn't know what he was talking about. There was nothing fine about any of this. Freya put on the last layer of lipstick and turned to go downstairs. She'd been in Fellingham almost six weeks now, and people were still talking about her. Yesterday yet another conversation had stopped abruptly the minute she'd walked into the farm shop.

'What do you think?' she asked, standing before her grandma and twisting round so she could see the low scooped back. Back in London she'd decided it was the most classic of all the evening dresses she possessed, but now she was wondering whether she should have just popped into Olban and bought something a little more restrained.

'You look lovely.'

'It's not too much?'

'It looks lovely,' Margaret repeated, looking up from her crossword. 'And it'll shock half the people there. As well you know,' she added.

'Too much?'

Margaret set her pencil down on her paper. 'Freya, you must have been to this type of thing before. They're inclined to be stuffy. Everyone stands about making mindless conversation and juggling silly little bites of food they probably wouldn't eat if they knew what they were. The point is, if you want Daniel you're going to have to go. And there's no point in pretending you're some kind of twinset and pearls woman, because you're not. You've always dressed to stand out from the crowd. And to shock.'

Margaret looked back down at her crossword and Freya fingered the single diamond nestling at her throat. It was the first time her grandma had let on that she knew about her fledging relationship with Daniel.

The elderly woman's mouth twitched into a smile. 'Of course I know. I saw you last week. And if Daniel kissed you as thoroughly as it looked from where I was standing, I'd say you had something worth the odd barb or two.'

'Will the Jamesons be there?'

'I imagine so.' The doorbell rang. 'Just do it.'

Just do it.

'And take your key. I doubt I'll be up when you get back.'

Freya leant forward and kissed her grandma's cheek.

'You do look lovely. And I'm so proud of you,' she added softly.

Tears smarted at the back of Freya's eyes. She blinked them away as she lifted her velvet wrap from the back of the chair and wrapped it round her shoulders. Then she picked up her clutch bag and went to open the door, letting in a blast of cold air.

Daniel looked quite different in his dinner jacket. She could imagine him as a City trader so much more easily than she could when he was dressed casually. He looked sharp, and scarily sexy.

'You look beautiful.'

Freya cleared her throat in an effort to dislodge the lump of fear that had settled there. 'You look fairly good yourself.'

He smiled and reached for her free hand. It felt better with her hand tucked in his. He led her towards the waiting taxi, watching while she settled herself in the rear passenger seat before shutting the door and walking round to join her.

'Have you told Mia we're dating?' Freya asked, turning her head to look at him as he sat beside her.

Daniel shook his head. 'It wasn't that kind of a night. Mia wants to go to a party.'

'Where?'

'She doesn't know. And she doesn't know what time she'll be back. What time it starts.'

Freya bit down on her lip. Daniel's voice was thick with a mixture of exasperation and frustration.

'And Steve will be driving her there.'

'What did you do?'

Daniel leant back on the headrest and turned to look at her. 'Shouted quite a bit.'

'Oh.'

'*God*, Freya, I don't know what I'm doing wrong with her.'

Freya slid her hand in his and squeezed his fingers. 'You're doing great. Just keep doing great.'

'So I've got poor Melinda Tilling from next door to come and sit in. I couldn't risk leaving her alone tonight. So, no, I didn't tell her anything about us.'

'Good decision.'

Daniel cracked a smile. 'I feel like I've gone two rounds with Mike Tyson.'

Kilbury seemed to loom quickly. The taxi driver took the second junction and followed the winding road out towards Kilbury Manor.

'Have you been here before?'

Freya looked out of the window at the predominantly Tudor-built house. 'No. Though I think my parents did a couple of times. What would that have been for?'

'Before my time,' Daniel said, with a shake of his head.

The taxi came to a stop, and the driver got out to open Freya's door. She swivelled round on her seat and climbed out with an easy flick of her legs.

Now she was actually here she felt strangely calm. Her grandma was right. She *did* know how these events worked. It was all about posturing, really. You just had to hold you head up high and look as though you were extremely comfortable.

Daniel appeared to *be* comfortable. His hand hovered at the small of her back and he steered her towards the heavy oak door which was standing open at the back of the central courtyard.

'Dan! Hi!'

He spun round, and Freya turned to look at the man who'd

hailed him. Cleanshaven, with hair slicked back, he wasn't someone she recognised.

'Hi.' The two men shook hands, and then Daniel stepped back. 'This is Freya Anthony.'

She fixed a smile to her face and held out her hand.

'Freya, this is Ben Taylor.'

'Hello.'

If she'd needed any confirmation that she looked good, Ben's eyes provided it. They took on that lascivious gleam men's eyes often held around her.

Daniel's hand moved to touch the small of her back again. It was both protective and possessive. Freya glanced up at him. A muscle pulsed in his cheek, and she knew he was completely aware of the other man's interest.

'Do men always react like that around you?' he asked quietly as they walked away.

'Not usually after they've talked to me a bit.'

Daniel gave a crack of laughter. 'You *are* very frightening up close.'

The room was a heavy mass of people. She'd instinctively tensed, but relaxed when she saw how easy it would be to hide from anyone she particularly wished to. The fear that she'd have to stand and talk with Professor Jameson and his wife receded.

'There's a makeshift cloakroom set up in the next room. Shall I take your wrap?'

Freya let it slip from her shoulders, the velvet slithering across bare skin. 'Thank you.'

'I'll be back in a minute.'

Kilbury Manor was exquisitely beautiful. Lord and Lady Harrold had filled the hall with exquisite flowers in shades of cream and white. Most impressive was the enormous fireplace right at the centre of the hall. It was blackened with age and a glorious fire had been lit in it. Perfect on a cold February night.

'Okay?'

Freya turned at the sound of Daniel's voice. Actually, she was. There was nothing here she couldn't cope with. Waitresses skilfully moved among the guests with trays of canapés and glasses of wine.

'I'm fine.'

'Shall we go further in?'

Freya nodded and led the way down the length of the hall. Only once did she think she'd been recognised, although that might have been simply on account of her dress. In London terms, Fellingham was a very conservative place.

'Where is Lady Harrold?'

Daniel nodded over towards a grey haired woman in a simple velvet dress. 'Talking to the Mayor and his wife. Lord Harrold doesn't seem to be here. Perhaps we passed him in the Great Hall.' He stopped one of the waitresses and took a glass of white wine. 'White or red?'

'White's fine. I'm happy with either.'

Daniel handed her the glass, noticing for the first time the narrow bangle she wore on her wrist. Everything about Freya was exquisitely understated. Her dark pink dress was deceptively simple. It looked like a silk sheath until she turned around. The back scooped low across her back, held in place by two criss-crossed straps.

Sexy wasn't the word to describe it. Every move she made had the fabric shimmering. So much so he could barely keep his hands off her. She carefully picked a tiny new potato topped with dill herring from a passing tray and bit it in half.

'This is nice—'

'And who do we have here?' Major Allingham interrupted, thrusting his body between them. 'I don't think we've met, have we, m'dear?'

Freya held up the other half of her canapé as though to ward him off. Or perhaps it was simply to show she didn't have a hand with which to take the one the Major was offering. 'I don't believe so.'

'We need to put that right, then. I'm Major Allingham. Arthur. And you're?'

'Freya Anthony.'

'Are you, now?'

Not by so much of a flicker did she show any kind of reaction. She merely took a sip of wine.

'You're the gal who ran off with that musician boy. Been hearing a fair bit about you. Simon!' The Major summoned one of his friends. 'This is the gal they've all been talking about.'

Simon, mid to late sixties, immediately came over. 'We were wondering when we were going to get a sight of you. I knew your father, of course. And your mother. Very highly strung was Christine.'

'What do you think you're doing?' a familiar voice hissed at Daniel's shoulder.

Daniel swung round to look down at his sister-in-law, elegant as ever in black, her dark auburn hair pinned up in a high chignon.

'Sophy! I was wondering if you'd be here tonight.'

'You knew damn well I'd be here.' She took him by the arm and led him slightly away from where Freya was still imprisoned by the Major and his friend. 'Why have you brought Freya here?'

'Why not?'

'*Why not?*' Sophy repeated, almost spluttering in indignation. He'd never seen her quite so agitated before. 'I've told you what she's like.'

'You don't know her.'

'I know her a damn sight better than you do.' She forced herself to calm down by taking a deep breath of air. 'And look at what's she's wearing. It's so inappropriate. What would Anna have thought?'

'Anna's dead.'

He'd spoken calmly, but his words had exactly the effect he'd intended. Sophy's head snapped round to look at him and her green eyes narrowed. 'Yes, she is. But,' she said, quite deliberately, 'her daughter doesn't need that kind of influence in her life.'

'What kind?'

'Look at her,' Sophy said, nodding back in Freya's direction.

Since he'd last looked she'd been surrounded by—presumably—a couple more of the Major's friends. Much longer and he would really need to go and rescue her.

'She's always been like that.'

'Like what?'

'Always behaved like a slut.' It was an ugly word, and it hung between them like a slap.

Daniel set his wine glass down on a nearby side table, and then he stepped in very close to his sister-in-law. 'I don't know what happened between you and Freya when you were younger. I don't even know what Anna thought about her. She never mentioned her, which would suggest she wasn't a very significant figure in her childhood. But I do know that much of what's being circulated in the village is coming from you, and I'd like it to stop.'

Sophy smiled. There'd been moments during her marriage to Russell when Daniel had felt incredibly sorry for his brother-in-law. Her smile seemed to conceal real malice.

'Dan, I haven't had to say a thing. Everyone knew Freya was the easiest girl in our year.'

Daniel found his hands had balled into fists.

Sophy spun round on her high-heeled shoes and slipped past him. 'Freya,' she murmured as she moved by her.

He watched Freya's long earrings swing as she looked round

o see who had called her name. He felt a surge of protectiveness. He so often felt that around her—although there was no
doubt she was more than capable of taking care of herself.

'Excuse me, Major,' he said, cutting through. 'I need to bor-
row my date, if I may?'

'Nicely saved,' Freya said moments later, looking up at him
with rich humour in her eyes.

'Why does Sophy hate you so much?'

The expression in Freya's eyes changed. They became
guarded, as though she were waiting to be hurt. 'Shouldn't you
be asking her?' She took another sip of wine.

'I'm asking you.'

She gave a faint shrug, as though she were resigned. 'I don't
honestly know. Not really. Except that boys liked me and I think
she was jealous.' Freya looked across the room towards Sophia,
who was leaning in towards a handsome man in his midthir-
ties. 'I'm fairly sure she started some rumours about me, and
they kind of took hold.'

'Freya—'

'They weren't true—but when does that make any difference
to rumours? And I told you I didn't go out of my way to make
people like me. In a way, I think I kind of enjoyed the reputation because my parents hated it so much.'

'But you *did* run away with someone?'

For the first time Freya's eyes sparked with anger. If he
could have bitten back the question he would have, but he so
wanted to know. Curiosity had been building inside him.

'That's common knowledge. His name was Jack. And he
was twenty-three and a drummer. He was absolutely everything
my dad hated—which made him incredibly attractive.

'And he told me he loved me, and that was exactly what I
wanted to hear. I thought everything would be just fine if we
could get away from Fellingham. Jack knew people who could

put us up, but what he didn't tell me was that it was a very unpleasant squat in South London.

'I thought we were going to play house—maybe have a
baby, build some kind of future together—but Jack wanted
to party. And when I wasn't so interested in that scene he
quickly found someone who was. Is that everything you
want to know?'

'Frey—'

She held up a hand to hold him off. 'Don't. This was your
idea. You knew I didn't want to do this, and I'm *damned* if I
like having to explain myself to you here.'

'She's Anna's sister.'

The look she shot him was full of contempt. 'Right. She's
Anna's sister. So we believe everything she says, do we?'

'Frey—'

But she'd swung away, easily cutting a swathe through the
room. Daniel raked a hand through his hair. If Sophy had meant
to cause trouble she'd certainly succeeded. A quick glance in
her direction suggested that she might have meant to do just that.

He swore silently and then went after Freya. He couldn't see
her and so walked back through to the Grand Hall, checking
each alcove in case she'd taken sanctuary in one of them.

Then he spotted a sudden flash of dusky pink and headed in
that direction—in time to see her stopped by a tall man who
then kissed her on both cheeks.

'I can't believe you're here.'

Daniel went to stand beside her.

'I was born here,' Freya answered the man tonelessly.

'What? Kilbury?'

She shook her head. 'Fellingham.'

The other man swore. 'I'm from Olban. Blimey, it's a small
world. And who's this?'

'Ross, this is Daniel Ramsay. Daniel—Ross Kestleman.'

The introduction meant absolutely nothing to him, but Daniel went through the motions. 'Nice to meet you.'

'I can't believe Freya's been hiding herself here. I've been trying to call you to congratulate you on your mega-millions. How much did you sell for?'

Freya named a figure which made Daniel's head swim.

'Actually, Ross, I was on the point of leaving. I'll ring you when I'm back in London.'

Oblivious to the tension, he said, 'Great.' And then he kissed her again on the cheek.

Without looking in Daniel's direction, Freya headed towards the makeshift cloakroom. Then, as though she'd thought through what she was doing, she stopped. 'Do I need a ticket to collect my wrap?'

Daniel pulled out a pink slip with the number fifty-nine on it and handed it across. 'What was that about?'

'Ross and I dated for a while.'

He quietly registered that.

'And the money?'

Freya stepped forward and picked up her wrap from the teenager who'd been given that particular job. 'Is there a phone I can use to call a taxi?'

Mutely, Daniel handed her his phone. She took it, but held it loosely in her hand.

'You owned your own company,' he stated quietly, as so many pieces of information fell into place. Her clothes, her car, her expectation that things would happen quickly and in the way she wanted.

'And now I've sold it.'

'Why?'

'Because I was bored.'

Her answer snapped back as though she wasn't taking time to think about anything she was saying.

'And now you're worth millions.'

'Funny, isn't it? The school drop-out has made good.'

Daniel didn't find it at all funny. There was too much information coming at him, too quickly, but he knew it wasn't remotely funny.

She was rich. Incredibly so. She had the kind of money which made pretty much anything a possibility. She could do all the travelling she wanted, stay in the best hotels. She could start a new business. Invest the money and do absolutely nothing for the rest of her life.

So what on earth could he offer her which would make sharing his life attractive?

The answer came back with resounding clarity—absolutely nothing.

CHAPTER ELEVEN

FREYA stood holding Daniel's phone. She should have told him. As she watched the expressions pass over his face she wished more and more that she had.

'I told you I was between jobs,' she said defensively.

'Yes, you did.'

'You never asked me where I'd worked.'

'Was there any reason why you didn't tell me?'

She'd hurt him. Every line of his body indicated that. And his eyes looked at her with an expression which ripped through her.

Freya moistened her lips. 'Most of the men I meet are more interested in my money than me.'

He drew a shaky hand through his hair. 'And you thought I was like that?'

'I didn't know you. When I first met you I thought you were married. You still wear your wedding ring.'

Daniel looked down at the gold band on the third finger of his left hand. 'And later?'

'I didn't think it mattered.' The phone in her hand rang shrilly. Mutely, she handed it across to him.

Everything was spoilt. She'd known it would be once they let other people into their world.

She watched as he struggled to get a good enough reception

to hear what was being said. He moved further away, and then came back towards her as he ended the call. 'It was Melinda. Mia's slipped out.'

His voice was without any expression at all.

Daniel pressed a couple of numbers and asked for a taxi to come out to fetch them as soon as was possible. 'Ten minutes,' he said, slipping his phone back into his inside pocket. 'I've no idea where she is. All I can do is sit about at home, waiting for her to come back.'

'Did she say anything else about this party? Who was holding it?'

Daniel shook his head. 'Only that they were friends of Steve's.'

'Well, that's a start.' Freya chewed at the side of her nails. She was sure Mia had mentioned something, but it hadn't made a lot of sense and she couldn't remember. 'Steve lives on the Wentworth Estate, doesn't he?'

'Yes.'

'Let's start there. If there's a party going on in any of the houses we're going to find it easily.' She pulled her wrap closer round her body. 'Let's wait nearer the door.'

'I'll kill her.'

'You can't do that until you find her. Have you tried ringing her mobile?'

Daniel swore, and pulled his phone out of his pocket, hitting a couple of keys. 'It's switched off.'

'It was worth a try.'

The taxi came more quickly than expected. Daniel was out in the courtyard and had the door open almost before the driver had pulled to a stop. 'I'm going home to pick up my car. I've only had half a glass of wine, so I'm fine to drive. Do you want me to drop you off at Margaret's first?'

Freya shook her head. 'I'd rather come with you, if that's okay?'

He nodded. She wished she felt she could reach out to touch him, comfort him. But she didn't feel she could. It was as though a sheet of glass had been put in between them.

'I'll get this,' she said, when the taxi pulled up outside his home. 'You get your car keys.'

'Fine.'

She pulled out a crisp twenty-pound note and handed it to the driver, watching as Daniel ran up the drive. He was out again seconds later, and was sitting in the driver's seat with the engine running by the time she came over to join him. Freya slid into the passenger seat. 'Did Melinda have anything else to say?'

'Just that she's sorry.' Daniel pulled the estate car away from the kerb and headed straight for the edge of the village.

The Wentworth Estate was more run-down than Freya remembered. 'Hang on a minute,' she said suddenly. 'Let's ask at the corner shop. They usually know if anything is happening round and about.'

'Where is it?'

'Left at the next mini-roundabout.'

But as they approached it was clear the newsagents had closed. 'We'll just have to drive about a bit.'

Daniel turned the car round in a small overgrown car park and headed back the way he'd come.

'Slow down a second,' Freya said, catching sight of someone she vaguely recognised. She wound down the window. 'Muriel?'

'Freya? Is that you?'

Jack's mum hadn't changed so very much in twelve years. 'Do you know of any parties going on tonight? We're looking for a fifteen-year-old who shouldn't be there.'

Muriel opened her handbag and pulled out a packet of cigarettes. 'There's a big one going on at the Farmans' place. You know—opposite the Plough?'

Freya frowned. 'Bill Farman's?'

'Well, he's dead now, but his sons stayed on there. Carl and Steve.'

Beside her, she heard Daniel set the car in gear. 'Thanks, Muriel.'

'You're welcome, love. Give us a call some time. It'd be good to hear how you're getting on.'

Freya gave a wave and then wound up the window as Daniel moved the car away.

'Where's the Plough?'

'Turn back the way we've come. The easiest way is to go back out onto the main road and come back into the estate through the other way. It's on that big looping road that goes round the back of the estate.'

'Okay.' His fingers clutched at the steering wheel. 'How do you know Muriel?'

'She's Jack's mum. She's brilliant. She brought up seven children by herself with absolutely no money. And when she found out Jack had left me she rang a couple of friends and got me a bedsit to tide me over.'

'She didn't think she ought to persuade you to come home?'

Freya looked across at him. 'I wasn't ever going to do that.' Then, 'Here you go. Take the first turning and follow the road round.'

Daniel did what she said, and before they'd gone a couple of hundred yards they saw the house where the party was happening. People milled about outside, drinking. Despite the cold, the windows were wide-open and there was loud music blaring out.

'She wouldn't be here?'

'Why not?'

'Why would she?'

Freya felt for the door handle. 'If she's got muddled up with the Farman brothers or any of their friends you need to get her out.' She slammed the passenger door shut.

It was only when someone grabbed at her stole that she remembered what she was wearing. Freya felt a moment's panic, and then experience kicked in. 'Is Mia here? About my height, red hair, fifteen?'

The youth took a swig of his beer. 'Came with Steve?'

'That's her,' Daniel said, coming to stand beside her.

'She's inside.' His words were slurred but he turned round and shouted, 'Mia!'

'It's okay—we'll find her,' Daniel said quickly.

They walked quickly up the overgrown path and straight in through the open front door. The music was deafening. So loud the beat seemed to hurt her heart. Freya pointed upstairs, and then did her best to indicate that Daniel should search the downstairs rooms.

She picked up the edges of her dress and hurried upstairs. Far too many of the rooms had the doors to them firmly shut. From the sound of the bathroom she heard the unmistakable sound of someone being violently sick.

'Mia?' She tapped firmly on the first bedroom door. 'Mia?'

A girl came up the stairs with a bottle of wine in her hand. 'Is that the young girl?'

Freya nodded.

'Red hair?'

'Yes.'

'She's locked herself in the toilet. Get her out. We're all dying for a pee.'

Freya sent up an urgent prayer of thanks and went to stand outside the door the girl had pointed at. 'Mia? It's Freya. Open the door.'

'Freya?'

'Yes. Open the door. I've come to take you home.'

There was the sound of a bolt being pushed back, and then Mia's tear-stained face peered through the crack. The minute she saw Freya she burst into tears, long streaks of mascara running down her face.

'Hey—come on, honey. Let's get you out of here.'

'I want to go home.'

'I know. Your dad is downstairs.'

'Dad?'

Freya pushed back Mia's hair from her face. 'Looking for you. Come on.' She took Mia by the hand and led her down the stairs.

From the other end of the hall Daniel spotted them. He lifted his hand in a wave, and Freya pointed at the door.

'How did you know where to find me?'

'You're forgetting this is where I used to hang out.' She almost couldn't believe it herself. It made it all the more incredible that her parents hadn't exerted themselves to stop her.

But they hadn't. And if it hadn't been for Muriel she'd have been a good deal worse off. Certainly hungrier, because Muriel had often put a plate of chips in front of her.

Daniel came up behind them and pulled Mia into his arms.

'Dad, I'm sorry.'

'What were you *doing*?'

'I know. I'm really sorry. I didn't think it would be like this.' Tears were coursing down her face.

'Are you okay?' Daniel held Mia away from him and searched her face.

'I just want to go home.'

He pulled the car keys from his pocket.

'Come on,' Freya said, tucking Mia into her arm.

Mia clutched at her velvet wrap. 'I'm sorry I spoilt your evening.'

'It wasn't that much fun anyway. I'm just glad you're safe,' she said, opening the back door. 'You get in and sit next to your dad.'

Mia shook her head and climbed into the back seat. Freya made a snap decision and climbed in beside her. She folded Mia against her and held her tight, placing a light kiss on the top of her hair. 'We've got you. You're safe.'

Daniel looked over his shoulder. 'You need to do up your seat belts.'

Freya helped Mia click the middle seat belt into position and then fumbled for her own. As soon as she was settled Mia curved in towards her once more. Freya gently stroked her hair and murmured words she hoped were comforting.

She looked up and caught Daniel's eyes in the rearview mirror, watching them. He'd been lucky tonight. He had to know that. The Farman family had always been synonymous with trouble. She didn't want to let her mind stray into what might have happened to Mia.

It was far better to concentrate on the fact that she was safe and unharmed. Though it wasn't surprising that Daniel's face had an ashen tone, and that he was incredibly quiet all the way back home.

He helped Mia out of the car. 'Let's get you inside and tucked up in bed.'

Freya stood back to let them pass, quietly shutting the front door as they started to climb the stairs. 'Shall I make a cup of tea or something?'

He nodded, but she wasn't entirely sure he'd heard her. She slipped off her stilettos and padded down to the kitchen, holding her long dress off the floor.

This had been Anna's house. As always, the thought popped into her head. It was *her* daughter upstairs. *Her* husband.

She dropped her wrap on one of the stools and placed her clutch bag on the work surface. She couldn't do this. She couldn't step into Anna's life.

And Daniel probably didn't want her to. He was attracted

to her. She knew that. But she wasn't sure that was enough. He'd need to love her enough to let her challenge the decisions he'd made with Anna.

She couldn't see that happening. This house was part of that. Being in Fellingham was. The auction house.

Freya set the kettle on to boil and calmly went about making tea. Had Anna chosen the kettle? The kitchen cupboards? Perhaps she'd even chosen them with her sister?

There was no sound from upstairs. No sign of Daniel reappearing, either. He was staying with Mia. And that was as it should be.

She wouldn't love Daniel as much as she did if he didn't put his child first. Freya poured tea into one mug and sat down to drink it, all the time listening for the first sounds that he might be about to join her.

It seemed interminable. Perhaps she should have called a taxi the minute she arrived? Maybe she should have asked him to take a small detour and drop her off at her grandma's?

At last she heard his footsteps on the stairs. Daniel walked slowly into the kitchen.

'Tea is in the pot. It's probably still okay.'

Daniel walked over and lifted the lid. What he saw must have been all right, because he poured himself a mug of tea.

'Is she okay?'

'She is now.' He pulled a tired hand through his hair. 'This Steve tried to persuade her to have sex with him.'

Freya's hands tightened on her mug.

'When she told him she didn't want to he left her to find someone who would.'

'Good for her for saying no.'

Daniel looked over at her.

'That can't have been easy.' She finished off her tea. 'Look, I'll call a cab to get me home. I just wanted to know she was fine before I left.'

'I can drive—'

'No, you need to be with Mia.' She swallowed, knowing what she was going to say next, but wishing she didn't feel she had to. 'And I think it's time I went back to London.'

Daniel slipped off his dinner jacket and laid it carefully across the breakfast bar. There must have been a part of her which had been hoping he'd say no, because pain ripped through her.

So strange—because she was taking control of this. It was time. And it was her decision. Except it wasn't. Daniel spread his hand out across his dinner jacket and she caught sight of his wedding ring.

Anna's ring.

'Anna's family are never going to be happy about me playing any part in Mia's life, are they? And she needs them.' She picked up her handbag. 'And she needs your undivided attention right now. My staying here is only going to make things more difficult.'

'That's it?'

Freya tried for a nonchalance she was far from feeling. 'We always knew this was going to be difficult. And I just think this is the time. Before it all gets horribly complicated…'

'You're going back to London?'

Freya nodded. 'I don't belong here. I never have.' She pulled in air. 'Maybe if we'd met in London…? If you'd not been married to Anna…?' She forced a smile and then shrugged. 'All a bit academic, really. I need to use your phone to call a cab.'

'I'll take you.' He left his jacket on the side and picked up his car keys. 'Mia's asleep. It's fine.'

This was it. Freya could feel the tears building up behind her eyes. She'd finished it. The one really lovely relationship she'd ever had was over.

He hadn't questioned her decision. Hadn't protested at all. Wrong place. Wrong time.

They walked out to the car in silence. The engine, when he turned the key, seemed over-loud. She was aware of every movement he made. His small adjustment to the rearview mirror. His leg as he changed gear.

'Thank you for your help tonight.'

Freya managed a hint of a smile. 'Give Mia my love.'

'I will. Of course.'

In no time at all he'd swung the car into Margaret's drive and pulled to a gentle stop. His hands moved on the steering wheel. 'I'll call you—'

'Don't!' Freya turned in her seat to look at him. 'Let's make this a clean break. You've got things you need to do, and I'd only make them difficult.'

He swallowed hard and then nodded.

Freya pulled her front door key out of her bag and then let herself out of the car. *Not much further and she could cry. One foot in front of the other.*

Even before she'd got her key in the lock Daniel had driven away.

'I shall miss you,' Margaret said, watching as Freya zipped the last things into her case.

'I'll be back.' She looked up and smiled. 'Have that hip operation and you can come up to London and stay with me.'

'What about your travelling?'

Freya shrugged. 'I don't know that I want to do that any more. I'm going to have to think about things.'

She was going to have to think about a lot of things. Aimlessly wandering about the world didn't hold any appeal any more. But neither did spending all her time in an office. Or being a lady of leisure. Maybe she ought to think about doing something for runaway teenagers?

'Why don't you ring him?' her grandma asked softly.

'No.'

'Don't you want to know how Mia is?'

Of course she did. But she couldn't phone. She had to believe things were going to be just fine for Mia from now on. For both of them.

And he could have phoned her if he'd wanted to. Except he knew she was right. And if she was right, she might as well experience the pain of loss now. She lifted her case off the bed.

'That's it. All done.' Freya leant over to give her grandma a tight hug. 'You don't need to come down.'

Margaret clutched at the apricot-coloured counterpane covering the bed and heaved herself to her feet. She stumbled painfully over to the window and pulled back the net curtain. 'Are you sure it's not going to be icy? Your car is covered with frost.'

'All the major roads are gritted. I'll be absolutely fine.'

She let the curtain fall and turned to look at her granddaughter. 'You drive safely—do you hear?'

Freya walked over and wrapped her arms tightly round her grandma. 'I always do. I'll go and get some of that ice off my car, and then I'll be back up to get my bag.'

Her grandma nodded and Freya ran down the stairs, stopping to put on her walking boots and throw on her sheepskin jacket.

She'd feel better when she was on her way. She'd always been like this. Once a decision was made she needed to get on with it. It was rather like pulling off a plaster.

The wind was icy cold. Freya pulled a face and paused long enough to do up her jacket before reaching into the glove department to pull out a plastic scraper. She set about de-icing the passenger window, shards of ice falling across her fingers.

She heard the approach of a car but didn't look up until it started to come into the driveway. *What the—?*

Freya stopped what she was doing and watched, mystified,

as Daniel brought his car in close up against her bumper. She pushed back the hair from her eyes.

'What are you doing?' she asked as he climbed out.

'Blocking you in. I thought we could make it a kind of family tradition.'

She frowned.

'Making it impossible for you not to listen to what I want to say.'

'We said everything last night.'

Daniel shook his head. 'No. You said everything last night. I just stood there too *damn* confused to know what was happening. But this is the morning after the night before, and I have some things to say.'

He walked up close to her—and stopped. His eyes were warm and full of emotion. 'You know, you talked a lot of rubbish last night.'

'Wh—?'

And then he kissed her. There was a moment when shock held Freya still, but it was only a moment. His lips were too persuasive. His tongue coaxed her response. She felt her hands move to hold him closer, her mouth open to him.

'I love the taste of you,' he said, pulling back. 'I don't think I'm ever going to get enough of that.' His eyes held a new energy, as though the fact she'd kissed him back had given him confidence. 'You'd better shut that door or Margaret will be losing all her heat.'

'Dan—'

He laughed and ran over to shut the front door himself.

'I haven't got my key!'

'I expect Margaret will let you back in later. Come,' he said, reaching for her hand. 'I've got something to say to you, and I want to say it in a particular place.'

Freya held back as uncertainty swamped her.

'You might as well come with me, because you're not going to get your car out unless you do,' he said, his dark eyes glinting down at her.

'Wh-where's Mia?'

'I'll tell you where she is in a bit, but she's great. Come.'

This time she let him take her hand, and he pulled her out of the drive and along the High Street. 'Daniel, where are we going?'

'Up to St Mark's.'

'Why?' She stopped. 'Daniel!'

He laughed. 'You just can't cope with not being in control, can you? But you're going to have to trust me.'

'My grandma won't know what's happened to me.'

'I think she'll have a pretty good idea when she sees my car blocking yours in. You know,' he said conversationally, 'that car of yours really bothered me.'

She started to feel a spurt of irritation. As though he sensed that, Daniel held her hand a little bit tighter.

'I've only just figured out why. Last night when I was thinking about you. *Us.* I've been incredibly slow to realise what Sophy's been doing. She just let it slip that it was the kind of thing you might choose to take away from a failed relationship and every time I looked at your car I wondered what he'd been like. Why you'd left him.'

'I bought the car.'

Daniel smiled. 'So I gather.'

'And Matt left me.'

'Hmm. Yes, well, we'll develop that part of the conversation later. Except to say he was an idiot. And I'm really glad he did, because if he hadn't you wouldn't have ever looked at me.'

Freya felt as though she'd stepped into a movie. One of those beautiful romantic ones where everything ended exactly as you wanted.

'And Sophy didn't just tell *me* about her theory. She dropped it around. By the time she'd told a few people it had become fact, and then it kind of spread,' he said, in an echo of what she'd told him before. 'She's quite good at that kind of subtle innuendo, isn't she? She carefully planted the idea that you always went for men with money. That spread, too. I don't think anyone stopped to question it.'

'Dan—'

'Shh. I haven't finished, and if you interrupt me I'm going to lose the thread of what I want to say because it's all really complicated.' He turned into Church Lane and walked briskly towards St Mark's. 'I'd just never realised quite how insidious remarks like that can be. Even though I've never rated Sophy's judgement, the things she said about you became lodged somewhere.'

'It doesn't matter.'

'It *does* matter. It's not fair.'

Daniel looked down at her with an expression which made her heart turn over.

'And she's certainly not right. After you'd gone last night I sat there and started to unpick it all. I've always known Sophy is inclined to be possessive. She was of Anna. And by extension she is of Mia. I know the last thing in the world she'd ever want is for me to introduce someone else into Mia's life. You are her worst nightmare. I don't know why that is. But she started undermining you from the moment she heard you were coming back to the village.'

Freya stopped. 'Daniel, this isn't just about Sophia and what she says about me. It's bigger than that. It's the whole thing. It's Mia. And Anna. And the fact you chose to live near her family. And—'

'I know. Just hear me out.'

She paused, and then nodded. She had no choice. She was blocked in. But the truth was she'd have listened anyway. Beside her Daniel had tensed, as though he were uncertain of the next thing he wanted to say.

He pushed open the gate that led into the graveyard which surrounded St Mark's, and purposefully led her to a white gravestone.

Anna Ramsay. Loved and still loved.

Freya read the inscription. It only told her what she already knew. Daniel had been in love with his wife. Would always love her.

Daniel moved to touch the headstone. 'You know, Anna was very lovely,' he said, without turning round, 'but hopelessly squashed by her family. You know the Professor. He's a very…*strong* personality.'

He was domineering and fairly unlikeable.

'As a child she was probably as unhappy as you. She just handled it differently. She tried to please everyone. Particularly her parents. And the Professor values success above all else, so Anna aimed to be the best. She worked hard to get top marks, top grades.'

Freya chewed at her bottom lip.

There was silence for a moment, and then Daniel turned. 'You didn't like her, did you?' he asked, with eyes that were incredibly soft.

His question pulled an honest answer from her. 'I didn't know her. But I really didn't like Sophia, and I transferred lots of that to her elder sister. I hated the way she always got the prizes and everyone said how perfect she was.'

Daniel touched her face, his thumb moving to stroke across her lips. 'You'd have mystified her. Never in a million years would Anna have spent her time in the kind of place we found Mia in yesterday. But she wasn't like Sophy, either. She wasn't a judgmental person. Incredibly accepting, in fact.'

His smile twisted. 'Which is kind of how we ended up in Fellingham. She never did see how controlling Sophy was. She was inclined to take what people said at face value. And she was brave. Really brave. Do you know, she told Mia that she'd always be her mother but that she really hoped I'd find someone who would be a mum to her? Mia told me that last night. I thought she'd feel I was being disloyal to her mum's memory if I fell in love with someone else. So I kept wearing Anna's ring, as though that would somehow make her feel safe.'

He held out his left hand, with a white band clearly visible where his wedding ring had been. 'Mia's got them both now. She's going to get them melted down into some kind of a necklace.'

Freya didn't know that tears had started to fall down her face until Daniel moved to brush them away, his fingers lightly wiping them.

'Don't cry. I don't want you to cry.'

She gave a kind of half-cry, half-hiccup, and then she was tightly wrapped in his arms. Arms which held her so close. She rested her cheek on his chest, feeling the roughness of his wax jacket and his soft kiss on the top of her head.

After a moment he pulled away and looked down into her face. 'You know I haven't finished, don't you?'

Freya brushed her hand across her face and nodded.

'Come over here.'

He led her to a bench immediately to the right of the main door which looked out across Fellingham. 'Anna and I never talked about after she'd gone. We just lived in the moment. And for the most part I never imagined I'd want to marry again.'

Freya's breath caught in her throat. It was painful to listen to him. She was so full of hope and yet so full of fear. Did he mean he was thinking about remarrying now?

He smiled. 'It hurt too much. The whole thing. Loving and losing it all seemed so pointless.' His voice deepened. 'But then I met you, and I wanted you like I've never wanted anyone before. You kind of blew me away. And I didn't know whether I was coming or going.

'On the one hand I had Mia messing up at school, and on the other I had Sophy dropping little vials of poison in my ear. I decided you were just one complication too many. But then I found I was falling for you anyway—and I felt so guilty.'

She knew this. All of this. Freya looked down at her hands, gripped tightly in her lap. All of that was why she needed to go. She didn't want to make his life difficult.

'Freya, I'm not good at this. The last time I proposed to a woman I said something like, "So we'd better get married, then".'

Daniel looked down at his feet and out across Fellingham. 'The thing is I love you. I love you so much it hurts.'

Freya stared at him, unbelieving.

His smile faltered. 'I'm scared of losing you. And I'm jealous as hell of the men you've shared part of your life with. I know I've picked a lifestyle you probably wouldn't want to live. And there's nothing I can ever give you that you couldn't buy several times over for yourself. But—' he turned to look directly into her blue eyes '—I love you, and I want to spend the rest of my life loving you.'

'You do?' Her words came out as a hoarse whisper.

'If that means I need to fold up the auction business, then that's what I'll do. If I have to follow after you as you explore Australia, I'll do that too.'

Her head was spinning. 'What about Mia?'

'Mia's definitely in favour.' Daniel stood up. 'Come.'

Freya put her hand in his and let him lead her down the steps into the old church.

Mia immediately stood up. 'Did she say yes?'

'I'd say it's all still hanging in the balance,' Daniel said, releasing Freya's hand. 'We want you, Freya. Part of our lives. Part of our family.'

She felt as though she were only just coming alive. Happiness was spreading out like a sunburst.

Freya looked at Mia. 'Really? You want to share your dad with me?'

The teenager nodded, her young face pinched with concentration.

Daniel moved. He reached out and interlaced his fingers with hers. 'Marry me? Let's change what we need to change to make this work. Let's just do it. Let's make a commitment and spend the rest of our lives making it work.'

Freya looked down at their hands, and then up into his eyes. 'I love you.'

With sudden energy Daniel moved to cradle her face. 'Is that a yes?'

'It's a yes.'

She heard Mia's laugh, and then she was only aware of Daniel's lips on hers. Warm and loving.

'Really a yes?' he said, pulling back so he could look in her eyes.

'Yes.' Laughter bubbled to the surface.

Daniel looked up and round at his daughter. 'I'm glad that's over. I've never done anything so hard in my life!' He held out his arm for Mia to come and join them. 'Let's go home and make some plans.'

She liked the sound of that. Particularly the 'home' bit. It didn't really matter what they decided, as long as they were together.

'What would you have done if I'd already left for London?' Freya asked.

'Followed you.' Daniel looked down at her, his eyes creating a private world that was just the two of them. 'You are my world. The light after a very dark night. I love you, and I will love you until the day I die.'

EPILOGUE

'*SOMETHING old, something new, something borrowed and something blue,*' Margaret said firmly.

Freya stroked the long lace dress she'd chosen to wear over an oyster silk shift. Simple and—hopefully—stunning. When it had actually come to choosing her wedding dress she'd decided she didn't want to go with her childhood dream of dressing in a meringue.

'This is new.'

'And the garter's blue,' Mia added.

Freya smiled at her grandma. 'And you've given me your old veil.'

'*Given.* So you will need something borrowed,' she said stoutly. 'It's bad luck if you don't have something borrowed.'

'I don't believe in luck.' Freya reached out for the white rose she was going to wear in her hair. 'Mia, will you put this in for me?' Mia came closer and set the rose in the centre of the veil. 'Thanks. How do I look?'

'Beautiful.'

'You need something borrowed.'

Mia looked uncertain for a moment. 'How about this?' She lifted up the pendant she'd had made from her parents' wedding rings. It was beautiful. Delicate and twisting.

'You'd lend me that?'

She unclipped it and handed it over. Freya's eyes filled with tears, and she reached out and hugged Mia hard. 'I love you, you know.'

Mia laughed. 'That's your job. You're my mum.'

'Just don't start crying, you two,' Margaret said, pulling herself out of the chair, 'or you'll make your mascara run. I think I hear my car.'

Freya picked up her hand-tied bouquet of white roses and helped her grandma out of the door.

'You ought to put a penny in your shoe,' she said as a parting shot. 'That's for wealth.'

'I'm not going to be happy if she's organised for a chimney sweep to come and kiss me,' Freya murmured to Mia as her grandma's car drove the short distance to St Mark's.

Mia was looking in the other direction and laughed. 'Dad said he'd done this.'

Freya turned to look as a pretty horse drawn carriage appeared round the corner. The tears she'd managed to control earlier threatened to spill out over her cheeks. 'When did he do it?'

'Last week. He said it was your dream when you were my age. You've got to admit it's pretty cool.'

Freya took the hand of the man who'd jumped down to help her into the carriage. 'What would he have done if it had been raining?'

Mia was helped in beside her. 'They bring a different carriage. This is so high.' She settled her bouquet on her lap. 'Do you wish your dad was giving you away?'

'I'd rather be with you.' Freya reached out and squeezed Mia's hand. 'And I'm probably too old to be given away.'

'Rubbish!' Mia laughed.

'Mr Ramsay asked me to give you this,' the driver said, handing Freya a single red rose.

She reached out and took it, unwinding the piece of paper wrapped around the stem.

'What does it say?'

Freya held it out. '"Hurry up!"'

The carriage lurched forward and Freya felt as though she'd wandered into a movie. After days of rain even the sun had come out to bless her. She could smell the hedgerow, and the fresh clean scent of an English summer day.

St Mark's Church was as beautiful as it had always been. Solid, permanent and loved. She had wondered whether Daniel would prefer to be married somewhere else, somewhere that didn't hold sad memories for him, but he'd said it held happy memories, too.

Freya smiled and tucked the red rose into her white bouquet before being helped out of the carriage.

'You can't do that,' Mia objected, pointing at the red rose. 'It spoils the theme.'

'It's romantic.'

Mia didn't look convinced, but she let it go. 'Ready?'

Freya nodded.

'Then let's go find Dad.'

The huge door was held open, and Freya stepped down into the church. St Mark's had been decorated to within an inch of its life. Her grandma's flower circle had been let loose, and the scent was overwhelming. Music from the old organ filled her ears, but all she was really aware of was Daniel.

Not even her parents' complicated seating arrangements had the power to distract her. Just Daniel. Tall, dark and handsome, as all heroes should be.

He turned to watch as she walked down the aisle. And then he winked before taking her hand. 'You took your time,' he whispered softly.

'Did you think I wasn't coming?'

His eyes hovered on her lips. 'That's why I insisted on you having Mia with you.'

'Ah.'

He led her up to the altar and leaned in close one last time before the service began. 'Happy Birthday. May all your wishes come true.'

At that moment, Freya wasn't sure she had a wish left that hadn't.